KAREN MARIE MONING

DARKFEVER

A MACKAYLA LANE NOVEL

Copyright © Karen Marie Moning 2006
Extract from *Bloodfever* copyright © Karen Marie Moning 2007
All rights reserved

The right of Karen Marie Moning to be identified as the author of
this work has been asserted by her in accordance with the
Copyright, Designs and Patents Act 1988.

First published in Great Britain in 2011 by
Gollancz
An imprint of the Orion Publishing Group
Orion House, 5 Upper St Martin's Lane, London WC2H 9EA
An Hachette UK Company

5 7 9 10 8 6 4

A CIP catalogue record for this book is available
from the British Library

ISBN 978 0 575 10849 3

Printed in Great Britain by Clays Ltd, St Ives plc

The Orion Publishing Group's policy is to use papers that are
natural, renewable and recyclable products and made from wood
grown in sustainable forests. The logging and manufacturing
processes are expected to conform to the environmental regulations
of the country of origin.

www.karenmoning.com
www.orionbooks.co.uk

This one's for Neil, for holding my hand
and walking into the Dark Zone with me.

Praise for Karen Marie Moning and the Fever series:

DARKFEVER
'A wonderful dark fantasy . . . give yourself a treat and read
outside the box'
Charlaine Harris

'Moning launches a remarkable new series that's exotic and treacherous'
Romantic Times

BLOODFEVER
'Addictively dark, erotic, and even shocking'
Publishers Weekly

'Moning brilliantly works the dark sides of man
and Fae for all they are worth'
Booklist

FAEFEVER
'The newest installment of this supernatural saga will have you
panting for the next. Breathtaking!'
Romantic Times

'A seductive mix of Celtic mythology and dark, sexy danger'
Chicago Tribune

DREAMFEVER
'This book is absolutely riveting. By far, the most fascinating book
I have read this year'
Penelope's Romance Reviews

'Freaking fabulous! So utterly wonderful that you must be
reading this series, if you're not already'
Literary Escapism

Also by Karen Marie Moning from Gollancz:

Darkfever

Bloodfever

Faefever

Dreamfever

Shadowfever

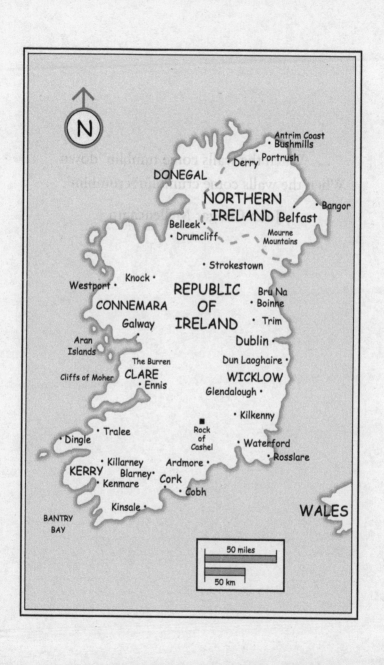

... When the walls come tumblin' down
When the walls come crumblin' crumblin'. ...

John Cougar Mellencamp

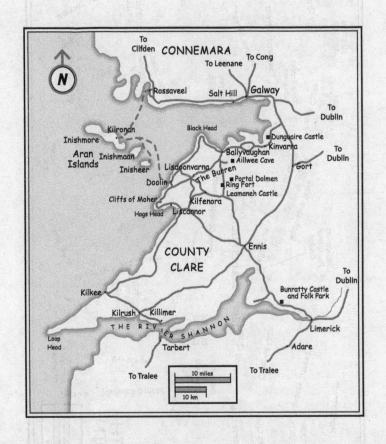

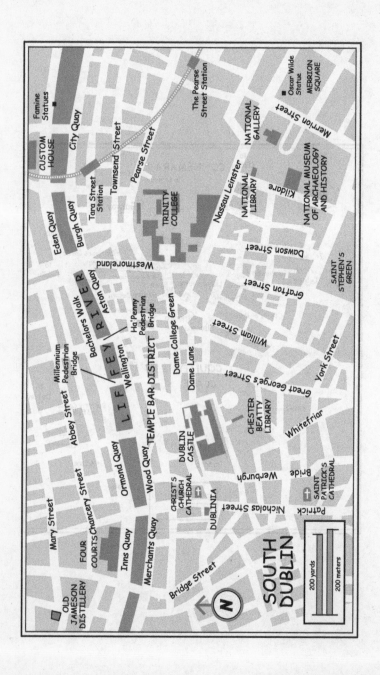

SOUTH DUBLIN

200 yards
200 meters

N

OLD JAMESON DISTILLERY

Mary Street

FOUR COURTS

Chancery Street

Inns Quay

Merchants Quay

Ormond Quay

Abbey Street

Millennium Pedestrian Bridge

Bachelor's Walk

L I F F E Y   R I V E R

Wellington

Aston Quay

Ha'Penny Pedestrian Bridge

Westmoreland

Eden Quay

Burgh Quay

Tara Street Station

Townsend Street

City Quay

CUSTOM HOUSE

Famine Statues

Pearse Street

TRINITY COLLEGE

The Pearse Street Station

Nassau Leinster

NATIONAL LIBRARY

NATIONAL GALLERY

Oscar Wilde Statue

MERRION SQUARE

Merrion Street

Kildare

NATIONAL MUSEUM OF ARCHAEOLOGY AND HISTORY

Dawson Street

Grafton Street

SAINT STEPHEN'S GREEN

Dame College Green

William Street

York Street

Whitefriar

Bride

Dame Lane

Great George's Street

CHESTER BEATTY LIBRARY

DUBLIN CASTLE

Wood Quay

TEMPLE BAR DISTRICT

CHRIST'S CHURCH CATHEDRAL

DUBLINIA

Nicholas Street

Werburgh

SAINT PATRICK'S CATHEDRAL

Patrick

Bridge Street

PROLOGUE

M y philosophy is pretty simple—any day nobody's trying to kill me is a good day in my
book.

I haven't had many good days lately.

Not since the walls between Man and Faery came
down.

But then, there's not a *sidhe*-seer alive who's had a
good day since then.

Before The Compact was struck between Man
and Fae (around 4000 B.C. for those of you who
aren't up on your Fae history), the Unseelie Hunters
hunted us down like animals and killed us. But The
Compact forbade the Fae to spill human blood, so
for the next six thousand years, give or take a few
centuries, those with True Vision—people like me
who can't be fooled by Fae glamour or magic—were
taken captive and imprisoned in Faery until they
died. Real big difference there: dying or being stuck

in Faery until you die. Unlike some people I know, I'm not fascinated by them. Dealing with the Fae is like dealing with any addiction—you give in, they'll own you; you resist, they never will.

Now that the walls are down, the Hunters are back to killing us again. Stamping us out like *we're* the plague on this planet.

Aoibheal, the Seelie Queen of the Light, is no longer in charge. In fact, nobody seems to know where she is anymore, and some people are beginning to wonder *if* she is anymore. The Seelie and Unseelie have been smearing their bloody war all over our world since her disappearance, and although some might say I'm being broody and pessimistic, I think the Unseelie are gaining the distinct upper hand over their fairer brethren.

Which is a really, *really* bad thing.

Not that I like the Seelie any better. I don't. The only good Fae is a dead Fae in my book. It's just that the Seelie aren't quite as lethal as the Unseelie. They don't kill us on sight. They have a use for us.

Sex.

Though they barely credit us with sentience, they have a taste for us in bed.

When they're done with a woman, she's a mess. It gets in her blood. Unprotected Fae-sex awakens a frenzy of sexual hunger inside a woman for something she should never have had to begin with, and will never be able to forget. It takes a long time for her to recover—but at least she's alive.

Which means a chance to fight another day. To

help try to find a way to return our world to what it once was.

To send those Fae bastards back to whatever hell they came from.

But I'm getting ahead of myself, ahead of the story.

It began as most things begin. Not on a dark and stormy night. Not foreshadowed by ominous here-comes-the-villain music, dire warnings at the bottom of a teacup, or dread portents in the sky.

It began small and innocuously, as most catastrophes do. A butterfly flaps its wings somewhere and the wind changes, and a warm front hits a cold front off the coast of western Africa and before you know it you've got a hurricane closing in. By the time anyone figured out the storm was coming, it was too late to do anything but batten down the hatches and exercise damage control.

My name is MacKayla. Mac for short. I'm a *sidhe*-seer, a fact I accepted only recently and very reluctantly.

There were more of us out there than anyone knew. And it's a damn good thing, too.

We're damage control.

ONE

A year earlier...

July 9. Ashford, Georgia.

Ninety-four degrees. Ninety-seven percent humidity.

It gets crazy hot in the South in the summer, but it's worth it to have such short, mild winters. I like most all seasons and climes. I can get into an overcast drizzly autumn day—great for curling up with a good book—every bit as much as a cloudless blue summer sky, but I've never cared much for snow and ice. I don't know how northerners put up with it. Or why. But I guess it's a good thing they do, otherwise they'd all be down here crowding us out.

Native to the sultry southern heat, I was lounging by the pool in the backyard of my parents' house, wearing my favorite pink polka-dotted bikini which went perfectly with my new I'm-Not-Really-a-Waitress-Pink manicure and pedicure. I was sprawled in a cushion-topped chaise soaking up the sun, my long blonde hair twisted up in a spiky knot on top of my head in one of those hairdos you really hope nobody ever catches you wearing. Mom and Dad were away on vacation, celebrating their thirtieth wedding anniversary with a twenty-one-day island-hopping cruise through the tropics, which had begun two weeks ago in Maui and ended next weekend in Miami.

I'd been working devotedly on my tan in their absence, taking quick dips in the cool sparkling blue, then stretching out to let the sun toast drops of water from my skin, wishing my sister Alina was around to hang out with, and maybe invite a few friends over.

My iPod was tucked into my dad's Bose Sound-Dock on the patio table next to me, bopping cheerily through a playlist I'd put together specifically for poolside sunning, composed of the top one hundred one-hit wonders from the past few decades, plus a few others that make me smile—happy mindless music to pass happy mindless time. It was currently playing an old Louis Armstrong song—"What a Wonderful World." Born in a generation that thinks cynical and disenchanted is cool, sometimes I'm a little off the beaten track. Oh well.

A tall glass of chilled sweet tea was at hand, and the phone was nearby in case Mom and Dad made ground sooner than expected. They weren't due ashore the next island until tomorrow, but twice now they'd landed sooner than scheduled. Since I'd accidentally dropped my cell phone in the pool a few days ago, I'd been toting the cordless around so I wouldn't miss a call.

Fact was, I missed my parents like crazy.

At first, when they left, I'd been elated by the prospect of time alone. I live at home and when my parents are there the house sometimes feels annoyingly like Grand Central Station, with Mom's friends, Dad's golf buddies, and ladies from the church popping in, punctuated by neighborhood kids stopping over with one excuse or another, conveniently clad in their swim trunks—gee, could they be angling for an invitation?

But after two weeks of much-longed-for solitude, I'd begun choking on it. The rambling house seemed achingly quiet, especially in the evenings. Around supper time I'd been feeling downright lost. Hungry, too. Mom's an amazing cook and I'd burned out fast on pizza, potato chips, and mac-'n'-cheese. I couldn't wait for one of her fried chicken, mashed potatoes, fresh turnip greens, and peach pie with homemade whipped-cream dinners. I'd even done the grocery shopping in anticipation, stocking up on everything she needed.

I love to eat. Fortunately, it doesn't show. I'm healthy through the bust and bottom, but slim through the waist and thighs. I have good metabolism, though Mom says, *Ha, wait until you're thirty. Then forty, then fifty.* Dad says, *More to love, Rainey* and gives Mom a look that makes me concentrate really hard on something else. Anything else. I adore my parents, but there's such a thing as TMI. *Too much information.*

All in all, I have a great life, short of missing my parents and counting the days until Alina gets home from Ireland, but both of those are temporary, soon to be rectified. My life will go back to being perfect again before much longer.

Is there such a thing as tempting the Fates to slice one of the most important threads that holds your life together simply by being too happy?

When the phone rang, I thought it was my parents.

It wasn't.

It's funny how such a tiny, insignificant, dozen-times-a-day action can become a line of demarcation.

The picking up of a phone. The pressing of an on button.

Before I pressed it—as far as I knew—my sister Alina was alive. At the moment of pressing, my life split into two distinct epochs: Before the call and After.

Before the call, I had no use for a word like "demarcation," one of those fifty-cent words I knew only because I was an avid reader. Before, I floated through life from one happy moment to the next. Before, I thought I knew everything. I thought I knew who I was, where I fit, and exactly what my future would bring.

Before, I thought I knew I *had* a future.

After, I began to discover that I'd never really known anything at all.

I waited two weeks from the day that I learned my sister had been murdered for somebody to do something—anything—besides plant her in the ground after a closed-casket funeral, cover her with roses, and grieve.

Grieving wasn't going to bring her back, and it sure wasn't going to make me feel better about who-ever'd killed her walking around alive out there somewhere, happy in their sick little psychotic way, while my sister lay icy and white beneath six feet of dirt.

Those weeks will remain forever foggy to me. I wept the entire time, vision and memory blurred by tears. My tears were involuntary. My soul was leaking. Alina wasn't just my sister; she was my best friend. Though she'd been away studying at Trinity College in Dublin for the past eight months, we'd e-mailed incessantly and spoken weekly, sharing everything, keeping no secrets.

Or so I thought. Boy was I ever wrong.

We'd been planning to get an apartment together when she came home. We'd been planning to move to the city, where I was finally going to get serious about college, and Alina was going to work on her Ph.D. at the same Atlanta university. It was no secret that my sister had gotten all the ambition in the family. Since graduating high school, I'd been perfectly content bartending at The Brickyard four or five nights a week, living at home, saving most of my money, and taking just enough college courses at the local Podunk university (one or two a semester, and classes like How to Use the Internet and Travel Etiquette didn't cut it with my folks) to keep Mom and Dad reasonably hopeful that I might one day graduate and get a *Real Job* in the *Real World*. Still, ambition or no, I'd been planning to really buckle down and make some big changes in my life when Alina returned.

When I'd said good-bye to her months ago at the airport, the thought that I wouldn't see her alive again had never crossed my mind. Alina was as certain as the sun rising and setting. She was charmed. She was twenty-four and I was twenty-two. We were going to live forever. Thirty was a million light-years away. Forty wasn't even in the same galaxy. Death? Ha. Death happened to really old people.

Not.

After two weeks, my teary fog started to lift a little. I didn't stop hurting. I think I just finally expelled the last drop of moisture from my body that wasn't absolutely necessary to keep me alive. And rage watered my parched soul. I wanted answers. I wanted justice.

I wanted revenge.

I seemed to be the only one.

I'd taken a psych course a few years back that said people dealt with death by working their way through stages of grief. I hadn't gotten to wallow in the numbness of denial that's supposed to be the first phase. I'd flashed straight from numb to pain in the space of a heartbeat. With Mom and Dad away, I was the one who'd had to identify her body. It hadn't been pretty and there'd been no way to deny Alina was dead.

After two weeks, I was thick into the anger phase. Depression was supposed to be next. Then, if one was healthy, acceptance. Already I could see the beginning signs of acceptance in those around me, as if they'd moved directly from numbness to defeat. They talked of "random acts of violence." They spoke about "getting on with life." They said they were "sure things were in good hands with the police."

I was *so* not healthy. Nor was I remotely sure about the police in Ireland.

Accept Alina's death?

Never.

"You're *not* going, Mac, and that's final." Mom stood at the kitchen counter, a towel draped over her shoulder, a cheery red, yellow, and white magnolia-printed apron tied at her waist, her hands dusted with flour.

She'd been baking. And cooking. And cleaning. And baking some more. She'd become a veritable Tasmanian devil of domesticity. Born and raised in the Deep South, it was Mom's way of trying to deal. Down here, women nest like mother hens when people die. It's just what they do.

We'd been arguing for the past hour. Last night the Dublin police had called to tell us that they were terribly sorry, but due to a lack of evidence, in light of the fact that they didn't have a single lead or witness, there was nothing left to pursue. They were giving us official notice that they'd had no choice but to turn Alina's case over to the unsolved division, which anyone with half a brain knew wasn't a division at all but a filing cabinet in a dimly lit and largely forgotten basement storeroom somewhere. Despite assurances they would periodically reexamine the case for new evidence, that they would exercise utmost due diligence, the message was clear: Alina was dead, shipped back to her own country, and no longer their concern.

They'd given up.

Was that record time or what? Three weeks. A measly twenty-one days. It was inconceivable!

"You can bet your butt if we lived over there, they'd never have given up so quickly," I said bitterly.

"You don't know that, Mac." Mom pushed ash-blonde bangs back from blue eyes that were red-rimmed from weeping, leaving a smudge of flour on her brow.

"Give me the chance to find out."

Her lips compressed into a thin white-edged line. "Absolutely not. I've already lost one daughter to that country. I will not lose another."

Impasse. And here we'd been ever since breakfast, when I'd announced my decision to take time off so I could go to Dublin and find out what the police had really been doing to solve Alina's murder.

I would demand a copy of the file, and do all in my power to motivate them to continue their investigation. I would give a face and a voice—a loud and hopefully highly persuasive one—to the victim's family. I couldn't shake the belief that if only my sister had a representative in Dublin, the investigation would be taken more seriously.

I'd tried to get Dad to go, but there just wasn't any reaching him right now. He was lost in grief. Though our faces and builds were very different, I have the same color hair and eyes as Alina, and the few times he'd actually looked at me lately, he'd gotten such an awful look on his face that it had made me wish I was invisible. Or brunette with brown eyes like him, instead of sunny blonde with green.

Initially, after the funeral, he'd been a dynamo of determined action, making endless phone calls, contacting anyone and everyone. The embassy had been kind, but directed him to Interpol. Interpol had kept him busy for a few days "looking into things" before diplomatically referring him back to where he'd begun—the Dublin police. The Dublin police remained unwavering. No evidence. No leads. Nothing to investigate. *If you have a problem with that, sir, contact your embassy.*

He called the Ashford police—no, they couldn't go to Ireland and look into it. He called the Dublin police again—were they sure they'd interviewed every last one of Alina's friends and fellow students and professors? I hadn't needed to hear both sides of *that* conversation to know the Dublin police were getting testy.

He'd finally placed a call to an old college friend of his that held some high-powered, hush-hush position in the government. Whatever that friend said had deflated him completely. He'd closed the door on us and not come out since.

The climate was decidedly grim in the Lane house, with Mom a tornado in the kitchen, and Dad a black hole in the study. I couldn't sit around forever waiting for them to snap out of it. Time was wasting and the trail was growing colder by the minute. If someone was going to do something, it had to be now, which meant it had to be me.

I said, "I'm going and I don't care if you like it or not."

Mom burst into tears. She slapped the dough she'd been kneading down on the counter and ran out of the room. After a moment, I heard the bedroom door slam down the hall.

That's one thing I can't handle—my mom's tears. As if she hadn't been crying enough lately, I'd just made her cry again. I slunk from the kitchen and crept upstairs, feeling like the absolute lowest of the *lowest* scum on the face of the earth.

I got out of my pajamas, showered, dried my hair and dressed, then stood at a complete loss for a while, staring blankly down the hall at Alina's closed bedroom door.

How many thousands of times had we called back and forth during the day, whispered back and forth during the night, woken each other up for comfort when we'd had bad dreams?

I was on my own with bad dreams now.

Get a grip, Mac. I shook myself and decided to head up to campus. If I stayed home, the black hole might get me, too. Even now I could feel its event horizon expanding exponentially.

On the drive uptown, I recalled that I'd dropped my cell phone in the pool—God, had it really been all those weeks ago?—and decided I'd better stop at the mall to get a new one in case my parents needed to reach me while I was out.

If they even noticed I was gone.

I stopped at the store, bought the cheapest Nokia they had, got the old one deactivated, and powered up the replacement.

I had fourteen new messages, which was probably a record for me. I'm hardly a social butterfly. I'm not one of those plugged-in people who are always hooked up to the latest greatest find-me service. The idea of being found so easily creeps me out a little. I don't have a camera phone or text-messaging capability. I don't have Internet service or satellite radio, just your basic account, thank you. The only other gadget I need is my trusty iPod—music is my great escape.

I got back in my car, turned on the engine so the air conditioner could do battle with July's relentless heat, and began listening to my messages. Most of them were weeks old, from friends at school or The Brickyard who I'd talked to since the funeral.

I guess, somewhere in the back of my mind, I'd made the connection that I'd lost cell service a few days before Alina had died and was hoping I might have a message from her. Hoping she might have called, sounding happy before she died. Hoping she might have said something that would make me forget my grief, if only for a short while. I was desperate to hear her voice just one more time.

When I did, I almost dropped the phone. Her voice burst from the tiny speaker, sounding frantic, terrified.

"Mac! Oh God, Mac, where *are* you? I need to talk to you! It rolled straight into your voice mail! What are you *doing* with your cell phone turned off? You've got to call me the *minute* you get this! I mean, the very instant!"

Despite the oppressive summer heat, I was suddenly icy, my skin clammy.

"Oh, Mac, everything has gone so wrong! I thought I knew what I was doing. I thought he was helping me, but—God, I can't believe I was so stupid! I thought I was in love with him and he's one of them, Mac! He's one of *them*!"

I blinked uncomprehendingly. One of who? For that matter, who was this "he" that was one of "them" in the first place? Alina—in love? No way! Alina and I told each other everything. Aside from a few guys she'd dated casually her first months in Dublin, she'd not mentioned any other guy in her life. And certainly not one she was in love with!

Her voice caught on a sob. My hand tightened to a death grip on the phone, as if maybe I could hold on to my sister through it. Keep *this* Alina alive and safe from harm. I got a few seconds of static, then, when she spoke again she'd lowered her voice, as if fearful of being overheard.

"We've got to talk, Mac! There's so much you don't know. My God, you don't even know what you *are*! There are so many things I should have told you, but I thought I could keep you out of it until things were safer for us. I'm going to try to make it home"—she broke off and laughed bitterly, a caustic sound totally unlike Alina—"but I don't think he'll let me out of the country. I'll call you as soon—" More static. A gasp. "Oh, Mac, he's coming!" Her voice dropped to an urgent whisper. "Listen to me! We've got to find the"—her next word sounded garbled or foreign, something like *shi-sadu*, I thought. "Everything depends on it. We can't let them have it! We've *got* to get to it first! He's been lying to me all along. I know what it is now and I know where—"

Dead air.

The call had been terminated.

I sat stunned, trying to make sense of what I'd just heard. I thought I must have a split personality and there were two Macs: one that had a clue about what was going on in the world around her, and one that could barely track reality well enough to get dressed in the morning and put her shoes on the right feet. Mac-that-had-a-clue must have died when Alina did, because *this* Mac obviously didn't know the first thing about her sister.

She'd been in love and never mentioned it to me! Not once. And now it seemed that was the least of the things she'd not told me. I was flabbergasted. I was betrayed. There was a whole huge part of my sister's life that she'd been withholding from me for *months*.

What kind of danger had she been in? What had she been trying to keep me out of? Until *what* was safer for us? What did we have to find? Had it been the man she'd thought she was in love with that had killed her? Why—oh *why*—hadn't she told me his name?

I checked the date and time on the call—the afternoon after I'd dropped my cell phone in the pool. I felt sick to my stomach. She'd needed me and I hadn't been there for her. At the moment Alina had been so frantically trying to reach me, I'd been sunning lazily in the backyard, listening to my top one hundred mindless happy songs, my cell phone lying short-circuited and forgotten on the dining-room table.

I carefully pressed the save key, then listened to the rest of the messages, hoping she might have called back, but there was nothing else. According to the police, she'd died approximately four hours after she'd tried reaching me, although they hadn't found her body in an alley for nearly two days.

That was a visual I always worked real hard to block.

I closed my eyes and tried not to dwell on the thought that I'd missed my last chance to talk to her, tried not to think that maybe I could have done something to save her if only I'd answered. Those thoughts could make me crazy.

I replayed the message again. What was a *shi-sadu*? And what was the deal with her cryptic *You don't even know what you are?* What could Alina possibly have meant by that?

By my third run-through, I knew the message by heart.

I also knew that there was no way I could play it for Mom and Dad. Not only would it drive them further off the deep end (if there *was* a deeper end than the one they were currently off), but they'd probably lock me in my room and throw away the key. I couldn't see them taking any chances with their remaining child.

But... if I went to Dublin and played it for the police, they'd have to reopen her case, wouldn't they? This was a bona fide lead. If Alina had been in love with someone, she would have been seen with him at some point, somewhere. At school, at her apartment, at work, somewhere. Somebody would know who he was.

And if the mystery man wasn't her killer, surely he was the key to discovering who was. After all, he was "one of *them*."

I frowned.

Whoever or whatever "they" were.

TWO

I quickly learned that it was one thing to *think* about going to Dublin and demanding justice for my sister—and entirely another to find myself standing there in the jet-lagged flesh, across an ocean, four thousand miles from home.

But standing there I was, in rapidly deepening dusk, on a cobbled street in the heart of a foreign city, watching my taxi drive away, surrounded by people speaking a version of English that was virtually unintelligible, trying to come to terms with the fact that, although there were more than a million inhabitants in and around the city, I didn't know a single soul.

Not in Dublin, not in Ireland, not on the entire continent.

I was as alone as alone could be.

I'd had a major blowout fight with Mom and Dad before I'd left, and they weren't speaking to me.

Then again, they weren't speaking to each other, either, so I was trying not to take it too personally. I'd quit my job and withdrawn from school. I'd drained my checking and savings accounts. I was a twenty-two-year-old single white female alone in a strange country where my sister had been killed.

Gripping a suitcase in each hand, I spun in a circle on the sidewalk. What in God's name did I think I was doing? Before I could entertain that thought long enough to go tearing off in a panic-stricken dash after my departing cab, I squared my shoulders, turned, and marched into The Clarin House.

I'd chosen this bed-and-breakfast for two reasons: It was close to where Alina had kept a small, noisy apartment over one of the many Dublin pubs, and it was one of the least expensive in the area. I had no idea how long I would be staying, so I'd booked the cheapest one-way flight I'd been able to find. I had limited funds and needed to watch every penny, or I could end up stuck abroad without enough money to make it home. Only when I was convinced the police—or *An Garda Síochána*, the Guardians of the Peace, as they were called over here—were doing the best job possible would I begin to even consider leaving Ireland again.

On the trip over, I'd devoured two slightly outdated guidebooks I'd found the day before at The Book Nook, Ashford's only used-book store. I'd pored over maps, trying to bone up on Ireland's history and acquaint myself with local customs. I'd passed a three-hour layover in Boston with my eyes closed, trying to recall every detail about Dublin I'd

ever picked up from Alina in our phone calls and
e-mails. I was afraid I was still as green as an un-
ripe Georgia peach, but hopefully I wouldn't be the
gauche tourist, stepping on toes every time I turned
around.

I entered the foyer of The Clarin House and hurried to the counter.

"Evenin' t'ye, m'dear," the desk clerk said cheer-
fully. " 'Opin you 'ave reserves, a'sure ye'll be
needin' 'em such a foine night th'season."

I blinked and replayed what he had just said in my
mind, much more slowly. "Reservations," I said. "Oh
yes." I handed my e-mail confirmation to the elderly
gentleman. With his snowy hair, neatly trimmed
beard, sparkling eyes behind round, rimless glasses,
and oddly small ears, he actually looked like a merry
leprechaun from the fabled Land o' Green. While he
confirmed my stay and checked me in, he thrust flyers
at me and prattled nonstop about where to go and
what to see.

At least I *think* he did.

Truth was, I understood little of what he was saying. Though his accent was charming, the suspicion
I'd formed at the airport had just been confirmed: It
was going to take my sadly monolingual American
brain time to acclimate to the Irish inflection and
unique way of phrasing things. As rapidly as the
clerk was speaking, he might as well have been
havering away (one of my new phrases from my
trusty guidebook) in Gaelic for all the sense it made
to me.

A few minutes later, and none the wiser about a

thing he'd recommended, I was on the third floor, unlocking the door to my room. As I'd expected for the price, it wasn't much. Cramped, only seven or eight feet in either direction, the room was plainly furnished with a twin bed perched beneath a tall narrow window, a small three-drawer dresser topped by a lamp with a stained yellow shade, a rickety chair, a pedestal sink for washing up, and a closet about as wide as I was with—I pushed it open—a whopping two wire hangers, badly bent. The bathroom was a shared deal down at the end of the hall. The only concession to atmosphere was a faded orange-and-pink rug and a matching drape over the window.

I dropped my bags on the bed, pushed the curtain aside, and looked out at the city where my sister died.

I didn't want it to be beautiful, but it was.

Full dark had fallen and Dublin was brilliantly lit. There'd been a recent rain, and against the coal of night, the shiny cobbled streets gleamed amber, rose, and neon-blue from reflected lamps and signs. The architecture was a kind I'd seen before only in books and movies: Old World, elegant, and grand. The buildings boasted ornate facades, some adorned by pillars and columns, others sported handsomely detailed woodwork and tall, majestic windows. The Clarin House stood on the outskirts of the Temple Bar District, which, according to my guidebook, was the most vibrant, alive part of the city, full of *craic*— Irish slang for something along the lines of "rollicking good fun."

People milled about in the streets, wandering from one of the countless pubs in the district to the next. "Good puzzle" James Joyce had written, "would be cross Dublin without passing a pub." *More than six hundred pubs in Dublin!* the headline on one of the many flyers the sprightly clerk had thrust into my hand proudly trumpeted. From what I'd seen on the drive in, I believed it. Alina had studied hard to be admitted to the exclusive study-abroad program at Trinity College, but I also knew she'd thoroughly enjoyed the energy, social life, and many and diverse pubs of the city. She'd loved Dublin.

Watching the people laughing and talking below, I felt as small as a dust mote glimmering in a shaft of moonlight.

And about as connected to the world.

"Well, *get* connected," I muttered to myself. "You're Alina's only hope."

At the moment, Alina's Only Hope was hungrier than she was tired—and after three layovers and twenty hours of travel, I was dog-tired. I'd never been able to sleep on an empty stomach, so I knew I would have to get something to eat before I could turn in. If I didn't, I'd just toss and turn all night, and wake up both hungrier and more exhausted, which wouldn't do. I had a busy day tomorrow and needed my wits about me.

It was as good a time to get connected as any. I splashed cold water on my face, touched up my makeup and brushed my hair. After changing into my favorite short white skirt that made the most of my sun-kissed legs, a pretty lilac camisole and matching cardigan, I swept my long blonde hair up into a high ponytail, locked up, and slipped out of the inn, into the Dublin night.

I stopped in the first pub that looked inviting and boasted authentic Irish fare. I selected a quaint Old World place over the flashier urban ones in the district. I just wanted a good hot meal without a lot of fuss. And I got it: a bowl of thick, hearty Irish stew, warm soda bread, and a slice of chocolate whisky cake, washed down by a perfectly stacked Guinness.

Though I was pleasantly sleepy after the filling meal, I ordered a second beer, sat back and looked around, drinking in the atmosphere. I wondered if Alina had ever come here, and indulged myself in a little fantasy of imagining her here with friends, laughing and happy. It was a beautiful pub, with cozy high-backed leather booths, or "snugs" as they were called, lining the brick walls. The bar occupied the center of the large room, a handsome, stately affair of mahogany, brass, and mirrors. It was surrounded by tall café tables and high stools. It was at one of those tables that I sat.

The pub was filled with an eclectic mix of patrons, from young university students to retired tourists, from fashionably attired to sporty-grunge. As a bartender, I'm always interested in what other clubs are like: what they offer, who they draw, and what soap operas unfold in them, because they inevitably do. There are always a few gorgeous guys, always a few fights, always a few romances, and *always* a few weirdos in any given bar, on any given night.

Tonight would prove no exception.

I'd already paid my tab and was just finishing my beer when he walked in. I noticed him because it was impossible not to. Though I didn't catch sight of him until he'd already passed me and his back was to me, it was the backside of a world-class athlete. Tall, strong, powerful muscle poured into black leather pants, black boots, and—yes, you guessed it, a real drama king—a black shirt. I've spent enough time behind a bar that I've formed a few opinions about what people wear and what it says about them. Guys who wear black from head to toe fall into two categories: they want to be trouble, or they are trouble. I tend to steer clear of them. Women who wear all black are a different story, but that's neither here nor there.

So I noticed his backside first, and as I'm scoping it out with a connoisseur's eye (trouble or not, he was serious eye-candy), he goes straight to the bar, leans over it, and *filches a bottle of top-shelf whisky.*

Not a soul seemed to notice.

I stiffened with instant indignation for the bar-keep; it was a good bet it was *his* pocket that the sixty-five-dollar bottle of single-malt scotch was going to end up coming out of at closing time when his accounts didn't zero-out.

I began to slide down from my stool. Yes, I was going to do it—stranger in a strange land, no less—I was going to rat him out. We bartenders have to stick together.

The guy turned.

I froze, one foot on the lower rung, halfway down. I think I even stopped breathing. To say he was movie-star material didn't cut it. To call him drop-dead gorgeous didn't either. To say that archangels must have been graced by God with such faces couldn't even begin to *begin* describing him. Long gold hair, eyes so light they looked silvery, and golden skin, the man was blindingly beautiful. Every hair on my body lifted, all over, in unison. And I got the strangest thought: *He's not human.*

I shook my head at my lunacy and backed up onto the stool. I still intended to tell the barkeep, but not until the man moved away from the bar. I was suddenly in no hurry to get close to him.

But he didn't move away. Instead he leaned back against it, broke the seal, unscrewed the cap, and took a long swig from the bottle.

And as I watched him, something utterly inexplicable happened. The fine hair all over my body began to vibrate, my meal turned to a lump of lead in my stomach and I was suddenly having some kind of waking vision. The bar was still there and so was he, but in *this* version of reality, he wasn't gorgeous at all. He was nothing but a carefully camouflaged abomination, and just beneath the surface of all that perfection, the barely masked stench of decay was rising from his skin. And if I got close enough, the foul odor might choke me to death. But that wasn't the full of it. I felt as if—if I could just open my eyes a little wider—I would see even more. I would see exactly what he was, if I could only look *harder* somehow.

I don't know how long I might have sat there, staring. Later, I would know that it was nearly long enough to get myself killed, but I knew nothing of that at the time.

I was saved from myself, from my story ending right here and now on this very page, by a sharp rap to the back of my head.

"Ow!" I hopped off my perch on the stool, turned around, and glared at my assailant.

She glared back at me—a tiny old woman, eighty if she was a day. Thick silvery-white hair was pulled back in a long braid from a fine-boned face. She was wearing black from head to toe and I was briefly aggravated to realize I might have to revise my theories about women's fashion. Before I could say, "Hey, what do you think you're doing?" she reached up and rapped me again, her knuckles cracking sharply against my forehead.

"Ow! Stop that!"

"How dare you stare at him like that?" the woman hissed. Fierce blue eyes glittered furiously at me from within nests of fine wrinkles. "Would you be jeopardizing us all, then, you damn fool?"

"Huh?" As with the elderly leprechaun of a desk clerk, I had to replay her words more slowly in my mind. Still they made no sense to me.

"The dark Tuatha Dé! How dare you betray us! And you—an O'Connor, no less! I'll be having a word with your kin, I will!"

"Huh?" It suddenly seemed the only word I could manage. Had I heard her correctly? What in the world was a *too-ah-day*? And who did she think I was? She raised her hand and I was afraid she was about to rap me again, so I blurted, "I'm not an O'Connor."

"Sure you are." She rolled her eyes. "That hair, those eyes. And that skin! Och, aye, you're an O'Connor through and through. The likes of him would snap a tasty little thing like you in two and be picking his teeth with your bones before you even managed to part those pretty lips to beg. Now get out of here, before you ruin us all!"

I blinked. "But I—"

She silenced me with a quelling stare no doubt perfected by half a century of practice. "Out! Now! And don't you be coming back in here. Not tonight, not ever. If you can't keep your head down and honor your bloodline, then do us all a favor—go die somewhere else."

Ow. Still blinking, I fumbled behind me for my purse. I didn't need to be hit over the head with a stick to know I wasn't wanted. A few knuckle-raps did just fine. Head high, eyes fixed straight ahead, I backed away just in case the nutty old woman got it in her mind to try to bean me again. At a safe distance, I turned and marched from the bar.

"And that's that," I muttered to myself as I stomped back to my cramped, unwelcoming room at the inn. "Welcome to Ireland, Mac."

I couldn't decide what had been more disturbing— my bizarre hallucination or the hostile crone.

My last thought before I fell asleep was that the old woman was obviously crazy. Either she was or I was, and it sure wasn't me.

THREE

It took me a while to find the Pearse Street Garda Station the next day. Things looked a lot different when I was walking on the pretty little map instead of looking down at it. The streets didn't branch off at quite the same tidy angles, and their names changed without rhyme or reason between one block and the next.

I wandered past the same outdoor café and independent newsstand three times. *Man Sees Devil in County Clare Cornfield, Sixth Sighting This Month,* one tabloid blared. *The Old Ones Are Returning, Claims Psychic,* another proclaimed. Wondering who the "Old Ones" were—an aging rock band?—on my fourth trip by I broke down and asked the elderly vendor for directions.

I couldn't understand a word he said. I was beginning to see a distinct correlation between age of

speaker and unintelligibility of accent. As the griz-
zled gentleman fired off a spate of lovely lilting
words that made no sense to me at all, I nodded and
smiled a lot, trying to look intelligent. I waited until
he wound down, then took a gamble—what the
heck? my odds were fifty-fifty—and turned to go
north.

With a sharp clucking sound, he grabbed my
shoulder, turned me in the opposite direction, and
barked, "Air ye deaf, lass?"

I think. He might have called me a hairy jackass.
Smiling brightly, I went south.

The morning desk clerk at The Clarin House, a
twenty-something woman named Bonita (whom I'd
understood with little difficulty), had assured me I
wouldn't be able to miss the Garda station once I got
there. She'd said the historic building looked a little
like an old English manor house, made of all stone,
with many chimneys and rounded turrets at each
end. She was right, it did.

I entered the station through a tall wooden door
set into a deep, high stone arch and checked in with
the receptionist. "I'm MacKayla Lane." I got right to
the point. "My sister was murdered here last month.
I'd like to see the detective that handled her case. I
have new information for him."

"Who've you been working with, luv?"

"Inspector O'Duffy. Patrick O'Duffy."

"Sorry, luv. Our Patty's out for a few days. I could
set you an appointment with him on Thursday."

An appointment on Thursday? I had a lead *now*. I

didn't want to wait three days. "Is there another inspector I could speak to about this?"

She shrugged. "Could. But you'll be having the best of luck with the one who worked her case. If it were my sister, I'd be waiting for Patty."

I shifted impatiently from foot to foot. The need to do something was burning a hole in my gut, but I wanted to do what was best for Alina, not what was the most immediate. "All right. I'll take an appointment on Thursday. Do you have something in the morning?"

She put me down for the first appointment of the day.

I went to Alina's place next.

Though her lease had been paid up through the end of the month—nonrefundable—I had no idea how long it might take to sort through her things and get everything boxed up to send back to Georgia, so I figured I'd better start now. I wasn't about to leave a single shred of my sister four thousand miles from home.

There was police tape over the door, but it had been cut. I let myself in with the key Inspector O'Duffy had mailed to us in the small package of personal effects found on her body. Her apartment smelled just like her room back home, of peaches-and-cream candles, and Beautiful perfume.

It was dark inside, the shutters drawn. The pub below hadn't yet opened for the day, so it was quiet as a tomb. I fumbled for the light switch. Though we'd been told her place was thoroughly ransacked, I wasn't prepared for it. Fingerprint dust was everywhere. Everything breakable was broken: lamps, knickknacks, dishes, even the mirror set into the mantel above the gas fireplace. The sofa was sliced, cushions torn, books ripped up, bookcases smashed, and even the drapes were shredded. CDs crunched beneath my feet when I stepped into the living room.

Had this been done before or after she'd died? The police had offered no opinion on the timing. I didn't know if what I was seeing was the by-product of mindless rage, or if the killer had been searching for something. Maybe the thing Alina had said *we* needed to find. Maybe he'd thought she had it already, whatever it was.

Alina's body had turned up miles away, in a trash-filled alley on the opposite side of the River Liffey. I knew exactly where. I'd seen the crime-scene photos. Before I left Ireland, I knew I would end up in that alley, saying my last good-byes to her, but I was in no hurry to do so. This was bad enough.

In fact, five minutes in the place was all I could stand.

I locked up and hurried back down the steps, bursting from the narrow, windowless staircase into the foggy alley behind the bar. I was grateful that I had three and a half more weeks to deal with the situation before her lease expired. Next time I came, I'd be braced for what I would find. Next time I came, I'd be armed with boxes, trash bags, and a broom.

Next time I came, I told myself, as I dragged a sleeve across my cheek, I wouldn't cry.

I spent the rest of the morning and a good part of a drizzly afternoon holed up in an Internet café, trying to track down the thing Alina had said we needed to find—a *shi-sadu*. I tried every search engine. I asked Jeeves. I ran text searches in local online newspapers hoping for a hit. Problem was, I didn't know how to spell it; I didn't know if it was a person, place, or thing, and no matter how many times I listened to the message, I still wasn't sure I understood what she was saying.

Just for the heck of it, I decided to hunt for the odd word the old woman had said last night—*too-ah-day*. I had no luck with that, either.

A few hours into my frustrating search—I shot off several e-mails too, including an emotional one to my parents—I ordered another coffee and asked two cute Irish guys behind the counter who looked about my age if they had any idea what a *shi-sadu* was.

They didn't.

"How about a *too-ah-day*?" I asked, expecting the same answer.

"*Too-ah-day?*" the dark-haired one repeated, with a slightly different inflection than I'd used.

I nodded. "An old woman in a pub said it to me last night. Any idea what it means?"

"Sure." He laughed. "It's what all you bloody Americans come here hoping to find. That and a pot

o' gold, wouldn't that be the right of it, Seamus?"
He smirked at his blond companion, who smirked
broadly back.

"What's that?" I said warily.

Flapping his arms like little wings, he winked.
"Why, that'd be a wee fairy, lass."

A wee fairy. Right. Uh-huh. With *Tourist* stamped
all over my forehead, I took the steaming mug, paid
for the coffee, and escorted my flaming cheeks back
to my table.

Crazy old woman, I thought irritably, closing
down my Internet session. If I ever saw her again,
she was going to get an earful.

It was the fog that got me lost.

I would have been okay if it had been a sunny
day. But fog has a way of transforming even the
most familiar landscape into something foreign and
sinister, and the place was already so foreign to me
that it quickly took on sinister attributes.

One minute I thought I was heading straight for
The Clarin House, plowing down block after block
without really paying much attention, the next I was
in a dwindling crowd on a street that I hadn't seen
before, and suddenly, I was one of only three people
on an eerily quiet fog-filled lane. I had no idea how
far I'd come. My mind was on other things. I might
have walked for miles.

I had what I thought was a really smart idea.
I would follow one of the other pedestrians and

surely they would lead me back to the main part of town.

Buttoning my jacket against the misting rain, I picked the closer of the two, a fiftyish woman in a beige raincoat and a blue scarf. I had to stick close because the fog was so thick.

Two blocks later, she was clutching her purse tightly to her side and darting nervous glances over her shoulder. It took me a few minutes to figure out what she was frightened of—*me*. Belatedly I recalled what I'd read in my guidebook about crime in the inner city. Innocent-looking youths of both genders were responsible for much of it.

I tried to reassure her. "I'm lost," I called. "I'm just trying to get back to my hotel. Please, can you help me?"

"Stop following me! Stay away," she cried, quickening her pace, coattails flapping.

"All right, I'm staying." I stopped where I stood. The last thing I wanted to do was chase her off; the other pedestrian was gone, I needed her. The fog was getting denser by the minute and I had no idea where I was. "Look, I'm sorry I scared you. Could you just point me toward the Temple Bar District? *Please?* I'm an American tourist and I'm lost."

Without turning or slowing in the least, she flung an arm out in a general leftward direction, then disappeared around the corner, leaving me alone in the fog.

I sighed. Left it was.

I went to the corner, turned, and began walking at a moderate pace. Taking stock of my surroundings as I went, I stepped it up a bit. I seemed to be heading deeper into a dilapidated, industrial part of the city. Storefronts with the occasional apartment above gave way to rundown warehouse-like buildings on both sides of the street with busted-out windows and sagging doors. The sidewalk whittled down to barely a few feet wide and was increasingly trash-littered with every step. I started to feel strongly nauseated, I suppose from the stench of the sewers. There must have been an old paper factory nearby; thick husks of porous yellowed parchment of varying sizes tumbled and blew along the empty streets. Narrow, dingy alleyways were marked at the entrances with peeling painted arrows, pointing to docks that looked as if the last time they'd received a delivery was twenty years ago.

Here, a crumbling smokestack stretched up, melting into the fog. There, an abandoned car sat with the driver's door ajar and, outside it, a pair of shoes and a pile of clothing, as if the driver had simply gotten out, stripped, and left everything behind. It was eerily quiet. The only sounds were the muted muffle of my footsteps and the slow dripping of gutters emptying into drainpipes. The farther I walked into the decaying neighborhood, the more I wanted to run, or at least give way to a vigorous sprint, but I worried if there were unsavory denizens of the human sort in the area, the rapid pounding of my heels against the pavement might draw their attention. I was afraid this part of the city was so deserted because the businesses had moved out when the gangs had moved in. Who knew what lurked behind those broken windows? Who knew what crouched beyond that half-open door?

The next ten minutes were some of the most harrowing of my life. I was alone in a bad section of a foreign city with no idea whether I was going the right way or headed straight for something worse. Twice I thought I heard something rustling about in an alley as I passed. Twice I swallowed panic and refused to run. It was impossible not to think of Alina, of the similar locale in which her body had been found. I couldn't shake the feeling that there was something wrong here, and it was something far more wrong than mere abandonment and decay. This part of the city didn't just feel empty. It felt, well...forsaken...like I should have passed a sign ten blocks ago that said Abandon Hope, All Ye Who Enter Here.

I was feeling increasingly nauseated and my skin was starting to crawl. I hurried down block after block, in as straight a general leftward direction as the streets would permit. Though it was only supper time, rain and fog had turned day to dusk and those few streetlamps that hadn't been broken out years ago began to flicker and glow. Night was falling and soon it would be as dark as pitch in those long shadowed stretches between the weak and infrequent pools of light.

I picked up my pace to a sprint. On the verge of hysteria at the thought of being lost in this awful part of the city at night, I nearly sobbed with relief when I spied a brightly lit building a few blocks ahead, blazing like an oasis of light.

I broke into that run I'd been resisting.

As I drew nearer, I could see that all the windows were intact, and the tall brick building was impeccably restored, sporting a costly updated first-floor facade of dark cherry and brass. Large pillars framed an alcoved entrance inset with a handsome cherry door flanked by stained-glass sidelights and crowned by a matching transom. The tall windows down the side were framed by matching columns of lesser size, and covered with elaborate wrought-iron latticework. A late-model sedan was parked out front in the street beside an expensive motorcycle.

Beyond it, I could see storefronts with second-floor residences. There were people in the streets; perfectly normal-looking shoppers and diners and pub-goers.

Just like that, I was in a decent part of the city again! *Thank God,* I thought. Though later I wouldn't be quite so certain about just who had saved me from danger that day, or if I'd been saved at all. We have a phrase back home in Georgia: Out of the frying pan and into the fire. The soles of my shoes should have been steaming.

Barrons Books and Baubles proclaimed the gaily-painted shingle that hung perpendicular to the building, suspended over the sidewalk by an elaborate brass pole bolted into the brick above the door. A lighted sign in the old-fashioned, green-tinted windows announced Open. It couldn't have looked more like the perfect place to call a taxi to me if it had sported a sign that said *Welcome Lost Tourists/Call Your Taxis Here.*

I was done for the day. No more asking directions, no more walking. I was damp and cold. I wanted hot soup and a hotter shower. And I wanted it more than I wanted to pinch precious pennies.

Bells jangled as I pushed open the door.

I stepped inside and stopped, blinking in astonishment. From the exterior I'd expected a charming little book and curio shop with the inner dimensions of a university Starbucks. What I got was a cavernous interior that housed a display of books that made the library Disney's Beast gave to Beauty on their wedding day look understocked.

I love books, by the way, way more than movies. Movies tell you what to think. A good book lets you choose a few thoughts for yourself. Movies show you the pink house. A good book tells you there's a pink house and lets you paint some of the finishing touches, maybe choose the roof style, park your own car out front. My imagination has always topped anything a movie could come up with. Case in point, those darned Harry Potter movies. That was *so* not what that part-Veela-chick, Fleur Delacour, looked like.

Still, I'd never imagined a bookstore like this. The room was probably a hundred feet long and forty feet wide. The front half of the store opened all the way up to the roof, four stories or more. Though I couldn't make out the details, a busy mural was painted on the domed ceiling. Bookcases lined each level, from floor to molding. Behind elegant banisters, platform walkways permitted catwalk access on the second, third, and fourth levels. Ladders slid on oiled rollers from one section to the next.

The first floor had freestanding shelves arranged in wide aisles to my left, two seating cozies, and a cashier station to my right. I couldn't see what stretched beyond the rear balcony on the upper floors but I guessed more books and perhaps some of those baubles the sign mentioned.

There wasn't a soul in sight.

"Hello!" I called, spinning in a circle, drinking it in. A bookstore like this was a fabulous find, a great end to an otherwise awful day. While I waited for my taxi, I'd browse for new reads. "Hello, is anyone here?"

"Be with you in a trice, dear," a woman's voice floated from the rear of the store.

I heard the soft murmur of voices, a woman's and a man's, then heels clacking across a hardwood floor.

The full-bosomed, elegant woman who came into view had once been stunning in the way of movie-star divas of old. In her early fifties now, her sleek dark hair was gathered back in a chignon from a pale-skinned, classic-boned face. Though time and gravity had traced the supple skin of youth with the lines of fine parchment and creased her brow, this woman would always be beautiful, right up to the day she died. She wore a long tailored gray skirt and a gauzy linen blouse that flattered her voluptuous figure and revealed a hint of a lacy bra beneath. Lustrous pearls glowed softly at her neck, wrist, and ears. "I'm Fiona. Is there something I can help you find, dear?"

"I was hoping I could use your phone to call a taxi. Of course, I'll buy something too," I added hastily. Many of the local businesses posted placards advising that phones and bathrooms were only for paying customers.

She smiled. "No need for that, dear, unless you wish. Certainly, you may use our phone."

After paging through the phone book and dialing up a cab, I set off to make good use of my twenty-minute wait, collecting two thrillers, the latest Janet Evanovich, and a fashion magazine. While Fiona was ringing me up, I decided to try a stab in the dark, figuring anyone who worked with so many books surely knew a little of something about a lot of everything.

"I've been trying to find out what a word means but I'm not sure what language it's in, or even if I'm saying it right," I told her.

She scanned the last of my books and told me the total. "What word would that be, dear?"

I glanced down, rummaging in my purse for my credit card. Books weren't in my budget and I was going to have to float them until I got back home. "*Shi-sadu*. At least that's what I think it is." I found my wallet, withdrew my Visa, and glanced up at her again. She'd gone still and looked white as a ghost.

"I've never heard of it. Why are you looking for it?" she said tightly.

I blinked. "Who said I was looking for it?" I

hadn't said I was looking for it. I'd just asked what the word meant.

"Why else would you be asking?"

"I just wanted to know what it means," I said.

"Where did you hear of it?"

"Why do you care?" I knew I'd started to sound defensive, but really, what was her deal? The word obviously meant something to her. Why wouldn't she tell me? "Look, this is really important."

"How important?" she said.

What did she want? Money? That could be a problem. "Very."

She looked beyond me, over my shoulder, and uttered a single word like a benediction. "Jericho."

"Jericho?" I echoed, not following. "You mean the ancient city?"

"Jericho Barrons," a rich, cultured male voice said behind me. "And you are?" Not an Irish accent. No idea what kind of accent it was, though.

I turned, with my name perched on the tip of my tongue, but it didn't make it out. No wonder Fiona had said his name like that. I gave myself a brisk inward shake and stuck out my hand. "MacKayla, but most people call me Mac."

"Have you a surname, MacKayla?" He pressed my knuckles briefly to his lips and released my hand. My skin tingled where his mouth had been.

Was it my imagination or was his gaze predatory? I was afraid I was getting a little paranoid. It had been a long, odd day after an odder night. *Ashford Journal* headlines were beginning to form in my mind: **Second Lane Sister Meets with Foul Play in Dublin Bookshop.** "Just Mac is fine," I evaded.

"And what do you know of this *shi-sadu*, just Mac?"

"Nothing. That's why I was asking. What is it?"

"I have no idea," he said. "Where did you hear of it?"

"Can't remember. Why do you care?"

He crossed his arms.

I crossed mine too. Why were these people lying to me? What in the world *was* this thing I was asking about?

He studied me with his predator's gaze, assessing me from head to toe. I studied him back. He didn't just occupy space; he saturated it. The room had been full of books before, now it was full of him. About thirty, six foot two or three, he had dark hair, golden skin, and dark eyes. His features were strong, chiseled. I couldn't pinpoint his nationality any more than I could his accent; some kind of European crossed with Old World Mediterranean or maybe an ancestor with dark Gypsy blood. He wore an elegant, dark gray Italian suit, a crisp white shirt, and a muted patterned tie. He wasn't handsome. That was too calm a word. He was intensely masculine. He was sexual. He attracted. There was an omnipresent carnality about him, in his dark eyes, in his full mouth, in the way he stood. He was the kind of man I wouldn't flirt with in a million years.

A smile curved his mouth. It looked no nicer than he did, and I wasn't deluded by it for a moment.

"You know what it means," I told him. "Why don't you just tell me?"

"You know something about it, as well," he said. "Why not tell me?"

"I asked first." Childish maybe, but it was all I could think of. He didn't dignify it with a response. "I'll find out what I want to know one way or another," I said. If these people knew what it was, somewhere in Dublin somebody else did, too.

"As will I. Have no doubt of that, just Mac."

I gave him my frostiest look, much-practiced on drunk, randy patrons at The Brickyard. "Is that a threat?"

He stepped forward and I stiffened, but he merely reached past me, over my shoulder. When he moved back, he was holding my credit card. "Of course not"—he glanced down at my name—"Ms. *Lane*. I see your Visa is drawn on SunTrust. Isn't that a southern U.S. bank?"

"Maybe." I snatched my card from his hand.

"What state in the South are you from?"

"Texas," I lied.

"Indeed. What brings you to Dublin?"

"None of your business."

"It became my business when you came into my establishment, inquiring about the *shi-sadu*."

"So you *do* know what it is! You just admitted it."

"I admit nothing. However, I will tell you this: You, Ms. Lane, are in way over your head. Take my advice and extricate yourself while it's still possible."

"It's too late. I can't." His condescending high-handedness was making me mad. When I get mad, I dig my heels in right where I am.

"A pity. You won't last a week as sophomorically as you're bludgeoning about. Should you care to tell me what you know, I might be able to increase your odds of survival."

"Not a chance. Not unless you tell me what you know first."

He made an impatient sound and his eyes narrowed. "You bloody fool, you have no idea what you're—"

"Somebody in here call a cab?" The bells on the door jangled.

"I did," I shot over my shoulder.

Jericho Barrons actually made the faint beginnings of a lunge toward me, as if to physically restrain me. Until that moment, although aggression had charged the air and threat had been implied, there'd been nothing overt. I'd been aggravated, now I was a little afraid.

Our gazes locked and we stood a moment in that frozen tableau. I could almost see him calculating the importance—if any at all—of our sudden audience.

Then he gave me a faint sardonic smile and inclined his head as if to say, *You win this time, Ms. Lane.* "Don't count on it twice," he murmured.

Saved by the bell, I snatched up my bag of books and backed away. I didn't take my eyes off Jericho Barrons until I was out the door.

FOUR

Communal bathrooms sucked.

I got my hot soup, but my shower was icy. Upon returning to The Clarin House, I made the unhappy discovery that apparently everyone in the inn waited until early evening to shower before going out for dinner and a night on the town. Inconsiderate tourists. The water was far too cold to endure washing my hair, so I phoned the desk for a six o'clock wake-up call when I would try again. I suspected some of the guests would just be getting in then.

I changed out of street clothes into a lacy peach sleep shirt and matching panties. That was another pain about communal bathrooms—you either got fully dressed again after your shower or risked a half-naked mad dash down the hall past dozens of doors that might pop open at any moment. I'd opted for fully dressed.

I finished unpacking the last of my luggage. I'd brought a few comfort items from home. I pulled out one of Alina's peaches-and-cream candles, two Hershey bars, my favorite pair of faded and much-loved cutoff jean shorts that Mom was always threatening to throw away, and a small framed picture of my folks, which I propped against the lamp on the dresser.

Then I rummaged through my backpack and dug out the notebook I'd bought a few weeks ago, and sat cross-legged on my bed. Alina had always kept a journal, ever since we were kids. As a bratty younger sibling, I'd ferreted out many of her hiding places—she'd gotten more inventive as the years had gone by; the last I'd found had been behind a loose base-board in her closet—and teased her mercilessly about whatever boyfriend she'd been mooning over, complete with annoying *kissy-kissy* sounds.

Until recently, I'd never written in one myself. After the funeral, I'd been in desperate need of an outlet and had poured out pages of grief into the thing. More recently I'd been writing lists: what to pack, what to buy, what to learn, and where to go first. Lists had become my anchors. They got me through the days. The oblivion of sleep got me through the nights. So long as I knew exactly where I was going and what I was doing the next day, I didn't flounder.

I was proud of myself for how well I'd blustered through my first full day in Dublin. But then, when bluster was all you had, it wasn't so hard to paste it on over your real face. I knew what I really was: a pretty young woman barely old enough to tend bar, who'd never been more than a few states away from Georgia, who'd recently lost her sister and who was—as Jericho Barrons had said—in way over her head.

Go to Trinity College, talk to her professors and try to find out names of friends was number one on my list for tomorrow. I had an e-mail copy of her class schedule, listing instructors and times. She'd sent it to me at the beginning of the term so I'd know when she was in class and when my odds were best of catching her at home to talk. With luck, someone I spoke to tomorrow would know who Alina had been seeing and be able to tell me who her mystery man was. *Go to local library, keep trying to track down* shi-sadu was next. I sure wasn't going back to that bookstore, which really pissed me off because it had been an amazing bookstore. I couldn't shake the feeling I'd been lucky to escape today. That if the cabbie hadn't arrived at just that moment, Jericho Barrons might have tied me to a chair and tortured me until I'd told him everything he wanted to know. *Buy boxes, bags, and broom to take to Alina's place* was third. That one was optional. I wasn't sure I was ready to go back there yet. I nibbled the tip of my pen, wishing I'd been able to see Inspector O'Duffy. I'd been hoping to get his reports and retrace whatever route the *Gardai* investigation had followed. Unfortunately, that possibility was now on hold for a few days.

I made a short list of things I wanted from a local drugstore: an adaptor to charge my iPod; juice; and a few cheap snacks to keep in my room, then turned out the light and fell almost immediately into a deep, dreamless sleep.

Someone knocking at my door awakened me.

I sat up, rubbing gritty, tired eyes that felt as if I'd just shut them seconds ago. It took me a few moments to remember where I was—in a twin bed in a chilly room in Dublin, with rain tapping lightly at the window.

I'd been having a fantastic dream. Alina and I were playing volleyball up at one of the many man-made lakes built by Georgia Power, scattered throughout the state. There were three near Ashford and we went to one or the other just about every weekend in the summer for fun, sun, and guy-watching. The dream had been so vivid I could still taste Corona with lime, smell coconut suntan oil, and feel the silk of trucked-in sand beneath my feet.

I glanced at my watch. It was two o'clock in the morning. I was sleepy and grumpy and didn't try to disguise it. "Who is it?"

"Jericho Barrons."

I couldn't have been slammed awake any harder if I'd been hit upside the head with my mom's cast-iron frying pan. What was *he* doing here? How had he found me? I shot up, my hand hovering over the phone, ready at any moment to call the front desk and ask for the police. "What do you want?"

"We have information to exchange. You want to know what it is. I want to know what you know about it."

I wasn't about to reveal how freaked out I was that he'd hunted me down. "Bright guy, aren't you? I figured that out back at the store. What took you so long?"

There was such a protracted silence that I began to wonder if he'd gone away. "I am unaccustomed to asking for what I want. Nor am I accustomed to bartering with a woman," he said finally.

"Well, get used to it with me, bud, because I don't take orders from anyone. And I don't give up anything for free." *Bluster, bluster, bluster, Mac.* But he didn't know that.

"Do you intend to open this door, Ms. Lane, or shall we converse where anyone might attend our business?"

"Do you really intend to exchange information?" I countered.

"I do."

"And you'll go first?"

"I will."

My shoulders slumped. I moved my hand away from the phone. I straightened my shoulders again quickly. I knew the value of putting a smile on a sad face—it made you feel happy after a while. Courage was no different. I didn't trust Jericho Barrons farther than I could throw him, which was a great big Not At All, but he knew what this *shi-sadu* was, and although I hoped I could find the information somewhere else, what if I couldn't? What if I wasted weeks looking with no success? Time was money and mine was finite. If he was willing to trade, I had to open that door. Unless... "We can trade through the door," I said.

"No."

"Why not?"

"I am a private person, Ms. Lane. This is not negotiable."

"But I—"

"No."

I blew out an aggravated breath. The tone in his voice said it would be a waste of time to argue. I stood and reached for a pair of jeans. "How did you find me?" I buttoned my fly and pushed my hands into my hair. It always got tangled when I slept because it was so long. I had major bed-head.

"You procured a hired conveyance at my establishment."

"We call them taxis where I come from. And bookstores." God, he was stuffy.

"We call them manners where I come from, Ms. Lane. Have you any?"

"You should talk. It's not my fault. Being threatened seems to bring out the worst in me." I opened the door a crack and glared up at him through the space afforded by the latch-chain. I couldn't imagine Jericho Barrons as a child, going to school, face freshly scrubbed, hair neatly combed, lunch box in hand. He'd surely been spawned by some cataclysmic event of nature, not born.

He cocked his head and studied me through the narrow opening, spending several seconds on each part of me: disheveled hair, sleep-swollen mouth and eyes, lacy sleep shirt, jeans, toes. I felt as if I'd been burned to CD by the time he was done. "May I come in?" he said.

"*I* wouldn't have let you up this far." I was furious the desk clerk had let him up. I'd thought the place had better security. I was going to have a word with the manager tomorrow.

"I told them I was your brother." He gleaned my thoughts from my face.

"Right. Because we look so much alike." If he was winter, I was summer. If I was sunshine, he was night. A dark and stormy one.

Not an ounce of amusement flickered in those dark eyes. "Well, Ms. Lane?"

"I'm thinking." Now that he knew where I was staying, if he wanted to harm me, he could do it anytime. No need to rush into it tonight. He could lie in wait for me and jump me somewhere tomorrow in the streets. I would be no safer in the future than I was from him now, unless I was willing to move about from inn to inn, trying to lose him, and I wasn't. I needed to be in this part of town. Besides, he just didn't look like the kind of creep that would messily murder a woman in her hotel room; he looked like the kind of creep that would line her up in the sights of an assassin's rifle without a shred of emotion. That I would use that as an argument in his favor should have worried me. Later I would realize I'd been walking around still more than a little numb from Alina's death during those first weeks in Ireland, and more than a little reckless from it as well. I sighed. "Sure. Come in."

I closed the door, unhooked the chain, opened it

again, then stepped back, allowing him to enter. I
pushed the door open all the way and left it flush to
the wall, so anyone walking past could see in and, if
I needed to, I could shout down the third floor with
my cries for help. Adrenaline was pumping through
my body, making me feel shaky. He was still wearing his impeccable Italian suit, his shirt just as crisp
and white as it had been hours ago. The cramped
room was suddenly stuffed to overflowing with
Jericho Barrons. If a normal person filled one hundred percent of the molecules they occupied, he
somehow managed to cram his to two hundred percent capacity.

He cast a brief yet thorough glance around and I
had no doubt, if questioned later, he would be able
to accurately recount every detail, from the rust-
colored water spots high up on the ceiling, down to
my pretty flowered bra lying on the rug. I nudged
the rug with my toe, pushing it and its cargo beneath the bed.

"So what is it?" I said. "No, wait—how do you
spell it?" I'd tried everything today, and assuming
he told me and I lived, I wanted to be able to re-
search it on my own.

He began pacing a small circle around me. I
turned with him, not willing to give him my back.
"S-i-n-s-a-r," he spelled.

"Sinsar?" I said it phonetically.

He shook his head. "*Shi-sa. Shi-sa-du.*"

"Oh, that makes great sense. And the 'du'?" He
stopped circling, so I stopped too, his back to the
wall, mine to the open door. In time, when I began to

see patterns, I would see that he always positioned himself in such a fashion, never with his back to an open window or door. It wasn't about fear. It was about control.

"D-u-b-h."

"*Dubh* is do?" I was incredulous. It was no wonder I hadn't been able to find the stupid word. "Should I be calling pubs poos?"

"*Dubh* is Gaelic, Ms. Lane. Pub is not."

"Don't bust a gut laughing." I'd thought I was being funny. Stuffy, like I said.

"Nothing about the *Sinsar Dubh* is a laughing matter."

"I stand corrected. So what is this gravest of graves?"

His gaze dropped from my face to my toes and back again. Apparently he was unimpressed by what he saw. "Go home, Ms. Lane. Be young. Be pretty. Get married. Have babies. Grow old with your pretty husband."

His comment stung like acid on my skin. Because I was blonde, easy on the eyes, and guys had been snapping my bra strap since seventh grade, I'd been putting up with the Barbie stereotype for years. That pink was my favorite color, that I liked matching accessories and eye-catching heels, didn't help much. But I'd never been turned on by the Ken doll—even before I looked down his pants and saw what was missing—I wasn't jonesing for a white picket fence and an SUV in the driveway, and I resented the Barbie implications—*Go procreate and die, I'm sure that's all someone like you can do.* I might not be the brightest bulb in the box, but I wasn't the dimmest, either. "Oh, screw you, Jericho Barrons. Tell me what it is. You said you would."

"If you insist. Don't be a fool. Don't insist."

"I'm insisting. What is it?"

"Last chance."

"Too bad. I don't want a last chance. Tell me."

His dark gaze bored into mine. Then he shrugged, his fine suit sliding over his body with suppleness and ease only exorbitant custom-made clothing could achieve. "The *Sinsar Dubh* is a book."

"A book? That's all? Just a book?" It seemed terribly anticlimactic.

"On the contrary, Ms. Lane, never make that mistake. Never think it just a book. It is an exceedingly rare and exceedingly ancient manuscript countless people would kill to possess."

"Including you? Would you kill to possess it?" I needed to know exactly where we stood, he and I.

"Absolutely." He watched my face as I took that in. "Reconsidering your stay, Ms. Lane?"

"Absolutely not."

"You'll be going home in a box, then."

"Is that another of your threats?"

"It is not I who will put you there."

"Who will?"

"I answered your question, now it's your turn to answer mine. What do you know of the *Sinsar Dubh*, Ms. Lane?"

Not nearly enough, obviously. What on earth had my sister gotten into? Some kind of shadowy Dublin underworld filled with stolen artifacts, peopled by murderers and ruthless thieves?

"Tell me," he pressed. "And don't lie. I'll know."

I glanced at him sharply, almost able to believe he would. Oh, not in some extrasensory way—I don't believe in that kind of stuff—but in the way of a man who scrutinizes people, gathers their tiniest gestures and expressions, and measures them. "My sister was studying here." He'd given me the bare minimum. I would give him nothing more. "She was killed a month ago. She left me a voice-mail message right before she died, telling me I had to find the *Sinsar Dubh*."

"Why?"

"She didn't say. She just said everything depended on it."

He made an impatient sound. "Where is this message? I must hear it myself."

"I accidentally deleted it," I lied.

He crossed his arms over his chest and leaned back against the wall. "Liar. You would make no such mistake with a sister you care enough about to die for. Where is it?" When I said nothing, he said softly, "If you are not with me, Ms. Lane, you are against me. I have no mercy for my enemies."

I shrugged. He wanted the same thing I wanted and he was willing to kill for it. That made us enemies in my book any way I looked at it. I glanced over my shoulder at the hallway beyond the open door and pondered my next move. His threat did not decide me. I wanted to see his face when I played the message for him. If he'd had any involvement with my sister or her death, I hoped he would betray something when he heard her voice and her words. I also wanted him to know that I knew as much as I did, and to believe the police did, as well.

"I already gave a copy of this recording to the Dublin *Gardai*," I told him, as I fished my cell phone out of my purse and thumbed up my saved messages. "They're working to track down the man she was involved with." *See Mac bluff.* Better than *See Mac run.* Way better than *See Mac get her stupid self killed.* He didn't challenge my words—so much for his boast that he would know if I lied. I pressed speakerphone, then play, and Alina's voice filled the small room.

I flinched. No matter how many times I listened to it, it made me cringe—my sister sounding so frightened, hours before her death. Fifty years from now, I would still hear her message, ringing in my heart's ear, word for word.

Everything has gone so wrong...I thought I was in love...he's one of them...we've got to find the Sinsar Dubh, *everything depends on it...we can't let them have it...he's been lying to me all along.*

I watched him intently as he listened. Composed, aloof, his expression told me nothing. "Did you know my sister?"

He shook his head.

"You were both after this 'exceedingly rare book' yet never ran into each other?" I accused.

"Dublin is a city of a million-odd people inundated daily by countless commuters and besieged by a never-ending wave of tourists, Ms. Lane. The oddity would be if we *had* encountered each other. What did she mean by 'you don't even know what you are'?" His dark gaze fixed on my face as if to gauge the veracity of my answer in my eyes.

"I wondered that myself. I have no idea."

"None?"

"None."

"Hmm. This was all she left you? A message?"

I nodded.

"Nothing more? No note or package or anything of the sort?"

I shook my head.

"And you had no idea what she meant by the *Sinsar Dubh*? Your sister didn't confide in you?"

"I used to think she did. Apparently I was wrong." I couldn't mask the note of bitterness in my voice.

"Who did she mean by 'them'?"

"I thought *you* might be able to tell me that," I said pointedly.

"I am not one of these 'them,' if that is what you're inferring," he said. "Many seek the *Sinsar Dubh*, both individuals and factions. I want it as well, but I work alone."

"Why do you want it?"

He shrugged. "It is priceless. I am a book collector."

"And that makes you willing to kill for it? What do you plan to do with it? Sell it to the highest bidder?"

"If you don't approve of my methods, stay out of my way."

"Fine."

"Fine. What else have you to tell me, Ms. Lane?"

"Not a thing." I retrieved my cell phone, resaved the message, and jerked a frosty glance from him to the door, encouraging him to leave.

He laughed, a rich dark sound. "I do believe I'm being dismissed. I can't recall the last time I was dismissed."

I didn't see it coming. He was nearly past me, nearly to the door, when he grabbed me and slammed me back against his body. It was like hitting a brick wall. The back of my head bounced off his chest, and my teeth clacked together from the impact.

I opened my mouth to scream, but he clamped a hand over it. He banded an arm beneath my breasts so tightly that I couldn't inflate my lungs to breathe. His body was far more powerful beneath that fine suit than I ever would have guessed, like reinforced steel. In that instant, I understood that the open door had been nothing more than a mocking concession, a placebo he'd fed me that I'd swallowed whole. Anytime he'd wanted, he could have snapped my neck and I wouldn't have gotten off a single scream. Or he could simply have suffocated me, as he was doing now. His strength was astonishing, immense. And he was only using a small fraction of it. I could feel the restraint in his body; he was being very, very careful with me.

He pressed his lips to my ear. "Go home, Ms. Lane. You don't belong here. Drop it with the *Gardai*. Stop asking questions. Do not seek the *Sinsar Dubh*

or you will die in Dublin." He released enough pres-
sure on my mouth to afford my reply, enough on my
ribs to permit me breath to fuel it.

I sucked in desperately needed air. "There you
go, threatening me again," I wheezed. Better to die
with a snarl than a sniffle.

His arm bit into my ribs, cutting off my air again.
"Not threatening—warning. I haven't been hunting
it this long and gotten this close to let anyone get in
my way and fuck things up. There are two kinds of
people in this world, Ms. Lane: those who survive
no matter the cost, and those who are walking victims." He pressed his lips to the side of my neck. I
felt his tongue where my pulse fluttered, tracing my
vein. "You, Ms. Lane, are a victim, a lamb in a city of
wolves. I'll give you until nine P.M. tomorrow to get
the bloody hell out of this country and out of my
way."

He let me go, and I crumpled to the floor, my
blood starved for oxygen.

By the time I picked myself up again, he was
gone.

FIVE

I was hoping you could tell me something about my sister," I asked the second-to-last instructor on my list, a Professor S. S. Ahearn. "Do you know who any of her friends were, where she spent her time?"

I'd been at this most of the day. With Alina's e-mail schedule clutched in one hand, and a campus map in the other, I'd gone from class to class, waited outside until it was over, then cornered her teachers with my questions. Tomorrow I would do the same all over again, but tomorrow I would go after the students. Hopefully the students would yield better results. So far what I'd learned wouldn't fill a thimble. And none of it had been good.

"I already told the *Gardai* what I know." Tall and thin as a rail, the professor gathered his notes with brisk efficiency. "I believe it was an Inspector O'Duffy conducting the investigation. Have you spoken with him?"

"I have an appointment with him later this week, but hoped you might spare me a few minutes in the meantime."

He placed the notes inside his briefcase and snapped it shut. "I'm sorry, Ms. Lane, I really knew very little about your sister. On those rare days she bothered to come to class at all, she hardly participated."

"On those rare days she bothered to come to class?" I repeated. Alina loved college, she loved to study and learn. She never blew off classes.

"Yes. As I told the *Gardai*, in the beginning she came regularly, but her attendance became increasingly sporadic. She began missing as many as three and four classes in a row." I must have looked disbelieving, perhaps a little stricken, because he added, "It's not so unusual in the study-abroad program, Ms. Lane. Young people away from home for the first time...no parents or rules...an energetic city full of pubs. Alina was a lovely young girl like yourself...I'm sure she thought she had better things to do than sit in a stuffy classroom."

"But Alina wouldn't have felt that way," I protested. "My sister loved stuffy classrooms. They were just about her favorite thing in the world. The chance to study at Trinity College meant everything to her."

"I'm sorry. I'm only telling you what I observed."

"Do you have any idea who her friends were?"

"I'm afraid not."

"Did she have a boyfriend?" I pressed.

"Not that I was aware. On those occasions I saw

her, if she was in the company of others, I didn't notice. I'm sorry, Ms. Lane, but your sister was one of many students who pass through these halls each term and if she stood out at all—it was through her absence, not her presence."

Subdued, I thanked him and left.

Professor Ahearn was the fifth of Alina's instructors that I'd spoken to so far, and the portrait they'd painted of my sister was that of a woman I didn't recognize. A woman that didn't attend classes, didn't care about her studies, and appeared to have no friends.

I glanced down at my list. I had a final professor to track down, but she taught only on Wednesdays and Fridays. I decided to head for the library. As I hurried out into a large grassy commons filled with students lounging about, soaking up the late-afternoon sun, I thought about possible reasons for Alina's unusual academic behavior. The courses offered through the study-abroad program were designed to promote cultural awareness, so my sister—an English major who'd planned to get a Ph.D. in literature—had ended up taking courses like *Caesar in Celtic Gaul* and *The Impact of Industry on Twentieth-Century Ireland*. Could it be she'd just not enjoyed them?

I couldn't see that. Alina had always been curious about everything.

I sighed and instantly regretted the deeply indrawn breath. My ribs hurt. This morning I'd awakened to find a wide band of bruises across my torso, just beneath my breasts. I couldn't wear a bra because the underwire hurt too much, so I'd layered a lacy camisole trimmed with dainty roses beneath a pink sweater that complemented my Razzle-Dazzle-Hot-Pink-Twist manicure and pedicure. Black capris, a wide silver belt, silver sandals, and a small metallic Juicy Couture purse I'd saved all last summer to buy completed my outfit. I'd swept my long blonde hair up in a high ponytail, secured by a pretty enameled clip. I might be feeling bruised and bewildered, but by God I looked good. Like a smile that I didn't really feel, presenting a together appearance made me feel more together inside, and I badly needed bolstering today.

I'll give you until nine P.M. *tomorrow to get the bloody hell out of this country and out of my way.* The nerve. I'd had to bite my tongue on the juvenile impulse to snap, *Or what?—you're not the boss of me*, second only to an even more juvenile impulse to call my mom and wail, *Nobody likes me here and I don't even know why!*

And his assessment of people! What a cynic. "Walking victim, my petunia," I muttered. I heard myself and groaned. Born and raised in the Bible Belt, Mom had taken a strong position about cussing when we were growing up—*A pretty woman doesn't have an ugly mouth*, she would say—so Alina and I had developed our own set of silly words as substitutes. Crap was fudge-buckets. Ass was petunia. Shit was daisies and the f-word, which I can't even recall the last time I used, was frog. You get the idea.

Unfortunately, we'd said them so often as children

that they'd become a habit just as hard to break as real cusswords. To my endless humiliation, the way it usually worked was the more upset I got, the more likely I was to fall back on my childhood vocabulary. It was a little difficult to get an out-of-hand bachelor party at the bar to take you seriously when your threat was they'd better "back off or the bouncer was going to kick the fudge-buckets out of them and toss their petunias right out the door." In this desensitized day and age, clean language got you laughed at more often than not.

I cleared my throat. "Walking victim, my *ass*."

Okay, I'll admit it; I'd been quaking in my proverbial boots by the time Jericho Barrons was done with me. But I'd gotten over it. There was no question in my mind that he was a ruthless man. But a *murdering* man would have killed me last night and been done with it. And he hadn't. He'd left me alive, and by my reasoning, that meant he would continue to do so. He might bully and threaten me, even bruise me, but he wouldn't kill me.

Nothing had changed. I still had my sister's murderer to find, and I was staying. And now that I knew how to spell it, I was going to find out exactly what the *Sinsar Dubh* was. I knew it was a book—but a book about what?

Hoping to miss the rush-hour crowds and conserve money by eating less frequently, I stopped for a late lunch/early dinner of crispy fried fish and chips, then headed for the library. A few hours later, I had what I was looking for. I had no idea what to make of it, but I had it.

Alina would have known some clever way to search computer indices and go straight to what she wanted, but I was one of those people who needed the placards at the ends of the aisles. I spent my first half hour at the library pulling books about archaeology and history off shelves and toting them to a corner table. I spent the next hour or so paging through them. In my defense, I did use the rear indexes, and midway through my second stack I found it.

Sinsar Dubh[1]: *a Dark Hallow*[2] *belonging to the mythological race of the Tuatha Dé Danaan. Written in a language known only to the most ancient of their kind, it is said to hold the deadliest of all magic within its encrypted pages. Brought to Ireland by the Tuatha Dé during the invasions written of in the pseudohistory Leabhar Gabhála*[3], *it was stolen along with the other Dark Hallows and rumored to have found its way into the world of Man.*

I blinked. Then I scanned down the page for the footnotes.

[1]*Among certain nouveau-riche collectors, there has been a recent surge of interest in mythological relics, and some claim to have actually beheld a photocopy of a page or two of this "cursed tome." The Sinsar Dubh is no more real than the mythical being said to have authored it over a million years*

ago—the "Dark King" of the Tuatha Dé Danaan. Allegedly scribed in unbreakable code, in a dead language, this author is curious to know how any collector proposes to have identified any part of it.

[2]The Tuatha Dé Danaan were said to possess eight ancient relics of immense power: four Light and four Dark. The Light Hallows were the stone, the spear, the sword, and the cauldron. The Dark were the mirror, the box, the amulet, and the book (Sinsar Dubh).

[3]Leabhar Gabhåla (The Book of Invasions) places the Tuatha Dé Danaan thirty-seven years after the Fir Bolg (who followed Cesair, the granddaughter of Noah, the Partholonians and the Nemedians) and two hundred and ninety-seven years before the Milesians or Q-Celtic Goidelic people. However, earlier and later sources contradict both the true nature of the Tuatha Dé and their date of arrival as put forth by this 12th-century text.

I closed *A Definitive Guide to Artifacts: Authentic and Legendary* and stared into space. You could have knocked me over with a feather. Seriously. One of those little down ones from inside a decorative pillow. If you'd just *swished* it at me, I would have toppled.

Mythological race? Dark King? Magic? Was this all some kind of joke?

Alina didn't get into woo-woo stuff any more

than I did. We both loved to read and watch the occasional movie, but we always went for your run-of-the-mill mysteries, thrillers, or romantic comedies, none of the bizarre paranormal stuff.

Vampires? Eew. Dead. Enough said. Time-travel? Ha, give me creature comforts over a hulking Highlander with the manners of a caveman any day. Werewolves? Oh please, just plain stupid. Who wants to get it on with a man who's ruled by his inner dog? As if all men aren't anyway, even without the lycanthrope gene.

No thank you, reality has always been good enough for me. I've never wanted to escape from it. Alina was the same way. Or so I'd always thought. I was seriously beginning to wonder if I'd ever really known my sister at all.

I just didn't get it. Why would she leave me a message telling me I had to find a book about magic that, according to T. A. Murtough of *A Definitive Guide*, didn't even exist!

I opened the book and read the first footnote again. Was it possible there were people out there in the world who believed in a book of magic written a million years ago, and my sister had been killed because she'd gotten in the way of their fanatical search?

Jericho Barrons believed it was real.

I thought about that a minute. Then he was nuts, too, I decided with a shrug. No matter how well it had been made, any book would have begun falling apart after a few thousand years. A million-year-old book would have crumbled to dust eons ago.

Besides, if nobody could read it, why would anybody want it?

Mystified, I began reading again, working through the second stack and into the third. Half an hour later I'd found the answer to that question too, in a book about Irish myths and legends.

> According to legend, the key to deciphering the ancient language and breaking the code of the Sinsar Dubh was hidden in four mystical stones. [Four is a sacred number to the Tuatha Dé: four royal houses, four Hallows, four stones.] In an accomplished Druid's hands, an individual stone can be used to shed light on a small portion of the text, but only if the four are reassembled into one will the true text in its entirety be revealed.

Great. Now we had Druids in the mix. I looked them up next.

> In pre-Christian Celtic society, a Druid presided over divine worship, legislative and judicial matters, philosophy, and education of elite youth to their order.

That didn't sound so bad. I kept reading. It went downhill quickly.

> Druids performed human sacrifices and ate acorns to prepare for prophecy. They believed day followed night, and held to a credo of metempsychosis in which the human soul does not die but is reborn in

*different forms. In ancient times it was believed
Druids were privy to the secrets of the gods, including issues pertaining to the manipulation of physical matter, space, and even time. Indeed, the old
Irish "Drui" means magician, wizard, diviner—*

Okay, that was it. I snapped the book shut and
decided to call it a night. My credulity had been
sapped. This was not my sister. None of it was. And
there was only one explanation for it.

Jericho Barrons had lied to me. And he was probably sitting in his fancy bookstore in his fancy five-
thousand-dollar suit, laughing at me right now.

He'd tossed me a red herring, and a whopper of a
smelly fish at that. He'd tried to throw me off the
trail of whatever it was Alina *really* wanted me to
find with a load of tripe about some stupid mythical book of dark magic. Like any good liar worth
his salt, he'd seasoned his deception with truth—
whatever it was, he genuinely *did* want it himself,
ergo the deception. Amused by my naïveté, he'd
probably not even bothered to change the spelling
of what she'd said very much. *"Shi-sadu."* I sounded
out the syllables, wondering how it was really
spelled. I was so gullible. Maybe there was only a
two- or three-letter difference between what Alina
had said in Gaelic and what Barrons had pretended
she meant, and those few letters were the difference
between an object of pure fantasy and some hard-
boiled, tangible item that would enable me to shed
light on her death. If, for that matter, he'd even told

the truth about the word being Gaelic. I could trust nothing he'd said.

Adding insult to injury, he'd tried to scare me with threats and chase me out of the country. And he'd bruised me too.

I was getting madder by the minute.

I left the library and stopped in a drugstore to pick up the few items I needed, then began walking through the busy Temple Bar District back to The Clarin House. The streets were packed with people. The pubs were brilliantly lit; doors were flung open to the temperate July evening and music spilled out onto the sidewalks. There were cute guys all over the place, and I got more than a few catcalls and whistles. A bartender, a young single woman and a music lover, this was my element. This was *craic*.

I didn't enjoy a bit of it.

When I get mad I have imaginary conversations in my head—you know, the kind where you say that really smart thing you always wish you'd think of at the time but never do—and sometimes I get so wrapped up in my little chats that I end up oblivious to everything around me.

That's how I found myself outside Barrons Books and Baubles instead of The Clarin House. I didn't mean to go there. My feet just took me where my mouth wanted to be. It was twenty past nine, but I didn't give a rat's petunia about Mr. Barrons' stupid deadline.

I stopped in front of the bookstore and snatched a

quick glance to my left, toward the deserted part of the city in which I'd gotten lost the other day. Four stories of renovated brick, wood, and stone, Barrons Books and Baubles seemed to stand bastion between the good part of the city and the bad. To my right, streetlamps spilled warm amber light, and people called to each other, laughing and talking. To my left, what few streetlamps still worked shed a sickly, pale glow, and the silence was broken only by the occasional door banging on broken hinges in the wind.

I dismissed the unpleasant neighborhood. My business was with Barrons. The open sign in the window was dark—the hours advertised on the door were noon to eight P.M.—and there were only dim lights on inside, but the expensive motorcycle was parked out front in the same place as yesterday. I couldn't imagine Fiona straddling the macho black-and-chrome hog any more than I could picture Barrons driving the sedate upper-middle-class gray sedan. Which meant he was here, somewhere.

I made a fist and pounded on the door. I was in a foul mood, feeling put-upon and wronged by everyone I'd encountered in Dublin. Since my arrival, few had been passably civil, none had been nice, and several had been unapologetically rude. And people said Americans were bad. I pounded again. Waited twenty seconds, pounded again. Mom says I have a redhead's temper, but I've known a few redheads and I don't think I'm nearly that bad. It's just that when I've got something stuck in my craw I have to do something about it. Like coming to Dublin in the first place to get Alina's investigation reopened.

"Barrons, I know you're in there. Open up," I shouted. I repeated the pounding and shouting for several minutes. Just when I was beginning to think maybe he wasn't there after all, a deep voice came out of the darkness on my left, marked by that untraceable accent that hinted of time spent in exotic climes. Like places with harems and opium dens.

"Woman, you are a thousand kinds of fool."

I peered into the gloom. Halfway down the block was a denser spot in the darkness that I took to be him. It was impossible to make out his shape, but that patch of darkness seemed to hold more substance, more potency than the shadows around it. It also made me shiver a little. Yes, that would be him.

"Not so much of a fool as you think, Barrons. Not so much of a fool that I fell for your stupid story."

"A lamb in a city of wolves. Which one will take you down, I wonder?"

"Lamb, my petu—*ass*. You don't scare me."

"Ah yes, a thousand kinds of fool."

"I know you lied to me. So what is it really, Barrons—this *shi-sadu*?" Though I'd not intended to emphasize the unfamiliar word, it seemed to ricochet off the surrounding buildings with the sharp retort of a gunshot. Either that or, for a weirdly suspended moment, a total hush fell over the night, like one of those untimely lulls in conversation that always happen just when you're saying something like, *Can you believe what a witch that Jane Doe is?* and Jane Doe's standing right across the suddenly silent room, and you just want to sink into the floor. "You may as well tell me, because I'm not going away until you do."

He was there before I could blink. The man had lightning reflexes. It made a difference that he wasn't where I thought he was to begin with. He detached from the shadows no more than ten feet from me and crushed me back against the door. "You bloody fool, do not speak of such things in the open night!" Crowding me back to the door, he reached past me for the lock.

"I'll speak of anything I—" I broke off, staring beyond him. The patch of darkness I'd mistaken for him had begun to move. And now there was a second spot slithering along the side of one of the buildings, a little farther down; an impossibly tall one. I glanced over to the other side of the street, to see what idiot was walking through that terrible neighborhood at night, casting the shadow.

There was no one.

I glanced back at the two darknesses. They were moving toward us. Quickly.

I looked up at Barrons. He was motionless, staring down at me. He turned and looked over his shoulder where I had been staring, then back at me.

Then he pushed open the door, shoved me inside, shut the door, and slid three dead bolts behind us.

SIX

"You will explain," he said roughly, shoving me deeper into the room, away from the door. He turned his back to me and began flipping light switches on the wall, one after another. Set after set of recessed lights and wall sconces came on inside the store. Outside, floodlights washed the night cold-white.

"Explain? Explain what? *You* explain. Why did you lie to me? God, I just don't get this place! Alina made it sound like Dublin was some kind of great city where everybody was so nice and everything was so pretty, but nothing is pretty and nobody is nice and I swear I'm going to do serious bodily harm to the next idiot that tells me to go home!"

"As if you could. You might break a nail." The gaze he shot me over his shoulder was contemptuous.

"You don't know a thing about me, Barrons." The

look I shot back was equally contemptuous. He finished with the last of the lights and turned around. I jerked a little at the sight of him beneath the blaze of illumination. I must not have looked at him very closely yesterday because he wasn't just masculine and sexual, he was carnal in a set-your-teeth-on-edge kind of way; he was almost frightening. He looked different tonight. He seemed taller, leaner, meaner, skin tighter on his body, features more starkly chiseled—and his cheekbones had been blades yesterday in that cold, arrogant face that was such an unlikely blend of genes. "What's your heritage, anyway?" I said irritably, backing away, putting more space between us.

He regarded me blankly, looking startled by the personal question, and as if he lacked a frame of reference for one. He paused as if debating answering, then, after a moment, shrugged. "Basque and Celt. Pict to be precise, Ms. Lane, but I doubt you're familiar with the distinction."

I was no slouch in history. I'd taken several college courses. I was familiar with both cultures, and it explained a lot. Criminals and barbarians. Now I understood the slightly exotic slant to the dark eyes, the deep gold skin, the bad attitude. I didn't think there could be a more primitive pairing of genes.

I didn't know I'd spoken my last thought aloud until he said coolly, "I'm sure there is somewhere. You will tell me what you saw out there, Ms. Lane."

"I didn't see anything," I lied. Truth was, I couldn't make sense of what I thought I'd seen and I was in no mood to discuss it. I was tired and I'd obviously gotten bad fish at dinner. In addition to food poisoning, I was grieving, and grief did funny things to a person's head.

He made a sound of impatience. "I have no patience for lies, Ms.—"

"Quid pro quo, Barrons." I got a juvenile kick out of cutting him off. The look on his face spoke volumes; no one ever did. I moved to one of the little conversation areas, dropped my bag of drugstore purchases and my Juicy purse on the table, and sank down on a camel-colored leather sofa. I figured I should get comfortable because I wasn't leaving until I'd gotten some answers, and as stubborn and tyrannical as Jericho Barrons was, we could be at this all night. I propped my pretty silver sandals on the coffee table and crossed my feet at the ankles. I would have caught heck from Mom for sitting that way, but Mom wasn't here. "You tell me something and I'll tell you something. But this time you're going to have to prove what you say before I give you anything back."

He was on me before my brain processed the fact that he was coming for me. It was the third time he'd pulled such a stunt and it was getting darned old. The man was either an Olympic sprinter or, because I'd never been jumped before, I just couldn't get a grasp on how quickly it happens. His lunges were way faster than my instincts to react.

Lips compressed, face tight with fury, he dragged me up off the couch with a hand in my hair, grabbed my throat with the other, and began walking me backward toward the wall.

"Oh, go ahead," I hissed. "Just kill me and get it over with. Put me out of my misery!" Missing Alina was worse than a terminal illness. At least when you were terminal you knew the pain was going to end eventually. But there was no light at the end of my tunnel. Grief was going to devour me, day into night, night into day, and although I might feel like I was dying from it, might even wish I was, I never would. I was going to have to walk around with a hole in my heart forever. I was going to hurt for my sister until the day I died. If you don't know what I mean or you think I'm being melodramatic, then you've never really loved anyone.

"You don't mean that."

"Like I said, you don't know me."

He laughed. "Look at your hands."

I looked. They were both wrapped around his forearm. Beautifully manicured pink nails with frosted tips were curled like talons into his suit, trying to loosen his grip. I hadn't even realized I'd lifted them.

"I know people, Ms. Lane. They think they want to die, sometimes even say they want to die. But they never mean it. At the last minute they squeal like pigs and fight like hell." He sounded bitter, as if he knew from personal experience. I was suddenly no longer quite so sure Jericho Barrons wasn't a murderer.

He thrust me against the wall and held me there, a hand at my throat, his dark gaze moving restlessly over my face, my neck, the rise and fall of my breasts beneath my lace camisole. Moving *majorly* over my breasts. I might have snorted if oxygen had been in plentiful supply. There was no way Jericho Barrons thought I was a hottie. We couldn't have been less each other's type. If he was Antarctica, I was the Sahara. What was his deal? Was this some new tactic he was going to threaten me with—rape instead of murder? Or was he upping the ante to both?

"I am going to ask you one more time, Ms. Lane, and I suggest you not trifle with me. My patience is exceedingly thin this evening. I've matters far more pressing than you to attend. What did you see out there?"

I closed my eyes and considered my options. I have a pride problem. Mom says it's my special little challenge. Since I'd initially taken such a strong defiant stance, any cooperation now would be caving. I opened my eyes. "Nothing."

"What a shame," he said. "If you saw nothing, I have no use for you. If you saw something, I do. If you saw nothing, your life means nothing. If you saw something, your life—"

"I get the point," I gritted. "You're being redundant."

"So? What did you see?"

"Let go of my throat." I needed to win something.

He released me and I staggered. I hadn't realized he was holding me on my tiptoes by my neck until my heels weren't touching the floor and suddenly needed to be. I rubbed my throat and said irritably, "Shadows, Barrons. That's all I saw."

"Describe these shadows for me."

I did, and he listened intently until I'd finished, his dark gaze boring into my face. "Have you ever seen anything like this before?" he demanded.

"No."

"Never?"

I shrugged. "Not really." I paused, then added, "I did have a kind of weird moment in a pub the other night."

"Tell me," he commanded.

I was still standing between him and the wall and I needed more space. Physical proximity to Barrons was disturbing, like standing next to a highly charged magnetic field. I slipped past him, taking great pains not to touch him—a fact that seemed to amuse him greatly—and moved toward the sofa. I began recounting the strange dual vision I'd had, the hostile old woman, what she'd said. He asked me many questions, pressing for minute details. I wasn't nearly as observant as Barrons, and I couldn't answer half of what he asked. He made no attempt to hide his disgust with my failure to be more investigative with either the odd vision or the old woman. When at last he finished his interrogation, he gave a sharp laugh of disbelief. "I never thought there might be one like you out there. Unaware, untrained. Unbelievable. You have no idea what you are, do you?"

"Crazy?" I tried to make a joke of it.

He shook his head and began walking toward me. When I instinctively backed up, he stopped, a faint smile playing at his lips. "Do I frighten you, Ms. Lane?"

"Hardly. I just don't like being bruised."

"Bruises heal. There are worse things in the night than I."

I opened my mouth to make a smart-aleck comment, but he silenced me with a wave of his hand. "Spare me your bluster, Ms. Lane. I see through it. No, you're not crazy. You are, however, a walking impossibility. I have no notion how you survived. I suspect you must have lived in a borough so provincial and uninteresting that you never encountered one of them. A cloistered town so utterly lacking distinction that it was never visited and never will be."

I had no idea who his "them" were that had or hadn't visited, but I couldn't argue with the rest of it. I was pretty sure Ashford was registered with the State of Georgia under *P* for provincial, and I seriously doubted our annual fried chicken cook-off or Christmas walk featuring the same half-dozen stately antebellums each year distinguished my town from any other scattered throughout the Deep South. "Yeah, well," I said defensively. I loved my hometown. "Point?"

"You, Ms. Lane, are a *sidhe*-seer."

"Huh?" What was a she-seer?

"A *sidhe*-seer. You see the Fae."

I burst out laughing.

"This is no laughing matter," he said roughly. "This is about life and death, you imbecile."

I laughed harder. "What, some pesky little fairy's going to get me?"

82 Karen Marie Moning

His eyes narrowed. "Just what do you think those shadows were, Ms. Lane?"

"Shadows," I retorted, my amusement fading. I was getting angry myself. I would not be made a fool of. There was no way those dark shapes had been anything more substantive. Fairies didn't exist, people didn't see them, and there were no books about magic that had been written a million years ago.

"The Shades would have sucked you dry and left a husk of skin scuttling down the sidewalk on the night breeze," he said coldly. "No body for your parents to claim. They would never know what happened to you. One more tourist gone missing abroad."

"Yeah, right," I snapped. "And how many other lines of bull are you going to try to feed me? That the *shi-sadu* really is a book of dark magic? That it really was written a million years ago by some Dark King? How stupid do you think I am? I just wanted to know what the word meant so I could maybe help the police find who killed my sister—"

"How did she die, Ms. Lane?" Barrons asked the question soft as silk, but it slammed into me like a sledgehammer.

I clenched my jaw and turned away. After a moment I said, "I don't want to talk about it. It's none of your business."

"Was it abnormal? Horrific, Ms. Lane? Tell me, did her body look as if animals had gone at her? Hard?"

I whirled back around. "*ShutupIhateyou*," I hissed.

Impatience blazed in his eyes. "Do you want to die like that too?"

I glared at him. I would not cry in front of him. I would not think about what I'd seen the day I'd had to identify Alina's body. Not in my worst nightmares did I want to die like that.

He peeled my answer from my face and half his mouth drew back in a smirk. "I didn't think so, Ms. Lane. Listen to me and learn, and I will help you."

"Why would you do that?" I scoffed. "You're hardly the Good Samaritan type. In fact, I think the word 'mercenary' has a little picture of you beside it in the dictionary. I don't have any money."

Both sides of his mouth drew back this time—in a snarl—before he quickly recomposed his face into a mask of smooth European urbanity. Wow, I'd sure struck a nerve. Something I'd said had pierced his thick hide and it seemed to have been the word "mercenary."

"I can hardly leave you to die. It wouldn't sit well with my conscience."

"You don't have a conscience, Barrons."

"You know nothing about me, Ms. Lane."

"And I'm not going to. I'm going to talk to the police and they're going to reopen my sister's case. I'm not going to see you again or any stupid shadows. I'm not even going to ask you what the shi-sadu really is, because you are beyond delusional. Stay away from me, or I'll tell the police all about you and your crazy ideas and threats." I snatched up my purse and drugstore bag and walked to the door.

"You're making a huge mistake, Ms. Lane."

I yanked it open. "The only mistake I made was yesterday, believing anything you said. It's a mistake I won't repeat."

"Don't cross that threshold. If you walk out that door you'll die. I give you three-day odds, at best."

I didn't dignify it with a response. I let the slam of the door behind me do that.

I think he might have yelled something through the door, something weird like, *Stay to the lights*, but I wasn't sure and I didn't care.

Jericho Barrons and I were done with each other.

Or so I thought. It would turn out to be just one more of those things I was wrong about. Soon, we would be living inside each other's hip pockets, whether we liked it or not.

And believe you me, we didn't.

SEVEN

L ater I would look back on the next few days as
the last normal ones of my life, though at the
time they seemed anything but. Normal was peach
pie and green beans, bartending and coaxing my car
to the garage for the latest two-hundred-and-fifty-
dollar Band-Aid, not investigating my sister's murder in Dublin.

I spent all day Wednesday on campus at Trinity
College. I spoke with the last professor on my list,
but she had nothing new to add. I talked with
dozens of Alina's classmates when their sessions let
out. The story they told was so identical from one to
the next that they were all either part of a vast
X-Files conspiracy—I always hated that show, it
was too vague and open-ended and I like my tidy
denouements—or this was really who my sister had
been while she was here.

They said for the first two or three months she was

friendly, outgoing, smart, someone others wanted to hang out with. That was the Alina I knew.

Then suddenly she changed. She began missing classes. When she did show up, if someone asked her where she'd been, she behaved strangely, secretively. She seemed excited and deeply preoccupied, as if she'd discovered something far more interesting to immerse herself in than her studies. Then, during her last months there, she lost weight and looked exhausted all the time, like she was going out drinking and partying all night, every night, and it was taking its toll. "Edgy" and "nervous" were two words I'd never associated with my sister, but her classmates used them liberally in describing her.

Did she have a boyfriend? I asked. Two of the people I spoke with said yes, two girls who seemed to have known Alina better than the others. She definitely had a boyfriend, they said. They thought he was older. Rich. Sophisticated and handsome, but no, they'd never seen him. No one had. She never brought him around.

Toward the end, on those rare days she showed up for class at all, it seemed she was making a last-ditch effort to try to get her life back, but she looked weary and defeated, as if she knew it was a battle she'd already lost.

Later that night I stopped in an Internet café and downloaded new tunes for my iPod. ITunes loves my Visa. I should be more frugal, but my weaknesses are books and music and I figure there are worse ones to have. I'd been hankering for the

Green Day *Greatest Hits* CD (the song that goes "sometimes I give myself the creeps, sometimes my mind plays tricks on me" had been majorly on my mind lately) and got it for the bargain price of $9.99, which was less than I would have paid in the store. Now you know how I justify my addictions—if I can pay less for it than I would at Wal-Mart, I get to have it.

I sent a long, determinedly upbeat e-mail to my folks and a few shorter ones to several of my friends back home. Georgia had never seemed so far away.

It was dark by the time I headed back to the inn. I didn't like to spend much time in my room. There was nothing comfortable or homey about it, so I tried to keep myself busy until I was ready to sleep. Twice, while walking home, I got the weirdest feeling I was being followed, but both times I turned around the scene behind me was a perfectly normal Dublin evening in the Temple Bar District. Brilliantly lit, warm and inviting, thick with throngs of pub-goers and tourists. Not a thing back there that should have sent a chill of foreboding up my spine.

Around three o'clock in the morning, I woke up strangely on edge. I pulled the drape aside and looked out. Jericho Barrons was on the sidewalk in front of The Clarin House, leaning back against a lamppost, his arms folded over his chest, staring up at the inn. He wore a long dark coat that went nearly to his ankles, a shirt of shimmering blood-red, and dark pants. He dripped casual European elegance and arrogance. His hair fell forward to just below his jaw. I hadn't realized it was so long because he

usually wore it slicked back from his face. He had
the kind of face you could do that with; chiseled,
symmetrical bone structure. In the morning, I decided I'd dreamt it.

Thursday I met with Inspector O'Duffy, who was
overweight, balding, and red-faced, with pants
belted low beneath a stomach that strained his shirt
buttons. He was British, not Irish, for which I was
grateful because it meant I didn't have to struggle
with his accent.

Unfortunately, the interview turned out to be
more depressing than quizzing Alina's classmates
had been. At first, things seemed to go well. Though
he told me personal notes on the case were not a matter of public record, he made me (yet another) copy
of the official report, and patiently recounted everything he'd told my father. Yes, they'd interviewed
her professors and classmates. No, no one had any
idea what had happened to her. Yes, a few had mentioned a boyfriend, but they'd never been able to
find out anything about him. Rich, older, sophisticated, not Irish, was all they'd been able to find out.

I played him her frantic phone message. He listened to it twice, then sat back and knitted his fingers together beneath his chin. "Had your sister
been using drugs long, Ms. Lane?"

I blinked. "Drugs? No, sir, Alina didn't use drugs."

He gave me that look adults get when they think
they're telling you something for you own good and
trying to be gentle about it. That look pisses me off
to no end when the adult is so obviously wrong. But
you can't tell grown-ups a thing when they've got

their minds made up. "The decline her classmates described follows the classic downward spiral of drug use." He picked up his file and read from it. "Subject became increasingly agitated, edgy, nervous, almost paranoid. Subject lost weight, looked exhausted all the time." He gave me that irritating brow-raised, expectant can't-you-see-what's-right-in-front-of-you look some people use, like they think they can cue the right response from you with it.

I stared at him stonily, resenting the word "subject" clear to my toes. "That doesn't mean she was doing drugs. That means she was in danger."

"Yet she never told you or your parents a thing about this danger? For months? You said yourself what a close family you have. Wouldn't your sister have told you if her life was in jeopardy? I'm sorry, Ms. Lane, but it's far more likely she was concealing drug use than her life was in danger and she never said a word to anyone. We see this kind of behavior in inner-city youth all the time."

"She said she was trying to protect me," I reminded him stiffly. "That's why she couldn't say anything."

"Protect you from what?"

"I don't know! That's what we need to find out. Can't you just reopen her case and try to find out who this boyfriend was? Surely someone somewhere saw the man! In her message, it sounded like she was hiding from someone. She said he was coming. She said she didn't think he'd let her out of the country. Obviously someone was threatening her!"

He studied me a moment, then sighed heavily.

"Ms. Lane, your sister's arms had holes in them. The kind of holes that needles make."

I flew to my feet, instantly livid. "My sister's *whole body* had holes in it, Inspector! Not just her arms! The coroner said they looked like teeth marks!" Not of any person or animal he'd been able to identify, though. "And parts of her were just *torn!*" I was shaking. I hated the memory. It made me sick to my stomach. I hoped she'd been dead when it had happened. I was pretty sure she hadn't been. The sight of her had pushed Mom and Dad right over the edge. It did the same to me, but I came back from that hellish place because somebody had to.

"We examined her ourselves, Ms. Lane. Neither animal nor human teeth made those marks."

"Needles didn't either," I said furiously.

"If you'll sit back d—"

"Are you going to reopen her case or not?" I demanded.

He raised his hands, palms upturned. "Look, I can't afford to send men out on cases that have no leads when we're up to our ears in ones that do. There's been a recent spike in homicides and missing persons like we've never seen before." He looked disgusted. "It's as if half the damn city's gone crazy. We're short-staffed as it is. I can't justify putting men on your sister's case when there's nothing to go on. I'm sorry for your loss, Ms. Lane. I know what it's like to lose a loved one. But there's nothing else that I can do for you. I suggest you go home and help your family get through it."

And that concluded our interview.

Feeling like a failure, needing to do something that would yield a tangible result, I trudged back to the inn and collected my trash bags, boxes, and broom, then sprang for a cab because there was no way I could carry it all to Alina's place. If I couldn't do anything else right, at least I could sweep up trash. I did every night I closed at The Brickyard and was darned good at it.

I cried the whole time I swept. Sorry for Alina, sorry for myself, sorry for the state of a world in which someone like my sister could be murdered so brutally.

When I was done sweeping and crying, I sat cross-legged on the floor and began packing. I couldn't bring myself to discard a thing, not even what I knew should get tossed, like torn clothing and broken knickknacks. Each item was lovingly crated away. Someday, years from now, I might pull the boxes from the attic at home in Georgia and sort through them more thoroughly. For now, out of sight was out of mind.

I spent the afternoon there and made a decent dent in it. It would take a few more days to finish up, clean the place, and see if there was any damage her deposit wouldn't cover. By the time I left, it was overcast and pouring rain. There were no cabs in sight. Because I had no umbrella and was starving, I splashed through puddles and ducked into the first pub I saw.

I didn't know it, but I'd just closed the book on the last normal hours of my life.

He was sitting at a table about a dozen feet from my booth, opposite a petite woman in her early thirties whose drab brown hair just brushed her collar.

She was a tad easier on the eye than mousy, which was why I noticed them, because he was drop-dead gorgeous. I mean, close-your-eyes-and-*wish*-some-guy-that-hot-would-ever-look-at-you gorgeous. Lots of times you see it the other way around, the sultry do-me-big-boy Betty Boop with a Jack Nicholson, but you don't often see a Fabio with an Olive Oyl.

Tall and hunky, with a ripped, tanned body beneath his white T-shirt and faded blue jeans, he had long blond hair that shimmered like gold. His face had that exotic model look, his eyes were sexy brown, his mouth full and sensuous. Everything about him was gorgeous. He looked elegant yet earthy, graceful yet powerful, managed even in jeans to appear rich as Croesus.

I admit I was fascinated. Though the woman wore a frothy short skirt, a silk blouse, and was smartly accessorized and polished right down to her French-manicured toenails, the kindest anyone would ever call her was plain, yet he seemed to positively dote on her. Couldn't stop touching her.

Then one of those stupid double visions began.

I'd just finished my cheeseburger and was leaning back in my booth, taking my time with my fries

(I adore fries, by the way, or I used to, anyway; I'd heavily salt and pepper the ketchup, then slather them with it and eat them slowly, one at a time, after everything else was gone), when his gestures suddenly seemed more unctuous than charming, and his face more gaunt than sculpted.

Then, abruptly, he was gone and for a split second something else occupied his chair. It happened so fast that I had no idea what had taken his place, just that it wasn't him for a moment.

I closed my eyes, rubbed them, then opened them again. The blond sex-god was back, stroking his companion's jaw with his hand, brushing his fingers to her lips—*with sharp yellow talons that protruded from a hand that looked as if a thin layer of rotting gray skin had been stretched over a corpse's bones!*

I shook my head brusquely, covered my face with my hands, and thoroughly rubbed my eyes this time, hard enough to smudge my mascara. I'd had two beers with my meal, and although I can usually handle three or four before copping a buzz, Guinness dark is stronger than what I drink back home. "When I open my eyes," I told myself, "I'm going to see what's really there." Meaning a man, not a hallucination.

I guess I should have specified that last part out loud, because when I opened my eyes again I nearly screamed. The sex-god was gone and the mousy woman had her mouth turned into the palm of a monster that was straight out of a horror movie, and she was *kissing* it.

Gaunt, emaciated to the point of death, it was

tall—and I'm talking like *nine feet* tall. It was gray and leprous from head to toe, covered with oozing, open sores. It was sort of human, by that I mean it had the basic parts: arms, legs, head. But that was where the resemblance ended. Its face was twice as tall as a human head and squished thin, no wider than my palm. Its eyes were black with no irises or whites. When it spoke, I could see that its mouth— which consumed the entire lower half of its hideous face—wasn't pink inside, it had a tongue and gums that were the same gray color as the rest of its rotting flesh and covered with the same wet sores. It had no lips and double rows of teeth like a shark. It was, in a word, putrid.

The blond sex-god was back. And he was looking at me. Hard. He was no longer conversing with the woman, but staring straight at me. He didn't look pleased.

I blinked. I don't know how I knew what I knew in that moment; it was like it was programmed into me on a cellular level somehow. My mind was split into separate camps. The first camp was insisting what I'd just seen wasn't real. The second was demanding I scramble up, grab my purse, throw money down on the table, and run out the door as fast as I could. Camps one and two sounded mildly hysterical, even to me.

The third camp was calm, cool, composed. And icily insisting that I had better do whatever I had to do to convince whatever was sitting at that table masquerading as human that I really couldn't see what it looked like beneath its facade—or I was dead.

That was the voice I obeyed without hesitation. I forced myself to smile at him/it and duck my head as if blushingly flustered to find myself the focus of such a sex-god's attention.

When I looked back up, it was the gray leprous thing again. Its head was way higher than where the sex-god's would have been, and it was all I could do to focus on the thing's navel (it didn't have one), which was where the sex-god's head *would* have been if I were still seeing it. I could feel its suspicious gaze on me. I gave its navel-region what I hoped was another flustered, self-effacing smile, then returned my attention to my fries.

I have never eaten french fries since. I forced myself to stay there and eat the entire platter, one by one. I forced myself to pretend the rotting monster was a gorgeous man. To this day, I believe it was only because I stayed that it found my bluff convincing. I still have to swallow the urge to vomit every time I see a plate of fries.

It was feeding off her each time it touched her. Stealing a little more of her beauty through the open sores on its hands. As I ate my fries, I watched her hair turn duller, her complexion muddier, she grew plainer, drabber, *grayer*, each time it touched her. I suspected she'd once been a stunningly beautiful woman. I wondered what would be left of her when it was done. I wondered if she would wake up tomorrow morning, look in the mirror and scream. I wondered if her friends and family would recognize her, know who she'd once been.

They left before I did, the short ugly woman and the nine-foot monster. I sat for a long time after they'd gone, staring into a third beer.

When at last I paid my tab and rose from the booth, I headed straight for Jericho Barrons.

EIGHT

I t was only seven-thirty, but the relentless, driving rain had ushered in the night while I'd been sitting in the pub. The streets were dark and mostly deserted, with few tourists thirsty enough to brave the downpour for a pint of stout when their hotel lounge would serve just as well. Tips in the pubs would be light for bartenders tonight.

A sodden, folded newspaper clutched to my head, I sloshed through puddles. I was glad I'd changed from the pretty yellow linen suit I'd worn for my interview with the inspector, into jeans, a lime-green V-neck T, and flip-flops to clean Alina's place, however I wished I'd had the presence of mind to grab a jacket too. The temperature had dropped sharply with the chilly rain. July in this part of Ireland wasn't real warm to begin with, especially for a girl used to the steamy summers of southern Georgia. Dublin's summer topped at highs of sixty-seven and could sink to as low as fifty. To-night was barely that.

I was relieved to find the bookstore still ablaze with light. I didn't know it yet, but I'd just crossed another of those lines of demarcation in my life. I used to need my bedroom completely dark in order to sleep, with no trickles of light stealing in through the blinds, no neon-blue glow cast by my stereo or laptop. I would never sleep in full dark again.

Barrons wasn't there, but Fiona was. She took one look at me past the queue of customers at her counter, and said brightly, "Well, hello again, dear. Just look at what the rain's done to you! Wouldn't you like to freshen up? Be back with you in a jiffy," she told her customers. Smiling fixedly, she took me by the elbow and practically dragged me to a bathroom in the back of the store.

When I saw my reflection in the mirror above the sink, I understood her reaction. I would have gotten me out of there, too. I looked awful. My eyes were huge, my expression shell-shocked. My mascara and liner had pooled into dark raccoon circles around my eyes. I was white as a sheet, had chewed off all my lipstick but for a streak at each corner of my mouth, and there was a big smear of ketchup down my right cheek. I was soaking wet, and the high ponytail I'd clipped my hair up in this morning was listing sadly behind my left ear. I was a mess.

I took my time freshening up. I stripped off my T-shirt and wrung it out in the sink, then paper-towel-dried my bra as best I could before putting my shirt on again. The bruises on my ribs were still dark but much less painful. I fixed my hair, then dampened more paper towels and dabbed at my face, gently removing the smudges from the delicate skin around my eyes. I dug out my on-the-go cosmetic pack from my purse—a sewing-kit-size collection of tiny amounts of the basics no proper southern belle should ever be without that Mom had bought for Alina and me this past Christmas. I moisturized and powdered, smoothed on a bit of blush and a touch of liner, then glossed my lips Moon-Silvered Pink again.

I opened the door, stepped out, walked right into Jericho Barrons' chest, and screamed. I couldn't help it. It was the scream I'd been holding down since I'd seen the hideous thing in the pub, and it had stayed inside me as long as it could.

He grabbed me by my shoulders—I think to steady me—and I punched him. I have no idea why. Maybe I was hysterical. Or maybe I was just mad because I'd begun to understand that something was very wrong with me and I didn't want it to be. When insane things start to arrange themselves in sane patterns around you, you know you've got problems. It was *his* fault. *He* was the one who'd told me impossible things to begin with. I hammered him with my fists. He just stood and took it, his hands clamped on my shoulders, his dark eyes fixed on my face. Don't get me wrong, he didn't suffer graciously, he looked pissed off to no end. But he let me hit him. And he didn't hit me back. Which was, I suspected, a pretty major concession from Jericho Barrons.

"What did you see?" he demanded when I finally

stopped. I didn't bother asking how he knew. We both knew I would have come back to him only if I needed something I couldn't get anywhere else—like the answers I'd refused the last time I was there. And that meant something had happened to change my mind.

His hands were still on my shoulders. Tonight, proximity to him was different but no less disturbing. I don't know if you've ever gotten out of your car near downed electric lines in the road during a storm, but I have. You can feel the energy sizzling and crackling in the air as the lines flop and twist on the ground, and you know you're standing next to raw power that could turn your way with killing force at any second. I shrugged in his grip. "Get off me."

He removed his hands. "You came to me. Remember that."

He never did let me forget it. *You chose,* he would remind me later. *You could have gone home.* "I think I'm going to be sick," I said.

"No, you won't. You want to be, but you won't. In time, you'll get used to the feeling."

He was right. I didn't throw up that night, but I never stopped feeling like I might hurl ketchup-soaked fries at any moment.

"Come." He led me back into the main part of the store and escorted me to the same camel-colored sofa I'd occupied a few nights ago. He spread a blanket over the leather to protect it from my wet jeans. Down south, a sofa is never more important than the person sitting on it; it's a little thing we call hospitality. It was impossible to miss how badly I was shivering and there was the small matter of the wet T-shirt, cold nipple problem I was having. I shot him a dark look and wrapped myself up in the blanket instead. With those lightning reflexes of his, he grabbed another wool throw and managed to toss it beneath my butt before it hit the sofa. He took a chair opposite me. Fiona was gone and the sign in the window was off. Barrons Books and Baubles was battened down for the night. "Tell me," he said.

I recounted what I'd seen. As before, he asked me many questions, demanding the tiniest details. He was more pleased with my observances this time. Even I felt they were keen, but then, when you see Death for the first time, it makes a heck of an impression.

"Not Death," he told me. "The Gray Man."

"The Gray Man?"

"I didn't know he was here," he murmured. "I had no idea things had gone so far." He rubbed his jaw, looking displeased with the turn of events.

I squinted. "What's that on your hand, Barrons? Blood?"

He started, glanced at me, then at his hand. "Ah yes," he said, as if remembering, "I was out for a walk. There was a badly injured dog in the street. I returned it to its owner's shop to die."

"Oh." Would wonders never cease. He seemed more the type to put it out of its misery where it lay, perhaps with a sharp twist of the neck or a well-placed kick, not take into account the human factor. I would later discover that my gut instinct was right; there'd been no dog that night. The blood on his hand was human. "So what is this Gray Man?"

"What you thought it was. It selects the loveliest

humans it can find and steals their beauty bit by bit until nothing is left."

"Why?"

He shrugged. "Why not? It is an Unseelie. They require neither rhyme nor reason. They are the Dark Ones. The old tales say the Gray Man is so ugly that even his own race mocks him. He steals the beauty of others out of corrosive envy and hatred. Like most of the Dark Fae, he destroys because he can."

"What happens to the women when he's done with them?"

"I suspect most kill themselves. Beautiful women rarely possess sufficient depth of character to survive without their pretty feathers. Strip them down and they crumble." The look he gave me was judge, jury, and executioner.

I made no effort to keep the sarcasm from my voice. "Flattered as I am that you count me among the beautiful people, Barrons, allow me to point out that I'm still alive. I encountered the Gray Man and I'm still here, just as pretty as always, dickhead."

He raised a brow. "Now, there's a visual for you."

I was chagrined. I never called people "dickheads." Oh well. It had been a rough day. *Sorry, Mom.* "What's wrong with me? And that's not an invitation for you to begin tallying your many perceived flaws in my character."

He smiled faintly. "I told you the other night. You are a *sidhe*-seer, Ms. Lane. You see the Fae. Though you are capable of seeing both Light and Dark, it seems thus far you've encountered only the unpleasant half of their race. Let us hope that continues, at least for a time, until I have trained you. The Seelie, or Light Fae, are as disconcertingly beautiful as their darker brethren are distressingly foul."

I shook my head. "This is impossible."

"You came to me, Ms. Lane, because you know it's not. You can rummage about in your repertoire of pretty self-delusions looking for a way to deny what you saw tonight, or you can look for a way to survive it. Remember what I said about walking victims? You watched one get preyed on tonight. What do you want to be, Ms. Lane? Survivor or victim? Frankly, I'm not certain even *I* can make you into the former, given the raw material I'm forced to work with, but it appears I'm the only person willing to try."

"Oh, you just *suck*."

He shrugged. "I call it like I see it. Get used to it. Stick around long enough and you might learn to appreciate it." He stood up and began walking toward the back of the store.

"Where are you going?"

"Bathroom. Wash my hands. Scared to be alone, Ms. Lane?"

"No," I lied.

He was gone long enough that I began peering into the corners of the room, making sure all the shadows were cast by objects and obeying known laws of physics.

"Okay," I said when he returned, "let's pretend I'm buying into your little story for a few minutes. Where have these monsters been all my life? Walking around all over the place and I just never noticed them before?"

He tossed me a wad of clothing. It hit me squarely in the chest. "Get out of those wet clothes. I'm no nursemaid. You get sick, you're on your own."

Though I was grateful for the clothing, he was in serious need of a lesson or two in manners. "Your concern is touching, Barrons." I practically ran to the bathroom to change. I was cold and shivering and the thought of being sick in Dublin in my cramped room by myself without Mom's homemade chicken noodle soup and TLC was more than I could bear.

The ivory sweater he'd given me was a blend of silk and hand-spun wool, and fell just past midthigh. I rolled up the sleeves four times. The black linen trousers were a joke. I had a twenty-four-inch waist. His was thirty-six and his legs were a good six to eight inches longer than mine. I rolled up the cuffs, tugged my belt from the loops of my jeans, and bunched his pants at my waist. I didn't care how I looked. I was dry and already starting to warm up.

"So?" He'd removed the damp blanket from the sofa and sponged it dry, and I sank down, cross-legged, on the tufted cushions and resumed our conversation without preamble.

"I told you the other night. You must have grown up in a town so small and uninteresting that it was never visited by any of the Fae. You've not traveled much, have you, Ms. Lane?"

I shook my head. Provincial with a capital *P*, that was me, just like my town.

"Additionally, these monsters, as you call them,

are a recent development. Previously, only the Seelie were capable of free passage among the realms. The Unseelie arrived on this planet already trapped in a prison. Those few that enjoyed brief paroles did so only at the Seelie Queen's or her High Council's behest."

I'd gotten stuck on a phrase. "Arrived on this planet?" I echoed. I thought about that a minute. "I see. So these monsters are really traveling space aliens. How silly of me not to have figured that out. Can they travel through time, too, Barrons?"

"You didn't think they were natives, did you?" He managed to sound a shade dryer than I had, an accomplishment I hadn't thought possible. "As for the time-traveling aspect, Ms. Lane, that would be a 'no, not right now.' But some of the Seelie used to— those of the four royal houses. Things have happened recently. Inexplicable things. No one knows for certain what is going on, nor even who holds power at the moment, but word is the Fae can no longer sift time. That for the first time in eons they are as trapped in the present as you and I."

I stared at him. It had been a joke, my time-travel crack. A snort of laughter escaped me. "Oh my God, you're being serious, aren't you? I mean, you really *believe* that—"

He was on his feet in one fluid motion. "What did you just see in that pub, Ms. Lane?" he demanded. "Have you forgotten so quickly? Or is this how fast you managed to concoct a pleasant little lie for yourself?"

I rose to my feet, too; my hands at my waist, my

chin high. "Maybe it was a hallucination, Barrons. Maybe I really *did* catch a cold and I have a fever and I'm sick in my hotel room right now, dreaming. Maybe I've gone NUTS!" My whole body shook from the vehemence with which I shouted the last word.

He kicked the table between us aside, sending coffee-table books flying, and stepped nose-to-nose with me. "How many of them will you need to see to believe, Ms. Lane? One every day? That could be arranged. Or perhaps you need a reminder right now. Come. Let me take you for a walk." He grabbed my arm and began dragging me toward the door. I tried to dig in and hold my ground but I'd left my flip-flops in the bathroom and my bare feet skidded across the polished wood floors.

"No! Get off me! I don't want to go!" I smacked at his arm, his shoulder. I was *not* going back out there.

"Why not? They're just shadows, Ms. Lane. Remember? You told me so yourself. Shall I take you down into the abandoned neighborhood and leave you with those shadows for a time? Will you believe me then?"

We were at the door. He'd begun sliding the dead bolts. "Why are you doing this to me?" I cried.

His hand went still on the third bolt. "Because you have one hope of survival, Ms. Lane. You *must* believe and you *must* fear, or you're wasting my time. Fuck you and your 'Let's pretend I believe your little story.' If you can't give me a 'Tell me, teach me everything, I want to live,' then get the bloody hell out of here!"

I felt like crying. I felt like collapsing in a puddle

right there at the door and whimpering, *Please make it all go away. I want my sister back and I want to go home and forget that I ever came here. I want to never have met you. I want my life back just the way it was.*

"Sometimes, Ms. Lane," he said, "one must break with one's past to embrace one's future. It is never an easy thing to do. It is one of the distinguishing characteristics between survivors and victims. Letting go of what was, to survive what is." He slid the last bolt and yanked open the door.

I closed my eyes. Even though I *knew* I'd seen what I saw tonight, a part of me was still denying it. The mind works hard to reject that which opposes its essential convictions, and Monster Fairies From Outer Space deeply opposed mine. You grow up thinking everything makes sense—it doesn't matter that you don't understand the laws that govern the universe— you know somewhere out there some geeky scientist does, and there's a degree of comfort in that.

I knew there wasn't a scientist alive that would believe my story, and there was no degree of comfort in that. Then again, I suspected there would be even less comfort in dying like Alina had.

I couldn't honestly say, *Tell me, teach me everything,* when all I really wanted to do was cover my ears and chant a childish, *I can't heeear you.*

But I could say with complete sincerity that I wanted to live.

"All right, Barrons," I said heavily. "Close the door. I'm listening."

NINE

Fae: a.k.a. the Tuatha Dé Danaan. Divided into two courts: the Seelie or Light Court, and the Unseelie or Dark Court. Both courts have different castes of Fae, with the four royal houses occupying the highest caste of each. The Seelie Queen and her chosen consort rule the Light Court. The Unseelie King and his current concubine govern the Dark.

I looked at what I'd just written in my journal and shook my head. I was sitting in my fourteenth pub of the day, or rather early evening. I'd spent the entire day pub-hopping, staring at people, trying to have another double vision. I'd not been successful and the longer I went without having one, the more removed and implausible the events of last night seemed. As did the insanity I was penning in these pages.

Shades: one of the lowest castes of Unseelie. Sentient but barely. They hunger—they feed. They cannot bear direct light and hunt only at night. They steal life in the manner the Gray Man steals beauty, draining their victims with vampiric swiftness. Threat assessment: kills.

Jericho Barrons had told me many things last night before packing me off in a cab for The Clarin House. I'd decided to write them down, fully aware that it read like something straight out of a badly scripted late-night sci-fi horror flick.

Royal Hunters: a mid-level caste of Unseelie. Militantly sentient, they resemble the classic depiction of the devil, with cloven hooves, horns, long, satyr-like faces, leathery wings, fiery orange eyes, and tails. Seven to ten feet tall, they are capable of extraordinary speed on both hoof and wing. Their primary function: sidhe-seer exterminators. Threat assessment: kills.

Which led us to the real kicker:

Sidhe-seer: a person Fae magic doesn't work on, capable of seeing past the illusions or "glamour" cast by the Fae to the true nature that lies beneath. Some can also see Tabh'rs, hidden portals between realms. Others can sense Seelie and Unseelie objects of power. Each sidhe-seer is different, with varying degrees of resistance to the Fae. Some are limited, some are advanced with multiple "special powers."

I snorted. Special powers. Somebody'd been watching too much *WB* and it wasn't me. The kicker was, *I* was supposedly one of these things. According to Barrons, this "True Vision" ran in bloodlines. He believed Alina must have had it, too, and that she'd been killed by one of the Fae she'd seen.

I closed my journal. It was already two-thirds full. Soon I would need a new one. The first half contained an outpouring of grief interspersed with disjointed memories of Alina. The next thirty or so pages were crammed with lists and ideas for tracking down her murderer.

And now the latest—I was filling page after page with absolute nonsense. Mom and Dad would lock me up and have me medicated if they ever got their hands on it. *We don't know what happened, Doctor,* I could hear Dad say, handing over my diary. *She went to Dublin and she just went crazy.* I suddenly understood why Alina had always hidden hers.

I blinked and replayed that in my mind—*Alina had always hidden hers.*

Of course, how could I have forgotten?

Alina had kept a journal all her life. Since we'd been kids, she'd never missed a day of writing in it. I used to watch her down the hall at night, before we closed our bedroom doors to sleep, sprawled on her bed, writing away. *Someday I'll let you read it, Junior,* she'd tell me. She'd started calling me little Mac (as opposed to Big Mac) when we were young, abbreviating it to Junior as I got older. *Like when we're both in our eighties, and it's too late for you to learn any bad habits from me.* She'd laugh and I'd laugh, too, because Alina didn't have any bad habits, and we both knew it. Her journal had been her confidante, her best friend. She'd told it things she'd never told me. I knew, because I'd found more than a few. As I'd matured, I stopped hunting for her diaries, but she hadn't stopped hiding them. Though she'd packed the ones she'd written in her younger years away in a locked trunk in the attic, she'd never stopped teasing me about how I would never find her latest, greatest hiding place.

"Oh yes, I will," I vowed. I'd find it even if it meant I had to dismantle her entire apartment, piece by piece. I couldn't believe I hadn't thought of it before—that somewhere right here in Dublin was a record of every single thing that had happened to my sister since she'd arrived, including all there was to know about the mystery man she'd been seeing—but I'd been blinded by my focus on the *Gardai* and packing and the strange things I'd been seeing.

I was struck by a sudden fear ... was that why her apartment had been ransacked? Because the man she'd been involved with had known she'd kept a journal and searched for it, too? If so, was I too late?

It had taken me too long to think of it as it was. I wasn't about to waste another second. I tossed down some bills, grabbed my journal and purse, and dashed for the door.

It was standing there—just *standing* there in the darkness; how the heck was I supposed to have known?—when I hurtled around the corner.

I was sprinting in my haste to get to Alina's place so I could find her journal and prove to myself that it was a perfectly normal man—albeit a homicidal maniac—who'd killed her, not some mythical monster. If I had rounded the corner and crashed into a person, it would have startled me. As it was, I slammed into something that made the Gray Man look like someone I might have considered taking to senior prom. My double vision lasted less than a heartbeat, from the instant I saw it to the moment I hit it.

I tried to dodge but didn't react fast enough. I crashed into it with my shoulder, bounced off it, and slammed into the side of a building. Dazed, I stumbled to my hands and knees on the sidewalk. I crouched there, staring up in horror. The glamour the thing cast was so faint it required no effort on my part at all to penetrate it. I couldn't see how it would fool anyone.

Like the Gray Man, it had *most* of the right parts. Unlike the Gray Man, it had a few extra ones, too. Parts of it were underdone, and parts of it were horrifyingly overdone. Its head was huge, hairless, and covered with dozens of eyes. It had more mouths than I could count—at least that's what I think the wet, pink leechlike suckers all over the misshapen head and stomach were—I could see the flash of sharp teeth as the moist puckers expanded and contracted in the gray, wrinkled flesh with what sure looked to me like hunger. Four ropy arms hung from its barrel-like body, two puny ones drooped limply at its sides. It stood on legs like tree trunks and its

male sex organ was distended and grotesquely over-
sized. I mean, as big around as a baseball bat and
hanging past its knees.

To my dismay, I realized it was leering at me—
with every one of those eyes and all of those mouths.
To my horror, it reached down and began stroking
itself hard.

I couldn't move. It's something I'm still ashamed
of. You always wonder how you'll handle a moment
of crisis; if you've got what it takes to fight or if
you've just been deluding yourself all along that
somewhere deep inside you there's steel beneath
the magnolia. Now I knew the truth. There wasn't. I
was all petals and pollen. Good for attracting the
procreators who could ensure the survival of our
species, but not a survivor myself. I was Barbie after
all.

I barely managed to choke out a squeak when it
reached for me.

TEN

DARKFEVER

"T his is becoming a habit, Ms. Lane," Barrons said
dryly, glancing briefly up from the book he was
examining when I burst into the store.

I slammed the door behind me and began locking it.

He raised his head again at the sound of dead
bolts ratcheting home and dropped the book on a
table. "What's wrong?"

"I think I'm going to be sick." I needed to wash.
With scalding water and bleach. Maybe a hundred
showers would be enough.

"No, you won't. Concentrate. The urge will pass."

I wondered if he was really so sure about that, or
if he was just trying to condition me with constant
denials, to keep me from puking on his precious
sofa or one of his priceless rugs.

"What happened? You're white as a sheet."

I glanced at Fiona behind the cashier's counter.

"You may speak freely in front of her," he said.

I moved to the counter and sank back against it for support. My legs were shaking, my knees weak. "I saw another one," I told him.

He'd turned with me as I'd moved. Now he stopped with his back to the end of a heavy, ornate bookcase. "So? I told you you would. Was it so hideous? Is that what this is about? It frightened you?"

I took a deep breath, fighting tears. "It knows I saw it."

Barrons' mouth fell open. He gaped at me a long moment. Then he turned and punched the end of the bookcase so hard books went crashing to the floor, shelf after shelf. When he whirled back around, his face was drawn with fury. "Bloody hell!" he exploded. "Un-*fucking*-believable! You, Ms. Lane, are a menace to others! A walking, talking catastrophe in pink!" If gazes could scorch, his would have incinerated me where I stood. "Didn't you hear a thing I told you last night? Weren't you even listening?"

"I heard every word you said," I said stiffly. "And for the record, I don't always wear pink. I often wear peach or lavender. You braced me for another Gray Man or Hunter or Shade. You didn't brace me for this."

"How much worse could it have been?" he said disbelievingly.

"Much," I told him. "You have no idea."

"Describe it."

I did, as succinctly as possible, stumbling a little over its proportions. I got nauseated all over again merely recounting its grotesque appearance. When I finished I said, "What was it?" *How does it kill?* was what I really wanted to know. I didn't care about their names. I didn't want to see them at all. But I was developing a burgeoning obsession with the various ways I might die. Especially given what the thing's intentions had seemed. I'd rather the Gray Man got me, or a Shade. I mean, really, just hand me over to the Royal Hunters, please. Let them skin and stake me as Barrons had said they'd once done.

"No idea. Was it alone or with others?"

"It was alone."

"Are you absolutely certain it knew you could see it? Could you be mistaken?"

"Oh no. No doubt there. It touched me." I shuddered, remembering.

He laughed, a hollow, humorless sound. "Funny, Ms. Lane. Now tell me what really happened."

"I just did. It touched me."

"Impossible," he said. "If it had, you wouldn't be here."

"I'm telling you the truth, Barrons. What possible reason could I have to lie? The thing grabbed me." And I wanted desperately to scrub, especially my hands, because I'd grabbed it right back, trying to fight it off. Its skin had been reptilian, slimy, and I'd gotten much too close a look at those many convulsively sucking, revolting mouths.

"And then what? Said, 'Oh, I'm so sorry, Ms. Lane, I didn't mean to wrinkle your lovely blouse. May I press that for you?' Or perhaps you gouged it with one of your pretty pink nails?"

I was really beginning to wonder what his hang-up with pink was, but I didn't resent the sarcasm in his voice. I couldn't make sense of what had happened next, either, and I'd been mulling it over for nearly half an hour. It certainly hadn't been what I'd expected. "Frankly," I said, "it seemed strange to me, too. It grabbed me and then it just stood there looking...well...if it had been human I would have said confused."

"Confused?" he repeated. "An Unseelie stood there looking confused? As in, perplexed, confounded, baffled, consternated?"

I nodded.

Behind me, Fiona said. "Jericho, that doesn't make any sense."

"I know, Fio." Barrons' tone changed when he addressed her, softened noticeably. It was sharp as a knife when he resumed his interrogation of me. "So, it looked confused. Then what, Ms. Lane?"

I shrugged. While the thing had stood there looking stymied, finally, *finally* a little steel had kicked in. "I punched it in the gut and ran. It chased me, but not right away. I think it stood there a minute. Long enough that I was able to flag down a taxi and get away. I made the cabbie drive me around for a while, to make sure I'd lost it." Also to try to muddle through what had just happened. I'd been grabbed by Death but granted a reprieve, and I had no idea why. I'd been able to think of only one person who might. "Then I came to you."

"At least you did one thing right and muddied your path here," he muttered. He stepped closer, peering down at me as if I were some strange new species he'd never seen before. "What the bloody hell are you, Ms. Lane?"

"I don't know what you mean." *You don't even know what you are,* Alina had said in her message. *If you can't keep your head down and honor your blood-line . . . go die somewhere else. . . .* the old woman in the bar had hissed. And now Barrons was demanding to know what I was. "I tend bar. I like music. My sister was murdered recently. I seem to have gone insane since then," I added this last almost conversationally.

He glanced beyond me, at Fiona. "See if you can uncover any record, however obscure, of this kind of thing happening."

"You don't need me to do that, Jericho," she said. "You know there is."

He shook his head. "She couldn't possibly be a Null, Fio. They're mythical."

Fiona's laugh was airy, musical. "So you say. As are many things. Aren't they, Jericho?"

"What's a Null?" I said.

Barrons ignored my question. "Describe this Unseelie for Fiona again, Ms. Lane, in as much detail as you can. She may be able to identify it." To Fiona, he said, "After the two of you have finished here, show Ms. Lane to a room. Tomorrow, purchase shears and buy an assortment of hair colors for her to choose from."

"A room?" Fiona exclaimed.

"Shears? Hair colors?" I exclaimed. My hands

flew to my hair. I'd address the room part in a minute. I had my priorities.

"Can't bear to shed your pretty feathers, Ms. Lane? What did you expect? It knows you saw it. It won't stop looking for you until you're dead—or it is. And believe me, they don't die easily, if at all. The only question is whether it will alert the Hunters, or come for you by itself. If you're lucky, it's one of a kind like the Gray Man. The lower castes prefer to hunt alone."

"You mean, maybe it won't tell any of the other Unseelie?" I felt a small surge of hope. One Unseelie might just be survivable, but the thought of being hunted by a multitude of monsters was enough to make me give up without even trying. I could too easily envision a horde of hideous creatures chasing me through the Dublin night. I'd keel over and die of a heart attack before they ever caught me.

"They have as many factions among themselves as humans do," he said. "The Fae, particularly the Unseelie, trust each other about as much as you might trust sharing a cage with a hungry lion."

Or a Jericho Barrons, I was thinking a quarter hour later, when Fiona showed me to a room. That's exactly what it felt like—preparing to spend the night at Barrons Books and Baubles—like I was taking up residence in the lion's den. *Out of the frying pan, into the fire.* That was me. But I'd thought twice about pitching a fit, because if my choices were staying at the inn by myself or staying here, I'd rather stay here, if only to minimize my odds of dying alone and unnoticed for several days like my sister had.

The bookstore extended farther back from the street than I'd realized. The rear half wasn't part of the store at all, but living quarters. Fiona briskly unlocked one door, led me down a short corridor, then unlocked a second door and we entered Barrons' private residence. I got a fleeting impression of understated wealth as she whisked me through an anteroom, down a hallway, and directly to a stairwell.

"Do you see them too?" I asked, as we climbed flight after flight, to the top floor.

"All myths contain a grain of truth, Ms. Lane. I've handled books and artifacts that will never find their way into a museum or library, things no archaeologist or historian could ever make sense of. There are many realities pocketed away in the one we call our own. Most go blindly about their lives and never see beyond the ends of their noses. Some of us do."

Which told me nothing about her, really, but she hadn't exactly been giving off warm and friendly vibes in my direction, so I didn't press. After Barrons left, I'd described the thing again. She'd taken notes with brusque efficiency, rarely looking at me directly. She'd gotten the same tight-lipped look my mom got when she vigorously disapproved of something. I was pretty sure the something was me, but couldn't imagine why.

We stopped at a door at the end of the hall. "Here." Fiona thrust a key into my hand, then turned back for the stairwell. "Oh, and Ms. Lane," she said over her shoulder, "I'd lock myself in if I were you."

It was advice I hadn't needed. I wedged a chair beneath the door handle, too. I would have barricaded it with the dresser as well, but it was too heavy for me to move.

The rear bedroom windows looked down four stories onto an alley behind the bookstore. The alley vanished into darkness on the left and semidarkness on the right, after bisecting narrow cobbled walkways that ran along each side of the building. Across the alley was a one-story structure that looked like a warehouse or a huge garage with glass-block windows that were painted black, making it impossible to discern anything within. Floodlights washed the area directly between the buildings white, illuminating a walkway from door to door. Dublin sprawled beneath me, a sea of roofs, melting into the night sky. To my left, so few lights pierced the darkness that it appeared that section of the city was dead. I was relieved to see there was no fire escape on the rear of the building. I didn't think any of the Unseelie I'd seen could scale the sheer brick face. I refused to dwell on the winged Hunters.

I double-checked all the locks and closed the drapes.

Then I dug my brush from my purse, sat down on the bed, and began brushing my hair. I worked on it for a long time, until it shimmered like blond silk.

I was going to miss it.

Don't leave the bookstore until I return, read the note that had been shoved beneath my door sometime during the night.

I crumpled it, irritated. What was I supposed to eat? It was ten o'clock. I'd slept late and was starving. I'm one of those people that needs to eat as soon as I wake up.

I removed the chair from beneath the knob and unlocked the door. Though my proper southern upbringing made me balk at the idea of intruding into another person's house without an invitation to make myself at home, I didn't see that I had any choice but to go hunting for his kitchen. I would get a sick headache if I went too long without food. Mom says it's because my metabolism is so high.

When I opened the door, I discovered someone had been busy while I'd slept. A bakery bag, a bottled latte, and my luggage were outside the door. Down South, store-bought food outside your bedroom door isn't a treat—it's an insult. Despite the presence of my personal belongings, Barrons couldn't have told me any more plainly not to make myself at home. *Stay out of my kitchen*, the bag said, *and don't go looking around*. Down South it meant, *Leave before lunch, preferably now*.

I ate two croissants, drank the coffee, got dressed, and retraced my steps of last night directly back to the bookstore. I didn't look either way as I went. Any curiosity I might have felt about Barrons was second to my pride. He didn't want me there—

fine—I didn't want to be there. In fact, I wasn't sure why I *was* there. I mean, I knew why I'd stayed, but I had no idea why he'd let me. I wasn't stupid enough to think Jericho Barrons had an ounce of chivalry in him; damsels in distress were clearly not his cup of tea.

"Why are you helping me?" I asked him that night, when he returned to the store. I wondered where he'd been. I was still where I'd spent the entire day: in the rear conversation area of the store, the one that was almost out of sight, back by the bathroom and set of doors that led to Barrons' private quarters. I'd pretended to be reading while I was really trying to make sense of my life and contemplating the various hair color shades Fiona had brought when she'd arrived to open the store at noon. She'd ignored my efforts to make conversation and hadn't spoken to me all day expect for the offer of a sandwich at lunch. At ten after eight, she'd locked up the store and left. A few minutes later, Barrons had appeared.

He dropped into a chair across from me: elegance and arrogance in tailored black pants, black boots, and a white silk shirt he'd not bothered to tuck in. The snowy fabric contrasted with his coloring, intensifying his slicked-back hair to midnight, his eyes to obsidian, his skin to bronze. He'd rolled the sleeves back at his wrists; one powerful forearm sported a platinum-and-diamond watch, the other an embossed, wide silver cuff that looked very old and Celtic. Tall, dark, and basely sexual in a way I supposed some women might find irresistibly attractive, Barrons exuded his usual unsettling vitality. "I'm not helping you, Ms. Lane. I'm entertaining the notion that you might be of use to me. If so, I need you alive."

"How could I be of use to you?"

"I want the *Sinsar Dubh*."

So did I. But I didn't see how my odds of getting it were any greater than his. In fact, in light of recent events, I didn't see that I had any odds of getting the darn thing at all. What could he need me for? "You think I can help find it somehow?"

"Perhaps. Why haven't you altered your appearance yet, Ms. Lane? Didn't Fiona provide you with the necessary items?"

"I was thinking maybe I could wear a ball cap."

His gaze flicked from my face to my feet and back again in a way that said he'd taken my measure and found me seriously lacking.

"I could tuck it up and pull the bill down really low," I said. "I've done it before, back home on bad hair days. With sunglasses on, you can hardly see me at all."

He folded his arms across his chest.

"It could work," I said defensively.

He shook his head once, just a few inches to the left and back. "When you've finished cutting and coloring your hair, return to me. Short and dark, Ms. Lane. Lose the Barbie look."

I didn't cry when I did it. I did, however—*damn* Jericho Barrons for doing what he did to me next—

throw up all over his Persian rug in the back of the bookstore when I came back down.

Looking back, I realized I began to feel it while I was upstairs washing my hair in the bathroom that adjoined my room. A wave of sudden nausea washed over me, but I thought it was an emotional reaction to changing my appearance so drastically. I'd already begun to wonder who I was and what was wrong with me; now I was going to *look* wrong, too.

The feeling intensified as I descended the stairs, and grew stronger as I made my way back to the bookstore. I should have paid more attention to it, but I was feeling sorry for myself to the point of obliviousness.

By the time I stepped through the second of the doors that separated Barrons' personal and professional domains, I was shivering and sweating at the same time, my hands were clammy, and my stomach was a churning mess. I'd never gone from feeling fine to feeling awful so quickly in my life.

Barrons was seated on the sofa I'd vacated, his arms stretched across the back of it, his legs spread, looking relaxed as a lion lazing after the kill. His gaze, however, was sharp as a hawk's. He studied me with voracious interest as I stepped through the door. There were some papers on the sofa next to him that I had yet to understand the significance of.

I closed the door and promptly doubled over and vomited what was left of my lunch. Most of the damage to his precious rug was water I'd drunk. I'm big on drinking lots of water. Hydrating one's skin from the inside out is even more important than using a good moisturizer on the surface. I heaved until there was nothing left, then I retched a few times more. I was on my hands and knees again, for the second time in as many days, and I didn't like it a bit. I dragged my sleeve across my mouth and glared up at him. I hated my hair and I hated my life and I could feel it blazing in my eyes.

He, on the other hand, looked pleased as punch.

"What just happened, Barrons? What did you do to me?" I accused. Improbable though it seemed, I was certain that somehow he'd had everything to do with my sudden malaise.

He laughed and stood up, looking down at me. "You, Ms. Lane, can sense the *Sinsar Dubh*. And you just became very, very useful to me."

ELEVEN

I don't *want* it," I repeated, backing away. "Get it away from me!"

"It won't harm you, Ms. Lane. At least not in this form," Barrons said again.

I didn't believe what he was saying the fifth time any more than I had the first. I flung an arm behind me, at the rug still damp from my cleaning efforts. "What do you call that? If I had anything left in my stomach at all, I'd still be on my hands and knees. I don't know about you, but I call impromptu vomiting harm." Not to mention the deep sense of dread I still couldn't shake. The fine hair on my body was standing on end as if I'd been hit with a high-voltage charge. I wanted to put as much distance between "it" and me as was possible.

"You'll get used to it—"

"So you keep saying," I muttered.

"—and your reactions will lessen in time."

"I have no intention of spending that much time around it." "It" was photocopies of two pages allegedly ripped from the *Sinsar Dubh*. Photocopies—not even the real thing—he was thrusting at me. Mere facsimiles had me plastered up against the wall in my frantic efforts to avoid it. I could feel a Spidey-moment coming on. If he didn't back off, I was going to scale the walls using only my Gentlemen-Prefer-Blondes-Blush nails as rappelling spikes, and I seriously doubted it was going to work.

"Take slow, deep breaths," Barrons said. "You can overcome it. Concentrate, Ms. Lane."

I gulped air. It didn't help.

"I said breathe. Not do a fish-out-of-water imitation."

I looked at him coldly, inhaled, and held it. After a long moment, Barrons nodded, and I exhaled slowly.

"Better," he said.

"Why is this happening to me?" I asked.

"It's part of being what you are, Ms. Lane. Thousands of years ago, when the Fae still ran the Wild Hunt, destroying anything in their path, this was what a *sidhe*-seer felt when the Tuatha Dé riders approached en masse. This was her warning to lead her people to safety."

"I didn't feel it when I saw any of the Unseelie," I pointed out. But as I reflected on those first two times, I realized I *had* gotten queasy, and both times a general, inexplicable sense of dread had preceded my "visions." I'd just not recognized it for what it was because I'd not been able to pin it on anything. With the last monster, I'd been so obsessed with getting to Alina's, and I'd crashed into it so fast, that I couldn't decide whether I'd felt anything in advance or not.

"I said, en masse," he said. "Alone, or in pairs, their impact is not as great. It is possible only the *Sinsar Dubh* will ever make you this sick—or perhaps a thousand Unseelie bearing down on you. The Dark Book is the most powerful of all the Fae Hallows. As well as the deadliest."

"Stay back," I snapped. He'd closed to less than a yard from me, holding those terrible pages. He took another step forward and I tried to make myself into wallpaper. Very yellow, very spineless wallpaper.

"Master your fear, Ms. Lane. They are mere copies of the real pages. Only pages of the Dark Book itself could do you lasting harm."

"They could?" That certainly put a problematic spin on things. "You mean even if we manage to find this book, I'm not going to be able to touch it?"

His lips curved but his eyes stayed cold. "You could. I'm not certain you would like yourself afterward."

"Why wouldn't I—" I broke off, shaking my head. "Forget it, I don't want to know. Just keep those pages away from me."

"Does this mean you're giving up the quest to find your sister's murderer, Ms. Lane? I thought she begged you to find the *Sinsar Dubh*. I thought she said everything depended on it."

I closed my eyes and sagged back against the wall. For a few minutes there I'd completely forgotten about Alina. "Why?" I whispered as if she were still there to hear. "Why didn't you tell me any of this? We could have helped each other. Maybe we could have kept each other alive." And that was the bitterest part of it all—how things *might* have turned out, if only she'd confided in me.

"I doubt you would have believed, even if she had. You've been a tough sell, Ms. Lane. As much as you've seen and heard, you're still trying to deny it."

His voice was much too close. Barrons had moved. I opened my eyes. He was standing right in front of me, yet my sickness hadn't intensified— because I hadn't seen him coming. He was right; my reaction was as much mental as it was physical, which meant at least part of it was controllable. I could retreat, go home, and try to forget everything that had happened to me since I'd arrived in Dublin, or I could figure out how to go forward. I touched my short, dark locks. I hadn't butchered my beautiful blonde hair for nothing. "You see the Fae, too, Barrons, yet you have no problem holding those pages."

"Repetition dulls even the keenest senses, Ms. Lane. Are you ready to begin?"

Two hours later, Barrons decided I'd had enough practice. I couldn't bring myself to touch the photocopied pages, but at least I was no longer retching in close proximity to them. I'd figured out a way to close my throat off against the involuntary heaves.

Nearness still made me feel perfectly miserable, but I could muster and maintain a presentable mask.

"You'll do," he said. "Get dressed. We're going somewhere."

"I am dressed."

He turned toward the front of the store and looked out the window at the night. "Go put on something more...grown-up...Ms. Lane."

"Huh?" I had on white capris, dainty sandals, and a sleeveless pink blouse over a lace-trimmed tank. I thought I looked perfectly grown-up. I circled around in front of him. "What's wrong with me?"

He gave me a brief glance. "Go put on something more...womanly."

With my figure, nobody could ever accuse me of not being womanly. Understanding might come slowly to me sometimes—but it comes. Men. Take them into a classy lingerie store and I guarantee you they'll find the only thing in there made of cheap black leather and chains. My eyes narrowed. "You mean sleazy," I said.

"I mean the kind of woman others are accustomed to seeing me with. A *grown* one, if you think you can manage that, Ms. Lane. Black might make you look old enough to drive. The new hair is...better. But do something with it. Make it look like it did the night I woke you."

"You want me to have bed-head on purpose?"

"If that's what you call it. Will an hour be enough?"

An hour implied that I needed a *lot* of help. "I'll see what I can do," I said coolly.

I was ready in twenty minutes.

My suspicions about the building behind the bookstore were confirmed; it *was* a garage, and Jericho Barrons was a very rich man. I guessed the books and baubles trade was pretty darned lucrative.

From the eye-popping collection of cars in his garage, he chose a modest-by-comparison black Porsche 911 Turbo that roared deep in its masterfully engineered five-hundred-and-fifteen-horsepower throat when he slid the key into the ignition on the wrong side of the steering wheel and turned it. Yes, I know cars. I love fast, pretty ones and the subtle class of the pricey Porsche appealed to every shallow bone in my twenty-two-year-old body.

He put the top down and drove much too fast, but with the expert aggressiveness any high-performance vehicle capable of running zero to sixty in three-point-six seconds demanded. One neighborhood melted into the next as he worked the engine, shifting up and down through the stop-and-go traffic of the city. Once past the outskirts of Dublin, he opened it up. Beneath a nearly full moon, we raced the wind. The air was warm, the sky brilliant with stars, and under other circumstances I would have tremendously enjoyed the ride.

I glanced over at him. Whatever else he might be—obviously a *sidhe*-seer himself and a royal pain in the petu—*ass* most of the time—Barrons was now just a man, lost in the pleasure of the moment, of the finely crafted machine in his hands, of the wide-open road and the seemingly limitless night.

"Where are we going?" I had to shout to make myself heard over the dual roar of the wind and engine.

Without taking his eyes off the road, for which I was eminently grateful at a hundred and four miles an hour, he said, "There are three main players in the city that have also been searching for the book. I want to know if they've found anything. You, Ms. Lane, are my bloodhound," he shouted back.

I glanced at the clock on the dash. "It's two in the morning, Barrons. What are we going to do, break and enter and creep around in their houses while they're sleeping?" It was a measure of how surrealistic my life had become that, if he replied in the affirmative, I suspected the first thing out of my mouth wouldn't be a protest but a complaint that he'd made me get overdressed for burgling. High heels and a short skirt would certainly make running from the police or angry, armed property owners very difficult.

He slowed a little so I could hear him better. "No, they're night people, Ms. Lane. They'll be up and just as willing to see me, as I am to see them. We like to keep tabs on one another. They, however, don't have *you*." A slow smile curved his lips. He was hugely pleased with the new secret weapon he had in me. I had a sudden dismal view of my future, of being led around and asked incessantly, like one of those Verizon commercials, *Do you feel sick now?*

He sped up and we drove another ten minutes or so in silence, then turned off the main road into the entrance of a walled estate. After being cleared by a pair of coldly efficient white-uniformed security guards who, after a quiet phone call, retracted an enormous steel gate, we purred down a long, winding drive, framed on both sides by huge, ancient trees.

The house at the end of the drive was anachronistic to its setting, which seemed to suggest a stately manor house had once stood there but had been razed to be replaced with this sprawling, chilly, brilliantly spotlighted Meet-the-Jetsons' affair of steel and glass. See-through skywalks connected five levels that slanted at slight upward angles, and metal-framed terraces sported New Age furniture that looked positively miserable to sit in. I admit it; I'm old-fashioned. Give me a wraparound porch with white wicker furniture, swings on each end, slow-paddling ceiling fans, ivy-covered trellises, and hanging baskets of ferns, all beneath the shade of waxy-blossomed magnolia trees. This place was way too artsy and not nearly homey enough for me.

As we got out of the car, Barrons said, "Keep your wits about you and try not to touch anything that doesn't look human, Ms. Lane."

I nearly choked on a nervous laugh. Whatever had happened to good, old, wholesome advice like, "Stick together, hold hands, and look both ways before you cross the street?" I glanced up at him. "Not that I would want to, but why shouldn't I?"

"I suspect Fiona is right," he said, "and you are a

Null, which means you'll give us away if you touch any of the Fae with your hands."

I looked at my hands, at the pretty pink nails that didn't complement my new look so well. My darker 'do would be better accented by slightly bolder tones. I would need to implement some wardrobe and accessorizing changes. "A Null?" I had to work to keep up with him in my heels as we hurried across the shimmering, white crushed-quartz drive.

"Old legends speak of *sidhe*-seers with the ability to freeze a Fae by touching it with their hands, immobilizing it for several minutes, preventing it from moving or even sifting place."

"Sifting place?"

"Later. Do you remember what to do, Ms. Lane?"

I eyed the house. It looked like there was a party going on. People milled on the terraces; laughter, music, and the clink of ice in glasses floated down to where we stood. "Yes. If I start to feel sick I should ask to use the bathroom. You'll escort me to it."

"Very good. And Ms. Lane?"

I glanced at him questioningly.

"Try to act like you like me."

When he put his arm around me and pulled me close, the shiver went clear down to my toes.

The house was decorated in unrelieved white and black. The people were, too. If it were up to me, I would carry a great big paintbrush around with me all the time, splashing color everywhere, decorating the world with peach and mauve, pink and lavender, orange and aquamarine. These folks seemed to think leeching the world of all color was cool. I decided they all must be deeply depressed.

"Jericho," a stunning raven-haired woman in a low-cut white evening gown and diamonds purred throatily. But her smile was teeth and viciousness, and for me, not him. "I almost didn't recognize you. I'm not sure we've ever seen each other with our clothes on."

"Marilyn." He acknowledged her with a brief nod that seemed to piss her off royally as we passed.

"Who's your little friend, Barrons?" a tall, anorexically thin man with a frightful shock of white hair asked. I wanted to pull him aside and give him the gentle advice that wearing all black only made him look thinner and sicker, but I didn't think now was a good time.

"None of your fucking business," Barrons said.

"Ah, we're in our usual fine form, aren't we?" the man sneered.

" 'We' implies we came from the same gene pool, Ellis. We didn't."

"Arrogant fuck," the man muttered to our backs.

"I see you've got a lot of friends here," I remarked dryly.

"No one has friends in this house, Ms. Lane. There are only users and the used at *Casa Blanc*."

"Except for me," I said. Weird name for a weirder house.

He gave me a cursory glance. "You'll learn. If you live long enough."

Even if I lived to be ninety, I would never become like the people in this house. The murmured acknowledgments continued as we passed through the rooms, some hungry—mostly from the women—and others damning—mostly from the men. It was an awful bunch of people. I suffered a sudden stab of homesickness, missed my mom and dad with a vengeance.

I didn't see anything that wasn't human until we came to that last room, at the far end of the house on the fifth floor. We had to pass through three sets of armed security guards to get there.

Reality check: I was at a party with armed security guards and I was wearing all black. It couldn't be my reality. I wasn't that kind of person. Sadly, despite the short skirt that bared my pretty, tanned legs to well above midthigh, a snug, bosom-enhancing top and high heels, compared to the rest of the women at *Casa Blanc*, I looked fifteen. I thought I'd turned my shoulder-length dark hair into something wild and sexy, but I obviously didn't know the meaning of those words. Nor did I understand a thing about the artful application of makeup.

"Stop fidgeting," Barrons said.

I took a deep breath and held it for a three count. "Next time a little more detail on our intended destination might help."

"Take a good look around, Ms. Lane, and next time you won't need it."

We stepped through a pair of enormous white doors, into a large white-upon-white room: white

walls, white carpet, white glassed-in cases interspersed with white columns upon which priceless
objets d'art rested. I stiffened, confronted with double double visions. Now that I knew such monsters
existed, it was easier to spot them. I decided these
two couldn't be putting much effort into the glamour they were throwing or else I was getting better
at penetrating it, because once I saw past their beefy
blond bouncer projections, they didn't flicker between the two, but remained Unseelie.

"Easy," Barrons murmured, sensing my tension.
To the man seated on the absurd white thronelike
chair in front of us, as if holding audience for his
subjects, he said in a bored voice, "McCabe."

"Barrons."

I don't generally like big-boned, hard-bodied,
auburn-haired men, and I was surprised to find
McCabe attractive in a rough-hewn Irish way that
would never polish up no matter the wealth he
managed to accumulate or the treasures with which
he chose to surround himself. But the two Unseelie
flanking him, left and right, weren't attractive at all.
They were huge, ugly, gray-skinned things that
reminded me of rhinoceroses with their bumpy,
oversized foreheads, tiny eyes, jutting underbites,
and lipless gashes for mouths. Wide, squat, barrel-
like bodies strained at the seams of ill-fitting white
suits. Their arms and legs were stumpy and they
were making a constant deep-in-the-throat snuffling
sound, like pigs rooting through the mud for whatever it was pigs rooted. They weren't scary; they
were just ugly. I focused on not focusing on them.

Aside from mild heartburn and a sense of increased agitation, they hardly made me feel sick at all. Of course, any Fae's impact would now and forever be diminished in the dark shadow of the *Sinsar Dubh*'s.

"What brings you to *Casa Blanc*?" McCabe said, adjusting the white tie on the white shirt beneath the jacket of his white suit. *Why bother?* I couldn't help but think. Ties fell into the accessory category and the very definition of accessorizing was accenting or enhancing by artful arrangement of color, texture, and style. Hello—had anyone heard the word "color" in there? He might just as well have *painted* himself white.

Barrons shrugged. "Nice night for a drive."

"Almost a full moon, Barrons. Things can get dangerous out there."

"Things can get dangerous anywhere, McCabe."

McCabe laughed, showing movie-star white teeth. He looked me over. "Into something a little different, Barrons? Who's the little girl?"

Don't speak, Barrons had told me on the way there, *no matter what anyone says. I don't care how pissed off you might get. Swallow it.* His derisive "little girl" ringing in my ears, I bit down hard and didn't say a word.

"Just the latest piece of ass, McCabe."

I no longer had to bite down. I was speechless.

McCabe laughed. "She talk?"

"Not unless I tell her to. Her mouth's usually too full."

I could feel my cheeks burning.

McCabe laughed again. "When she grows up,

pass her my way, will you?" He looked me over thoroughly, ice-blue eyes lingering on my bosom and bottom, and by the time he was done, I felt as if he'd not only seen me nude but somehow knew I had a tiny heart-shaped mole on the left cheek of my behind, and another on my right breast, just east of my nipple. His expression changed, his nostrils widened, his eyes narrowed. "On second thought," he murmured, "don't let her grow up too much. What would you take for her now?"

Barrons flashed a mocking smile. "There's a book I might be interested in."

McCabe snorted, brought the tip of his index finger to his thumb, and flicked an imaginary speck of lint from his sleeve. "No bitch is that good. There are women and there's power—and only one of those holds its value." His expression changed again, his lips thinned out and his eyes went chillingly empty.

Just like that, McCabe lost interest in me, and I had the startling realization that, to him, I wasn't even human. I was more like...well, a condom... something he'd use, then toss the soiled remains away from his person—and if we happened to be in a speeding car on the autobahn, or a jet crossing the Atlantic at the time, so what?

Had Alina been in this world? Had she known this obsessive-compulsive man in white? I could certainly see him killing her, or killing anyone for that matter. But could I see Alina believing herself in love with a man like him? Granted, he was rich, worldly, and attractive in a brutish, powerful way. But the inspector and the two girls I'd spoken with had been absolutely certain Alina's boyfriend wasn't native to the Emerald Isle, and McCabe—despite his enormous pretensions—was salt-of-the-earth Irish, through and through.

"Heard anything about it?" Barrons lost interest in me, too, and moved on to a new subject. Simply two men going about their business, with walking, talking—or rather mute—sex-on-heels nearby in case anyone wanted any, just a convenient platter of oysters on the half shell.

"No," McCabe said flatly. "You?"

"No," Barrons replied just as flatly.

McCabe nodded. "Well, then. Leave her and go. Or just leave." It was obvious he couldn't have cared less which option Barrons chose to exercise. In fact, if I'd gotten left, I wasn't sure McCabe would even notice me again for several days.

The King of White had dismissed us.

TWELVE

Glamour: illusion cast by the Fae to camouflage their true appearance. The more powerful the Fae, the more difficult it is to penetrate its disguise. The average human sees only what the Fae wants them to see, and is subtly repelled from bumping into or brushing against it by a small perimeter of spatial distortion that is part of the Fae glamour.

And *that* was why the monster in the alley with mule-size genitals and leechlike sucking mouths had instantly known what I was—I'd been unable to avoid crashing into it.

Any other person would have been repelled the instant they'd rounded the corner, and stumbled clumsily, careening off nothing they could see. You know all those times you say, "Geez, I don't know what's wrong with me—I must have tripped over my own feet?" Think again.

According to Barrons, McCabe had no idea his "bodyguards" were Unseelie who'd addressed each other as Ob and Yrg when they'd escorted us from the Throne Room in guttural tones Barrons and I had pretended not to hear. McCabe's usual staff of bodyguards had disappeared three months ago and been replaced by the Rhino-boys, a type of Unseelie Barrons believed were low-to-mid-level caste thugs dispatched primarily as watchdogs for the highest-ranking Fae.

After thinking about that for a minute and following it to the logical conclusion, I'd said, *Does that mean an Unseelie is hunting for the* Sinsar Dubh, *too?*

It looks that way, Barrons replied. *And a very powerful one, at that. I keep catching wind of someone the Unseelie call the "Lord Master," but so far I've had no luck discovering who or what this Lord Master is. I told you, Ms. Lane, that you had no idea what you were getting into.*

The Unseelie were terrifying enough. I had no desire to encounter whatever they addressed as their ruler. *Well, maybe now's a real good time for me to get right back out of it,* I'd said.

Try, the look he'd given me had said. Even if I managed to close my heart and turn my back on my sister's murder, Jericho Barrons wasn't about to let me go.

Sad fact was we needed each other. I could sense the *Sinsar Dubh* and he had all the pertinent information about it, including a few ideas about where it might be and who else was looking for it. Left to my own devices, I would never be able to find out about parties like the one at *Casa Blanc* and get myself invited there. Left to his own devices, Barrons would never know if the book was nearby, perhaps even in the same room with him. He could be standing right next to it, for all he knew.

I'd gotten a good idea just how important I was to him last night. If the book was metal, I was Jericho Barrons' own private state-of-the-art metal detector. After Ob and Yrg had returned to McCabe, Barrons had escorted me through floor after floor of the starkly decorated house. When I'd felt nothing, he'd marched me all over the manicured estate, including the outbuildings. He'd insisted we cover the grounds so thoroughly that I hadn't gotten back to my borrowed bedroom to sleep until just before dawn. Reluctant though I was to feel something so awful again, I'd been almost disappointed when my newly discovered Spidey-sense hadn't picked up the faintest tingle anywhere.

Still, to me, the bottom line wasn't about the Dark Book at all. It was about uncovering the details of my sister's secret life. I didn't want the creepy thing. I just wanted to know who or what had killed Alina, and I wanted him or it dead. Then I wanted to go home to my pleasantly provincial Podunk little town in steamy southern Georgia and forget about everything that had happened to me while I was in Dublin. The Fae didn't visit Ashford? Good. I'd marry a local boy with a jacked-up Chevy pickup truck, Toby Keith singing "Who's Your Daddy?" on the radio, and eight proud generations of honest, hardworking Ashford ancestors decorating his

family tree. Short of essential shopping trips to Atlanta, I'd never leave home again.

But for now, working with Barrons was my only
option. The people I met during our search could be
people Alina had met too. And if I could somehow
find and retrace the path she'd taken through this
bizarre film-noir world, it should lead me straight to
her killer.

I would be seriously rethinking the wisdom of
that before long.

I picked up my pen. It was Sunday afternoon and
Barrons Books and Baubles was closed for the day.
I'd woken up disoriented and badly missing Mom,
but when I'd called, Dad had said she was in bed
and he didn't want to wake her. She hadn't been
sleeping well, he said, even though she'd been taking something that was supposed to help her. I'd
carried on an achingly one-sided conversation with
him for a few minutes, but his efforts had been so
painfully halfhearted that I'd given up. At a loss for
what to do, I'd finally grabbed my journal and gone
downstairs to the bookstore.

Now I was sprawled on my stomach on the
comfy sofa in the rear conversation area of the bookstore, notebook propped on a pillow in front of me.

Sifting: a method of Fae locomotion, I wrote.

I nibbled the tip of my fine-point, felt-tipped
fuchsia pen and tried to figure out how to write this
one down. When Barrons had explained it to me, I'd
been horrified.

You mean they can just think *themselves somewhere*

and that's how instantly it happens? They just want to be someplace—and then there they are?

Barrons nodded.

You mean I could be walking down the street and one could just pop in alongside me and grab me?

Ah, but there you have a tremendous advantage, Ms. Lane. Grab it back and you'll freeze it like you did the one in the alley. But do it fast, before it sifts you to someplace you really don't want to be.

And then what am I supposed to do? Start toting weapons around with me so I can kill them while they're frozen? No matter how horrific the Unseelie were, the thought of carving something up while it couldn't even move was abhorrent to me.

I doubt you could, Barrons said. *Both Seelie and Unseelie are virtually indestructible. The higher the caste, the harder they are to kill.*

Great, I said. *Any ideas what I should do once I turn them into all-too-temporary statues?*

Yes, Ms. Lane, he'd replied, with that dark, sardonic smile of his. *Run like hell.*

I brushed the tips of my lashes with sable mascara, and wondered what one wore to visit a vampire.

The chic red sweater set I'd brought with me from home not only didn't go so well with my darker hair, I was afraid it might be construed as a flirtatious invitation to color me bloodier. The dainty silver cross earrings my aunt Sue bought me for my last birthday would no doubt be considered provocative, as well. I glanced at my watch. Indecision over my outfit was making me late for my midnight appointment with Barrons. I wasn't going to have time to dash to the church down the street and dab holy water at my wrists and behind my ears; my version of *Eau de Don'tbiteme*.

I stared in the mirror. I couldn't make myself look like the women at *Casa Blanc* if I wanted to, and I didn't. I liked me. I liked my colors. I missed my hair so bad it hurt.

Sighing, I turned my head upside down, hair-sprayed it liberally, then set the lacquer with a blast of heat from my dryer. When I tossed it back again and finger-combed it—thanks to Ms. Clairol's Medium Hot Rods—I had a head of shoulder-length, tousled Arabian-Nights curls that framed my face seductively and made my green eyes stand out even more than they usually did. Slightly uptilted at the outer corners, with long dark lashes, my eyes were one of my best features, a brilliant shade of green, the color of new young grass at Easter. I have clear, even-toned skin that tans really well and goes with pretty much any shade. I didn't look bad with dark hair. I just didn't look like me. I looked older, especially with the candy-apple red I'd just glossed on my mouth, a concession to Barrons since I was sure he wasn't going to like the outfit I'd just decided on.

As I slipped into my clothes, I remembered how Alina and I used to make fun of vampire movies and novels, and of the whole paranormal craze in general that had been launched by the creation of one small, pale, bespectacled boy who lived beneath the stairs.

That was before I knew there really *were* things out there in the night.

"What the bloody hell do you have on, Ms. Lane?" Barrons demanded.

What I had on was a luscious gauzy skirt of nearly every pastel hue on the color wheel that hugged my hips and kicked frothily at my ankles, a form-fitting rose sweater with silk-trimmed cap sleeves and a plunging silk-edged neckline that made much of my bust, and dainty pink high heels that laced around my ankles. The colors went stunningly with my sun-kissed skin and dark curls. I looked feminine, soft, and sexy in a wholesome young woman way, not a *Casa Blanc* way. I strode briskly past rows of bookcases to where he stood waiting impatiently by the front door of the shop, and stabbed a finger in his direction. "If you treat me like one of your skanks again tonight, Barrons, you can just forget about our little arrangement. You need me as much as I need you. That makes us equal partners in my book."

"Well, your book is just wrong," he said flatly.

"No, yours is," I said just as flatly. "Figure out another way to explain me. I don't care what you come up with. But if you call me your latest piece of petunia again or make uncalled-for references to my mouth and oral sex with you, you and I are through."

He raised a brow. "Petunia, Ms. Lane?"

I scowled. "Ass, Barrons."

He crossed his arms and his gaze dropped to my

glossy Lip-Venom red lips. "Am I to understand there are called-for references to your mouth and oral sex with me, Ms. Lane? I'd like to hear them."

Eyes narrowed, I sidestepped his idiotic taunting. "Is this Mallucé guy really a vampire, Barrons?"

He shrugged. "He claims to be. He is surrounded by people who believe he is." He scanned me from head to toe. "Last night you said you wanted to know what to expect so you could better select your attire. I told you we were going to visit a vampire in a Goth-den tonight. Why, then, Ms. Lane, do you look like a perky rainbow?"

I shrugged in kind. "Take me or leave me, Barrons."

He took me. As I'd known he would.

There are a few things a hunting man can't do without. His bloodhound is one of them.

McCabe lived twenty minutes to the north of the city, in my idea of a modernistic nightmare.

Mallucé lived ten minutes to the south of Dublin, entombed in garish tatters of the past. The Victorian Era, to be precise—those sixty-three years from 1837 to 1901 during which Queen Victoria ruled Great Britain and called herself Empress of India—immortalized, erroneously perhaps, by opulent, velvet-draped, sensualistic, and often cluttered home decor.

Steampunk was the theme of the night at Mallucé's: Victorian-style clothing tweaked in edgy ways, ripped, distorted, and blended with Goth,

Rivet, and Punk—although I admit sometimes I have a hard time picking up the subtle details that differentiate the individual pockets of the Dark Fashion world. I think you have to live in it to get it.

We left the Porsche with an Unseelie Rhino-boy valet at the door, whose glamour looked like unvarnished deathpunk to me. In contrast, I did indeed resemble a perky rainbow.

Mallucé's lair was a monstrous, rambling affair of brick and stone that was a mishmash of various types of Victorian architecture, leaning heavily toward *Addams Family* Goth, with an embarrassment of turrets and porticos, wrought-iron balustrades and battlements, oriel windows and transoms, and enough ornate cornices and brackets to dizzy the eye, not to mention baffle the soul.

Four tall stories were stacked haphazardly on top of each other, cresting in a black roofline against the cobalt night sky that made no sense, but leapt whimsically from flat to dangerously steep and back again. Trees with skeletal limbs, badly in need of a trim, scraped against slate, like oaken nails on the lid of a coffin.

The house rambled over an acre and I wouldn't have been at all surprised to learn it had upward of sixty or seventy rooms. On the top floor, strobe lights flickered beyond tall narrow windows, in tempo with raucous, driving music. On the lower floors the ambience was different: black and crimson candles were the light of choice, and the music was soft, dreamy, and voluptuous.

Barrons had given me a good bit of background

about our soon-to-be host on the way over. Mallucé had been born John Johnstone Jr. to old British money some thirty years ago. When the senior Johnstones had died in a suspicious car accident, leaving their twenty-four-year-old son sole heir to a several-hundred-million-dollar fortune, J. J. Jr. had turned his back on his father's vast financial empire, sold off one company after the next, and liquidated all assets. He'd cast off his embarrassingly redundant name, gotten it legally changed to the singular, romantic Mallucé, dressed himself in the height of refined steampunk, and presented himself to Goth society as one of the newly undead.

Over the years, several hundred million dollars had bought him an extensive cult of true believers and hardcore groupies, and in some quarters, the name Mallucé was nearly synonymous with Lestat.

Barrons had never met him face-to-face but had seen him on several occasions in the trendier night-clubs. He'd made it his business to track Mallucé's interests and acquisitions. "He goes after many of the same artifacts as I," he told me. "Last time he tried to outbid me in an exclusive Internet auction— a wealthy recluse in London, Lucan Trevayne, disappeared and within days a large portion of his collection was up for grabs on the black market—I had a hacker standing by who took down Mallucé's entire computer network at the crucial moment." Dark eyes glittering, Barrons smiled, a predator relishing the memory of a cherished kill.

But his smile faded as he continued. "Unfortunately, what I'd been hoping to find in

Trevayne's collection was no longer there. Someone had beaten me to it. At any rate, Mallucé must have learned of the *Sinsar Dubh* in the years preceding his father's death. The senior Johnstone dabbled in artifacts and there was a considerable uproar in the antiquities world some time back when photocopied pages of what most believed to be mythical—indeed, a joke of an icon—debuted on the black market. I have no idea how many photocopied sets are out there, but I do know Mallucé saw the pages at some point. The undead fuck's been getting in my way ever since." Barrons said "undead fuck" as if he strongly wished Mallucé dead—not believed him undead.

"You don't think he's a vampire," I said in a hushed voice, as we picked our way through room after room of stoned-looking people draped across low-backed velveteen divans, passed out on brocade chaises, and sprawled in various stages of undress on the floor. We were searching for an entrance to the sub-basement, where a dazedly compliant sloe-eyed Goth-girl had told us "the Master" would be. I tried not to notice the rhythmic thrusts, grunts, and moans as I stepped carefully over half-naked tangles.

He laughed briefly, a hollow, humorless sound. "If he is, the one that made him should be drowned in holy water, defanged, gelded, skinned, staked, and left to blister agonizingly in the sun." He was silent a moment, then, "Feeling anything, Ms. Lane?"

I didn't think he meant embarrassment about what I'd just stepped over, so I shook my head.

We passed half a dozen more Unseelie by the time we found the sub-basement. Mingled in with the white-skinned, pierced and chained, black-nailed, black-lipped Goth-youth, casting similar noir glamours, the Dark Fae were doing things to their unwitting victims I refused to see. Though I saw none as horrific as the Gray Man or the Many-Mouthed-Thing, I was beginning to realize that there was no such thing as an attractive Unseelie.

"Not true," Barrons said when I remarked upon it. "Unseelie royalty, the princes and princesses of the four houses, are every bit as inhumanly beautiful as Seelie royalty. In fact, it is virtually impossible to tell them apart."

"Why are there so many Unseelie here?"

"Morbidity is their oxygen, Ms. Lane. They breathe richly in places like this."

We'd been navigating a maze of subterranean corridors for some time. Now we turned down a long dim hallway that ended in an immense, square black door belted by bands of steel. A dozen men stood guard between Mallucé and any of his too-fervent faithful, shoulders slung with ammunition, toting automatic weapons.

A large bull of a man with a shaved head stepped into our path, blocking our way. The safety pins in his ears didn't bother me. The ones in his eyelids did.

"Where do you think you're going?" he growled, fixing his rifle on Barrons with one hand, resting the heel of the other on the butt of a gun tucked into the waistband of his black leather pants.

"Inform Mallucé that Jericho Barrons is here."

"Why would the Master give a fuck?"

"I have something he wants."

"Oh yeah? Like what?"

Barrons smiled and for the first time I saw a glint of genuine humor in his dark eyes. "Tell him to try to access any of his bank accounts."

Ten minutes later the door to Mallucé's inner sanctum burst open. The shaven-headed messenger stumbled out, his face ashen, his shirt covered with blood.

He was followed by two Unseelie Rhino-boys who jammed guns into our sides and marched us through the doorway and into the vampire's lair. Nausea flooded my stomach and I gripped my purse tightly with both hands so I wouldn't inadvertently touch either of our ugly escorts.

The chamber beyond the steel-belted door was so sumptuously decorated in velveteens, satins, gauzes, and brocades, and so busily furnished in Neo-Victorian that it was difficult at first to locate our host in the clutter. It didn't help that his attire matched his surroundings, the very height of Romantic Goth.

I spotted him at last. Motionless on a low-backed, richly embellished chaise scattered with gilt pillows and tasseled throws, Mallucé was wearing stiff, textured brown-and-black-striped trousers and fine-tooled Italian slippers. His eggshell linen shirt dripped lace at his wrists and throat, and blood at his jabot. He wore a brocade-and-velvet vest of amber, russet, crimson, and gold, and as I watched, he withdrew a snowy handkerchief from a pocket in the inner lining and gently dabbed blood from his chin, then licked a few remaining drops from his lips. Muscular and graceful as a cat, he was pale and smooth as a marble bust. Dead yellow eyes lent a feral cast to his sharply chiseled, too-white face. Long blond hair pulled back in an old-fashioned, amber-beaded queue emphasized his abnormally rigid pallor.

The vampire separated sinuously from the settee and rose, holding an incongruously modern laptop. With a graceful flick of his fingers, he snapped the chrome case shut, tossed it carelessly on a velvet-draped table, then glided to a halt in front of us.

As he stood there in all his undead stillness, face-to-face with the carnal maleness and disturbing vitality of Jericho Barrons, I was startled to realize that, although I was deep in the belly of a vampire's lair, surrounded by his worshipers and monster minions—if pressed to decide which of the men before me was more dangerous—it wouldn't have been Mallucé. Eyes narrowed, I looked back and forth between them. Something nagged at me, something I couldn't quite put my finger on. It was a thing that I would stupidly fail to put my finger on until it was too late. Before long, I would understand that nothing had been what it seemed that night, and the reason Barrons had faced-off so coolly with the blood-sucking Master was because he'd gone in with the quiet assurance that, no matter what happened, he would walk out alive, and *not* because he had Mallucé by the proverbial fiscal balls.

"What did you do with my money?" the vampire inquired, his silken voice unmatched by the steel in his strange citron eyes.

Barrons laughed, teeth flashing white in his dark face. "Think of it as an insurance policy. I'll return it when we're through, Johnstone."

The vampire's lips drew back, revealing long, sharp, pointed fangs. There was still blood on them. An expression of utter, mindless rage flashed over his icy face. "The name's Mallucé, asshole," he hissed.

Score one for Barrons, I thought. J. J. Jr. still hated his name. Losing control of an immense fortune didn't seem to bother him nearly as much as merely being addressed by the name with which he'd been christened.

Barrons flicked a contemptuous gaze over the vampire, from frothy, bloody jabot to pointy-toed, silk-trimmed leather slippers. "Mallucé asshole," he repeated. "And here I thought your last name was 'fashion nightmare.'"

Mallucé's inhuman yellow eyes narrowed. "Do you have a death wish, human?" He'd recovered quickly, his face was blank again, his voice once more controlled, so light and melodic it was nearly a verbal caress.

Barrons laughed again. "Might. Doubt you'll be helping me with it, though. What do you know about the *Sinsar Dubh*, Jr.?"

Mallucé flinched, almost imperceptibly, but it was there. If I hadn't been watching him so closely, I wouldn't have caught it. Twice now he'd betrayed an emotion, a thing I was willing to bet he rarely did. With a glance at his guards, then to the door, he said, "Out. Except you." He pointed at Barrons.

Barrons wrapped an arm around my shoulder and I instantly shivered, just as I had last night when he'd touched me. The man packed a seriously weird physical punch.

"She stays with me," Barrons said.

Mallucé gave me a deprecating once-over. Slowly, very slowly, his lips curved. The smile didn't work with those chilling, dead, animal-eyes of his. "Someone certainly took that passé Rolling Stones song to heart, didn't they?" he murmured.

Everyone's a fashion critic. I knew which song he meant: "She's a Rainbow." Whenever I listened to it on my iPod, I would close my eyes and spin around, pretending I was in a sun-dappled clearing, with my arms spread wide and my head thrown back, while colors of every hue sprayed from my fingertips like brilliant little airbrush guns, painting trees, birds, bees, and flowers, even the sun in the sky, glorious shades. I *loved* that song. When I didn't answer him—Barrons and I might have reached an agreement about how he would and wouldn't refer to me, but I was still under orders to keep my mouth shut—Mallucé turned to his bodyguards, who hadn't moved an inch, and hissed, "I said *out*."

The two Unseelie looked at each other, then one

spoke in a gravelly voice, "But O Great Undead One—"

"You've got to be kidding me, Jr.," Barrons muttered, shaking his head. "Couldn't you come up with something a little more original?"

"Now." When Mallucé bared his fangs at them, the Rhino-boy bodyguards left. But they didn't look at all happy about it.

THIRTEEN

Well, that was a pure waste of time," Barrons growled as we picked our way back through the antique furnishings and all-too-modern morals of Mallucé's house.

I didn't say anything. The Unseelie Rhino-boys were right behind us, making sure we left. "The Master" was not at all happy with us.

Once he'd dismissed his guards, Mallucé had simply pretended not to know what Barrons was talking about, acting as if he'd never heard of the *Sinsar Dubh* before, even though a blind man could see that not only had he, but he knew something about it that disturbed him deeply. He and Barrons had gotten into a pissing match, trading barbs and insults, and within moments, they'd completely forgotten about me.

Ten minutes or so into their little testosterone war, one of Mallucé's guards—one of the human ones—had been stupid enough to interrupt and I'd seen something that had convinced me J. J. Jr. was the genuine article, or at least *something* supernatural. The vampire had picked up the nearly seven-foot bruiser with one pale hand around his throat, raised him in the air, and flung him backward across the chamber so hard he'd slammed into a wall, slumped to the floor, and lay there, his head lolling at an impossible angle on his chest, blood leaking from his nose and ears. Then he stood there, his yellow eyes blazing unnaturally, and for a moment, I'd been afraid he was going to fall slathering on the bloody bundle and feast.

Time to go, I'd thought, on the verge of hysteria. But Barrons had said something nasty and he and Mallucé had gotten right back into it, so I'd stood there hugging myself against the awfulest chill, tapping a foot nervously, and trying not to throw up.

The Rhino-boys didn't leave us at the door but escorted us all the way to the Porsche, and waited while we got inside. They were still standing there with their valet-buddy as we sped away. I watched them in my side-view mirror until they disappeared from sight, then heaved a huge sigh of relief. That had been singularly the most nerve-wracking experience of my life, surpassing even my encounter with the hideous Many-Mouthed-Thing. "Tell me we never have to go back there again," I said to Barrons, blotting clammy palms on my skirt.

"But we do, Ms. Lane. We didn't get the chance to cover the grounds. We'll have to return in a day or two for a thorough look around."

"There's nothing on the grounds," I told him.

He glanced at me. "You can't know that. Mallucé's estate covers hundreds of acres."

I sighed. I had no doubt, if Barrons had his way, he'd run me over every dratted inch of it, back and forth, his own indefatigable psychic lint brush. "There's nothing on the grounds, Barrons," I repeated.

"Again, Ms. Lane, you can't know that. You didn't start sensing the photocopies of the *Sinsar Dubh* until I'd removed them from the vault three floors beneath the garage and brought them into the bookstore."

I blinked. "There are three floors beneath the garage? Why on earth?"

Barrons locked his jaw, as if he regretted the admission. I could see I was going to get nothing further from him on the subject so I pressed my point instead. I was *not* going back to the vampire's den; not tomorrow, not the day after tomorrow, not even next week. If they caught me, they'd kill me, of that I was certain. I'd not exactly been discreet.

"I don't agree," I said. "I think Mallucé would keep anything he valued nearby. He would want it close at hand, to pull it out and gloat over it, if nothing else."

Barrons slanted me a sideways look. "Now you're an expert on Mallucé?"

"Not an expert, but I think I know a thing or two," I said defensively.

"And why is that, Ms. Rainbow?"

He was such a jackass sometimes. I shrugged it

off because it was only going to make this next part even sweeter. It had almost been worth leaving my on-the-go cosmetics pack Mom had given me, my brush, my favorite pink fingernail polish, and two candy bars on a table in the vampire's den just to see the look on Barrons' face when I unzipped my purse, withdrew an enameled black box, held it up and waggled it at him. "Because that was where *this* used to be," I said smugly. "Close at hand."

Barrons shifted down and slammed on the brakes so hard the tires squealed and the pads smoked.

"I did good. Go ahead and say it, Barrons," I encouraged. "I did good, didn't I?" Not only could I sense the *Sinsar Dubh,* apparently I could sense all Fae Objects of Power—or OOPs for short, as I would soon be calling them—and I was darned proud of myself for how neatly I'd purloined my first.

We'd returned to the bookstore at just slightly under the speed of light, and were now seated in the rear conversation area where he was examining the spoils of my novice kill.

"Short of leaving your calling card on the table for all to see, Ms. Lane," he said, turning the elaborate box in his hands, "which was beyond idiotic, I suppose one could say at least you didn't get yourself killed. Yet."

I snorted. But I suspected damned by faint praise was probably the best anyone ever got from Jericho Barrons. When we'd smoked to a stop in the middle of the road—not nearly far enough from Mallucé's lair—and I'd confessed to having left a few personal items behind, he'd jammed the Porsche into gear again and we'd raced the moon back to the city.

"I didn't have a choice," I said for the umpteenth time. "I told you, I couldn't fit it in my purse otherwise." I glared at him but he had eyes only for the OOP, which he was trying to figure out how to open. "Next time I'll know better and just leave it," I said crossly. "Would that make you happier?"

He glanced up, his dark gaze dripping icy Old World hauteur. "That's not what I meant, Ms. Lane, and you know it."

I imitated his expression and shot it back at him. "Then don't berate me for doing something the only way it could be done, Barrons. I couldn't figure out a way to smuggle it out beneath my skirt, and I could hardly stuff it down my bra."

His gaze flicked to my chest and stayed there a moment.

When he returned his attention to the box, I caught my breath and stared blankly at the top of his dark head. Barrons had just given me the most carnal, sexually charged, *hungry* look I'd ever seen in my life, and I was pretty sure he didn't even know he'd done it. My breasts felt hot and flushed and my mouth was suddenly uncomfortably dry. Jericho Barrons might be only seven or eight years older than me, and he might be what most women would consider extremely attractive in a dark, forbidding way, but he and I came from different worlds; we didn't see life the same way. Gazelles didn't lie down with lions, at least not unbloodied and alive. After a long, puzzled moment, I shook my head, thrust the inexplicable look from my mind—there was simply no room for it in my reality—and employed a swift change of subject.

"So, what is it? Any idea?" The feeling I got from it wasn't the same as the one I'd gotten from the photocopies of the *Sinsar Dubh*. Though I'd begun feeling nauseated the instant I'd stepped into the chamber, it hadn't approached incapacitating, not even when I'd located and stood right next to the thing. I'd taken advantage of Barrons' and Mallucé's ridiculous posturing and made my stealthy swap. Handling the box hadn't been pleasant, but I'd been able to contend with my queasy stomach.

"If it's what I think it is," Barrons replied, "it's nearly as important as the Dark Book itself, indispensable to us. Ah," he said with satisfaction, "there you are." With tiny steely *clicks*, the box popped open.

I leaned forward and peered inside. There, on a bed of black velvet, lay a translucent blue-black stone that looked as if it had been cleaved in sharp, clean strokes from a much larger one. Both the smooth outer surfaces and rough inner faces were covered with raised runelike lettering. The stone emitted an eerie blue glow that deepened to coal at its outer edges. I got an icy chill just from looking at it.

"Ah yes, Ms. Lane," Barrons murmured, "you are indeed to be commended. Maladroit methods aside, we now have two of the four sacred stones necessary to unravel the secrets of the *Sinsar Dubh*."

"I see only one," I said.

"I have its mate inside my vault." He traced his

fingers lightly over the raised surface of the faintly humming stone.

"Why is it making that noise?" I was beginning to feel a great deal of curiosity about just what else might be tucked away beneath Barrons' garage.

"It must sense the proximity of its counterpart. It is said if the four are brought together again they will sing a Song of Making."

"You mean, they'll create something?" I asked.

Barrons shrugged. "There are no words in the Fae language equivalent to 'create' or 'destroy.' There is only Making, which also includes the unmaking of a thing."

"That's odd," I said. "They must have a very limited language."

"What they have, Ms. Lane, is a very precise language. If you think about it a moment, you'll see it makes sense; case in point, if you're making sense, you've just unmade confusion."

"Huh?" My confusion hadn't been unmade. In fact, I could feel it deepening.

"In order to make something, Ms. Lane, you must first unmake what *is* in the process. Should you begin with nothing, even nothing is unmade when it is replaced with something. To the Tuatha Dé there is no difference between creating and destroying. There is only stasis and change."

I'm a bottom-line girl. I barely managed Cs in my college philosophy courses. When I tried to read Jean-Paul Sartre's *Being and Nothingness*, I developed an unshakable case of narcolepsy that attacked every two to three paragraphs, resulting in deep, coma-like fits of sleep. The only thing I remember about Kafka's *Metamorphosis* is the awful apple that got impacted in the bug's back, and Borges' stupid story about the avatar and the tortoise didn't teach me a thing, except how much better I like *Little Bunny Foo Foo;* it rhymes and you can jump rope to it.

The way I saw it, what Barrons had just told me was this: A Faery not only wouldn't care whether I lived or died, it wouldn't even really register that I *was* dead, just that, before, I could walk and talk and change my clothes by myself, but afterward I couldn't, as if someone had yanked the batteries out of me.

It occurred to me that I could really learn to hate the Fae.

With a muttered apology to my mom, I snatched up a shredded pillow, hurled it across the ransacked bedroom, and cried, "Damn, damn, *damn!* Where did you *put* it, Alina?"

Feathers showered the room. What remained intact of the slashed-up pillow crashed into a framed picture of a thatch-roofed seaside cottage above the headboard—one of the few items in her apartment that had been left undisturbed—and knocked it off the wall. Fortunately, it fell on the bed and the glass didn't break. Unfortunately, it didn't reveal a convenient hidey-hole.

I sank to the floor and leaned back against the wall, staring up at the ceiling, waiting for inspiration to strike. It didn't. I'd run out of ideas. I'd checked every place Alina had ever hidden a journal at home and then some, with no luck. Not only hadn't I found her journal, I'd discovered a few other things missing as well: her photo albums and her floral-paged Franklin Planner were gone. Alina carried her planner as faithfully as she wrote in her journal, and I knew she had two photo albums in Dublin: one of our family and home in Ashford to show to new friends, and a blank one to fill while she was there.

I'd had no luck finding any of them. And I'd done a thorough search.

I'd even stopped at a hardware store on the way over and bought a hammer, so I could tear apart the baseboard in her bedroom closet. I'd ended up using the claw handle to pry at *all* the moldings and casings in the place, looking for loose trim. I'd tapped at the wood nooks and crannies of the fireplace facade. I'd hammered at floor planks, listening for hollow spots. I'd examined every piece of furniture in the place, tops, sides, and bottoms, and even checked inside, as well as beneath, the toilet tank.

I'd found nothing.

If her journal was hidden somewhere in the apartment, she'd outdone me this time. The only thing left for me to try was complete demolition of the place: smashing out the walls, ripping off the cabinets, and tearing up the floors, at which point I'd have to buy the darned building just to pay for all the damages, and I didn't have that kind of money.

I caught my breath. But Barrons did. And I could offer him an incentive to want to find her notebook.

I wanted Alina's journal for the clues it might hold to the identity of her killer, but there was a good possibility it also contained information about the location of the *Sinsar Dubh*. After all, the last thing my sister had said in her message was, *I know what it is now, and I know where—*, before her words had abruptly terminated. The odds were high she'd written something about it in her diary.

The question was, could I trust Jericho Barrons, and if so, how far?

I stared into space, wondering what I really knew about him. It wasn't much. The darkly exotic half Basque, half Pict was a self-contained mystery I was willing to bet he never let anyone get close enough to unravel. Fiona might know a thing or two about him, but she was a mystery herself.

I knew this much: He was going to be royally pissed at me by the time he saw me again, because the last thing he'd said to me, in his typical high-handed manner, before I'd stumbled exhaustedly off to bed early this morning was, "I have things to do tomorrow, Ms. Lane. You will remain in the bookstore until I return. Fiona will procure anything you might need."

I'd ignored his orders and, shortly after I'd awakened at half past two in the afternoon, slipped out the back way, down the alley behind the store. No, I wasn't being stupid and I didn't have a death wish. What I had was a mission, and I couldn't afford to let fear shut me down, or I might as well reserve the first seat available on the next flight back to Georgia, tuck tail and run home to the safety of Mom and Dad.

Yes, I knew the Many-Mouthed-Thing was out there looking for the blonder, fluffier version of me. Yes, I had no doubt that while Mallucé slumbered his daylight hours away, tucked in a garish Romantic-Goth coffin somewhere, dripping blood-encrusted lace, his men were already scouring Dublin for the thieving Ms. Rainbow.

But nobody would be looking for *this* me. I was incognito.

I'd scraped my dark hair tightly back into a short ponytail and tucked it up beneath a ball cap, pulled down low. I was wearing my favorite faded jeans, a sloppy oversized, nearly threadbare T-shirt I'd swiped from Dad before I left, which had once been black a few hundred washings ago, and scuffed-up tennis shoes. I didn't have on a single accessory and I'd used a brown paper bag as a purse. I'd applied no makeup; zip, zilch, nada, not even lipstick, even though my mouth felt really weird without it. I'm pretty addicted to moisturizers. I think it comes from living in the heat of the South. Even the best skin needs a little extra care down there. But the crowning triumph of my disguise was a truly hideous pair of magnifying spectacles I'd purchased at a drugstore on the way over that I currently had hooked on the neck of my dingy tee.

You might not think it sounds like much of a disguise, but I know a thing or two about people. The world notices pretty, well-dressed young women. And it tries real hard not to see the unattractive, sloppy ones. If you're bad enough, you get the thousand-yard stare that slides right off you. There was no doubt that I looked worse than I'd ever looked in my life. I wasn't proud of it, yet at the same time I was. I might never manage ugly, but at least I bordered on invisible.

I glanced at my watch and pushed to my feet. I'd been searching Alina's place for hours; it was nearly seven. Barrons seemed to have a habit of showing up at the bookstore shortly after eight, and I wanted to be back before he arrived tonight. I knew Fiona would rat me out anyway, but I figured he wouldn't be half as irritated if his personal OOP-detector had already returned safe and sound by the time he showed up, as he would be if I left him to stew over the potential loss of it for a while.

I collected my paper-bag purse, stuck the awful glasses back on my nose, pulled my ball cap down as low as it would go, turned out the lights, and locked up.

The air was warm, the sky streaked with the orange and crimson of a magnificent sunset when I stepped from the building. It was going to be a beautiful midsummer's eve in Dublin. Alina's place and Barrons' were on opposite ends of the busy Temple Bar District, but I didn't mind that I had to push through crowds of festive pub-goers to get back to the bookstore. I might not be happy myself, but it was kind of nice to see others who were. It made me feel more optimistic about my own chances.

As I hurried down the cobbled streets, not a single person spared me a glance. I was pleased with my invisibility, and determinedly tuning out my increasingly alien and depressing world by tuning in to my iPod. I was listening to one of my favorite one-hit wonders, "Laid," by James—*this bed is on fire with passionate love, the neighbors complain about the noises above, but she only comes when she's on top*—when I saw it.

I wanted to fuck the moment I laid eyes on it.

I told you before, cusswords don't come easily to me, especially not that particular one, so you can see the measure of the Fae's impact that the word marched into my mind and assumed immediate control of the front. Ego and superego were dispatched with a single swift, killing blow and in swaggered my new ruler—that primitive little hedonistic bastard, the id.

I was instantly wet, hot, and slippery in my panties, every cell ripe and swollen with need. My breasts and loins *plumped* just from looking at it; grew soft, fuller, heavier. The friction of my nipples against my bra was suddenly an unthinkable sexual torture device, my panties more binding than ropes and chains, and I needed desperately to have something between my legs, pounding into me, cramming me full inside. I needed friction. I needed thick, hot, long, rough friction pushing in and pulling out. Pushing in and pulling out, over and over, oh God, please, I needed *something*! Nothing else would stop my pain, nothing else would satisfy my sole purpose in life—to fuck.

My clothes were an offense to my skin. I needed them off. I grabbed the bottom of my T-shirt and began to pull it over my head.

The breeze on my naked skin startled me. I froze, my shirt half over my face.

What in the *world* was I doing?

My sister was dead. Buried and rotting in a grave outside the church we'd gone to since we were children. The church we'd both dreamed of one day getting married in. She never would.

Because of a Fae, I had no doubt. After the events of the past few days I was certain one or several of them had been responsible for her brutal murder. For ripping and tearing into her with their teeth and claws, and for God only knew what else they'd done to her. No, the coroner hadn't found semen inside her, but what he *had* found inside her, he'd not been able to explain. Most of the time I tried not to think about it too much.

"I don't think so," I hissed, yanking my shirt back down. I took advantage of that moment to pluck the ear buds from my ears as well. Listening to James sing about obsessive-compulsive sex was proving the equivalent of tossing gas on an open flame. "Whatever it is you're doing to me, you can just turn it off. It's a waste of your time."

"It is nothing I do, *sidhe*-seer," it said. "It is what I *am*. I am every erotic dream you've ever had and a thousand more you've never thought of. I am sex that will turn you inside out and burn you down to ashes." It smiled. "And if I choose, I can make you whole again."

Its voice was deep, rich, and melodic and had all the impact of a soft, sensual suckling at my swollen nipples. The erotic inferno began to rage inside me again. I backed away, straight into the window of the pub behind me. I pressed against it, shivering.

Alina is dead because of one of these things. I clung to that thought like a lifeboat.

The Fae stood in the middle of the cobbled street, fifteen to twenty feet away from me, making no move to approach farther. Cars were prohibited in this part of the district and those pedestrians crossing the street were detouring placidly around it without giving it a second glance.

Nor was anyone looking at me, which I wouldn't have found particularly interesting except that I had my T-shirt up again and was flashing the world my favorite pink lace push-up bra as well as most of my breasts. Inhaling sharply, I yanked my shirt back down.

Even today, after all that I've seen, I couldn't begin to describe V'lane, prince of the Tuatha Dé Danaan. There are some things that are simply too immense, too rich to be contained in words. This is the best I can offer: imagine a tall, powerful, mighty archangel, frighteningly male, terrifyingly beautiful. Then paint him the most exquisite shades of chestnut, bronze, and gold you can possibly imagine. Give him a mane shimmering with strands of cinnamon gilded by sunlight, skin of tawny velvet, and eyes of liquid amber, kissed by molten gold.

The Fae was unutterably beautiful.

And I wanted to fuck and fuck and fuck until I died.

I understood then. Each Fae I'd encountered so far had a "thing," its own personal calling card. The

Gray Man stole beauty. The Shades sucked life. The Many-Mouthed-Thing most likely devoured flesh.

This one was death-by-sex. Immolation by orgasm; the worst of it was that its victim would be fully aware with some distant part of her brain that she was dying, even as she begged and pleaded for the very thing that was killing her. I had a sudden, horrific vision of myself, right there in the street, naked, pathetic, writhing with insatiable need at the thing's feet, invisible to passersby, dying like that.

Never.

I had one hope: If I could get close enough, I could freeze it and run. Steeling my will with the hellish memory of how Alina had looked the day I'd identified her body, I peeled myself from the window and stepped forward.

The Fae stepped back.

I blinked. "Huh?"

"Not retreat, human," it said coldly. "Impatience. I know what you are, *sidhe*-seer. We need not play your silly game of tag."

"Oh right," I snapped, "but we sure were going to take the time to play your silly game of death-by-sex, weren't we?"

It shrugged. "I would not have killed you. You have value to us." When it smiled at me, I went blank for a heartbeat, as if the sun had come out from behind clouds to shine down only on me, but it was so hot that it charred all my wiring. "I would have given you only the pleasure of my magnificence," it told me, "not the pain. We can do that, you know."

I trembled at the thought—all that heat, but no

ice; all that sex, but no death. The night air felt suddenly cool on the scorching skin of my breasts, frigid to the fire of my nipples. I glanced down. My shirt and bra were lying in the gutter at my feet, mixed with the daily trash and grime of the city.

Jaw set, hands shaking, I bent to retrieve my clothing. Blushing a half-dozen shades of red, I put my bra back on and pulled my shirt over my head again. I reclaimed my paper-bag purse and my iPod from the gutter as well, jammed my ball cap back on my head, but didn't bother fishing out my hideous glasses—I didn't want the thing looking any larger than it already did. Then, without hesitation, I stood and lunged straight for the Fae. I *had* to freeze it. It was my only hope. God only knew what I might do next.

Before I was able to reach it, however, it vanished. One moment it was there, the next it was gone. I was pretty sure I'd just witnessed Fae "sifting" firsthand. But where had it gone?

"Behind you, human," it said.

I turned sharply to find it standing on the sidewalk, a dozen feet to my left, pedestrians parting around it like the Red Sea drawing back from Moses, giving it increasingly wider berth. In fact, foot traffic on the entire street seemed to be thinning substantially and, here and there, a pub door suddenly slammed closed against a distinctly un-summery chill in the July air.

"We do not have time for fool's play, MacKayla Lane."

I jerked. "How do you know my name?"

"We know much about you, Null," it said. "You

are one of the most powerful *sidhe*-seers we've yet encountered. And we believe you have only begun to realize your potential."

"Who are 'we'?" I demanded.

"Those of us who are concerned with the future of both our worlds."

"And who would these 'those' be?"

"I am V'lane, prince of the Tuatha Dé Danaan, and I am here on behalf of Aoibheal, exalted High Queen of our race. She has a task for you, *sidhe*-seer."

I barely resisted the urge to burst out laughing. The last thing I'd have expected to hear from any Fae was something along the lines of: *Your mission, should you choose to accept it...* "Uh, on the off chance that you've forgotten—not that I'm trying to remind you or anything—but aren't the Fae more inclined to *kill* *sidhe*-seers than to assign them helpful little tasks?"

"We haven't made examples of your kind for some time now," it said. "As a gesture of our good will and a token of the Queen's esteem, we have a gift for you,"

"Oh no." I shook my head. "No gifts, thank you." I was familiar with the whole Trojan-horse-beware-of-Greeks-bearing-gifts debacle and there was no doubt in my mind that a Fae bearing gifts would certainly be worse.

"It is my understanding you have betrayed yourself to one or more of the Unseelie," it said coolly.

I stiffened. How did it know? And what did it mean by "or more"? Had the Royal Hunters been alerted too? "So?" I shrugged, falling back on my best, last defense: bluffing.

"Our gift offers you no small protection from those who would harm you."

"Including you?" I blurted. Though I'd been managing to hold my own in conversation with it—and believe me, with what I was feeling, it was hard enough to string together consecutive words, to say nothing of trying to make them intelligible—twice now I'd had to pull my shirt back down and I'd just caught myself unzipping my jeans.

"There is no protection against one such as I, *sidhe*-seer. We of the royal houses affect humans in this manner. There is nothing that can be done to prevent it."

One day I would know that for the lie it was. But not before I'd been burned by the truth in it. "Then what good is your stupid gift?" Crossly, I hooked my bra again. My breasts were so hot and tight they hurt. I cupped one in each hand, squeezed and kneaded, but my desperate massage provided no relief.

"Our gift would allow you to defend against many who would kill you," it said, "just not against those with the right to kill you."

My eyes narrowed and my hands dropped to my sides where they fisted. My nails gouged half-moon crescents on my palms. "The *right* to kill me?" I snapped. Was that what they'd thought of my sister, the ones who'd murdered her? That they'd had the *right*?

It studied me. "Not that any of us would."

Yeah, right—and piranhas were vegetarians. "What is this gift?" I demanded.

The Fae extended a gold arm cuff, etched with

silver, flashing with ruby fire. "The Cuff of Cruce. It was made long ago for one of his prized human con- cubines. It permits a shield of sorts against many Unseelie and...other unsavory things."

"What about the Seelie? Does it work against them?"

It shook its frighteningly beautiful head.

I thought a minute. "Would it keep me safe from the Royal Hunters?" I asked.

"Yes," it replied.

"Really?" I exclaimed. I could want it for that alone! Ever since I'd heard of the devil-like Hunters, the mere thought of them made my skin crawl, as if a special fear of that caste of Unseelie beyond all others was programmed into my much preyed upon genes. "What's the catch?" I asked. A stupid question, I knew. As if it would tell me. I couldn't trust a thing it said. I'd not forgotten Barrons' com- ment that Seelie and Unseelie royalty were nearly impossible to tell apart. Though this Prince V'lane of the Tuatha Dé Danaan claimed to be here on the Seelie Queen's behalf, I had no proof of that, nor even that it was who and what it claimed to be.

"There is no catch," it said.

Like I said, stupid question. "I stand with my ini- tial position," I informed it. "No thank you. There, that's done. Now let's get to the point: What do you want from me?" I yanked my shirt back down. I wanted our little job-offer interview over and done with, the sooner the better.

The air around me chilled, as if iced by the Fae's displeasure with my attitude. "There is trouble in

Faery, *sidhe*-seer," it said, "and as you have seen, in your world, as well. After an eternity of confinement, some of the lower-caste Unseelie have begun escaping their prison. Despite our efforts to isolate the weakness in the fabric of our realms, we have not been able to determine how they are breaking free."

I shrugged. "So, what do you want me to do about it?"

"Queen Aoibheal wants the *Sinsar Dubh, sidhe*-seer."

I was beginning to think it might be easier to start tallying everyone I knew in Dublin that *didn't* want the *Sinsar Dubh*. Gee, that would be nobody. "Well, what's stopping her from getting it? Isn't she supposed to be the most powerful of all the Fae?" I was pretty sure that was what Barrons had told me. Except for the Unseelie King, who some claimed outranked all, while others contended he was a mere figurehead, that the "children of the goddess Danu" were a matriarchal line. According to Barrons, nobody really knew anything for sure about the Unseelie King.

"We have a small difficulty. We are unable to sense our own sacred objects. It is only the rare *sidhe*-seer who can. We do not know where it is." The Fae could not have seemed more affronted by its admission. How dare the world not bow and scrape at its feet? How dare the universe not conspire to arrange everything in its favor? How dare a mere human possess an ability that was beyond theirs? "Other things have gone missing, as well, that we would like to recover."

"And just what does she want *me* to do about it?"

I didn't like where things seemed to be going. I wasn't certain I could survive it.

"She merely wishes you to continue searching as you have been and from time to time we will check on your progress. Should you learn anything—however small—about any of our hallowed relics, especially the *Sinsar Dubh*, you will alert me immediately."

I sighed with relief. I'd been afraid it was planning to stay around while I searched. Thank God, it wasn't. "How am I supposed to do that?"

Again, it offered me the Cuff of Cruce. "With this, I will show you how to use it."

I shook my head. "I'm not taking it."

"Don't be a fool. Your world is suffering, too."

"I have only your word for any of this," I said. "For all I know, you're lying about everything and that cuff might just kill me the instant I put it on."

"By the time you find proof that satisfies you, *sidhe*-seer," it said coldly, "it may well be too late for your race."

"That's not my problem," I retorted. "I never wanted to be a *sidhe*-seer and I'm not even admitting that I am one now." In college, I'd known a few people with superhero aspirations, who'd wanted to make a difference: join the Peace Corps, or become doctors and cut people open so they could fix them and sew them back up again, but personally, I'd never had any desire to save the world. Decorate it? Yes. Save it? No. Until a short time ago, I'd been a small-town girl with small-town dreams and perfectly content with my lot in life. Then someone had crapped on my world and forced me out of my happy little hole. I'd come to Dublin with a single purpose at heart: to avenge my sister's death. Then and only then could I return to Ashford with some kind of closure for Mom and Dad. Then maybe we could heal, and try to be a family again. That was the only world I cared about saving—mine.

"You will change your mind," it said.

The Fae was gone.

I stared blankly for several moments at the space it had been occupying, before snapping out of it. Despite the recent horrors I'd witnessed, I wasn't in the least inured, and watching something vanish right before my eyes had been profoundly disturbing.

I glanced around to make sure it hadn't popped back in behind me to sneak up on me or anything like that, but I was alone on the street. I was startled to realize the temperature in my immediate vicinity had dropped so significantly that I could see my breath in the air. A thin perimeter of fog encased me some twenty feet away, where iced air met heat again. I would soon learn it was characteristic of royalty; their pleasure or displeasure often reshaped the environment in small ways around them.

I did another quick scan. Yes, the street was empty, all the doors were closed, and there wasn't a soul around.

As fiercely ashamed of myself as I was aroused, I slipped a hand down my jeans.

I came the moment I touched myself.

FOURTEEN

I t was a quarter past eight by the time I made it back to the bookstore. I knew Barrons was there as soon as I turned the corner. His big black-and-chrome hog was parked outside the brilliantly spot-lighted front, playing kissing cousins with Fiona's sedate sedan.

I rolled my eyes. My day continued to cruise downhill. I'd been hoping that Fiona had left on time, before Barrons had arrived, and before she could rat me out.

No such luck.

I detoured around back, deciding I would sneak in from the rear, pretend to have been upstairs all day—with my iPod on in case anyone claimed to have knocked—and see if I could pull it off. You never knew what you could get away with until you tried. Maybe nobody had bothered checking on me.

When I rounded the rear of the building, my gaze

automatically shot to the end of the alley, past the store, to the dark perimeter of the abandoned neighborhood beyond the rear floodlights. I paused, searching for shadows that shouldn't be there. A humorless smile curved my lips; the strangest things were becoming instinctive.

I spotted four clusters of darkness that were wrong. Three clung to the shadowy eaves of a building two doors down on the right; the fourth was on my left and behaving far more boldly. It was creeping back and forth along the stone foundation of the shop directly adjacent to Barrons, shooting and retracting dark tendrils of itself, testing the edges of the pool of light flooding the rear entrances.

All four of them pulsed hungrily at my approach.

Stay to the light, Barrons had told me, *and you will be safe. The Shades can only get you in full darkness. They are unable to tolerate even the smallest amount of light. You must never, Ms. Lane,* ever *enter the abandoned neighborhood at night.*

Well, why doesn't somebody go in there during the day and fix all those broken streetlamps? I'd asked. *Wouldn't that get rid of them? Or at least help?*

The city has forgotten that section exists, he'd replied. *You will not find a district of the* Gardai *that claims it, and if you ask city power or water they will have no record of service to any address within its bounds.*

I'd snorted. *Cities don't just lose entire neighborhoods. That's impossible.*

He'd smiled faintly. *In time, Ms. Lane, you will cease using that word.*

As I climbed the steps to the rear door, I raised my

fist and shook it angrily at the Shades. I'd had my fill of monsters for the night. The Shade that was creeping along the foundation startled me by bristling visibly back at me. I found its display of sentient hostility chilling.

The rear door was locked, but the third window I tried slid up easily. I muttered beneath my breath about Barrons' appalling lack of safety-consciousness, as I boosted myself up and over the sill. After a quick bathroom stop, I headed for the front of Barrons Books and Baubles.

I don't know what made me hesitate when I went to open that second door that separated residence from store, but something did. Maybe I heard my name as I was reaching for the knob, or my curiosity was piqued by the urgent undertone in Fiona's voice that was carrying clearly through the door, although her words did not. Whatever the reason, rather than betray my presence, I nudged the door slightly ajar, pressed my ear to the crack, and displayed a dearth of manners that would have appalled every woman in my family ten generations back; I eavesdropped on the conversation taking place beyond it.

"You have no right, Jericho, and you know it!" Fiona cried.

"When will you learn, Fio?" Barrons said. "Might makes right. That's all the right I need."

"She doesn't belong here. You can't let her stay. I won't stand for it!"

"*You* won't stand for it? When did you become my keeper, Fio?" There was danger in the very gentleness with which Barrons asked the question, but Fiona either didn't hear it, or chose not to heed it.

"When you started needing one! It's not safe to have her here, Jericho. She must go—tonight, if possible, tomorrow at the very latest! I can't be here all the time to make sure nothing happens!"

"No one asked you to," Barrons said coldly.

"Well, someone needs to," she cried.

"Jealous, Fio? It doesn't become you."

Fiona sucked in an audible breath. I could almost see her standing there: eyes bright with passion, two spots of color high on the cheekbones of her aging movie-star face. "If you must take this to a personal level, then yes, Jericho, I am. You know I don't want her here. But it's not just about me and what I want. That *child* is as ignorant and innocent as the day is long—"

Okay, I really resented that.

"—and she doesn't have the slightest idea what she's doing. She has no notion of the danger she's in, and you have no right to continue placing her in it."

"Not right, Fio, might. Remember? I'm not interested in rights. I never have been."

"I don't believe that, Jericho. I know you."

"No, Fio, you only think you know me. You really don't know me at all. Stay out of this or leave. I'm sure I can find another to"—he paused a moment as if searching for precisely the right words—"serve my needs."

"*Oh!* Serve your—*oh!* Is that what I do? Serve your needs? You'd do that, too, wouldn't you? Find someone else. Just pack me off on the nearest train. I bet you wouldn't even say good-bye, would you? You'd probably never even think of me again!"

Barrons laughed softly, and although I couldn't see either of them, I pictured him taking her by the shoulders, maybe brushing his knuckles to the pale, soft curve of her cheek. "Fio," he said, "my foolish, sweet, faithful Fio; there will always be a place for you in my thoughts. But I am not the man you believe me to be. You have romanticized me unforgivably."

"I have never seen any more in you than I know you could be, if you wanted to, Jericho," Fiona declared fervently, and even I—a child as ignorant and innocent as the day was long, to coin a recently minted phrase—could hear the blind conviction of love in her voice.

Barrons laughed again. "And there, my dear Fio, you make one of Womankind's greatest mistakes: falling in love with a man's potential. We so rarely share the same view of it, and even more rarely care to achieve it. Stop pining for the man you think I could be—and take a good, long, hard *look* at the one I am." In my mind, Barrons grabbed her when he emphasized the word "look" and was now shaking her, not quite so gently.

There was another silence, then a sharp, pained feminine gasp, and a much longer silence.

"She stays, Fio," Barrons murmured after some time. "And you *will* keep your peace about it, won't you?"

I was beginning to think I'd missed her reply

when Barrons spoke again, harshly. "I said 'won't you,' Fio?"

"Of course, Jericho," Fiona replied softly. "Whatever you wish." Her voice was dreamy, as carefree as a child's.

Taken aback by her sudden, drastic change of heart, I closed the door with careful stealth.

Then I turned and beat a hasty path for the dubious security of my borrowed bedroom.

Later that evening, hours after Barrons had come to yell at me through my closed door for going out today and risking the safety of his personal OOP-detector, then gone—yes, Fiona had ratted me out—I stood at my bedroom window and stared out into the night. There was no order to my thoughts. They jumbled and tumbled like autumn leaves in a whirlwind.

Where was Alina's journal? There was no way she hadn't been keeping one. If she'd thought she was falling in love, she would have written page after page about her new boyfriend every night, especially if she'd not been talking to me or anyone else about him. Though I'd been considering asking Barrons to help me search for it, after the conversation I'd just overheard, that was a big, fat no. Nor was I about to confide in him about my little visit from the death-by-sex Fae.

Was V'lane really a Seelie prince? The proverbial "guy in the white hat"? It sure didn't seem like it. But then, would any Fae ever seem good to a *sidhe*-seer?

Not that I was admitting that I *was* one or anything. I was still holding out hope that something else was going on. Like maybe I was sleeping and stuck in a long, awful nightmare that would end if only I could wake up. Or maybe I'd been hit by a car and was lying in a hospital bed back in Ashford, having coma-induced hallucinations.

Anything would be preferable to calling myself a *sidhe*-seer. It felt like an admission of defeat, a willful embracing of the strange dark fever I seemed to have caught the moment I'd set foot in Ireland. The craziness had begun that very night, with the Fae at the bar and the batty old woman.

In retrospect, I could see the old woman hadn't been crazy, she'd been a *sidhe*-seer, and she'd actually saved my life that night. Who could say how things might have turned out if she hadn't stopped me from betraying myself? *Honor your bloodline*, she'd said.

What bloodline? A bloodline of *sidhe*-seers? Every question I thought of only bred a host of other questions. Did that mean my mom was supposed to be one, too? That thought was simply ludicrous. I couldn't see Rainey Lane, spatula in one hand, dish towel in the other, pretending not to see the Fae any more than I could see Mallucé forgiving me for stealing his stone and inviting me along on a shopping trip for the latest in shabby-chic Goth fashions. Nor could I see my tax-attorney father faking Fae-blindness.

My thought bounced back to V'lane. What if the Fae was lying and was actually an Unseelie, working to free more of his brethren to prey upon my world? And if it was telling the truth, why did the Seelie Queen want the book containing "the deadliest of all magic"? What did Aoibheal plan to do with it, and how had this highly sought-after book gotten lost in the first place?

Who could I trust? Where could I turn?

Had Alina known any of what I was learning? Had she been to McCabe's and Mallucé's? What had happened to her when she'd first arrived in Dublin all those months ago? Whatever it was—when it had begun—she'd found it exciting. Had she met a man who'd dragged her into this dark underworld, as I had? Had she met a Fae who seduced her into it? *He's been lying to me all along,* she'd said. *He's one of them.* By "them" had she meant "Fae"? "Oh God," I whispered, stunned by the thought. Had Alina thought she was in love with a Fae? Had it wooed her, used her? Had she been an OOP-detector, too? And a Null, like me?

Was I unwittingly following the same steps she'd taken, down the same path to the same eventual destination—death?

I mentally tallied everyone that was looking for the *Sinsar Dubh:* There was Barrons, McCabe, Mallucé, V'lane, and according to V'lane, the Seelie Queen, and from the presence of the Unseelie watchdogs at McCabe's and Mallucé's, at least one big, bad Unseelie that might or might not be called the Lord Master. Why? What were all these, er ... people, for lack of a better word, after? Did they all want it for the same reason? And if so, what was that reason?

We can't let them have it, Alina had said of the *Sinsar Dubh.* "Gee, sis, could you have been a little more specific?" I muttered. "*Who* shouldn't get it?" Even if by some fluke of fate I found the darn thing, not only would I probably not be able to touch it, according to Barrons, I wouldn't have any idea what to do with it.

I sighed. I had nothing but questions and nobody to ask. I was thick in the middle of people who guarded secrets and pursued hidden agendas as naturally as they lived and breathed and—probably—killed. Just look at the "men" I'd met in the past week: McCabe, Mallucé, V'lane, Barrons. Not a normal one among them. Not a safe one in the bunch. *A lamb in a city of wolves,* Barrons had called me shortly after we'd met. *Which one will take you down, I wonder?*

Secrets. Everyone had secrets. Alina had taken hers to the grave. I had no doubt that trying to ask V'lane questions when I saw the Fae again—I wasn't stupid enough to think it was done with me—would be an exercise in futility. The alleged prince might answer me, but I was only an OOP-detector, not a lie detector. And Barrons was no better. As Fiona's little dispute with him revealed, he was keeping secrets, too, and I was somehow in even more danger than I already knew.

That was a cheerful thought. As of this morning I'd pretty much figured out that any time I walked out the door I was taking my life in my own hands, but apparently I was in danger while I was here, too.

God, I was homesick! I missed my life. I missed The Brickyard. I missed Saturday night closes with my bartending buddies. I missed our obligatory three A.M. Huddle House stop for pancakes, where we'd try to unwind enough to sleep before dawn and, in the summer, plan what lake to meet at later that day.

We'll be seeing Roark O'Bannion tomorrow, Ms. Lane, Barrons had told me through my locked and barricaded door when he'd climbed four flights to chew my head off. *He's the third big player on the field. Among other things, he owns O'Bannion's, a posh bar in downtown Dublin. It's Old World with wealthy clientele. As you seem to have a problem dressing yourself, Fiona will fetch you appropriate attire. Do not leave the bookstore again without me, Ms. Lane.*

It was three in the morning before I slept, and when I did, it was with the closet door wide open, and every single light in the bedroom and adjoining bathroom ablaze.

FIFTEEN

Roark "Rocky" O'Bannion had been born Irish Catholic, dirt-poor, and with genes that would give him the strength, stamina, and body of a prize-fighter before his eighteenth birthday.

With his looks, some would call him Black Irish, but it wasn't Spanish or Melungeon blood in his veins, it was an unspoken-of Saudi ancestor that had bequeathed something fierce, dark, and ruth-less to the O'Bannion line.

Born in a city controlled by two feuding Irish crime families—the Hallorans and O'Kierneys—Roark O'Bannion fought his way to the top in the ring, but it wasn't enough for the ambitious champ; he hungered for more. One night, when Rocky was twenty-eight years old, the Halloran and O'Kierney linchpins, every son, grandson, and pregnant woman in their families were killed. Twenty-seven people died that night, gunned down, blown up, poisoned, knifed, or strangled. The city had never seen any-thing like it. A group of flawlessly choreographed killers had closed in all over the city, at restau-rants, homes, hotels, and clubs, and struck simulta-neously.

Horrific, most said. *Bloody brilliant*, some said. *Good riddance*, nearly all said, including the cops. The very next day, when a suddenly wealthy Rocky O'Bannion, champion boxer and many a young boy's idol, retired from the ring to take over control of various businesses in and around Dublin previ-ously run by the Hallorans and O'Kierneys, he was hailed by the working-class poor—whose hope and bank accounts were as tiny as their TVs and dreams were big—as a hero, despite the fresh and obvious blood on his hands, and the rough pack of ex-boxers and thugs he brought with him.

That he was a "damned fine-looking man" didn't hurt any. Rocky was considered quite the charmer and ladies' man, but one with a fine point of honor that endeared him to his faithful; he didn't sleep with other men's wives. Ever. The man who had no respect for life, limb, or law, respected the sacrament of marriage.

Did I mention he was Irish Catholic? A joke around the city was that the young O'Bannion had missed school the day the priest had given the sermon about the Ten Commandments, and on makeup day little Rocky only got the short list: *Thou shalt not covet thy neighbor's wife—but everything else is up for grabs.*

Despite the colorful background Barrons had

given me on our soon-to-be third host—and unsuspecting victim, as I was coming to think of them—I
would still find myself unprepared for the dichoto-
mies that were Rocky O'Bannion.

"Uh, Barrons," I said. "I really don't think stealing from this guy is a very good idea." I'd seen my
share of mafia movies. You didn't march up to the
Godfather and rip him off—and expect to survive
for very long afterward, anyway. I already had too
many scary things after me.

"We'll burn that bridge when we come to it, Ms.
Lane," he replied.

I glanced over at him. My life was so surreal.
Tonight Barrons had selected a 1975 Lamborghini
Countach, one of only three "Wolf" Countachs ever
made, from his absurd collection.

"I think the expression is cross that bridge,
Barrons, not torch it. What do you want—every
freak, vampire, Fae, and Mafia don in the city hunting me down? How many different ways do you
think I can do my hair? I refuse to be a redhead. I
draw the line there. As much as I like color, I have no
desire to paint my head orange."

He laughed. Unguarded humor was such a rare
expression to see on that chiseled, urbane face that I
blinked, staring.

"Funny, Ms. Lane," he said. Then he added,
"Would you like to drive?"

"Huh?" I gaped. What was wrong with him?
Ever since I'd come down at shortly after eleven,
wearing Fiona's disturbing dress—when I'd first
slipped it over my head I'd waited a few seconds to

see if it was laced with some awful poison that would make me itch my skin off—he'd been acting like this, and I just didn't get it. He seemed... well...playful, for lack of a better word. In high spirits. Almost drunk, though with a clear head. If he were any other man, I might have suspected him of substance abuse, of being coked up or something. But Barrons was too much a purist for that; his drugs were money, power, and control.

Still, he was so electrically alive tonight that the air around him seemed to crackle and hiss.

"Just kidding," he said.

And that was out of character, too. Jericho Barrons didn't indulge in humor. "That wasn't nice. I've *dreamed* of driving a C-c—Lamborghini."

"Can't say Countach, Ms. Lane?" With his unplaceable accent, *Kuhn-tah* came out sounding even more foreign.

"Can," I said irritably. "Won't. Mom taught me better."

He slanted me a sideways look. "And why is that, Ms. Lane?"

"Cussing in any language is still cussing," I said primly. I knew what Countach meant. My dad was the one that got me addicted to fast cars. I'd been a little girl of seven when he'd begun dragging me from one Exotic Car Show to the next, in lieu of a son to share his passion with. Over the years we'd developed a deep bond over our love of all things fast and shiny. The Italian Countach was the near equivalent of "holy fucking cow" in English, which was exactly how I felt every time I saw one, but that was still no reason to say it out loud. If I managed to hold on to nothing else in the midst of the insanity my life had become, at least I could maintain my dignity and decorum.

"You seem to know your cars, Ms. Lane," Barrons murmured.

"Some," I said modestly. It was the only thing modest about me at the moment. We'd just begun crossing the first of two sets of railroad tracks and my bosom jiggled in—or rather mostly out—of my revealing dress like it was made of molded Jell-O. Okay, so sometimes I could maintain my dignity and decorum. At other times, it seemed half of Dublin was going to see my breasts up close and personal; although I did derive some comfort from the thought that when I'd done my impromptu strip for the death-by-sex Fae yesterday, I was pretty certain no one else had seen me, thanks to the glamour it had been throwing.

We were about to hit the second set of tracks, so I folded my arms in an attempt to hold myself still. As we crossed them, I could feel the weight of Barrons' gaze on my bosom, the heat of it, and I knew without even looking that he had that raw, hungry look on his face again. I refused to glance his way, and we rode for several miles in silence, with him using up entirely too much room in the car, and a weird tension eating up what little space there was between us.

"Seen the new Gallardo Spyder?" I blurted finally.

"No," he said instantly. "Why don't you tell me

about it, Ms. Lane?" The playful edge in his voice was gone; it was guttural, tight.

I pretended not to notice and began waxing poetical about the V-10 with its razor-sharp lines and 512 horses that, although it couldn't beat the Porsche 911 turbo in a zero-to-sixty speed test, it still packed a flashy, muscular punch, and before I knew it, we were pulling up in front of O'Bannion's and waiting while valets cleared space for us between a Maybach sedan and a limo. They were human, not Rhino-boys, which made for a nice change.

I confess I left fingerprints on the Maybach. I had to pet it as I walked by, if only to be able to tell Dad I'd touched one. If I'd been living another life, one where Alina hadn't been killed and I wasn't currently up to my neck in nightmares, I would have rung him up on my cell phone right then and there and described the twin-turbo, V-12, 57S touring sedan "for those who want to drive their own Maybach," right down to the interior trim done in black piano-lacquer finish that gleamed in exquisite contrast to an abundance of creamy leather. He would have excitedly demanded more details—and couldn't I go to the nearest drugstore and buy a disposable camera or ten?

But Alina *had* been killed, my parents were still off the deep end, and calling Dad right now would have served no purpose. I knew, because I'd called home earlier, after I'd finished getting dressed. Ten-forty-five Dublin time was still early evening in Georgia. I'd sat on the edge of my borrowed bed, staring down at stockings that were hooked to an embarrassment of a garter belt, spiky high heels, and the egg-size blood-red ruby nestled between my breasts, and wondered what I was becoming.

Dad had been drunk when he'd answered. I'd not heard him drunk in years. Six and a half, to be exact. Not since his brother had died on the way to his own wedding, leaving his bride-to-be a pregnant widow and my dad standing at the altar, best man to a dead man. I'd hung up as soon as I'd heard Dad's deeply slurred voice, unable to deal with it. I needed a rock—not to have to be one for someone else.

"Wits about you, Ms. Lane," Barrons cautioned, close to my ear, jerking me from the dark place I'd been about to get lost in. "You'll need them here." With his left arm around my waist, his right hand on my shoulder, fingers lightly brushing the swell of my breast, he steered me toward the entrance, locking gazes with any man brave or stupid enough to let his gaze dip below my eyes, holding it until the man looked away. He could not have more clearly branded me his possession.

As soon as we entered the bar, I understood. That was what the women were here: beautiful, impeccably waxed, coifed and groomed, softly laughing, brightly dazzling possessions. Trophies. They weren't people in and of themselves, but reflections upon their men. As tightly guarded as they were lavishly cosseted, they sparkled and shined like glittering diamonds, showing the world what successes their husbands were, what giants among men.

Rainbow Mac would have been as out of place here as a porcupine in a petting zoo. I straightened my spine, held my head high, and pretended that two-thirds of my supple young body wasn't exposed by the short, sleek black dress with the bare back and plunging neckline.

Barrons was known here. As we passed, nods were exchanged and greetings were murmured, and all was soft and lovely at O'Bannion's, if you were careful not to notice the steel every man in the room was packing.

I leaned close to whisper my next question up at Barrons' ear; even with heels on, he was a head taller than me. "Do you have a gun on you somewhere?" I really hoped he did.

His lips quirked, brushing my hair when he replied, "A gun would only get you killed faster in a place like this, Ms. Lane. Don't worry, I don't plan to piss anyone off." He nodded to a short, cigar-chomping, enormously fat man with a beautiful woman on each mammoth arm. "Not yet, anyway," he murmured after we'd passed.

We took a booth in back where he ordered dinner and drinks for both of us.

"How do you know I like my steak medium-well?" I demanded. "Or that I wanted a Caesar salad? You didn't even ask."

"Look around and learn, Ms. Lane. There's not a waiter in here that will take an order from a woman. At O'Bannion's, you eat what is chosen for you, whether you like it or not. Welcome to a time gone by, Ms. Lane, when men provided and women accepted. And if they didn't like it, they pretended they did."

Wow. And I'd thought the Deep South was bad. Fortunately, I liked my steak anywhere from rare to medium-well, could eat just about any kind of salad, and was thrilled to have someone else springing for an expensive meal, so I made short work of it. All I'd eaten today was two bowls of cereal, and I was starved. When I finished, I saw Barrons' plate was still nearly full and raised a brow.

He pushed it toward me. "I ate earlier," he said.

"So why'd you order, then?" I asked as daintily as I could around a bite of rare filet mignon.

"You don't go to an O'Bannion business and not spend money," Barrons said.

"Sounds like he's got a lot of stupid rules," I muttered.

Just then a barrel of a man with big-knuckled hands, a flattened nose, and cauliflowered ears approached. "Good to see you again, Mr. Barrons. Mr. O'Bannion invites you and your companion to drop by the back and say hello."

It wasn't really an invitation and no one pretended it was. Barrons rose immediately, collected me, tucked me into his body again, and steered me along behind the battered ex-boxer as if, without guidance, I might blindly bounce off walls, a short-circuited Stepford Wife.

I was going to be really glad to get out of this place.

"By the back" meant another building quite some distance behind the pub. We got there underground, following O'Bannion's man through the kitchens, down a long flight of stairs, and into a well-lit, damp stone tunnel. As we hurried past openings to more tunnels that were either blocked up with stone and concrete or sealed by heavily padlocked steel doors, Barrons murmured close to my ear, "In some parts of Dublin, there's another city beneath the city."

"Creepy," I muttered, as we ascended another long flight of stairs.

I guess I was expecting something out of a movie: a pack of dissolute, heavy-jowled men crammed into a smoke-filled room, gathered around a table, wearing sweat-stained shirts and gun holsters, chewing cigars and playing high-stakes poker, with centerfolds of naked women tacked to the walls.

What I got was a dozen or so well-dressed men talking quietly in a spacious, handsomely appointed room of mahogany and leather, and the only woman on the walls here was the *Madonna and Child*. But the Madonna wasn't alone; the august room was virtually wallpapered with religious icons. Interspersed with built-in bookcases graced by a collection of Bibles that I suspected might make even the Pope covetous, hung crucifixes of silver, gold, wood, and even one of those glow-in-the-dark plastic ones. Behind a stately desk hung a series of twelve paintings depicting Christ's last moments. Over the fireplace was a reproduction of *The Last Supper*. At the far end of the room were two prayer shrines covered with brightly flickering candles, flanking a larger shrine that held an elaborate antique reliquary containing heavens only knew what—perhaps the tooth or heel bone of some obscure saint. A powerfully built, dark-haired man stood before the ancient religious *chasses*, his back to us.

I pretended to stumble at the threshold of the door. Barrons caught me. *"Oops,"* I said meaningfully. Though we'd not agreed on a code, I thought saying OOPs was pretty clear. I was telling him there was an Object of Power somewhere nearby. Not in this room, but close. From the sudden acid in my stomach that seemed to be boiling up through the soles of my feet, I suspected whatever it was lay directly beneath us, in Barrons' "city beneath the city."

If Barrons got my not-so-subtle message, he gave no sign of it. His eyes were focused on the man at the shrine, his jaw set.

As the man turned from the reliquary, the two Unseelie flanking him turned also. Whoever the big, bad Unseelie was that was after the *Sinsar Dubh*, he'd stationed his watchdogs here, too. Our unknown competitor was watching the same people Barrons was interested in: McCabe, Mallucé, and now O'Bannion. Unlike the Rhino-boys at McCabe's and Mallucé's, however, these were casting no glamour of being human whatsoever, which perplexed me until I realized that they really had no need. In their natural state, they were invisible to everyone but *sidhe*-seers like Barrons and me, and we seemed a pretty rare breed. I had no idea why these Rhino-boys had chosen to remain invisible rather than in-serting themselves into O'Bannion's tangible reality as others had done with McCabe and Mallucé, but they had, which meant I had to determinedly not look at them at all. At least when Unseelie were fak-ing passing as humans, I could notice whatever illu-sion they were presenting and not give myself away, but when they weren't, I didn't dare observe the space they occupied, which was easier said than done. Sliding your gaze over something that looks so alien is a little tricky.

I took a cue from Barrons and focused my atten-tion on the man between them who was, no doubt, Rocky O'Bannion.

I could instantly see how he'd gotten where he was. In any century, this man would have been a fighter, a leader of men. Dark, brawny, six feet of graceful, glistening muscle in black trousers, a white shirt, and a fine, soft Italian-made black leather jacket, he moved with the confidence of a man who knew his slightest wish was the rest of the world's command. His short black hair was thick, his teeth the perfect white of an ex-boxer with money, and when he smiled, which he did now at Barrons, it was lightning quick and full of dark Irish deviltry.

"Good to see you again, Barrons."

Barrons nodded. "O'Bannion."

"What brings you here tonight?"

Barrons murmured something complimentary about the pub and then the two men moved swiftly into a conversation about recent trouble O'Bannion had been having at one of his shipping concerns down by the docks. Barrons had heard something out on the streets that might be useful, he said.

I watched them while they talked. Rocky O'Bannion was a lodestone, six feet of pure muscle-packed charisma. He was the kind of man men wanted to be and women wanted to be dragged off to bed by—and I did mean dragged off—there would be no dominating this man by any woman. There was no doubt in my mind that the powerful, ruggedly attractive Irishman with the stone-hewn jaw was also a stone-cold killer, and from the way he was trying to pave his way to heaven by plastering over his sins with the putty of religious zeal, he was also a borderline psychopath.

Yet none of it diminished my attraction to him one bit—*that* was the true measure of the man's presence. I was revolted by him, and at the same time, if he were to focus that devilish Irish charm my way, if those dark, heavy-lidded eyes would turn with favor in my direction, I was afraid I would flush with pleasure even as I knew I should be running as fast as I could the other way, and for that reason alone, the man scared the living bejeezus out of me.

I was surprised to notice that Barrons didn't look much more comfortable than I, and that worried me even more. Nothing disturbed Jericho Barrons, yet I could clearly see tension in the angles of his body and strain in the lines of his face, around the mouth and eyes. Every bit of earlier playfulness in him was gone. He was lean, mean, and hard again, even seemed a little pale beneath that exotic golden skin. Though he stood inches taller than our host and was even more powerfully built, though he usually exuded comparable vitality and presence, at the moment he seemed...diminished, and I got the sudden, weirdest impression that ninety-nine percent of Jericho Barrons was currently focused somewhere else, and being nearly used up, leaving only one percent of him here and now, in this room, paying attention to O'Bannion.

"Beautiful woman, Jericho," O'Bannion said then, turning his gaze—as I'd feared—my way. And as I'd feared, I blushed. The boxer stepped closer, circled me, looking me up and down, and made a rough sound of masculine approval in the back of his throat.

"She is, isn't she?" Barrons replied.

"Not Irish," O'Bannion observed.

"American."

"Catholic?"

"Protestant," Barrons said.

I didn't bat an eyelash at the lie.

"Too bad." Rocky turned his attention back to Barrons and I breathed again. "Good to see you, Jericho. If you should hear anything further about my troubles at the dock..."

"I'll be in touch," said Barrons.

"You like him," I said later, as we picked our way back through the nearly deserted four A.M. streets of downtown Dublin. The information Barrons had given him had actually been pertinent, identifying several members of a local gang as the thorns in O'Bannion's side.

"No, Ms. Lane," Barrons replied.

"Okay, maybe not like," I corrected, "respect. You respect O'Bannion."

Again Barrons shook his head.

"Well, what, then?" Barrons had accorded Rocky O'Bannion a certain solemn distance he'd not shown any of the others and I wanted to know why.

He thought a moment. "If I were in the middle of Afghanistan's mountains and could choose either one man to fight barehanded by my side, or a full complement of sophisticated weapons, I'd take O'Bannion. I neither like nor respect him, I merely recognize what he is."

We hurried along for a few blocks in silence.

I was grateful to be out of the stilettos I'd worn earlier and back in comfortable shoes. When we'd left O'Bannion's, Barrons had whisked us back to the bookstore, where he'd demanded a full report of what I'd sensed. After I'd told him, he'd left me alone in the bookstore while he'd gone off by himself somewhere to "get reacquainted with some of the finer points of the city's sewage system," he'd said.

In his absence, I'd gone upstairs and changed. I could figure out proper sewer-crawling attire all by myself—something old, dark, and grungy.

We'd returned to the general vicinity of O'Bannion's Pub & Restaurant in a dark, nondescript sedan I'd never have noticed parked in the shadowy rear of Barrons' fascinating garage, left it at the curb several blocks from our intended destination, and hoofed it from there.

"Stay here a minute." A hand on my shoulder, Barrons stopped me on the sidewalk, then strode into the middle of the street. He was his usual self again, occupying more space than was his due. He'd changed, too, into faded jeans, a black T-shirt, and scuffed black boots. It was the first time I'd ever seen him in something so ... well, *plebian* for him, and the hard, muscled body those clothes showcased was nothing short of incredible, if you went for that kind of man. Thankfully, I didn't. It was like seeing a powerful, stalking black panther, blood frothing its muzzle, wearing street clothes—very weird.

"You've *got* to be kidding me," I said when, shoulders bunching and biceps bulging, he lifted the manhole cover, slid it aside, and beckoned me.

"How did you think we were going to get into the sewer system, Ms. Lane?" Barrons said impatiently.

"I didn't. I must have purposely bypassed that thought." I walked over. "Are you sure there's not a convenient flight of stairs around here somewhere?"

He shrugged. "There is. It's not, however, the best point of access." He glanced up at the sky. "We need to get in and out as quickly as possible, Ms. Lane."

I understood that. In very little time it would be dawn, and the streets in Dublin began bustling with people as early as daybreak. It would hardly do to come popping out of a manhole right in front of them, or worse, inches from a car's front bumper.

I stood over the open hole in the street and peered down into the darkness. "Rats?" I asked, a bit sadly.

"Undoubtedly."

"Right." I took a deep breath and blew it out slowly. "Shades?"

"Not enough to feed on down there. They prefer the streets. Take my hand and I'll lower you down, Ms. Lane."

"How will we get back up?" I worried.

"I have a different route in mind for our return trip."

"Does it involve stairs?" I asked hopefully.

"No."

"Of course not. How silly of me. And for our return adventure," I said, in my best game-show-announcer voice, "we will be scaling the side of Mount Everest, hiking boots to be provided by our trusty sponsor, Barrons Books and Baubles."

"Amusing, Ms. Lane." Barrons could not have looked more unamused. "Now move."

I took his outthrust hand, let him dangle me over the edge and drop me down. Destination: a darker, even scarier Dublin, deep underground.

SIXTEEN

It turned out not to be so scary after all.

In fact, not nearly as scary as upside had been lately.

Down there, in the dreary, dirty sewers beneath the city, I realized how drastically my world had changed, and in such a small amount of time.

How could a beady-eyed, twitchy-nosed rat—or even a few hundred—compare to the Gray Man? What consequence raw sewage and stench next to one's likely fate at the hands of the Many-Mouthed-Thing? What significance ruined shoes or nails torn scrabbling over rocks in collapsing parts of the city's underbelly, when measured against the brazen theft I was about to commit? Against a man who'd taken out twenty-seven people in a single night just because they were in the way of his bright and shining future, no less.

We turned one way, then the next, through

empty tunnels with unobstructed walkways, into ones fouled by slow-moving sludge. We sloped down deeper into the earth, veered up, and descended again.

"What is that?" I pointed to a wide stream of fast-moving water, visible beyond an iron grill mounted in the wall. We'd passed many such grills, though smaller and set lower into the walls. Most were affixed in sunken spots, with large pools of black water collected around them, but I'd seen nothing like this. This looked like a river.

It was. "The River Poddle," Barrons said. "It runs underground. You can see where it meets the River Liffey through another such grill at the Millennium Bridge. In the late eighteenth century, two rebel leaders escaped Dublin castle by following the sewer system to it. One can navigate the city fairly well, if one knows where things connect."

"And you do," I said.

"I do," he agreed.

"Is there anything you don't know?" Ancient artifacts, how to freeze obscenely large bank accounts, the seedy subculture of the city, not to mention the exact layout of its dark, dirty underbelly.

"Not much." I could discern no arrogance in his reply; it was simply fact.

"How did you learn it all?"

"When did you become such a chatterbox, Ms. Lane?"

I shut up. I told you pride is my special little challenge. He didn't want to hear me? Fine, I didn't want to waste my breath on him, anyway. "Where were you born?" I asked.

Barrons stopped short, turned around and looked at me, as if bewildered by my sudden spate of talkativeness.

I raised my hands, bewildered too. "I don't know why I asked that. I had every intention of shutting up but then I started thinking about how I know nothing about you. I don't know where you were born, whether you have parents, siblings, a wife, children, or even exactly what it is you do."

"You know all you need to know about me, Ms. Lane. As I do about you. Now move. We've precious little time."

A dozen yards later, he motioned me up the rungs of a steel ladder bolted into the wall and, at the top of it, I became instantly, deeply nauseated.

There was one extremely potent OOP—dead ahead.

"Beyond that, Barrons," I said apologetically. "I guess we're kind of screwed, huh?"

"That" was what looked like a bulkhead door. You know, the kind they use on bank vaults that are several feet thick, made of virtually impenetrable alloys, and open with that big spinning wheel thing like on submarine doors. It was just too bad "the handle" wasn't on our side. "Don't suppose you have a convenient stash of explosives on you somewhere?" I joked. I was tired and afraid and I was getting a little slaphappy, or maybe it was just the general, ever-increasing absurdity of my life that was making it difficult for me to take anything too seriously.

Barrons eyed the massive door a moment, then closed his eyes.

I could actually see the internal analysis he was performing. His eyes moved rapidly beneath closed lids, as if scanning the blueprints of Dublin's sanitation system as they flashed across his retinas, Terminator-style, while he targeted our exact position, and searched for a point of entry. His eyes flew open. "You're sure it's beyond that door?"

I nodded. "Absolutely. I could puke right here."

"Try to restrain yourself, Ms. Lane." He turned and began walking away. "Remain here."

I stiffened. "Where are you going?" A single flashlight suddenly seemed grossly inadequate company.

"He's counting on natural barriers to protect it," Barrons tossed over his shoulder. "I'm a strong swimmer."

I watched his flashlight bob as he hurried down a tunnel to my left and disappeared around a corner, then there was nothing but blackness and I was alone in it, with only two batteries standing between myself and a serious case of the heebie-jeebies. I hate the dark. I didn't used to, but I sure do now.

It felt like hours, although according to my watch, it was only seven and a half minutes later that a dripping-wet Barrons opened the bulkhead door.

"Oh God, what *is* this place?" I said, turning in a slow circle, transfixed. We were in a rough-hewn stone chamber that was crammed with yet more religious artifacts displayed side by side with ancient weapons. It was evident from the high-water marks on the stone that the subterranean structure flooded occasionally, but all of O'Bannion's treasures were mounted well above the highest, suspended on brackets bolted into the walls or displayed on top of tall stone pedestals.

I could just see the dark, handsome, psychopathic ex-boxer standing here, gloating over his treasures, the frightening gleam of religious fanaticism in his heavy-lidded eyes.

Wet footprints led from an iron grate low in the wall, beyond which lay deep black water, straight to the door. Barrons hadn't even paused to look around when he'd entered.

"Find it, get it, and let's go," Barrons barked.

I'd forgotten he couldn't know which item it was. Only I could. I turned in a slow circle, stretching my newfound Spidey-sense.

I retched. Dryly. Fortunately, it seemed I was getting a little better at this. My supper stayed in my stomach. I had a sudden vision of O'Bannion coming down to discover his artifact missing, with neat little piles of puke all over the place and wondered what he would make of it. I snickered; a measure of how completely freaked out I was. "That." I pointed to an item mounted just above my head, almost lost amid the assortment of similar items surrounding it, and turned to look at Barrons who was standing behind me, just outside the bulkhead door. He was staring down the corridor. Now he turned slowly and glanced in.

"Fuck," he exploded, punching the door. "I didn't even see it." Then louder, "*Fuck.*" He turned away. His back to me, he snapped, "Are you sure that's it?"

"Absolutely."

"Well, get it, Ms. Lane. Don't just stand there."

I blinked. "Me?"

"You're standing right next to it."

"But it makes me feel sick," I protested.

"Now's the perfect time to start working on that little problem of yours. *Get it.*"

Stomach heaving all the while, I lifted the thing from the wall. The metal brackets suspending it popped up with an audible *click* when I removed its weight. "Now what?" I said.

Barrons laughed and the sound echoed hollowly off the stone. "Now, Ms. Lane, we run like hell, because you just set off a dozen alarms."

I jerked. "What are you talking about? I don't hear anything."

"Silent. Straight to every house he owns. Depending on where he is at the moment, we have little, or even less, time."

Barrons wasn't turning out to be a good influence on me at all. In a single night he'd gotten me to dress like a floozy, burgle like a common thief, and now he had me cussing like a sailor as I seconded his opinion. "*Fuck,*" I exclaimed.

It occurred to me as I raced through the predawn streets of Dublin, with a spear longer than I was tall tucked beneath my arm, that I didn't expect to live much longer.

"Lose the pessimism, Ms. Lane," Barrons said when I informed him of my thoughts. "It's a self-fulfilling prophecy."

"Huh?" I said, gasping for breath. I tried to fling myself into the car, but succeeded only in getting wedged in the open door by the spear.

"Slide it over the top of the seat and into the back," he barked.

I managed to unjam myself and did just that. I had to roll the window down so part of the shaft could protrude. Barrons slid behind the wheel at the same moment I dropped into the passenger seat and we both slammed our doors.

"Expect to die," he said, "and you will. The power of thought is far greater than most people ever realize." He started the car and pulled away from the curb. "*Fuck,*" he said again. It seemed to be the word of the night.

A *Gardai* car was passing us, moving very slowly. Fortunately it was on Barrons' side, not mine, and the cop couldn't see the butt of the spear sticking out.

"We're not doing anything wrong," I said instantly. "Well, I mean, not that *he* knows, right? Surely the alarm hasn't been reported to the police yet, has it?"

"Whether or not it has, he just got a good look at us, Ms. Lane. We're on O'Bannion turf. Who do you think pays to have his streets patrolled at these hours?"

Understanding dawned slowly. "You're saying that even if the cop doesn't know now, once he finds out O'Bannion was robbed..." I trailed off.

"He'll pass on our descriptions," Barrons finished for me.

"We're dead," I said matter-of-factly.

"There's that pessimism again," said Barrons.

"Realism. I'm talking about reality here, Barrons. Pull your head out. What do you think O'Bannion's going to do to us when he finds out? Give us a little slap on the wrist?"

"Attitude shapes reality, Ms. Lane, and yours, to coin a grossly overused American phrase, sucks."

I didn't get what he was trying to tell me that night, but later, when it counted, I would remember and understand. The single greatest advantage anyone can take into any battle is hope. A *sidhe*-seer without hope, without an unshakable determination to survive, is a dead *sidhe*-seer. A *sidhe*-seer who believes herself outgunned, outmanned, may as well point that doubt straight at her temple, pull the trigger, and blow out her own brains. There are really only two positions one can take toward anything in life: hope or fear. Hope strengthens, fear kills.

But I understood little of such things that night and so I rode in white-knuckled silence as we sped through deserted Dublin streets until at last we pulled in to the brightly lit alley between Barrons' garage and residence. "What the heck did we just steal, anyway, Barrons?" I said.

He smiled faintly as the garage door rose. Our headlamps illuminated the gleaming grilles of his auto collection. We drove inside and parked the old sedan in the rear. "It has been called many things, but you might know it as the Spear of Longinus," he said.

"Never heard of it," I said.

"How about the Spear of Destiny?" he asked. "Or the Holy Lance?"

I shook my head.

"Do you subscribe to any religion, Ms. Lane?"

I climbed out of the car and reached in back for the spear. "I go to church sometimes."

"You are holding the spear that pierced Christ's side as he hung on the cross," he said.

I nearly dropped it. "This thing killed Jesus?" I exclaimed, dismayed. And I was *holding* it? I hurried after him toward the open garage door. I didn't consider myself a particularly religious person, but I had the sudden fiercest urge to fling it away, scrub my hands, then go to the nearest church and pray.

We ducked beneath the door as it slid soundlessly down, and headed across the alley. Shades lurked to my right just beyond the reach of the floodlights illuminating the rear entrances, but I didn't spare them a glance. I was intent on getting inside and out of the wide-open night where a crime lord's bodyguard might pick me off at any moment with a well-aimed bullet.

"He was already dead when it happened, Ms.

Lane. A Roman solider, Gaius Cassius Longinus, did it. The next day was the Passover and the Jewish leaders didn't want the victims hanging on display throughout their holy day. They asked Pilate to hasten their deaths so they might be taken down. Crucifixion," Barrons explained, "was a slow business; it could take days for the hanged man to die. When soldiers broke the legs of the two men beside Christ, they could no longer use them to push up for breath and expired quickly of suffocation. However, Christ appeared already dead, so instead of breaking his legs, one of the soldiers pierced his side to prove it. Perversely, the so-called Spear of Longinus has been coveted ever since, for alleged mythic powers. Many have claimed to possess the sacred relic: Constantine, Charlemagne, Otto the Great, and Adolph Hitler, to name but a few. Each believed it to be the true source of all his power."

I stepped into the rear foyer of Barrons' residence, slammed the door behind me, and rounded on him with disbelief. "So let me get this straight. We just broke in to a mobster's private collection and stole what he believes to be the true source of all his power? And we did this *why*?"

"Because, Ms. Lane, the Spear of Destiny has another name, the Spear of *Luin*, or *Luisne*, the Flaming Spear. And it is not a Roman weapon at all but one brought to this world by the Tuatha Dé Danaan. It is a Seelie Hallow and just happens to be one of only two weapons known to man that can kill a Fae. *Any* Fae. No matter the caste. Even the Queen herself is said to fear this spear. But if you like, I can ring up

O'Bannion and see if he might forgive us if we bring it back. Shall I, Ms. Lane?"

I gripped the spear. "This could kill the Many-Mouthed-Thing?" I asked.

He nodded.

"And the Gray Man, too?"

He nodded again.

"Hunters?"

A third nod.

"Even Fae royalty?" I wanted to be perfectly clear on this.

"Yes, Ms. Lane."

"Really?" I breathed.

"Really."

I narrowed my eyes. "Do you have a plan for dealing with O'Bannion?"

Barrons reached past me, turned on the bright overhead in the anteroom, and flipped off the exterior floodlights. Beyond the window, the back alley went dark. "Go to your room, Ms. Lane, and do not come out again—for any reason—until I come for you. Do you understand me?"

There was no way I was going to go sit somewhere and passively await my death, and I told him so. "I will not go upstairs and cower—"

"Now."

I glared at him. I hated it when he cut me off with one of those one-word commands of his. I had news for him: I wasn't like Fiona, pining away for crumbs of his affection, willing to yield to any demand he might make to get them. "You can't order me around like I'm F—" This time I was glad he cut me off before I betrayed that I'd eavesdropped.

"Do you have somewhere else to go, Ms. Lane?" he asked coolly. "Is that it?" His smile chilled me, shaped as it was by the satisfaction of a man who knows he has a woman exactly where he wants her. "Will you go back to The Clarin House and hope Mallucé isn't out looking for you? I have news for you, Ms. Lane, you could be swimming in a lake of holy water, dressed in a gown of garlic, denying an invitation at the top of your lungs, and it wouldn't stop a vampire who's fed richly and recently enough. Or will you try for a new hotel, and hope O'Bannion doesn't have anyone there on his payroll? No, I have it; you'll go back home to Georgia. Is that it? I hate to break it to you, Ms. Lane, but I think it's a little too late for that."

I didn't want to know why it was too late for that: whether he meant O'Bannion would come after me, dazed-eyed Goth slaves would cross water to return me to their Master, or Barrons himself would hunt me down.

"You bastard," I whispered. Before he'd dragged me from one bizarre "player's" house to the next, before he'd gotten me to rip off both a vampire and a mobster, I'd still had a chance. It might have been a slim one, but it had been a chance. Now it was a whole different ball game and I was playing in the dark and somehow, everyone but me had night-vision goggles and understood the rules of play. And I suspected this had been part of Barrons' plan all along: to shave down my options, to whittle away my choices until he'd left me only one—to need him to survive.

I was furious with him, with myself. I'd been such a fool. And I couldn't see any way out. Still, I wasn't entirely helpless. I needed him? I could swallow that if I had to, because he needed me, too, and I was *never* going to let him forget it. "Fine, Barrons," I said, "but I'm keeping this. And that's nonnegotiable." I raised the spear I was gripping. Maybe I couldn't fight off vampires and mobsters, but at least I could give the Fae a decent battle.

He looked at the spear for several moments, his dark gaze unfathomable. Then he said, "It was for you all along, Ms. Lane. I suggest you remove the shaft and make it portable. It's not the original and only the head itself matters."

I blinked. It was for me? Not only did the relic have to be worth an absolute fortune on the black market, but Barrons was also a *sidhe*-seer and could use it to protect himself, too, yet he was going to let *me* hang on to it? "Really?"

He nodded. "Obey me, Ms. Lane," he said, "and I will keep you alive."

"I wouldn't need to be kept alive in the first place," I snapped, "if you hadn't dragged me into this mess."

"You came looking for this mess, Ms. Lane. You sauntered in here all innocence and stupidity asking for the *Sinsar Dubh*, remember? I told you to go home."

"Yeah, well, that was before you knew I could

find things for you. Now you'd probably tie me up and drug me to keep me here," I accused.

"Probably," he agreed. "Though I suspect I'd have no problem at all finding more effective means."

I looked at him sharply. He wasn't joking. And I never wanted to know what those "more effective means" might be.

"But considering everything that's after you, I don't need to, do I, Ms. Lane? Which puts us right back where we started: Go to your room and do not come out again *for any reason* until I come for you. Do you understand me?"

Mom says humility isn't one of my strengths, and she's right. To reply would have reeked of capitulation, or at the least, acquiescence, and although he might have won this particular battle, I sure didn't have to admit it, so I stared down at the spear in stony silence. The spearhead shimmered like silvery alabaster in the brightly lit anteroom. If I broke it off to a short shaft, it would be only about a foot long. The tip was razor-sharp, the base about four inches wide. It would no doubt fit nicely in my largest purse, if I could figure out a way to keep the lethal point from puncturing the side.

When I looked back up, I was alone.

Barrons was gone.

SEVENTEEN

My folks have some funny sayings. They were born in a different time, to a different generation. Theirs was the "hard work is its own reward" generation. Admittedly it had its problems, but mine is the "entitlement generation" and it has its fair share, too.

The EG is made up of kids who believe they deserve the best of everything by mere virtue of having been born, and if parents don't arm them with every possible advantage, they are condemning their own children to a life of ostracism and failure. Raised by computer games, satellite TV, the Internet, and the latest greatest electronic device—while their parents are off slaving away to afford them all—most of the EG believe if there's something wrong with them, it's not their fault; their parents screwed them up, probably by being away too much. It's a vicious little catch-22 for the parents any way you look at it.

My parents didn't screw me up. Any screwing up that might have been done, I did to myself. All of which is my roundabout way of saying that I'm beginning to understand what Dad always meant when he said, "Don't tell me you didn't *mean* to do it, Mac. Omission or commission—the end result is the same."

I understand now. It's the difference between involuntary manslaughter and homicide: the dead person is still dead, and I highly doubt the corpse appreciates any legal distinctions we make over it.

By omission or commission, one orange, two candy bars, a bag of pretzels, and twenty-six hours later, I had blood on my hands.

I'd never been so happy to see the first rays of dawn in my life as I was that next morning. I'd ended up doing exactly what I'd sworn I wouldn't do: I'd cowered in my brilliantly lit, borrowed bedroom from one daybreak to the next, trying to make my meager snacks last, and wondering what plan Barrons could possibly have devised that might guarantee our safety from Rocky O'Bannion, quite pessimistically certain there was none. Even if he managed to scare off a few of O'Bannion's men, there would only be more. I mean, really, how could one man hope to stand up to a ruthless mobster and his loyal pack of ex-fighters and thugs who'd once taken out twenty-seven people in a single night?

When the first rays of a rosy sunrise pressed at the edges of the drapes, I hurried to the window and pulled back the curtain. I'd lived through yet another Dublin night and that, in and of itself, was swift becoming cause for celebration in my badly warped little world. I stared dumbly down into the alley for a long moment, as the sight that greeted me slowly sunk in.

Or didn't, I guess, because before I knew it, I'd raced from my fourth-floor retreat and was pounding bare-heeled down the back stairs for a closer look. I burst out into the early, chilly Irish morning. The concrete steps were damp with cold dew beneath my bare feet as I hurried down them, into the rear alley.

A dozen or so feet away, in the early morning light, a black Maybach gleamed, with all four of its doors ajar. It was making that annoying *bing-bing* sound that told me the keys were still in the ignition and the battery hadn't yet run down. Behind it, hood to trunk, stretching down into the beginnings of the abandoned neighborhood, were three more black vehicles, all with their doors wide open, emitting a chorus of *bings*. Outside each car were piles of clothing, not far from the doors. I had a sudden flashback to the day I'd gotten lost in the abandoned neighborhood, to the derelict car with the pile of clothing outside the driver's door. Comprehension slammed into my brain and I flinched from the horror of it.

Any fool could see what had happened here.

Well, at least any *sidhe*-seer fool who knew what

kind of things that went bump in the night around these parts could.

The cop who'd seen us yesterday morning had apparently reported to O'Bannion, and at some unknown hour after dark, the mobster had come looking for us with a full complement of his men, and as evidenced by their stealthy backdoor approach, they'd not been coming to pay us a social call.

The simplicity of Barrons' plan both astounded and chilled me: He'd merely turned off the outside lights, front and rear, allowing darkness to swallow the entire perimeter of the building. O'Bannion and his men had stepped out of their cars, directly into an Unseelie massacre.

Barrons had *known* they would come. I was even willing to bet he'd known they would come in force. He'd also known they would never make it farther than the direct vicinity of their own cars. Of course, I'd been safe in the store. With the interior lights ablaze and the exterior lights extinguished, neither man nor monster could have reached me last night.

Barrons had baited a death trap—one that my theft had made necessary. When I'd reached up and blithely removed that weapon from the wall, I'd signed death warrants for sixteen men.

I turned and stared up at the bookstore, now seeing it in an entirely different light: It wasn't a building—it was a *weapon*. Only last week I'd stood out front, thinking it seemed to stand bastion between the good part of the city and the bad. Now I understood it *was* a bastion—this was the line of demarcation, the last defense—and Barrons held the encroachment of the abandoned neighborhood at bay with his many and carefully placed floodlights, and all he had to do to protect his property from threat at night was turn them off and let the Shades move in, hungry guard dogs from Hell.

Drawn by grim fascination, or perhaps some long-dormant genetic need to understand all I could about the Fae, I approached the Maybach. The pile of clothing outside the driver's door was topped by a finely made black leather jacket that looked just like the one I'd seen on Rocky O'Bannion the night before last.

Barely repressing a shudder, I reached down and picked it up. As I lifted the supple Italian leather, a thick husk of what looked like badly yellowed, porous parchment fell out of it.

I jerked violently and dropped the coat. I'd seen that kind of "parchment" before. I'd seen dozens of them, blowing down the deserted streets of the abandoned neighborhood that day I'd gotten lost in the fog, all different shapes and sizes. I remembered thinking that there must be a defunct paper factory somewhere nearby with broken windows.

But it hadn't been paper blowing past me—it had been *people*. Or what had been left of them, anyway. And that day, if I'd not made it out before nightfall, I would have become one of these...these...dehydrated rinds of human matter, too.

I backed away. I didn't need to peer beneath any more coats to know those husks were all that was left of Rocky O'Bannion and fifteen of his men, but I did anyway. I lifted three more, and that was all I

could take. The men hadn't even been able to see
what was killing them. I wondered if the Shades had
attacked simultaneously, waiting for all of them to
get out of their cars, or if only the front two men had
stepped out of each car and then, when the two in
the rear had seen them go down, sucked into little
scraps of whatever it was the Shade palate found in-
digestible in humans, they too had lunged out, guns
blazing, only to fall victim to the same unseen foe. I
wondered if the Shades were clever enough to wait,
or merely driven by mindless, insatiable hunger.

If they'd gotten me that first night I'd been lost,
I'd have been able to see what was coming—great
big oily darknesses—but I'd not have known I was a
Null, or even a *sidhe*-seer, and although I probably
would have raised my hands to try to fend it off, I
wasn't sure the Shades had a tangible form that I
could touch to freeze.

I made a mental note to ask Barrons.

I stared at the four cars, at the piles that were all
that remained of sixteen men: clothing, shoes, jew-
elry, guns; there were lots of guns. They must have
been packing at least two each; blue steel littered the
pavement around the cars. Apparently Shades killed
quickly or all the guns had silencers, because I hadn't
heard a single shot last night.

No matter that these men had been criminals and
killers, no matter that once before they'd wiped out
two entire families, I could not absolve myself of
their deaths. By omission or commission, my hand
was in it, and I would carry it inside me for the rest

of my life in a place that I would eventually learn to live with, but never learn to like.

Fiona arrived at eleven-fifty to open the bookstore. By midafternoon, the day had turned overcast, drizzly, and cold, so I flipped on the gas logs in the fireplace in the rear conversation area, curled up with some fashion magazines, and watched the customers come and go, wondering what kind of lives they had and why I couldn't have one like that, too.

Fiona chatted brightly with everyone but me and rang up orders until eight o'clock on the dot, when she locked up the store and left.

Mere hours after its urbane owner had killed sixteen men, all was business as usual at Barrons Books and Baubles again, which begged the question: Who was the stone-*colder* killer—the overzealous ex-boxer turned mobster, or the car-collecting bookstore owner?

The mobster was dead. The very-much-alive bookstore owner stepped in from the rain, a little later than usual but no worse for the wear, at half past nine that night. After relocking the front door, he stopped at the cash register to check on notes Fiona had left him about two special orders placed that day, then joined me, taking an armchair opposite my perch on the sofa. His blood-red silk shirt was splattered with rain and molded to his hard body like a damp second skin. Black trousers clung to his long muscular legs, and he was wearing black boots that had wicked-looking silver toes and heels.

He had on that heavy silver Celtic wrist cuff again that made me think of arcane chants and ancient stone circles, complemented by a black-and-silver torque at his throat. He radiated his usual absurd amount of energy and dark, carnal heat.

I looked him straight in the eye, and he gazed straight back at me, and neither of us said a word. He didn't say, *I'm sure you saw the cars out back, Ms. Lane* and I didn't say, *You cold-blooded bastard, how could you?* And he didn't counter with, *You're alive, aren't you?* So I didn't remind him that he'd been the one to jeopardize my life to begin with. I have no idea how long we sat there like that, but we had a complete conversation with our eyes. There was knowledge in Jericho Barrons' gaze, a bottomless pit of it. In fact, for a moment, I imagined I saw The Tree Itself in there, smothered with delicious, shiny red apples just begging to be eaten, but it was only a re-flection of flames and crimson silk on irises so dark they served as a black mirror.

There was one thing we hadn't covered in our wordless communiqué that I just had to know. "Did you even think twice, Barrons? Did you feel any hesitation at all?" When he didn't answer, I pressed, "For just a few moments, did you wonder about their families? Or worry that maybe one of them was a last-minute substitute who'd never done any-thing worse in his life than steal some kid's lunch in fourth grade?" If eyes were daggers, mine would have killed. These were all things I'd been thinking about throughout the long day; that somewhere out there were wives and children whose husbands and fathers were never coming home again, who would never know what had happened to them. Should I gather their personal effects—minus their ghastly remains—and ship them anonymously to the police department? I understood the grim comfort of knowing for a fact that Alina was dead, of having seen her body and laid her in the ground. If she'd simply disappeared, I'd have gone through every day of the rest of my life driven by an unquenchable, desperate hope, searching every face in every crowd, wondering if she was alive out there somewhere. Praying she wasn't in the hands of some psycho.

"Tomorrow," said Barrons, "you'll go to The National Museum."

I hadn't realized I was holding my breath, hoping for an answer that might assuage some of the guilt I'd been stewing in, until it came out in a derisive snort. Typical Barrons. Ask for an answer—get an order. "What happened to 'You will remain here until I return, Ms. Lane?'" I mocked. "What about Mallucé and his men? Have you forgotten about that little problem?" O'Bannion might be gone, and I might have a way of protecting myself from the Fae, but there was still one very pissed-off vampire on the loose out there.

"Mallucé was summoned away last night by someone whose orders he apparently could not, or would not, refuse. His followers expect him to be gone for several days, perhaps as long as a week," said Barrons.

My battered spirits lifted a little. That meant, for a few days at least, I could venture out into the city and move about almost like a normal person again, with only the Fae to worry about. I wanted to go back to Alina's apartment and decide just how much damage I was willing to inflict on it to further my search for her journal, I wanted to buy more snacks for my room in case I got stuck up there again, and I'd been itching to pick up a cheap SoundDock for my iPod. Earbuds were fast becoming a thing of my past; I was turning into too paranoid a person to stand not being able to hear the approach of whatever might jeopardize my life next. But at least I could listen to music in my room if I had a SoundDock, and since I was saving money by not paying for a room anymore, I'd neatly justified the purchase. "Why am I going to the museum?"

"I want you to scour it for OOPs, as you call them. I've long wondered if there are Fae artifacts being hidden in plain view, catalogued as something else. Now that I have you, I can test that theory."

"Don't you know what all the OOPs are, and what they look like?" I asked.

He shook his head. "If only it were that simple. But not even the Fae themselves recall all their own relics." He gave a short, dark laugh. "I suspect it comes from living too long. Why bother to remember or keep track of things? Why care? You live today. You'll live tomorrow. Humans die. The world changes. You don't. Details, Ms. Lane," he said, "go the way of emotions in time."

I blinked. "Huh?"

"The Fae, Ms. Lane," he said. "They aren't like

humans. Extraordinary longevity has made them something else. You must never forget that."

"Believe me," I said, "I wasn't about to mistake them for human. I know they're monsters. Even the pretty ones."

His eyes narrowed. "The pretty ones, Ms. Lane? I thought all the ones you'd seen so far were ugly. Is there something you're not telling me?"

I'd almost slipped about V'lane, a topic I had no desire to discuss with Barrons. Until I knew who I could trust—if anyone—and how far, I would keep my own counsel about some things. "Is there something *you're* not telling *me*?" I countered coolly. How dare he poke at me for keeping secrets when he was chock-full of them? I didn't bother trying to hide that I was trying to hide something. I just used one of his methods on him—evasion by counter-question.

We had another of those wordless communiqués, this time about truths and deceptions and bluffs and calling people on them, and I was getting better at reading him because I saw the very moment Barrons decided pushing me wasn't worth giving up anything himself.

"Try to wrap the museum up as quickly as possible," he said. "After you've finished there, we've a list of places longer than your arm in and about Ireland to search for the remaining stones and the *Sinsar Dubh*."

"Oh God, this is my life now, isn't it?" I exclaimed. "You expect me to just trudge around from place to place as you select them, with my nose pressed to the ground, sniffing out OOPs for you, don't you?"

"Have you changed your mind about trying to find the *Sinsar Dubh*, Ms. Lane?"

"Of course not."

"Do you know where to look yourself?"

I scowled. We both knew I didn't.

"Don't you think the surest way to find both the Dark Book and your sister's killer is to immerse yourself in the very world that killed her?"

Of course I did. I'd thought of that all by myself last week. "So long as that world doesn't kill me first," I said. "And it certainly seems to be trying its darnedest."

He smiled faintly. "I don't think you understand, Ms. Lane. I won't *let* it kill you. No matter what." He stood and walked across the room. As he opened the door, he shot over his shoulder, "And one day you *will* thank me for it."

Was he kidding? I was supposed to thank him for staining my hands with blood? "I don't think so, Barrons," I told him, but the door had already swung closed and he'd disappeared into the rainy Dublin night.

EIGHTEEN

S*hades: perhaps my greatest enemy among the Fae*, I
wrote in my journal.

Dropping my pen between the pages, I checked
my watch again; still ten more minutes to go until
the museum opened. I'd had bad dreams last night,
and I'd been so eager to get out of the bookstore and
into the sunny morning, to go do something touristy
and refreshingly normal, that I hadn't thought to
check what time the museum opened. After stopping for coffee and a scone, I'd still arrived a half an
hour early and was one of many people milling outside, standing in groups or waiting on benches near
the domed entrance of the Museum of Archaeology
and History on Kildare Street.

I'd managed to snag a bench for myself and was
making good use of my extra time by updating
recent events in my notebook and summarizing
what I'd learned. My obsession with finding Alina's

journal was shaping what and how I chose to write in my own: about everything, and in great detail. Hindsight was twenty-twenty and you never knew what clues someone else might be able to pick up on in your life that you were blinded to by living it. If anything happened to me, I wanted to leave behind the best possible record I could, in case someone else would take up my cause—although frankly, I couldn't imagine anyone who would—and I hoped Alina had done the same.

I picked up my pen.

According to Barrons, I wrote, *the Shades lack substance, which means I can neither freeze nor stab them. It appears I have no defense against this low-level caste of Unseelie.*

The irony was not lost on me. The Shades were the most base of their kind, barely sentient, yet— despite the spearhead in my purse (tip securely cased in a wad of foil) allegedly capable of killing even the most powerful shark in the Fae sea—I was still helpless against the bottom-feeders.

Well, I was just going to have to stay off the bottom, then, and arm myself tooth and nail with what *did* work against them. I jotted a quick addition to a shopping list I'd been compiling: several dozen flashlights in varying sizes. I would begin carrying two or more on me at all times and scatter the rest around the bookstore, in every corner of every room, bracing for the horrifying possibility that the power might, one night, go out. Despite the bright morning sun, I shivered, just thinking about it. I'd not been able to get the Shades off my mind ever since yesterday when I'd discovered those piles of clothing collapsed around their papery remains.

Why do they leave clothing behind? I'd asked Barrons when I'd passed him in the rear hall, late last night on my way to bed. The man was a serious night owl. At my tender age—in my defense, I'd like to point out that I've had a very stressful life lately—I'd been bleary-eyed and exhausted by one in the morning, yet he'd looked disgustingly energized and awake, and in high spirits again. I knew my question was hardly important in the overall scheme of things, but sometimes it's the tiniest, insignificant details that nag at my curiosity the most.

In the same way the Gray Man hungers for beauty that will never be his, Ms. Lane, Barrons had said, *the Shades are drawn to steal that which they can never possess as well: A physical manifestation of life. So they take ours and leave behind what has no animation. Clothing is inert.*

Well, what are those papery things? I'd asked, gripped by a revolting fascination. *I'm assuming they're parts of us, but which ones?*

Morbid tonight, are we, Ms. Lane? How would I know? Barrons' shrug was a Gallic ripple of muscle beneath crimson silk. *Perhaps condensed skin, bones, teeth, toenails and such, sucked dry of life. Or perhaps our brains are unpalatable to them. Maybe they taste like frog, Ms. Lane, and Shades hate frog.*

"Ugh," I muttered, as I scribbled the gist of our nocturnal conversation on a new page.

While I was finishing up, there was a sudden mass exodus around me, and I glanced up at the now-open doors of the museum. Tucking my journal carefully into my purse so it didn't hamper easy access to my spearhead, I slung my bag over my shoulder and rose, pleased to realize I was barely registering the nausea caused by such close contact with the OOP. I was determined to carry the thing with me everywhere, so I'd forced myself to sleep with it last night, hoping the more contact I had with it, the less disturbing I would find it over time. It seemed to be working.

My mood perked up as I stepped into the grand rotunda entrance. I've always liked museums. I should probably pretend it's because I'm so erudite and scholarly and love to learn, but the truth is I just love shiny, pretty things, and from what I'd heard about this place, it was packed full. I couldn't wait to see them.

Unfortunately, I wasn't going to get very far.

One day I would stop taking off my clothes in V'lane's presence, but the cost of that resistance would be a piece of my soul.

Today, here and now, strolling through the National Museum of Archaeology and History, dazzled and delighted by the Ór exhibit, a treasure trove of Ireland's gold, I had no idea that pieces of one's soul *could* be lost.

Back then, I was so blind to everything that was going on around me. Back then, I was twenty-two and pretty and up until the month before, my biggest concern had been whether Revlon would discontinue my favorite Iceberry Pink nail polish, which would be a disaster of epic proportions as it would leave me without the perfect complement for the short pink silk skirt I was wearing today with a clingy pearly top, and shimmery gold sandals, flattered by just the right heel to show off my golden, toned legs. A polished pearl-drop necklace swung between my full breasts, matching earrings and a pearl bracelet at my wrist gave me just the right look of youthful glam. My Arabian Nights curls were soft around my face and I was turning more than a few male heads. I notched my chin a bit higher and smiled inside. Ah, the simple pleasures in life...

A few display cases down, over by the stairs, a really cute guy was checking me out. He was tall, athletically built, with short dark hair, great skin, and the dreamiest blue eyes ever. He looked to be about my age, maybe a few years older—a college student, I was willing to bet—and he was exactly the kind of guy I'd have gone out with back home. He gave me an appreciative nod and a smile, making his interest plain. *Distinguish yourself,* my mom had told Alina and me, *in an age where girls often make themselves too available to boys, by making him work a little for your attention. He'll think he's won a prize when he gets it, and he'll work that much harder to keep it. Boys turn into men and men put a premium on what's hardest to get.*

Have I mentioned what a wise woman my mother is? My dad is still head over heels for her after thirty years, still thinks the sun rises and sets on Rainey Lane's head, and if one day she didn't get out of bed, neither would the morning. And neither would he. Alina and I never lacked for love, but we always knew our parents loved each other a little bit more. We found it disgusting and, at the same time, reassuring that they never stopped locking us out of the bedroom at the weirdest times of day, sometimes *twice* in the same day. We'd roll our eyes at each other, but in a world where the divorce rate is more alarming than oil prices, their ongoing love affair was our Rock of Gibraltar.

I started to give the guy a demure smile, but the moment my lips began to curve, they froze. Why bother? It wasn't as if dating was something I could schedule neatly in, right between vampires, life-sucking Fae, mobsters, and OOP-detecting. Would he come pick me up at Barrons' for our date? Gee, what if my enigmatic and cold-blooded host chose that night to turn off the outside lights again?

Bye-bye cute boy, hello pile of clothes.

That thought iced the blood in my veins. I stepped up my pace and left the boy behind in a hurry. Continuing through the exhibit, I focused on my recently discovered raison d'être, stretching my Spidey-sense in all directions, waiting for a tingle.

I got nothing.

I moved through room after room, past artifact after relic, display after display, without getting the faintest twinge of nausea. I was, however, getting a few other twinges. Apparently the cute boy had stirred up my hormones, because I was suddenly having downright kinky thoughts about him and wondering if he had a brother. Or two. Maybe even three.

That was *so* not me. I'm a one-man woman. Even in my fantasies I go for good old-fashioned steamy sex, not multipartnered porn. A particularly graphic image of cute boy plus brothers swam up in my mind and I nearly staggered from the raw eroticism of it. I shook my head sharply, and reminded myself what I was doing here: looking for OOPs—not orgiastic, mindless sex.

I'd nearly given up hope of encountering anything of interest when my gaze was drawn to a scrap of pink silk and lace lying on the floor a few feet away to my left, back in the direction from which I'd come.

I couldn't help but think how pretty it was and walked back over toward it, to see what it was.

My cheeks flamed. Of *course* I'd liked it.

It was my panties.

I snatched them up and performed a hasty inventory of myself.

Skirt, check. Shirt, check. Bra on, good. Thank you, God. Apart from the draft on my bare bottom, and the excruciatingly painful state of arousal I was in, I seemed to be okay. Apparently I'd gone straight to the panties, reached beneath my skirt, slipped them off, and continuing walking without even noticing. If I weren't so enamored of pink, if I weren't so into fashion, I might have continued blithely disrobing, thinking all kinds of happy, horny thoughts, until I'd have been strolling the museum naked. As it was, I'd been sidetracked by the vision of my own good taste lying there on the floor. I wasn't sure if I should be relieved or appalled by how shallow I was.

"Where *are* you?" I snapped, stepping back into my panties and smoothing my skirt down over my hips. Though I stood in the middle of a large room full of people exclaiming over various treasures, not one person was paying me the slightest bit of attention. There was no doubt in my mind what had just brought me to such an intense, base state of sexual arousal that I'd begun subconsciously stripping.

A Fae was here somewhere, glamouring things up, and it was one of the death-by-sex ones. I assumed it was V'lane, mostly because the thought that there might be multiple, terrifyingly beautiful, mind-bending, libido-distorting Fae in my world was more than I could handle.

From somewhere behind me, laughter rolled like smooth, round, cool pearls sliding slowly over my clitoris, and I was suddenly a great, bottomless abyss of excruciating sexual need. My legs were shaking, my panties were gone again, my inner thighs were soaking wet, and I was so hungry for sex that I knew for a fact I was going to die if I didn't get it right here and now.

A clatter drew my gaze to the floor. Next to my panties was my pearl bracelet. I wasn't sure if I'd done what I'd just felt between my legs, or if it had. "V'lane," I whispered, through lips swollen and plumped, just like my breasts were swelling and plumping. My body was changing, making itself ready for its Master, growing softer and wetter and riper and fuller.

"Lie down, human," it said.

"Over my dead body, Fae," I snarled.

It laughed again and my nipples were on fire. "Not yet, *sidhe*-seer, but one day you might beg for death."

Anger. That was it. Anger had worked before. Anger and another A-word. But what was it, that word? What had saved me before? What was that unhappy thought, that miserable thought that could make me go cold inside and feel like Death myself?

"Apple," I muttered. No, that wasn't it. Artifact? Adam? Alleged? Allowed? Wasn't I? Allowed to have sex right here and now? Hadn't it said, "Lie down, human?" Who was I to disobey?

I knelt on the cool marble floor of the museum and slipped my skirt up over my hips, baring, presenting. Here I am. Take me.

"On all fours," it said behind me, laughing again, and again I felt the cool slip of pearls being dragged slowly between my thighs, over my taut bud, between my swollen, slick lips. I dropped forward on my hands and knees. My spine arched, my bottom lifted, and I made a sound that wasn't at all human.

My mind was going. I could feel it and I still didn't even know if it was V'lane behind me or some other Fae that was going to nail me to the floor and slowly screw me to death. Then its hands were on my bottom and it was positioning me, and if I was a Null, I'd forgotten I had hands, and if there was a spear nearby, I'd forgotten I had a purse, and if I'd once had a sister who'd been killed somewhere in Dublin—

"*Alina!*" The word exploded from me with such vehemence and desperation that spittle sprayed from my lips.

I wrenched myself free, reared around, and slammed both palms into V'lane's chest. "You *pig!*" I scuttled sideways, a bare-bottomed crab, desperate to reach the purse I'd dropped several yards away, along with my shirt and shoes.

By the time I reached my small pile of abandoned possessions, the Fae was already unfrozen again. Barrons had been right, the higher the caste, the more powerful the Fae. Apparently I could only freeze royalty for mere moments. It wasn't enough. Not nearly enough.

"We are not pigs," it said coldly, rising. "It is humans who are the animals."

"Yeah, right. I'm not the one that almost just raped me!"

"You wanted it and you still do," it said flatly. "Your body burns for me, human. You *want* to worship me. You *want* to be on your knees."

The horror of it was—it was right. I did. Even now, my back was still arched with sensual invitation, my bottom was questing up like a cat in heat, and my every move was supple, sinuous. I was one great big come-hither. There was a mindless nymphomaniac inside me and it didn't care how many orgasms it took to die. With trembling hands, I grabbed my purse. "Stay away from me," I warned.

Its expression said it was in no hurry to get close

to me at the moment. Its expression said it was revolted by my all-too-brief power over it, by a mere
human having dominion in any manner over something so glorious as itself. "Why have you come
here? What of ours is here, *sidhe*-seer?" it demanded.

Unzipping my purse, I nudged the ball of foil
from the tip and closed my hand on the spear, but
left it tucked inside. I wanted to preserve the element of surprise. "Nothing."

"You lie."

"No, really, there's nothing here," I said truth-
fully, not that I would have told it if there had been.

"It has been five days, *sidhe*-seer. What did you
take from O'Bannion?"

I blinked. How in the world did it know that?

"He died trying to get it back, that's how. I know
where you stay," it said. "I know where you go. It is
useless to lie to me."

I preferred to believe the Fae had read the
thoughts on my face, not plucked them from my
mind. I bit my tongue to keep from whimpering. It
was doing something to me again. It had my pearls
again. And was working between my legs with
them, one hard, cool ball after the next.

"Talk, *sidhe*-seer."

"You want to know what we took? I'll show you
what we took!" I curled my fingers tightly around
the base of the spearhead, yanked it from my purse,
and drew it back threateningly. "This!"

It was the first time I ever saw such a look on a
Fae's face and it would not be the last. It filled my
veins with such a heady rush of power that it was

very nearly equal to the insane sexual arousal I was feeling.

V'lane, prince of the Tuatha Dé Danaan, *feared* something.

And it was in *my* hand.

The imperious Fae was gone. Just like that. Blink of an eye, if I'd blinked. I hadn't. He'd vanished.

I sat, breathing deeply, clutching the spear, and trying to regroup.

The room seeped slowly back into my consciousness: a buzz of noise, a blur of color, and finally, snippets of conversation here and there.

"What do you suppose she's doing?"

"No idea, man, but she's got a great ass. And talk about your tits to die for!"

"Cover your eyes, Danny. *Now.*" A mother's tight, pinched voice. "She's not decent."

"Looks better than decent to me." Accompanied by a low whistle and the flash of a camera.

"What the hell is in her hand? Should somebody call the cops?"

"I dunno, maybe the paramedics? She doesn't look so well."

I glanced around, wild-eyed. I was on the floor, surrounded by people on all sides, a circle of them, pressing in on me, staring down at me with greedy, curious eyes.

I sucked in a ragged breath that wanted to come back out as a sob, crammed the spear back in my purse—how in the world would I explain having it?—yanked my skirt back down over my bottom, clasped my bra over my bare breasts, fumbled for my shirt, yanked it over my head, picked up my shoes, and scrambled to my feet.

"Get out of my way," I cried, plunging blindly into the crowd, shoving them aside, vultures, one and all.

I couldn't help it. I burst into tears as I raced from the room.

For such an old woman, she sure could move fast.

She cut me off less than a block away from the museum, darting in front of me, blocking my path.

I veered sharply left, and detoured around her without missing a beat.

"Stop," she cried.

"Go to hell," I snapped over my shoulder, tears scalding my cheeks. My victory over V'lane with the spear had been completely overshadowed by my public humiliation. How long had I been sitting there with parts of me sticking out that no man had ever gotten a good look at in broad daylight unless armed with a speculum and a medical license? How long had they been watching me? *Why* hadn't someone tried to cover me up? Down South, a man would have draped a shirt around me. He would have taken a quick glance while he did it, I mean, really, breasts are breasts and men are men, but chivalry is not entirely dead where I come from.

"Voyeurs," I said bitterly. "Sick scandal-starved people." Thank you, reality TV. People were so used to being taken straight into other people's most intimate moments and viewing the sordid details of their lives that they were now far more inclined to sit back and enjoy the show than make any effort to help someone in need.

The old woman got in front of me again and I veered right this time, but she veered with me and I crashed into her. She was so elderly and tiny and fragile-looking that I was afraid she might topple over, and at her age, a fall could mean serious broken bones and a long recovery period. Good manners—unlike those creeps in the museum, *some* of us still had them—temporarily eclipsed my misery, and I steadied her by the elbows. "What?" I demanded. "What do you want? You want to bean me in the head again? Well, go ahead! Do it and get it over with! But I think you should know that I couldn't help seeing this one and the situation is— well, it's complicated."

My assailant was the old woman from the bar that first night I'd arrived in Dublin; the one who'd rapped me with her knuckles and told me to stop staring at the Fae and go die somewhere else and— although now I knew she'd saved my life that night, she might have done it more nicely—I was currently in no mood to thank her.

Tilting her silvery-white head back, she stared up at me, a flabbergasted expression on her wrinkled face. "Who *are* you?" she exclaimed.

"What do you mean, who am I?" I said sourly. "Why are you chasing me if you don't know who I am? Do you make a habit of chasing strangers?"

"I was in the museum," she said. "I saw what you

did! Sweet Jesus, Mary Mother of God and all the saints, who *are* you, lass?"

I was so disgusted with people in general that I shrieked, "You *saw* what that thing was trying to do to me and didn't try to *help* me? If it had raped me, would you have just stood there and watched? Thanks a lot! Appreciate it. Gee, it's getting to the point where I'm not sure who the bigger monsters are—us or them." I spun sharply and tried to walk away but she latched onto my arm with a surprisingly strong grip.

"I couldn't help you and you know it," she snapped. "You know the rules."

I shook her hand off my arm. "Actually, I don't. Everyone else seems to. Just not me."

"One betrayed is one dead," said the old woman sharply. "Two betrayed is two dead. We count precious each of our kind, never more so than now. We cannot take risks that might betray more of us, especially not me. Besides, you held your own in a way I've never seen—and against a prince, no less! Sweet Jesus, how did you do it? What are you?" Her sharp blue gaze darted rapidly from my left eye to my right and back again. "At first your hair fooled me, then I knew it was you, from the bar. That skin, those eyes, and the way you walk—*och*, just like Patrona! But you can't be Patrona's, or I'd have known. From what O'Connor line do you come? Who is your mother?" she demanded.

I tossed my head impatiently. "Look, old lady, I told you that night in the bar that I'm *not* an O'Connor. My name is Lane. MacKayla Lane, from

Georgia. My mom is Rainey Lane and before she married my dad, she was Rainey Frye. So there you have it. Sorry to disappoint you, but there's not a single O'Connor anywhere in my family tree."

"Then you were adopted," the old woman said flatly.

I gasped. "I was *not* adopted!"

"Ballocks!" the old woman snapped. "Though I've no notion the hows and whys of it, you're an O'Connor through and through."

"The nerve!" I exclaimed. "How dare you come up to me and tell me I don't know who I am? I'm MacKayla Lane and I was born in Christ Hospital just like my sister and my dad was right there in the room with my mom when I was born and I am *not* adopted and you don't know the first thing about me or my family!"

"Obviously," the old woman retorted, "you don't, either."

I opened my mouth, thought better of it, shut it, and turned and walked away. I would only be giving credence to the old woman's delusions by rebutting them. I wasn't adopted and I knew that for a fact, as certainly as I knew she was one crazy old woman.

"Where are you going?" she demanded. "There are things I must know. Who you are, if we can trust you and *how*, by all that's holy, did you get your hands on one of their Hallows? That night in the bar I thought you *Pri-ya*"—she spat the word like the foulest of epithets—"from the moonstruck way you were staring at it. Now I've no idea what you are. You must come with me now. *Stop right there, O'Connor.*" She used a tone of voice that, not so long ago, would have stopped me dead in my tracks and turned me around, out of respect for my elders if nothing else, but I wasn't that girl anymore. In fact, I was no longer even certain who that girl had really been, as if Mac BTC—Before The Call that day by the pool—hadn't quite been real, just an empty, pretty amalgam of fashionable clothes, happy music, and coltish dreams.

"Stop calling me that," I hissed over my shoulder, "and stay away from me, old woman." I broke into a sprint but wasn't fast enough to outrun her next words, and I knew as soon as she said them that they were going to chafe like sharp pebbles in my shoes.

"Then ask her," rang out the old woman's challenge. "If you're so certain you're not adopted, MacKayla *Lane,* talk to your mother and ask her."

NINETEEN

W hat's on the agenda tonight?" I asked Barrons the moment he stepped into the bookstore. I'd been pacing near the front windows with all the lights blazing, both interior and exterior, watching as night fell beyond the illuminated fortress.

I guess my tone was a little tight, because he raised a brow and looked at me hard. "Is something wrong, Ms. Lane?"

"No. Not at all. I'm fine. I just wanted to know what I have to look forward to tonight," I said. "Robbing somebody we get to let live, or somebody we have to kill." I sounded brittle even to myself, but I wanted to know just how much worse a person I was going to be by tomorrow morning. Every day I looked in the mirror it was getting harder to recognize the woman looking back at me.

Barrons paced a slow circle around me. "Are you sure you're all right, Ms. Lane? You seem a little tense."

I rotated at the center, turning with him. "I'm just ducky," I said.

His eyes narrowed. "Did you find anything at the museum?"

"No."

"Did you search every exhibit?"

"No."

"Why not?"

"I didn't feel like it," I said.

"You didn't feel like it?" For a moment Barrons looked perfectly blank, as if the idea that someone might disobey one of his orders just because they didn't feel like it was even more inconceivable to him than the possibility of human life on Mars.

"I am not your workhorse," I told him. "I have a life, too. At least, I used to. I used to do perfectly normal things like date and go out to eat and see movies and hang out with friends and never once think about vampires or monsters or mobsters. So don't go getting all over my case because you think I haven't performed up to your exacting standards. I don't plan your days for you, do I? Even an OOP-detector needs a break every now and then." I gave him a disgusted look. "You're lucky I'm helping you at all, Barrons."

He closed in on me and didn't stop until I could feel the heat coming off his big, hard body. Until I had to tilt my head back to look up at him, and when I did, I was taken aback by his glittering midnight eyes, the velvety gold of his skin, the sexy curve of his mouth, with that full lower lip that hinted at voluptuous carnal appetites, and the upper one that smacked of self-control and perhaps a bit of cruelty, making me wonder what it would be like—

Whuh. I shook my head sharply, trying to clear it. From my two brief encounters with V'lane, I knew that merely being in the same general vicinity with a death-by-sex Fae caused an extreme hormonal spike in a woman that did not go away until it was released somehow. What V'lane had done to me today had left me so awfully, icily aroused that it had taken more orgasms than I'd thought possible and a long frigid shower to calm me. And now it seemed I hadn't done a good enough job, because I was still suffering residual effects. There was no other way to explain why I was standing there wondering what it would be like to kiss Jericho Barrons.

Fortunately, he chose that moment to open the mouth I'd been finding so disturbingly sexual and begin speaking. His words abruptly restored my perspective.

"You still think you can walk away from this, don't you, Ms. Lane?" he said coolly. "You think this is about finding a book, you think it's about figuring out who killed your sister—but the truth is, your world is going to Hell in a handbasket and you're one of the few people that can do something about it. If the wrong person or thing gets its hands on the *Sinsar Dubh,* you won't be ruing the loss of your rainbow-hued, prettily manicured world, you'll be regretting the end of human life as you know it. How long do you think you'll last in a world where someone like Mallucé, or the Unseelie who's got his Rhino-boy watchdogs stationed all over the city, gets the Dark Book? How long do you think you'll *want* to? This isn't about fun and games, Ms. Lane. This isn't even about life and death. This is about things that are worse than death."

"Do you really think I don't know that?" I snapped. Maybe I hadn't been *talking* about everything he'd just said, but I'd sure been thinking about it. I knew there was a bigger picture going on out there than just what had been happening to me, in my little corner of the world. I'd eaten ketchup-soaked fries and watched the Gray Man destroy a helpless woman and I'd wondered every night since who was falling victim to him now. I'd gotten an up close look at the Many-Mouthed-Thing's many mouths and knew it was out there somewhere, feeding on someone. I'd wondered—if I could jump forward in time a year or two—what Dublin would look like then. I had no doubt the dark territory of the abandoned neighborhood was expanding even as Barrons and I spoke, that somewhere out there another streetlamp had fizzled, emitting a final, weak flicker of light before burning out, and the Shades had instantly slithered in around it and to-morrow, according to Barrons, the city wouldn't even remember that block had ever existed.

Such worries weren't just on my waking mind; they were invading my dreams. Last night I'd had a nightmare in which I'd been floating over a Dublin that was pitch-black except for a single, blazing four-story stronghold in the middle of it. In the sur-real manner of dreams, I'd been both above the city and down inside the store, looking out the front door. So much of Dublin had fallen to darkness that I'd known, even if I'd begun walking the instant the morning sun crested the horizon, I wouldn't be able to make it to another lighted sanctuary before nightfall, and that I was stuck at Barrons Books and Baubles for the rest of my life.

I'd woken up thinking about things like prophetic dreams and apocalypses instead of entertaining my usual blissful early-morning thoughts of what I was going to eat that day and what pretty outfits I might wear.

Oh yes, I knew this was about worse things than death. Like being expected to go on living after your sister was killed. Like watching everything you believed about yourself and the world in general get unveiled as one great big, fat lie. But the big picture going on out there wasn't my problem. I'd come to Dublin to find Alina's killer, get whatever justice I could, then go home, and that's what I still planned to do. O'Bannion was no longer a threat, and maybe out of sight was out of mind for Mallucé. Maybe Barrons could save the city from the Fae. Maybe the Queen—if anything V'lane had said was true—would find the Dark Book without my help just fine, send the Unseelie back to prison, and our world would go back to normal. Maybe after I left, all the evil things hunting the *Sinsar Dubh* would fight themselves to death over it. There were a great many possibilities and none of them had to involve me. I was sick of this place. I wanted out before one more strand of reality unraveled around my ears.

"Then what's with the attitude," Barrons demanded, "and why didn't you finish at the museum?"

"I had a bad day today, okay?" I said coolly, though inside I felt like a volcano about to blow at any moment. "Isn't everybody entitled to one, now and then?"

He searched my face for a long moment, then shrugged. "Fine. Finish up tomorrow."

I rolled my eyes. "So what are we doing tonight?"

He gave me a faint smile. "Tonight, Ms. Lane, you learn how to kill."

I know what you're wondering; I'd be wondering it, too: Did I call my mom?

I'm neither that stupid nor that insensitive. She was still reeling from the shock of Alina's death and I wasn't about to upset her more.

Still, I had to prove the old biddy wrong, so after I left the museum and stopped at a hardware store for a cache of flashlights, I'd made a beeline back to Barrons Books and Baubles so I could call the hospital where I'd been born and lay the old woman's ridiculous claim to rest.

One great thing about small towns is that the people are so much more helpful than they are in big cities. I think it's because they know the person on the other end of the line is somebody they might run into at their kid's softball practice on Tuesday, or at Wednesday night bowling league, or one of the town's many church picnics and festivals.

After being transferred a half a dozen times and

put on hold a few more, I finally got through to the woman in charge of the Records Department, Eugenia Patsy Bell, and she was just as nice as could be. We chatted for a few moments during which I learned I'd gone to high school with her niece, Chandra Bell.

I told her what I was looking for, and she told me yes, they kept both paper and electronic files on every birth in the hospital. I asked if she could find mine and read it to me over the phone. She said she was terribly sorry, she wasn't allowed to do that, but if I could confirm some personal information, she could pull it up right now on her computer, print it off, and get it out to me in the afternoon mail.

I gave her Barrons' address and was just about to hang up, when she asked me to hold on a moment. I sat on the other end of the line, listening to her tap away at her keyboard. She asked me to reconfirm my information twice, and I did so, each time with a growing sense of dread. Then she asked if she could put me on hold one more time while she went and checked the physical files. It was a long hold, and I was glad I'd made the call on the bookstore's phone.

Then Eugenia came back and said—wasn't it just the darnedest thing?—she couldn't explain it, because she knew for certain their records were complete. Their database went all the way back to the early nineteen hundreds and was painstakingly maintained by none other than herself.

And she was so sorry that she couldn't help me, but there was absolutely no record, electronic or otherwise, of a MacKayla Lane born at Christ Hospital twenty-two years ago. And no, she said when I pressed, nothing twenty-four years ago for Alina Lane, either. In fact, there was no record at all of any Lane born at Christ Hospital during the past fifty years.

We couldn't find a single Unseelie.

We walked down street after street, went into pub after pub, but found nothing.

There I was, armed with a Fae-killing spear and a seriously bad attitude, only to be denied the chance to blow off some steam by taking out one of the monsters responsible for turning my life into the mess it was.

Not that I was entirely certain I *could* have taken one of them out. Oh, I was pretty sure my head was in the right place. I just didn't know if my body would perform the way it was supposed to. I was pretty sure I was feeling the same thing a guy must feel before he proves himself in his first fistfight: wondering if he has what it takes to knock out his opponent, or if he'll humiliate himself by swinging like a girl, or worse, miss completely.

"That's why I brought you out tonight," Barrons said, when I told him my concerns. "I'd rather you screw up while I'm with you, so I can manage the situation, than have you attempt your first kill on your own and get yourself killed instead."

I had no idea how prophetic his words would prove. "Just a hard night's work, out protecting your investment, huh?" I said dryly as we exited yet another pub filled with only people, no monsters.

Sarcasm aside, I was glad he was along to save me if I needed saving. I might not trust Barrons, but I'd developed a healthy respect for his ability to "manage" situations. "So, how am I supposed to do it?" I asked. "Is there some trick to this?"

"Just freeze it and stab it, Ms. Lane. But do it fast. If it sifts you somewhere else, I won't be able to save you."

"Is there any particular place I'm supposed to stab it? Assuming, of course, whatever we stumble across has the equivalent of human body parts." Were they like vampires? Was a direct hit to the heart necessary? For that matter, did they even have hearts?

"The gut's always good."

I glanced down at my lavender shirt and short, purple, floral-patterned skirt. The outfit went fabulously with my new darker 'do. "Do they bleed?"

"Some of them. In a manner of speaking, Ms. Lane." He gave me a quick, dark flash of a smile that wasn't nice at all, and I knew right then and there that whatever came out of some of the Unseelie was going to seriously gross me out. "You might try wearing black next time. Then again, we could always just hose you off back at the garage."

I scowled as we stepped into our fourteenth pub of the night. "Don't any of them just poof?" Wasn't that what monsters were supposed to do when you killed them? Disintegrate instantly into dust that promptly scattered on an opportune wind?

"Poof, Ms. Lane?"

The bar we'd just entered featured a live band tonight, and was jam-packed with people. I pushed into the crowd, following Barrons' broad back. "You know, vanish. Remove all need to waste time cleaning up, or explain away inexplicable corpses littering the world," I clarified.

He glanced back at me, one dark brow raised. "Where do you get your ideas?"

I shrugged. "Books and movies. You stake a vampire, it goes poof and disappears."

"Really?" He snorted. "Life is rarely so convenient. The real world is considerably messier." As he moved toward the bar in the center of the pub, he tossed over his shoulder, "And don't trust a stake to work on a vampire, Ms. Lane. You'll be sorely disappointed. Not to mention dead."

"Well, then, how *does* a person kill a vampire?" I asked his back.

"Good question."

Typical Barrons answer—no answer at all. One of these days I was going to corner him with questions and not let him off the hook, one of these days when I didn't have so many other things on my mind. I shook my head and turned my attention to the people around me, searching faces, looking for the one that would waver and run like melting candle wax, and betray the monster within.

This time, I wasn't disappointed. Barrons saw it at the same time I did. "Over by the hearth," he said quietly.

My eyes narrowed and my hands curled into fists. Oh yes, I'd like to kill this one. It would put an end to some of my nightmares. "I see it," I said. "What do I do?"

"Wait until it leaves. We don't fight our battles in public. Dead, its glamour fails. The whole bar would see its true form."

"Well, maybe the whole bar *should* see its true form," I said. "Maybe they should know what's going on and what's out there."

Barrons gave me a look. "Why? So they can fear things they can't do anything to defend themselves against? So they can have nightmares about monsters they can't see coming? Humans are of no use in this battle."

I pressed a hand to my mouth and concentrated on keeping my supper of microwave popcorn down. It felt like it was popping again in my stomach and the bag was about to blow. "I can't stand here and watch this," I said. I didn't know if my sudden nausea was in reaction to the Unseelie, or to the sight of its victim.

"It's almost over, Ms. Lane. He's nearly done. In case you couldn't tell."

Oh, I could tell. The moment I'd spotted the Gray Man and his companion I'd known he was nearly done. The woman the gaunt, nine-foot-tall monster was feeding off had good bones. Model-worthy bones: the kind that make all the difference between a pretty face and an agency-quality one. Me, I have a pretty face. This woman had once been exquisitely beautiful.

Now those great bones were all that was left of her, beneath a veneer of thin, pallid, sagging flesh. And still the ravaged woman was staring up at the leprous Unseelie with worship in her eyes. Even from here I could see the bloodshot jaundice of her whites, from dozens of tiny exploded capillaries. I had no doubt that her teeth had once been pearly, but they were now gray and had a brittle, crumbling appearance. A small, vicious-looking, pus-filled sore had blossomed in the corner of her mouth, and there was another budding on her forehead. As she tossed her head, smiling flirtatiously up at her destruction— in her eyes, a gorgeous blond man—two clumps of her hair fell out, one onto the floor, the other onto the shoe of a man standing behind her. The man glanced down, saw the tuft of scalp and hair on his shoe, and kicked it off his foot with a shudder. He took one look at the Gray Man's victim, grabbed his date's hand, and dragged her off through the crowd like he was fleeing the black plague.

I looked away. I couldn't watch. "I thought it just made them ugly. I thought it didn't feed on them until they died."

"It usually doesn't."

"It's killing her, Barrons! We have to stop it!" Even I heard the edge of hysteria in my voice.

He spun me by my shoulders and shook me. His touch crackled through me like heat lightning. "Get a grip, Ms. Lane! It's too late. We can't do anything for her now. That woman has no hope of recovering from what it has done to her. She's going to die. It's only a question of when. Tonight by the Gray Man, tomorrow by her own hand, or in a few weeks from a severe wasting disease doctors won't be able to identify or arrest by any means known to man."

I stared up at him. "Are you kidding me? You

mean, even if the victim tries to go on with her life to whatever degree she can, she dies in time anyway?"

"If the Gray Man takes it this far, yes. It usually doesn't. It usually leaves its victims alive because it likes to revisit them, to savor their pain for a long time. Occasionally, however, it finds one so beautiful it doesn't seem able to bear that she exists, so it kills her on the spot. At least she'll never have to look at herself in a mirror, Ms. Lane. At least her sojourn in hell will be brief."

"That's supposed to be a comfort?" I cried. "That it will be brief?"

"You underestimate the pricelessness of brevity, Ms. Lane." His eyes were ice, his smile colder. "What are you, all of twenty-one, twenty-two?"

There was a *tinkle* of breaking glass, a dull *thud* like that of a body hitting the floor, and a collective gasp behind me. Barrons looked over my shoulder. His arctic smile faded.

"Oh God, is she dead?" a woman cried.

"It looks like her face is rotting!" a man exclaimed, aghast.

"Now, Ms. Lane," Barrons ordered. "It's on the move. Headed for the door. Go after it. I've got your back."

I tried to glance over my shoulder. I don't know if I wanted to make sure the woman was really no longer suffering, or if there's just some innate human instinct to look at dead people—it would certainly explain our funeral practices, not to mention all those rubberneckers clogging up the roads around Atlanta at the scenes of traffic accidents. But Barrons caught my chin in his hand and forced me to look straight into his eyes. "Don't," he barked. "The dead ones stick in your memory. Just go kill the fuck that did it."

Sounded like good advice to me. We left the pub.

I followed the Gray Man and Barrons followed me, a dozen paces behind. The last time I'd seen this Unseelie, I'd had long blonde hair. I doubted it would recognize me with my new look. It didn't know I was a *sidhe*-seer or a Null, or that I had the spear, so I figured my odds of killing were high, if I could get close enough.

Getting close enough, however, was going to be the problem. Inhumanly tall, it was also inhumanly fast. I was already sprinting to keep pace with it. In order to catch it, I was going to have to break into a run. It's a little hard to sneak up on an enemy at a full gallop, especially in heels.

"It's getting away, Ms. Lane," Barrons growled behind me.

"Do you think I don't know that?" I snapped. It was nearly halfway down the block and seemed to have suddenly amped up its glamour-repellent; pedestrians were scattering in its wake, detouring wide, out into the street. Abruptly, I had a clear view of it down the sidewalk, which was not good. I could hardly shadow something without any camouflage between us. I was going to have to make a dash for it.

It stopped, turned around, and looked straight at me.

I froze. I had no idea how it knew, but it knew I knew, and I knew it, and there was no point in faking.

"Bloody hell!" I heard Barrons curse softly, followed by the scrape of steel on stone, the rustle of fabric, then silence behind me.

We stared at each other, the Gray Man and I. Then it smiled with that awful mouth that used up half its tall, thin face. "I see you, *sidhe*-seer," it said. Its laugh was the sound of cockroaches scuttling over dried leaves. "I saw you in the bar. How do you want to die?" It laughed again. "Slow or slower?"

I wished I'd thought to ask Barrons earlier if my suspicion about the strange word the old woman had used today was correct. I was pretty sure from the context she'd used it in that I'd gotten the gist of it, but there was only one way to find out. I wet my lips, batted my eyes, and praying I was right, said breathlessly, "Whatever you wish, Master. I am *Pri-ya*."

The Gray Man sucked in a long, hissing breath that showed shark teeth in its lipless mouth. Its mocking amusement faded and its black eyes gleamed with sudden interest that married sexual excitement to homicidal sadism in a way that chilled me to the bone.

I bit my tongue to keep from betraying my revulsion. I was right. *Pri-ya* meant something along the lines of Fae-addict or Fae-whore. I would ask Barrons for an exact definition when this was over. Right now, I had to get closer to it. The Gray Man might have somehow clued into me watching it, but it didn't know I was a Null, or that I had a weapon capable of killing it.

There was no mistaking that it wanted what it thought I was offering, wanted it enough to believe I was the real deal. This was its weakness, I realized, its Achilles' heel. It could steal beauty, it could cast a glamour to make even the most beautiful human woman desire it, but it would never be desired in its true form and it knew it.

Except...maybe...by one who was *Pri-ya*. A woman that was Fae-struck, Fae-blind, a whore for anything Seelie or Unseelie. Such sick devotion would be the closest thing to true attraction this monster could ever know.

It rubbed its leprous hands together and leered. At least, unlike the Many-Mouthed-Thing, it only had one mouth to leer with. "On your knees, *Pri-ya*," it said.

I wondered what the deal was with Fae liking women on their knees. Did they all have worship fetishes? I pasted a smile on my lips like the one I'd seen on the blankly compliant face of the Goth-girl at Mallucé's, and sank to the sidewalk, bare knees to cold stone. I could no longer hear Barrons or anyone else on the street behind me. I had no idea where everyone had gone. It looked like the Gray Man's glamour-repellent was on a par with V'lane's.

My purse was unzipped, my hands ready. If it would just stay frozen half as long as the Many-Mouthed-Thing, I'd have more than enough time to kill it. Once it approached, it was dead.

It could have worked that way, it *should* have worked that way, but I made a critical error. What can I say? It was my first time. My expectations weren't in line with reality. It had walked down the street and I expected it to walk back.

It didn't.

It *sifted* back.

It had me, one yellow-taloned hand in my hair, before I even knew what was happening. Inhumanly strong, it jerked me up off the ground, its gray fist tight to my scalp.

Fortunately, my *sidhe*-seer instincts kicked in and I slammed both hands into its chest as it lifted me into the air.

Unfortunately, it froze exactly like that, with its hand in my hair, and me dangling. Fact of some significance: I have arms of normal human length. My spear was in my purse. My purse was on the sidewalk, a foot below my feet.

"Barrons," I hissed desperately. "Where are you?"

"Unbelievable," a dry voice said above me. "Of all the potential scenarios I'd envisioned, this was not one of them."

I tried to look up but aborted the painful effort and clamped both my hands to my head instead. What was he doing on the roof? For that matter, *how* had he gotten on the roof? I didn't recall passing any convenient ladders. And wasn't that building two stories high? "Hurry, it hurts!" I cried. I knew how lucky I was that he was there. If I'd gotten into this predicament by myself, I would have had to tear the hair out of my skull to escape, and frankly, I wasn't sure that could even be done. I have really strong hair and it was holding a huge handful of it. "Come on, hurry! Get my purse! I don't know how long it'll stay frozen."

Barrons dropped to the sidewalk in front of me

with a soft *thud* of boots hitting stone, his long black coat billowing out around him. "You probably should have thought about that before you froze it, Ms. Lane," he said coolly.

Hanging as I was put me eye-to-eye with him. I transferred my grip from my scalp to the Gray Man's immobilized arm and used all my strength to take some of the weight off my hair. "Can we talk about this *after* you've gotten me down?" I gritted.

He crossed his arms over his chest. "You wouldn't be having an after if I weren't here to save you. Let's talk about where you went wrong, shall we?"

It wasn't a question, but I tried to answer it anyway. "I'd rather not just now."

"One: It was obvious you didn't expect it to sift in on you and you weren't prepared for it. Your spear was down at your side. Your purse should have been up and you should have been ready to stab the Gray Man through it."

"Okay, I messed up. Can I have my purse now?"

"Two: You let go of your weapon. Never let go of your weapon. I don't care if you have to wear fat-clothes and strap it to your body beneath them. *Never* let go of your weapon."

I nodded, but not really. I couldn't move my head that much. "Got it. Had it the first time you said it. Now can I have my purse?"

"Three: You didn't think before you acted. Your greatest advantage in any one-on-one battle with a Fae is that it doesn't know you're a Null. Unfortunately, this one does now."

He retrieved my purse—*finally*—and I reached

for it with both hands but he held it beyond my grasp. I clamped my hands back on the Gray Man's arm. I was getting a headache the size of Texas. I tried to kick him but he sidestepped it easily. Jericho Barrons had those kind of flawless reflexes that I've only ever seen before in professional athletes. Or animals.

"*Never* freeze a Fae, Ms. Lane, unless you are absolutely, one-hundred-percent sure you can kill it before it unfreezes again. Because this one"—he tapped the rigid Unseelie coat hanger upon which I was draped—"is perfectly conscious even though it's frozen, and the very instant it unfreezes it's going to sift out with you. You'll be gone before your brain even manages to process that it *has* unfrozen. Depending on where it takes you—you might materialize surrounded by dozens of its kind—you will be there, your spear will be here, and I won't have any idea where to begin looking—"

"Oh, for God's sake, Barrons," I exploded, kicking wildly in midair, "enough already! Will you just *shut up* and give me my purse?"

Barrons glanced down at the spear, which was half-poking out of my purse, and plucked the ball of foil from the lethal tip. Then he leaned forward and got right in my face. Up close I could see how truly furious he was with me. The corners of his mouth and rims of his nostrils were white, and his dark eyes burned with anger. "Never get separated from this thing again. Do you understand me, Ms. Lane? You will eat with it, shower with it, sleep with it, fuck with it."

I opened my mouth to tell him not only didn't I have anyone I was currently doing that last thing with, I never called it that, and didn't appreciate him calling it that, when my perspective changed abruptly. I'm not sure if the Gray Man began moving before Barrons stabbed it in the gut, or after, but something wet suddenly sprayed me, and it let go of my hair. I fell to my knees and got a face full of sidewalk.

The Gray Man slumped next to me. I instantly backed away on my hands and knees. A deep wound in its abdomen oozed the same grayish-green stuff that I was revolted to discover was also on my shirt, my skirt, and my bare legs. The Unseelie looked from Barrons to the spearhead—half-wrapped in what *used* to be my favorite purse, and might still have been if not for the slime dripping all over it—its eyes blazing with disbelief, hatred, and rage.

Though its wrath was for Barrons, it swung its head around and the last words it uttered were for me. "The Lord Master is back, you stupid bitch, and he's going to do the same thing to you he did to the last pretty little *sidhe*-seer. You'll *wish* you'd died at my hands. You'll beg for death the same way she did."

A few moments later, when Barrons gave me my purse back, even though I knew it was already dead, I pulled out the spear and stabbed it again anyway.

TWENTY

In the year since the day I got on a plane to fly to Dublin, determined to find my sister's killer and bring him to justice, I've learned that you can discover just as much from what people don't say to you, as what they do.

It's not enough to listen to their words. You have to mine their silences for buried ore. It's often only in the lies we refuse to speak that any truth can be heard at all.

Barrons disposed of the Gray Man's body that night—I didn't ask how. I just went back to the bookstore, took the longest, hottest shower of my life, and scrubbed my hair three times. Yes, I took the spear into the shower with me. I'd learned my lesson.

The next day, I finished up at the museum without incident. No V'lane, no old woman, and not a single OOP in the entire place.

For the first time since I'd been staying at the bookstore, Barrons didn't make an appearance that night. I guessed he must have slipped out while I was upstairs, answering e-mails on my laptop. It was a Saturday, so I thought he might have a date and wondered where a man like him went on one. I couldn't see him doing the movie-and-dinner routine. I wondered what kind of woman he went out with, then remembered the one from *Casa Blanc*. Out of sheer boredom, I imagined them having sex, but when the woman began looking more and more like me, I decided there were wiser ways to kill time.

I spent the evening watching old movies by myself on a small TV that Fiona kept behind the counter in the bookstore, trying not to stare at the phone, or think too much.

By Sunday morning, I was a wreck. Alone with too many questions and no one to talk to, I did what I'd sworn I wouldn't do.

I called home.

Dad answered, as he had every time I'd called from Ireland. "Hi," I said brightly, crossing my legs and twirling the phone cord around my finger. I was sitting on the comfy couch in the rear conversation area of the bookstore. "How's it going?"

We chatted halfheartedly for several minutes about the weather in Georgia and the weather in Dublin, before moving on to comparing and contrasting the food in Georgia to the food in Dublin, then he launched into a rambling diatribe that supposedly linked climates with high per-annum rainfall to dour personalities and, just when I was thinking he'd surely exhausted his run of banality and we could begin a real conversation, he started in on one of his favorite filler topics about which he'd been known to pontificate for hours: the ever-fluctuating price of gas in America and the role the president was playing in our current economic woes.

I almost burst into tears.

Was this what we'd come to—stilted conversation between strangers? For twenty-two years this man had been my rock, my skinned-knee-kisser, my Little League coach, my fellow sports-car enthusiast, my teacher, and—although I knew I'd never been the most ambitious daughter—I hoped he counted me among his pride and joys. He'd lost a daughter and I'd lost a sister; couldn't we manage to comfort each other somehow?

I fidgeted with the phone cord, hoping he'd wind down but he didn't, and finally, I could wait no longer. I wasn't going to get anywhere with him. "Dad, can I talk to Mom?" I interrupted.

I got his canned reply: She was sleeping and he didn't want to disturb her because she so rarely did anything but toss and turn, despite all the medication she was on, and the doctor had said only time and rest could help her heal, and he wanted his wife back, and didn't I want my mother? So we should both let her rest.

"I *need* to talk to Mom," I insisted.

There was no budging him. I think I get my stubbornness from him. We both dig our heels in and sprout roots if somebody tries to push us. "Is something wrong with her that you're not telling me?" I asked.

He sighed and it was such a sad, deeply exhausted sound that I suddenly knew if I saw him right now, he would look like he'd aged ten years in the two weeks since I'd left. "She's a little out of her head with grief, Mac. She blames herself for what happened to Alina and there's no reasoning with her about it," he said.

"How could she possibly blame herself for Alina's death?" I exclaimed.

"Because she let her go to Ireland in the first place," he said tiredly, and I could tell it was a conversation he'd had with her a dozen times but made no headway. Maybe I get my stubbornness from both sides. Mom digs in, too.

"That's ridiculous. That's like saying if I decided to take a cab somewhere and the cab wrecked, it was your fault. It was my choice to take the cab. You couldn't know something would go wrong and neither could Mom."

"Unless somebody warned us in the first place," he said in a voice so low that I nearly missed it, and then I wasn't sure I'd heard him right.

"Huh?" I said. "What did you say? Did somebody tell you not to let Alina go to Ireland? Oh, Dad, people are always full of gloom and doom! Everybody's a prophet in retrospect. You can't listen to them!" Though I love Ashford, we have our share of busybodies, and I could just see some of the nosier and less-kind inhabitants of the town gossiping in the grocery store, and not quietly, when my parents went by. Saying snide things like, *Well, what did they expect—sending their daughter four thousand miles away by herself, anyway?*

Right on cue, Dad said, "What kind of parents let their daughter go four thousand miles away from home by herself?"

"All *kinds* of parents let their kids study abroad," I protested. "You can't blame yourselves."

"And now you're gone, too. Come home, Mac. Don't you like it here? Wasn't it good? We always thought you and your sister were happy here," he said.

"We were!" I exclaimed. "I was! Then Alina got killed!"

There was a weighty silence that I spent most of wishing I'd kept my big, fat mouth shut, then he said, "Let it go, Mac. Just walk away. Let it go."

"What?" I was stunned. How could he say that? "You mean, come home and let the monster who did this to Alina just get away with it? Go on walking around out there to kill someone else's daughter next?"

"I don't give a grand, glorious *shit* about anyone else's daughter!"

I flinched. In my entire life, I'd never heard my father cuss. If he did so at all, he did it in private, or beneath his breath.

"I care about *mine*. Alina is dead. You're not. Your mother needs you. *I* need you. Get on a plane. Pack up right now and come home, Mac!"

I swear, I prefaced it a thousand different ways in my head; from a several sentence buildup, to a five-minute explanation and apology for what I was about to ask, but none of it came out. I opened my mouth, it stayed open, and I merely managed to breathe into the phone as I thought about all the things I could or should say, including just shutting up and never asking.

I was in sixth grade when I learned about things like brown eyes and blue eyes, about dominant and recessive genes and what kind of parents make what kind of babies and then went home that night to look really hard at my mom and dad. I'd said nothing because Alina had green eyes just like me, so we were obviously family, and I've always had ostrich tendencies; if I can wedge my head far enough down into the sand that I can't see whatever's staring at me, then it can't see me, either, and no matter how people try to dispute it, perception *is* reality. It's what you choose to believe that makes you the person you are. Eleven years ago, I chose to be a happy daughter in a happy family. I chose to fit, to belong, to feel safe and cherished right down to my deep, strong, proud southern roots. I chose to believe DNA theory was wrong. I chose to believe teachers didn't always know what they were talking about and scientists might never understand all there was to know about the complexities of human physiology. I'd never discussed it with anyone. I'd never had to. I knew what I thought and that was enough. I'd barely squeaked by with a *D* in my high-school science requirement and I'd never taken another biology course since.

"Dad, was I adopted?" I said.

There was a soft explosion of air on the other end of the line, as if someone had hit Jack Lane in the stomach with a baseball bat.

Say no, Daddy, say no, Daddy, say no.

The silence stretched.

I squeezed my eyes shut against the burn of tears. "Please, say something."

There was another long, terrible silence, punctuated by a bone-deep sigh. "Mac, I can't leave your mother right now. She can't be alone. She's too heavily medicated and unstable. After you left for Dublin, she...well, she just...fell apart. The best thing you can do right now for all of us is come home. Now. Tonight." He paused, then said carefully, "Baby, you are our daughter in every way."

"Really?" My voice was kind of squeaky in the back of my throat. "Like birth? Am I your daughter that way too, Daddy?" I opened my eyes but they wouldn't focus properly.

"Stop it, Mac! I don't know where this came from! What are you doing, bringing something like this up now? Come home!"

"It doesn't matter where it came from. It matters where it's going. Tell me Alina and I weren't adopted, Daddy," I insisted. "Tell me that. Say it! Just say those words and we can end this conversation. That's all you need to say. Alina and I weren't adopted. Say it. Unless you can't."

There was another of those horrid, horrid silences. Then he said, "Mac, baby, we love you. Come *home*." His deep, usually strong baritone cracked on the last word. He cleared his throat and when he spoke again he was using his in-control tax-attorney voice that conveyed years of expertise coupled with the bone-deep assurance that you could trust him to know what was best. Calm, confident, powerful, backed by six feet two inches of self-assured, strong southern man, it used to work on me. "Look, I'm booking a flight for you the second we hang up, Mac. Go pack your bags right now and get yourself to the airport. I don't want you to do or think about anything. Don't even check out. I'll take care of any bills you have over the phone. Do you hear me? I'm going to call you back and tell you what flight you're on. Pack and go. Do you *hear* me?"

I stared out the window. It had begun to rain. There it was: the lie he refused to speak. If we hadn't been adopted, Dad would have told me that without hesitation. He would have laughed and said, "Of course you weren't adopted, you goon." And we would both think it was funny that I could be so stupid. But he wouldn't say it, because he couldn't. "God, Daddy, who *am* I?" It was my turn for my voice to crack.

"My daughter," he said fiercely into the phone. "That's who you are! Rainey and Jack Lane's baby girl!"

But I wasn't, really. Not by birth. And we both knew it. And I guess some part of me had sort of known it all along.

1. *Fairies exist.*
2. *Vampires are real.*

3. *A mobster and fifteen of his henchmen are dead because of me.*
4. *I'm adopted.*

I stared down at the journal that would soon be full, ignoring the wet splash of tears that was making the ink run on the page.

Of the four things I'd listed, only one of them had the power to cut me off at the knees. I could wrap my brain around any weirdness, realign myself to any new reality, except for one.

I'm adopted.

I could deal with fairies and vampires and I could live with blood on my hands, so long as I could stand and proudly say, *I'm MacKayla Lane, you know, from the Frye-Lanes in Ashford, Georgia? And I follow the same genetic recipe as everyone else in my family. We're yellow cake with chocolate frosting, all of us, from great-grandparent down to the tiniest tot. I fit with them. I belong somewhere.*

You have no idea how important that is, how deeply reassuring, until you lose it. All my life, up until that moment, I'd had a warm, protective blanket wrapped around me, knitted of aunts and uncles, purled of first and second and third cousins, knot-tied with grandmas and grandpas and greats.

That blanket had just dropped from my shoulders. I felt cold, lost and alone.

O'Connor, the old woman had called me. She'd said I had their skin and eyes. She'd mentioned a name, an odd name: Patrona. *Was* I an O'Connor? Did I have relatives somewhere in Ireland? Why hadn't I been kept? Why had Alina and I been given up? Where had Mom and Dad gotten us? When? And how had all my talkative, chatty, gossipy aunts, uncles, and grandparents kept such a conspiracy silent? Not one of them had ever slipped. How young had we been when we were adopted? I must have barely been born, because I had no memories of any other life, nor had Alina ever mentioned a thing. Since she was two years older than me, it stood to reason she would have been the one with anachronistic recall. Or would her memories of another life and place simply have blurred into our new life and merged seamlessly over time?

I'm adopted. The thought had me whirling, rootless, in a tornado, and still that wasn't quite the worst of it.

The part that really bit, the part that had its teeth in me and wouldn't let go, was that the only person I knew for a fact I'd been related to was dead. My sister. Alina. My only blood relative in the world, and she was gone.

I was stricken by an awful thought: Had she known? Had she found out we were adopted and not told me? Was this one of the things she'd meant by, *There are so many things I should have told you?*

Had she been here in Dublin, like me right now, feeling this confused and disconnected?

"Oh God," I said, and my tears turned to great shuddering, hurtful sobs. I wept for me, for my sister, for things I couldn't even begin to put into words, and might never be able to explain. But it felt something like this: I used to walk on my feet. Now all I knew how to do was crawl. And I wasn't sure how long it was going to take for me to get up off my knees and regain my balance, but I suspected that when I did, I would never walk the same way again.

I don't know how long I sat there and cried, but eventually my head was pounding too hard for me to weep anymore.

I told you back at the beginning of this story that Alina's body had turned up miles away from The Clarin House, in a trash-filled alley on the opposite side of the River Liffey. That I knew exactly where because I'd seen the crime-scene photos, and that before I left Ireland I would end up in that alley myself, saying good-bye to her.

I dragged myself up off the couch, went to my borrowed bedroom, stuffed money and my passport in my jeans pocket so nothing would interfere with a swift extraction of the contents of my purse, slung it over my shoulder, yanked a ball cap down over my eyes, jammed on sunglasses, and went outside to flag down a cab.

It was time to go to that alley. But not to say good-bye—to say hello to a sister I'd never known and never would: the Alina that was my only true kin, the one who'd been tempered in Dublin's forge, who'd learned hard lessons and made hard choices. If, after all her months here, she'd stumbled across even half of what I had, I understood why she'd done everything she'd done.

I remember that Mom and Dad had tried to visit Alina on two occasions. Both times, she'd refused.

The first time she'd said she was sick and terribly behind on classes. The second time she'd used a punishing round of exams as an excuse. She'd never once invited me to fly over, and the one time I'd talked about trying to save up the money, she'd instantly told me not to waste it, but to spend it on pretty clothes and new music and go out dancing for her—a thing we used to love to do together— while she studied, and before I knew it she'd be home.

I understood now what those words must have cost her.

Knowing what I knew was out there stalking and slithering along Dublin's streets, would I have permitted anyone I loved to come over here and see me?

Never. I'd have lied through my teeth to keep them away.

If I'd had a baby sister that was my only blood relative, safe at home, would I have told her about any of this and risked dragging her into it? No. I would have done exactly what Alina had done: protected her to my dying breath. Kept her happy and whole as long as I could.

I'd always looked up to my sister, but now I had a whole new appreciation for her. Gripped by it, I needed to be somewhere I knew she'd been. Some place imprinted by her, and her apartment didn't fit the bill. Aside from the scent of peaches and Beautiful perfume, I'd never gotten a very strong sense of her there, as if she'd not spent much time in it, except when talking to me on the phone or sleeping. I'd gotten no real feeling for her on campus, either, but I could think of one place I knew I'd feel her intensely.

I needed to go where she'd been run to ground, four hours after she'd called me. I needed to confront the final awful grief of standing in the same spot on the cobbled pavement where my sister had drawn her last breath and closed her eyes forever.

Morbid, maybe, but *you* lose a sister and find out you're adopted and see what you feel compelled to do. Don't accuse me of being morbid when I'm merely the product of a culture that buries the bones of the ones they love in pretty, manicured flower gardens so they can keep them nearby and go talk to them whenever they feel troubled or depressed. *That's* morbid. Not to mention bizarre. Dogs bury bones, too.

I see lines of demarcation everywhere I turn now. The River Liffey is one of them, dividing the city, not merely north and south, but socially and economically as well.

The south is the side I've been staying on, with the Temple Bar District, Trinity College, The National Museum, and Leinster House to name but a few of its many attractions, and is generally considered the affluent side: rich, snobby, and liberal.

The northside has O'Connell Street with its fine statues and monuments, the Moore Street Market, St. Mary's Pro-Cathedral, the Customs House overlooking the Liffey, and is generally held to be the home of the working-class: industrial, blue-collar, and poor.

As you'll find with most divisionary boundaries, it's not absolute. There are pockets of the opposite on each side of the river: wealth and fashion to the north, poverty and decay to the south; however, no one will argue that the overall *feel* of the southside is different than the northside and vice versa. It's hard to explain to someone who hasn't spent time on opposing banks of the river, heard the talk and watched the walk.

The cabbie that drove me to the northside didn't seem real happy about dropping me on Allen Street by myself, but I tipped him handsomely and he went away. I'd seen too many truly scary things lately for a rundown neighborhood to have much of an impact on me, at least not in the daytime, anyway.

The dead-end alley in which Alina's body had been found didn't have a name, was cobbled in the old way, with stone that time and weather had heaved and cracked, and stretched a good several hundred yards back from the road. Trash cans and Dumpsters were wedged between windowless brick walls of a decaying subsidized-income tenement building on the right and a boarded-up warehouse on the left. Old newspapers, cardboard boxes, beer bottles, and debris littered the alleyway. The ambience was similar to that of the abandoned neighborhood. I had no intention of remaining in the area long enough to find out if the streetlamps still worked.

Dad didn't know I'd seen the crime-scene photos he'd tucked beneath the blue-and-silver folder containing the financial plan he'd been working on for Ms. Myrna Taylor-Hollingsworth. In fact, I had no idea how *he'd* gotten them. I was under the impression the police didn't ordinarily release such things to grief-crazed parents, especially not shots so graphic and gruesome.

Identifying her body had been bad enough. I'd found those pictures the day before I'd left for Ireland, when I'd gone into his office to swipe a stash of pens.

Now, as I walked to the end of the alley, I was seeing the photos superimposed on the scene. She'd been lying just *there*, to my right, a dozen feet away from the twelve-foot brick wall that cut off the alley and had aborted her run. I didn't want to know if bits of her fingernails were broken off in those bricks from a frantic attempt to climb the sheer face and escape whatever had been pursuing her, so I looked away, down at the spot where she'd died. They'd found her slumped back against the brick wall. I'll spare you the details I wish I didn't know.

Driven by some awful darkness inside me, I dropped down onto the dirty cobblestones and slumped into the exact position in which my sister had been found. Unlike in the pictures, there was no blood splashing the stones and brick walls. Rain had washed away all signs of her struggle weeks ago. Here she'd taken her last breath. Here all of Alina Lane's hopes and dreams had died.

"God, I miss you *so much*, Alina!" I felt every bit

as brittle as I sounded, and once more the tears came. I swore it would be the last time I cried. And it would be, for quite some time.

I don't know how long I sat there before I noticed the cosmetic pack Mom had given Alina for Christmas, half-buried beneath the trash. Twin to the one I'd had to abandon at Mallucé's, the tiny quilted gold bag had been badly weathered, bleached by the sun and soaked by rain. I pushed aside old newspapers, picked it up, and cradled it in my hands.

I know what you're thinking. I thought it, too—that there would surely be a clue in it. That Alina had tucked away some clever reduction of her entire journal or some sophisticated little computer chip that held all the information I needed to know, and miraculously the police had overlooked it and serendipity had steered me to this alley at just the right moment to find it.

Life is rarely so convenient, as Barrons would say. We've all seen too many movies, I would say.

There was nothing inside the battered pack except for the items Mom had chosen for us, minus the tiny metal fingernail file. Nothing in the lining, nothing tucked away in a compact or lipstick. I know, because I practically ripped everything apart looking for it.

I won't burden you with my thoughts of Alina as I sat there, or the grieving I did. If you've lost someone, then you know what kind of things go through your head and need no reminder from me. If you've not yet lost someone—good—I hope it's a small eternity before you do.

I said good-bye and I said hello, and as I was pushing myself up to go, my eye was caught by the silvery glint of metal near my feet. It was the tip of Alina's fingernail file, badly scraped and dented. I bent and pushed aside the trash to retrieve it, not about to leave one bit of her behind, and sucked in a sharp breath of disbelief.

I'd comforted myself with the hope that Alina had died quickly. That she hadn't laid in that alley alone, bleeding to death for a long time. But she couldn't have died too quickly, because she'd used her fingernail file to gouge something into the stone.

I knelt on the pavement and brushed away the trash, then blew off the dust and grime.

I was both disappointed and grateful she hadn't written more. Disappointed because I needed some major help here. Grateful because it meant she'd died in minutes, not hours.

1247 LaRuhe, Jr. was all it said.

TWENTY-ONE

I nspector O'Duffy, please," I said briskly. I'd snatched up the phone as soon as I'd let myself into Barrons Books and Baubles and rung up the Pearse Street Garda Station. "Yes, yes, I can hold." I drummed my fingers impatiently on the cashier's counter at Fiona's station while I waited for the duty officer on the other end of the line to transfer my call to the detective who'd handled Alina's case.

I had another clue for him and this one was etched in stone: 1247 LaRuhe. I was going with him when he went to check it out, and if he wouldn't let me, then I'd just have to tail him. Surely with all the slinking around in the shadows I'd been doing lately, I'd acquired a measure of stealth.

"Yes, Ms. Lane?" The detective sounded harried when he picked up, so I explained quickly where I'd been and what I'd found. "We've been over this," he said when I was done.

"Who's been over what?" I asked.

"The address," he said. "First, there's nothing to prove she wrote that. Anyone might have—"

"Inspector, Alina called me Junior," I interrupted. "And her fingernail file was right there at the scene, dented and scarred from gouging at the stone. Even without knowing the significance of 'Jr.,' I'm surprised one of your people didn't find it and put two and two together." Not to mention the cosmetic pack. Hadn't they examined the scene at all?

"We saw the address, Ms. Lane, but by the time we were notified of the body, the scene had been contaminated by onlookers. If you were just there yourself, you saw how much trash is in that alley. We could hardly catalogue everything on the pavement. We had no way of knowing if anything in the area originated inside her purse."

"Well, didn't you think it a little odd there was an address gouged in stone right next to her body?" I demanded.

"Of course we did."

"So? Did you track it down? Did you go there?" I asked impatiently.

"Couldn't, Ms. Lane. It doesn't exist. There *is* no 1247 LaRuhe in Dublin. Not an avenue, street, boulevard, or lane. Not even an alley named that."

I bit the inside of my lip, thinking. "Well, maybe it's outside of Dublin. Maybe it's in another city nearby."

"We tried that, too. We were unable to find any such address, anywhere in Ireland. We even tried variations of the spelling from Laroux to something as simple as La Rue. No 1247 anywhere."

"Well, maybe it's in...London or something," I persisted. "Did you check out other cities?"

Inspector O'Duffy sighed deeply and I could picture him on the other end of the line, shaking his head. "Just how many countries do you think we should search, Ms. Lane?" he asked.

I took a breath and let it out slowly, biting my tongue on: *However many you need to in order to find my sister's killer. I don't care if it's a thousand.*

When I didn't reply, he said, "We sent her file to Interpol. If they'd found anything, they'd have notified us by now. I'm sorry, but there's nothing else we can do."

Armed with spear and flashlights, I hurried down the darkening streets to a gift shop/café in the Temple Bar District that offered a wide selection of maps, ranging from beautifully laminated close-ups of Dublin to detailed spreads of Ireland, to the equivalent of Rand McNally road map books. I bought one of each, tossed in England and Scotland for good measure, then went back to my borrowed bedroom and, as full night fell, sat cross-legged on the bed and began searching. A foreign country's *Gardai* couldn't be half as motivated as a vengeance-hungry sister.

It was nearly midnight before I stopped, and then only because five hours of squinting at tiny print had turned the pounding of my earlier headache

into an all-out attack on my skull with small jackhammers. I'd found many variations of LaRuhe, but
none at 1247, or 1347, or even 1427, or any other
number that seemed close enough that Alina might
have made a mistake, not that I believed she had.
She'd carved out a message with her dying breath
and I just couldn't see her getting it wrong. There
was something here, something I was missing.

I massaged my temples gently. Headaches aren't
a common thing for me, but when I do get one, it's
usually a killer and leaves me drained the next day. I
folded the maps and stacked them on the floor next
to my bed. Barrons might know, I decided. Barrons
seemed to know everything. I would ask him tomorrow. Right now I needed to uncramp my legs
and try to get some sleep.

I stood, stretched gingerly, then padded over to
the window, pushed the drape aside, and stared out
into the night.

There was Dublin, a sea of rooftops. Down in
those streets was a world I'd never imagined.

There was the darkness of the abandoned neighborhood. I wondered if I'd still be looking out this
window in a month—God, I hoped not!—and if so,
would the darkness have spread?

There sat three of the four cars of the O'Bannion
entourage. Someone had taken the Maybach and
closed the doors of the others. All sixteen piles of
clothing were still there. I was really going to have
to do something about them. To someone in the
know, it was the same thing as staring out the window at sixteen corpses.

There were the Shades, those lethal little bastards, moving around down in the alley at the edge of the Dark Zone, pulsing at the perimeter as if angry at Barrons for keeping them at bay with his toxic barrier of light.

I gasped.

And *there* was the man himself: stepping into the abandoned neighborhood, moving from the safety of his floodlights into complete darkness.

And he didn't have a flashlight!

I raised my hand to knock on the windowpane. I don't know what I was thinking, I guess to get his attention and call him back before he did something stupid.

Then I paused, my knuckles half an inch from the glass. Barrons was *anything* but stupid. He did nothing without a reason.

Tall, dark, and graceful as a midnight panther, he wore unrelieved black beneath his long black coat, and as he walked, I caught the glint of steel on his boots. Then even that was gone, absent the light to reflect it, and he was just a lighter shadow in the shadows.

You must never, Ms. Lane, ever enter the abandoned neighborhood at night, he'd said not so long ago.

Okay, then why was he? What was going on? I shook my head and paid for it instantly, as tiny jackhammers fell over, then righted themselves and renewed their attack with vigor: *rat-a-tat-tat-TAT-TAT!* I clutched my skull and stared down uncomprehendingly.

The Shades weren't paying Barrons the slightest

bit of attention. In fact, if I were a woman given to fancy, I would have said the oily darknesses actually peeled back with distaste as Jericho Barrons passed by.

I'd seen the husks the Shades left. I'd seen the evidence of their voracious appetite. The only thing they feared was light. *They kill with vampiric swiftness*, Barrons had told me. I'd written that in my journal, appreciating the phrase.

I watched him move deeper into the abandoned neighborhood, black on black, until he and the night became one. I stared blankly down the alley after him for a long time after he'd gone, trying to make sense of what I'd just seen.

There were really only two possibilities I could think of: either Barrons was lying to me about the Shades, or he'd struck some kind of dark bargain with the life-sucking Fae.

Whichever it was, I finally had my answer to whether or not I could trust him.

That would be a great, big NOT.

When I finally turned away, brushed my teeth, flossed, washed my face, moisturized, ran a brush through my hair, slipped on my favorite sleep shirt and matching panties, and crawled beneath the covers, I wasn't sure of much, but I did know this: I wasn't going to be asking Barrons any questions about addresses tomorrow.

I woke up the next morning with the answer burning in my brain.

Years ago, in some book I'd read, the author had postulated that the human mind was little different from a computer, and that one of the primary functions of sleep was downtime to integrate new program files, run backup subroutines, defrag, and dump minutiae so we could start fresh the next day.

While I'd slept, my subconscious had attended to my consciousness' dreck, determining data or detritus, dispatching it accordingly, allowing me to see what I would have seen much sooner if I had not been blinded by inner chaos. I would have slapped myself in the forehead if I hadn't been in that delicate just-recovered-from-a-headache state.

I scrambled from bed—I didn't need to turn on a light, I slept with every one of them lit, and would for years to come—and picked up map after map, examining the copyright date. Each was current, as any good tourist map would be, compiled from information collected over the past year.

But Barrons had told me the city had "forgotten" one entire section existed—the abandoned neighborhood. That no district of the *Garda* would claim it, that city utilities would contend no such addresses existed. Did that mean there were streets in Dublin nobody remembered anymore? And if so, had they "fallen off the map," so to speak?

If I were to examine another map—say, one from five years ago—would the Dublin preserved in shamrock-embossed laminate look identical to the one I had now? Or would parts of it be missing?

Could it be the answer I was looking for had been

staring me in the face all the while from just the other side of my windowpane?

"Bingo!" I stabbed the map with the fuchsia tip of my favorite pen. "There you are!"

I'd just found LaRuhe Street, and—as I'd suspected—it was deep in the abandoned neighborhood.

Last night, when I'd needed a map, I'd gone automaton-like to the first place I remembered seeing a prominent display. It hadn't occurred to me that Barrons would have some in the bookstore. Up on the third floor I'd found a large collection of atlases and maps, gathered up a dozen or so, and toted them down to my favorite sofa to begin my search all over again.

What I'd discovered shocked and horrified me. The Dark Zone abutting Barrons' wasn't the only part of Dublin that was missing. There were two other areas, which had existed on maps in previous years, that did not exist on any of them now. They were considerably smaller, and on the outskirts, but there was no doubt in my mind that they were areas that had become Shade-infested, too.

Like a cancer, the life-sucking Unseelie were spreading. I couldn't begin to guess how they'd gotten all the way out in those nearly rural areas, but then I couldn't begin to guess how they'd gotten here in the city, either. Perhaps someone had transported them from one place to the next, unknowing, like roaches in a cardboard box. Or perhaps...I had a terrible thought...was that the basis for Barrons' truce with the parasites? Did he take them to new feeding grounds in exchange for safe passage? Were they sentient enough to make and keep bargains? Where did the Shades go during the day? What dark places did they find? How small could they be in repose if they had no real substance? Could a hundred of them travel in a matchbox? I shook my head. I couldn't ponder the horrors of Shades spreading right now. Alina had left me a clue. I'd finally managed to stumble upon it, and all I could think about was finding whatever it was she'd wanted me to find.

I lay the laminated maps of the city on the table in front of me, side by side, and looked at them a long moment. The map on the right was current; the one on my left had been distributed seven years ago.

On the current map, Collins Street was one block over and ran directly parallel to Larkspur Lane. On the map from seven years ago, there were *eighteen city blocks* between those two streets.

I shook my head, shrugged, and snorted, all at the same time, an explosive expression of how completely freaked-out I was. This was awful. Did anyone *know*? Were Barrons and I—and God only knew what Barrons really was; *I* sure didn't—the only two with any clue that such things were happening?

The truth is, your world is going to hell in a handbasket, Barrons had said. Recalling his words, I caught something in them I'd missed before. He'd said "your" world. Not "our" world. Mine. Was it not his world also?

As usual, I had a million questions, no one to trust, and nowhere to go but forward. Backward was a path forever barred me now.

I tore a page out of my journal—there were only four blank pages left—laid it over the laminated map and traced out my path, block by block, scribbling in street names. The map itself was too bulky to carry. I needed my hands free. LaRuhe was at the end of a zigzagging path, roughly fourteen blocks into the Dark Zone; the street itself was only two blocks long, one of those short jogs that connect two main roads near multiple five-point intersections.

In retrospect, I'm still stunned that I went into the abandoned neighborhood alone that day. It's a wonder I survived. I don't know quite what I was thinking. Most of the time, as I look back on things and tell you my tale, I'll be able to give you a good idea what was in my head at the time. But this is one of those days that—although the middle hours bear the permanent and highly stamped details of a fiery brand in my mind—began in a bit of a fog and ended in a worse one.

Maybe I was thinking it was still early in the day, the Shades were only a threat at night, and I had my spear, so I'd be safe. Maybe I was numb from so many shocks that I wasn't feeling the fear I should have been.

Maybe, after everything I'd lost so recently, I just didn't care. Barrons had called me Ms. Rainbow the night we'd robbed Mallucé. Despite his disparaging tone, I'd liked the nickname. But rainbows needed sunshine to exist, and there hadn't been a lot of that in my world lately.

Whatever the reason, I got up, showered, chose my outfit with care, gathered my spearhead and flashlights, and went to find 1247 LaRuhe, by myself.

It was nearly noon and I heard the quiet purr of Fiona's luxury sedan pulling up behind me as I walked into what all *sidhe*-seers would one day be calling what I'd christened it, what would one day, and not too far off, begin showing up in cities scattered around the entire globe: a Dark Zone.

I did not look back.

TWENTY-TWO

Though it was only two weeks from the day I'd first gotten lost in the eerie, deserted streets of the abandoned neighborhood, it felt like another lifetime.

Probably because it was.

The Mac who'd followed a woman's outflung arm into an urban wasteland that day had been wearing a killer outfit of pink linen, low-hipped, wide-legged capris, a silk-trimmed pink tee, her favorite silver sandals, and matching silver accessories. She'd had long, beautiful blonde hair swept up into a high ponytail that brushed the middle of her back with the spring of each youthful step.

This Mac had shoulder-length black hair: the better for hiding from those monsters hunting Mac Version 1.0. This Mac wore black jeans and a black T-shirt: the better for potentially being bled upon. Concealing her Iceberry Pink manicured toenails were tennis shoes: the better for running for her life in. Her drab outfit was finished off with an over-sized black jacket she'd swiped from a coat hook by the front door as she'd left: the better for concealing the foot-long spearhead tucked into the waistband of her jeans (tip stuck in a wad of foil), the only silver accessorizing this carefully selected ensemble.

There were flashlights jammed into her back pockets and more stuffed into her coat.

Gone was the energetic step that had bounced so prettily on air. Mac 2.0 strode with determination and focus on feet that were rooted firmly to the ground.

This time, as I moved deeper into the Dark Zone, I understood what I'd been feeling my first time through: the blend of nausea, fear, and that edgy, intense urge I'd had to run. My *sidhe*-seer senses had been triggered the moment I'd crossed Larkspur Lane and unwittingly begun traversing the missing eighteen-block section between it and Collins Street. Though the Shades retreated during the day and went somewhere utterly dark, their lightless sanctuary had to be here somewhere in this forgotten place. All around me I could feel the presence of Unseelie—as I had that day—but I'd not yet known what I was, or understood what I'd been in the middle of.

This time, there was something more, too. I was willing to bet the little map I'd drawn myself would prove unnecessary. Something was tugging at me from a southeasterly direction, both luring and re-pelling. The feeling made me think of a nightmare I'd once had that had left an indelible impression on my memory.

In my dream, I'd been in a cemetery at night, in the rain. A few graves over from the sepulchre where I stood, was my own tomb. I hadn't actually seen it. I just knew it was there with that irrefutable dream-kind-of-knowing. Part of me wanted to run away, to flee the rain-slicked grass and stones and bones as fast as I could, and never look back, as if merely beholding my own grave might seal my fate. But another part of me had known that I would never have another moment's peace in my life if I was afraid to walk over there and look at my own headstone, stare down at my own name, and read aloud the date I'd died.

I'd woken from that nightmare before I'd had to choose.

I wasn't foolish enough to think I was going to wake from this one.

Fixedly ignoring the dehydrated human husks blowing like tumbleweeds down the fog-filled, deserted street, I left the map I'd drawn myself in the left front pocket of my jeans, and gave myself over to the dark melody of my personal Pied Piper. I saw the abandoned neighborhood a little differently this time as I walked into it.

As a graveyard.

I recalled Inspector O'Duffy's complaint the first time I'd met him: *There's been a recent spike in homicides and missing persons like we've never seen before. It's as if half the damn city's gone crazy.*

Not nearly half by my count, not yet anyway—although I could well imagine his consternation over corpses such as the one the Gray Man had left in the pub the other night—but *here* were O'Duffy's missing persons.

All around me. I was passing them, block after block.

They were outside abandoned cars, in neat piles. They were scattered up and down sidewalks, half-buried beneath litter that would never get collected again because these streets didn't show up on any maps used by city employees. Though a conscientious sweeper or trash-collector might occasionally take a look while passing by and say, "Gee, what a mess down there," it was no doubt followed swiftly by a "not my route, not my problem."

The danger of the Dark Zone was this: Although these lanes and avenues wouldn't show up on any map, there was nothing to keep people from driving down them, or walking in, just as I had on my first day in Dublin. As close as it was to the Temple Bar District, there was a lot of foot traffic, and I'd seen myself just how much of that traffic was tourists too inebriated and full of *craic* to notice a radical change in environment until it was too late. A car might have a decent chance of getting through at night, with headlamps and interior lights ablaze, so long as the driver didn't stop and get out for any reason—like to indulge in a drunken urination—but I wouldn't take that gamble myself.

I noticed another thing that had eluded me on my first time through: There were no animals here. Not a single hissing alley cat, no beady-eyed rats, not one pooping pigeon. It was truly a dead zone. And those very small husks now made sense to me, too.

Shades ate everything.

"Except Barrons," I muttered, more deeply aggrieved by that than I cared to admit. The other night when we'd taken on the Gray Man, I'd felt a kinship with my enigmatic mentor. We'd been a *team*. We'd rid the city of a monster. Maybe I'd fumbled my first try, but the end result had been good, and I'd do better next time. I'd frozen it—he'd stabbed it. No more women would be robbed of their beauty and youth. No more would die horrific deaths. It had been a *good* feeling. And I guess in the back of my mind I'd been thinking that when I finally found out who or what had killed Alina, Barrons would help me go after it.

I suffered no delusions that the police or a court of law would be able to help me in my quest for justice. I had no doubt her murderer(s?) would be something only Barrons, I, and other *sidhe*-seers could see, and I only knew of one other *sidhe*-seer. Not only didn't I think the old woman would be much help taking down an Unseelie or ten, I didn't *want* her help. I never wanted to see her again. I know the old "kill the messenger" adage is hardly fair, but adages become adages because they resonate. I resented that woman every bit as much as her message.

I shook my head and turned my thoughts back to my sister. *1247 LaRuhe, Jr.*, Alina had written with her dying breath. She'd wanted me to come here to find something. I hoped it was her journal, though I couldn't imagine why she would have hidden it in the abandoned neighborhood. I doubted it was the mysterious, deadly *Sinsar Dubh*, because—although

I was feeling the typical Fae-induced queasiness, which, by the way, I was finding easier to deal with—I wasn't suffering anything close to the killer nausea mere photocopies of the book had induced. All I was picking up from whatever was push-pulling me in a southeasterly direction was a sense of supernatural danger, but it was muted, as if what-ever awaited me was...well...dormant.

I wasn't able to derive much comfort from that because dormant is just another word for "liable to explode at any moment," and from the way my life had been going lately, if there was a volcano in the vicinity, it was going to spew lava in my face sooner rather than later.

Sighing, I pressed on through the fog.

1247 LaRuhe was not what I'd expected at all.

I'd expected a warehouse or one of those dilapi-dated tenement buildings that had sprung up, re-placing residences in the area when industry had moved in and taken over.

What I got was a tall, fancy brick house dressed up with an ornate limestone facade, smack in the middle of blocks upon blocks of commercial facto-ries and warehouses.

The owner had obviously refused to sell, holding his or her bitter stand against the transition and decay of the neighborhood until the very end. The residence looked as out of place here as a Bloomingdale's would in the center of a low-income housing project.

There were three skeletal trees in the large, foggy,

wrought-iron-fenced front yard with no leaves, no birds in the branches, and I was willing to bet, if I dug at their bases, not one worm in the ground. The terraced gardens were barren and the stone fountain at the grand, arched entrance had long ago run dry.

This was Wasteland.

I looked up at the elegant residence warily. Its veneer of civility and wealth was sharply undermined by what had been done to the many tall mullioned windows.

They'd all been painted black.

And I had the creepiest feeling that something was pressed up against those big dark eyes, watching me.

"What now, Alina?" I whispered. "Am I really supposed to go in there?" I *so* didn't want to.

I didn't expect an answer and I didn't get one. If angels really watch over us like some people believe, mine are deaf-mutes. It had been a purely rhetorical question, anyhow. There was no way I could turn my back on this place. Alina had sent me here and I was going in, if it was the last thing I did. It occurred to me that it might just be.

I didn't bother with stealth. If someone or something was watching me, it was too late for that now. Squaring my shoulders, I took a deep breath, marched up the curved walkway of pale pavers, climbed the front stairs, and banged the heavy knocker against the door.

No one answered. I did it again a few moments later, then tried the door. Its owner suffered no security concerns; it was unlocked and opened on an opulent foyer. Black-and-white marble floors gleamed beneath a glittering chandelier. Beyond an ornate round table topped with a huge vase of showy silk flowers, an elegant spiral staircase curved up the wall, adorned by a handsome balustrade.

I stepped inside. Though the exterior was time-worn and in need of things like gutter and roof repair, the interior was furnished in high Louis XIV style, with plush chairs and sofas set against palatial columns and pilasters, richly carved marble-topped tables, and beautiful amber-and-gold light fixtures. I had no doubt the bedroom furniture would be ornate and enormous in true Sun King style. Huge gilt-framed mirrors and paintings of vaguely familiar mythological scenes adorned the walls.

After listening for a few moments, I began moving through the dimly lit house, one hand on a flashlight, the other on my spearhead, trying to get a mental picture of its inhabitant. The more rooms I glanced into, the less I understood. I'd seen so much ugliness in my short time in Dublin that I'd been expecting more of it, especially here in these desolate barrens, but the occupant appeared to be a wealthy, cultured person of highly sophisticated tastes and—

I mentally smacked myself in the forehead—was this where Alina's boyfriend lived? Had she sent me straight to the address of her murderer?

Ten minutes later I found my answer in an upstairs bedroom, beyond a massive bed, in a spacious walk-in closet filled with finer clothing than even Barrons wore. Whoever, whatever the owner was, he bought only the best. I mean, the *ridiculously* best—the stuff you paid insane amounts for just to ensure no one else in the world could wear it, too.

Tossed carelessly on the floor, beside a collection of boots and shoes that could have shod an army of Armani models, I found Alina's Franklin Planner, her photo albums, and two packets of pictures that had been developed at one of those one-hour photo joints in the Temple Bar District. I thrust the planner and albums inside my bulky jacket but kept the plastic packs of photos in my hand.

After a quick but thorough look around both the closet and the rest of the bedroom, to make sure I wasn't overlooking anything else of hers, I hurried back downstairs so I'd be closer to an escape if I needed one.

Then I sat down on the bottom stair, beneath the gold-and-crystal-encrusted chandelier and opened the first pack of photos.

They say a picture's worth a thousand words.

These certainly were.

I'll finally admit it: Ever since I'd heard the description of Alina's boyfriend—older, worldly, attractive, not Irish—I'd been having a perfectly paranoid thought.

Was I following in Alina's footsteps, *exactly*? Right down to the man who'd betrayed her? Had my sister been in love with Jericho Barrons? Was my mysterious host and alleged protector the one who'd killed her?

When I'd walked into this place earlier, a part of

me had thought, *Aha, so this is where he was going the other night. This is his real home, not the bookstore, and he's really a Dark Fae and for some reason I can't pick up on it any more than Alina could.* How was I to know? It certainly would explain those strange flashes of attraction I'd felt toward him on a couple of occasions, if he were really a death-by-sex Fae somewhere under all that domineering authority. Maybe there were Fae that could hide it somehow. Maybe they had talismans or spells to conceal their true nature. I'd seen too many inexplicable things lately to consider anything beyond the realm of possibility.

I'd been vacillating back and forth on the issue: one day thinking there was no way Barrons was the one, the next day nearly convinced he had to have been.

Now I knew for certain. Alina's boyfriend was most definitely *not* Jericho Barrons.

I'd just taken a photographic journey through a part of my sister's life I'd never thought to see, beginning with the first day she'd arrived in Ireland, to pictures of her at Trinity, to some of her laughing with classmates in pubs, and still more of her dancing with a crowd of friends. She'd been happy here. I'd flipped through them slowly, lovingly, touching my finger to the flush of color in her cheeks, tracing the sleek line of her long blonde hair, alternately laughing and trying not to cry as I got a glimpse of a world I'd never expected to see—of Alina *alive* in this crazy *craic* and monster-filled city. God, I missed her! Seeing her like this was a kick in the stomach! Looking at them, I felt her presence so strongly it was almost as if she were standing right behind me saying, *I love you, Jr. I'm here with you. You can do this. I know you can.*

Then the pictures changed, about four months after she arrived in Dublin, according to the dates on the photos. In the second packet of photos there were dozens of Alina alone, taken in and around the city, and it was obvious from the way she was looking at the person behind the camera that she was already deeply in love. Much as it chafed me to admit, the man behind the lens had taken the most beautiful pictures of my sister that I'd ever seen.

You want to believe in black and white, good and evil, heroes that are truly heroic, and villains that are just plain bad, but I've learned in the past year that things are rarely so simple. The good guys can do some truly awful things, and the bad guys can sometimes surprise the heck out of you.

This bad guy had seen and captured the very best in my sister. Not just her beauty, but that unique inner light that defined her.

Right before he'd extinguished it.

I found it impossible to understand that no one had been able to describe him to me. He and my sister must have turned heads all over the city, yet no one had even been able to tell me what color his hair was.

It was shimmering copper, streaked with gold, and it fell to his waist. Now, how could people not remember that? He was taller than Barrons and beneath his expensive clothing was the kind of body a man only got from weight lifting and intense self-discipline. He looked to be somewhere around thirty, but could easily have been younger or older; there was a timelessness about him. His skin was tanned gold and smooth. Though he was smiling, his strange copper eyes held the arrogance and entitlement of aristocracy. Now I understood why he'd furnished his home with the extravagant opulence of the Sun King who'd built the palace at Versailles—it fit him like a glove. I wouldn't have been at all surprised to learn he *was* the king of one of those small foreign countries few people ever heard of. The only thing that marred his perfection was a long scar running down his left cheek, from cheekbone to the corner of his mouth, and it didn't really mar him at all. It only made him more intriguing.

There were many pictures of them together that had obviously been taken by someone else—yet not one person had been able to describe him to the police, or tell them his name.

Here, they were holding hands and smiling at each other. There they were shopping. Here, they were dancing on top of a table down in the Temple Bar District.

There they were kissing.

The more I looked at the pictures, the harder it was to see this man as a villain. She looked so happy with him and he looked just as happy with her.

I shook my head sharply. She'd thought so, too. She'd believed in him right up to the day she'd called and left me her frantic message: *I thought he was helping me,* she'd said, *but—God, I can't believe I was so stupid! I thought I was in love with him and he's one of them, Mac! He's one of* them!

One of who? An Unseelie that could somehow

pass for human, duping even a *sidhe*-seer? I wondered again if such a thing was possible. If he wasn't Unseelie, what was he, and why would he ally himself with monsters? The man was clearly a consummate actor to have fooled Alina. But she'd found him out in the end. Had she grown suspicious and followed him here? To his home in the Dark Zone, smack in the middle of where my Spidey-sense was getting all kinds of warnings about supernatural danger?

Speaking of supernatural danger, I'd been so intent on investigating the address Alina had sent me to, then gotten so sidetracked by the photos, I'd not realized whatever had push-pulled me in this direction wasn't even in the house. It was out back, beyond it.

And it was getting stronger.

Way stronger. Like it just had woken up.

I slipped the photos back in their envelopes, stuffed them into an inner pocket of my jacket, and got up. As I hurried through the first floor of the house again, looking for a rear exit, I noticed that there was something really wrong with the mirrors on the walls. So wrong, in fact, that after glancing into the first few, I stopped looking and stepped up my pace sharply. Those surreal-looking glasses were my first taste of the true "otherness" of the Fae. Although some Seelie and Unseelie walk and talk just like we do, we are *so* not the same species.

I found a back door, let myself out, and headed straight for the half-raised corrugated steel dock door of a warehouse that sat back off the alley about fifty feet behind 1247 LaRuhe. Whatever was pulling me was in there.

I must have been crazy that day is all I can figure. Though I moved with stealth and kept to the side of the entrance, I walked straight in. The temperature plummeted the moment I crossed the threshold and entered the shadowy interior. The building could easily have housed several football fields. It was an old distribution center, with racking systems a good thirty feet high to my left and right, and a central aisle between them, wide enough to drive two delivery trucks down, side by side. The long aisle was littered with plastic-wrapped pallets stacked ten to fifteen feet high that had not yet been unloaded and transferred to the racking. The chipped and scarred concrete was strewn with haphazard piles of wooden crates and forklifts that looked as though they'd been abandoned midlift. Far down the long aisle, I could see a stark, heavy light, and hear voices.

I crept toward the light, slipping from stack to forklift to crate, working my way stealthily along, drawn by an instinct I could neither understand nor refuse. The nearer I got, the colder it grew. By the time I reached the third-to-last row of racking between me and whatever was ahead, I was shivering and watching my breath puff tiny ice crystals into the air.

By the second-to-last row of racking, the metal of the forklift I crouched behind was painfully icy to the touch.

By the last row, I was so nauseated I had to sit down and stay put awhile. All that remained between me and whatever was ahead were stacks and stacks of pallets in a disorganized row that looked as if they'd been shoved back to clear a large area of floor space. Beyond those stacks, I could see the top parts of what looked like massive stones. The dense light that pressed into the gloom where I crouched wasn't natural. It was a heavy, somehow dark light, and not one of the objects it was shining on threw a shadow.

I have no idea how long it took me to get my queasy stomach under control. It might have been five minutes, it might have been half an hour, but eventually I was able to stand up again and forge on. It occurred to me that perhaps I *shouldn't* forge on; I should just "run like hell" as Barrons had once counseled me and not look back, but there was that whole "pull" part of the push-pull thing going on. I *had* to see what was up there. I had to know. I'd come too far to turn back now.

I peered around the corner of a stack of pallets— and jerked back violently.

I eased myself to the floor on legs that were shaky again, a hand pressed to my pounding heart, wishing fervently that I'd never gotten out of bed this morning.

After a few deep, careful breaths, I leaned forward and looked again. I think I was hoping I'd just imagined it.

I hadn't.

Though I'd seen pictures in guidebooks and on postcards, I would have expected to find this kind of thing in the middle of a farmer's pasture, not in the rear of an industrial warehouse in the heart of a commercial district, midcity. I'd also gotten the impression they were more moderately sized. This one was huge. I tried to imagine how it had gotten here, then remembered I wasn't dealing with human methods of locomotion. With the Fae, anything was possible.

Looming behind about a hundred Rhino-boys and other assorted Unseelie—who threw no shadows in the oppressive, strange light spilling from it—was a dolmen. Two towering stones stood upright about twenty-five feet apart, and a single long slab of rock lay across the top, making a doorway of the ancient megaliths.

All around the doorway, symbols and runes were chiseled into the concrete floor. Some glowed crimson, others pulsed that eerie blue-black of the stone we'd stolen from Mallucé. A red-robed figure stood facing the dolmen, a deep cowl concealing its face.

An arctic wind so cold it made my lungs hurt blasted through the stones, chilling more than my flesh; the dark wind bit into my soul with sharp, icy teeth, and I suddenly knew if I had to withstand it for very long I would slowly begin to forget every hope and dream that had ever warmed my heart.

But it wasn't the soul-searing wind or the Rhino-boys or even the red-robed figure the Fae watchdogs were addressing as "my Lord Master" that had me cowering in shadows.

It was that the immense stone doorway was open. And through it was pouring a *horde* of Unseelie.

TWENTY-THREE

I won't bore you with the details of the monsters that came through the doorway that day. Barrons and I would discuss them later and try to identify their castes, and you'll meet most of them soon enough, anyway.

Suffice to say, there were hundreds of them, tall and short, winged and hoofed, obese and gaunt, all of them pretty much horrific, and as they stepped through, they grouped off, ten or so to each Rhino-boy. From the bits I gathered, the Unseelie watch-dogs had been assigned the task of acclimating their new charges to the world.

My world.

I cringed behind the stack of pallets, watching, too terrified to move. Finally, the last one came through. With more chanting and the sharp rapping of a gold-and-black scepter upon some of the glowing symbols, the red-robed Lord Master closed the doorway. The symbols went dark and the bitter wind ceased. The light in the warehouse brightened, became lighter somehow, and the Unseelie began casting shadows again. Feeling returned to my chilled face and fingers, and dreams to my heart.

"You have your instructions," the Lord Master said, and I wondered how such an evil thing could have such a beautiful voice.

Genuflecting as if to a god, the Rhino-boys began herding their newly arrived brethren toward the aisle. A group of about thirty assorted monsters remained behind with the Lord Master.

I plastered myself against the stack of pallets as every single one of the new arrivals passed within a dozen feet of me, accompanied by its "trainer." They were some of the most harrowing few minutes of my life. I got an up-close-and-personal look at things we've never even come close to creating in our scariest horror flicks.

After the last of them had marched, slithered, flapped, or crawled down the long aisle and exited the building, I slumped back against the pallets, closed my eyes, and kept them closed.

So *this* was what Alina had wanted me to know: That behind 1247 LaRuhe was a gate to hell, and here the Lord Master was bringing his dark servants through from their previously inescapable Unseelie prison and turning them loose on our world.

Okay, now I knew.

Just what was I supposed to do about it? Alina had seriously overestimated me if she thought I could, or would, do anything about this problem. It wasn't *my* problem. My problem was finding the bastard who'd betrayed her and bringing him to whatever justice I could. If he was human, I might let the courts have him. If he was an Unseelie masquerading as human, he'd die at the end of my spear. That was all I cared about.

We've got to find the Sinsar Dubh, Alina had said. *Everything depends on it.*

What depended on it? I had a sinking feeling the answer to that question was one of those Fate-of-the-World things. I didn't do Fate-of-the-World things. That wasn't in my job description. I poured drafts and mixed drinks, wiped counters and washed glasses. After work I swept up.

Had Alina wanted me to find the Dark Book because somewhere within its dangerous, encrypted pages was the way to defeat the Lord Master and destroy his Unseelie portal? Why should I care? It was in Dublin, not Georgia! It was Ireland's problem. They could handle their own troubles. Besides, even if I managed to accomplish the impossible and find the stupid Dark Book, how was I supposed to translate it? Barrons had two of the stones necessary, but I had no clue which team he was playing for. Nor did I have any idea where the other two stones were, how to find them, or how to use them—assuming I ever actually managed to get my hands on them.

What had Alina expected me to do? Commit to staying in Dublin indefinitely, searching for all this woo-woo stuff and living in constant fear? Devote my *life* to this cause? Be willing to die for it?

It was one heck of a tall order for a short-order bartender. I would have snorted if I hadn't been on the uncomfortable verge of peeing my pants with fear for the past half hour.

She'd died for it.

I clenched my jaw and squeezed my eyes shut even harder.

I'd never measured up to Alina, and I never would. I had no desire to open my eyes. I might see something *else* she thought I should be responsible for, I thought resentfully. I was getting out of here. I was going to put as much distance as possible between me and the prison-portal and the red-robed Lord Master and the whole Dark Zone.

I sighed.

I really was. Just as soon as I took just one last small look around the corner to see if there was anything else I should know. Not that I planned to *do* anything with the information. I just figured since I was already here, I might as well gather all of it I could. Maybe I could pass it on to that interfering old woman, or V'lane, and one of *them* could do something about it. If V'lane really was one of the good guys, then he and his queen should take immediate, decisive action to plug this unacceptable hole between our worlds. Hadn't Barrons mentioned something about a Compact? Wasn't there some kind of agreement this violated?

I opened my eyes.

And failed miserably at both my attempt to climb

out of my own skin, and my efforts to sink into the floor.

Barrons and I had wondered where Mallucé was. Now I knew.

Less than a dozen feet away from me, fangs bared, flanked by six beady-eyed Rhino-boys.

TWENTY-FOUR

Trying to disappear hadn't worked, so I exploded up, hissing and kicking and slamming my hands into everything I could, well, lay my hands on.

Unlike the other night, when I'd tried to kill the Gray Man, I didn't have time to think about what I was doing, I just acted on instinct.

It turned out my instincts were *amazing*.

I left the spearhead tucked into my waistband, so I could use both hands. There was something inside me that worked like the missile-targeting system of a stealth bomber, locating and locking onto anything Fae once it was within a few feet of me.

As Mallucé dropped back and let the six Rhinoboys close in, I slammed my palms out in opposite directions, hitting two of them smack in their barrel chests. I spun, slammed out again, catching another two in the ribs, then dropped to the floor and slammed out a third time.

On my knees, I tossed my hair out of my eyes and assessed the situation. I'd frozen all six of them in two seconds flat.

But how long would they stay frozen? That was the critical question.

Mallucé looked startled—I guess he'd never seen a Null in action before—then glided toward me in that sinuous way of his. I reached inside my jacket for the spearhead, then remembered what Barrons had said, or rather hadn't said about how to kill a vampire. Mallucé wasn't Fae, so I could neither freeze nor stab him and expect it to work. Nor, according to Barrons, would a stake through his heart do the job, so I didn't see any reason my spear would, either. I removed my hand from my jacket. I didn't want to show my ace-in-the-hole until I had no other choice. Maybe, just maybe, I could get close to the Lord Master. And maybe I could use the spear to kill him. And then maybe I could freeze all the Unseelie *and* outrun a vampire. It sounded like a plan to me. The only one I could think of.

I pushed up and began backing away. It seemed it was what the vampire'd wanted, anyway. I held his too-bright yellow gaze as he backed me past the pallet, onto the rune-chiseled floor in front of the dolmen, and into a circle of Unseelie Rhino-boys and assorted monsters.

"What is this, Mallucé?" Though he was behind me and I couldn't see him, I would never mistake the voice of the Lord Master. It was rich, multitonal, and musical, like V'lane's.

"I thought I heard something behind the pallets," Mallucé said. "She is a Null, Lord Master. *Another* one."

I couldn't help it. I had to know. "You mean Alina, don't you? The other Null, she was Alina Lane, wasn't she?" I accused.

The vampire's creepy citron eyes narrowed. He exchanged a long glance with the red-robed thing behind me.

"What do you know about Alina Lane?" the Lord Master said softly, in that melodious voice. It was the voice of something larger than life, an archangel, perhaps—the one that fell.

"She was my *sister*," I snarled, whirling around. "And I'm going to *kill* the bastard that killed her. What do *you* know about her?"

The crimson cowl shook with laughter. I fisted my hands at my sides to keep from whipping out my spear and lunging for the red-robed figure. Stealth, I told myself. Caution. I doubted I'd get more than one chance.

"I told you she would come, Mallucé," said the Lord Master. "We will use her to finish what her sister began." He raised his hands as if to encompass the group and addressed all the Unseelie gathered there. "When everything is in place, I will open the portal and unleash the entire Unseelie prison on this world, as I promised you. Restrain her. She comes with us."

"Now, that was just stupid, Ms. Lane," Barrons

said, shaking his head, as he dropped onto the floor next to me, his long black coat fluttering. "Did you have to go and tell them who you were? They would have figured it out soon enough."

I blinked, stupefied.

I guess the Lord Master, Mallucé, and all the rest of them were just as stunned by the unexpected entrance as I was, because we all gaped at him, and then we all looked up. *I* just wanted to see where in the world he'd come from. I think they were checking to see if there were any others up there. He had to have been on the ceiling girders. They were thirty feet high. I didn't see a convenient rope dangling anywhere.

When I looked back down, the Unseelie ruler had pushed back his crimson cowl and was looking at Barrons, hard. He didn't seem to like what he saw.

I gasped, stunned.

I stared in disbelief and confusion at Alina's boyfriend, the Lord Master. The leader of the Unseelie wasn't even Fae! Even Barrons looked a little thrown.

The Lord Master barked a command, then he turned in a whirl of red robes. Dozens of Unseelie closed in on us instantly.

Things got kind of crazy then, and I still have a hard time sorting them out. As his minions cut off any chance of pursuit, the prick who'd used and killed my sister and had been planning to do the same to me ordered them to take me *alive, or else, and kill the other one.*

Then I was surrounded by Unseelie and I couldn't

see Barrons anymore. Somewhere in the distance, I heard chanting, and the runes in the concrete beneath my feet began to glow again.

I closed my mind to everything but battle. I fought.

I fought for my sister, who'd died alone in an alley. I fought for the woman the Gray Man had fed on while I'd eaten french fries, and the one he'd consumed two days ago, while I'd watched in helpless horror. I fought for the people the Many-Mouthed-Thing had killed. I fought for the dehydrated human husks blowing down the forgotten streets between Collins Street and Larkspur Lane. I might have even fought for a few of O'Bannion's henchmen. And I fought for the twenty-two-year-old young woman who'd arrived in Dublin pretty darned sure of herself, who no longer had any idea where she'd come from or where she was going, and who'd just broken her *third* Iceberry Pink nail.

The alabaster spearhead seemed to blaze with holy light in my hand as I ducked and twisted, slammed and stabbed. I could feel myself turning into something else and it felt *good*. At one point I caught sight of Barrons' startled face, and I knew that if he was looking at me like that, I was truly something to see. I *felt* like something to see. I felt like a well-built, well-oiled machine with one purpose in life: to kill Fae. Good or bad. Take 'em all.

And I did, one after another. Duck, slam, stab. Whirl, slam, stab. They went down fast and hard. The spear was pure poison to them, and I was getting a weird kind of high off watching them die. I have no idea how long I could have kept it up, if they'd all been Fae, but they weren't and I screwed up.

I'd forgotten about Mallucé.

When he crept up behind me, I sensed him there just like a Fae—apparently my radar picked up on anything otherworldly within a certain perimeter—and I spun and stabbed him in the gut.

I realized my error instantly, although I had no idea how to correct it. The vampire was a more serious threat to me than any of the Unseelie, even the Shades—at least I knew how to drive those life-suckers back: light. I didn't have any idea what *this* life-sucker's weakness was, or even if he had one. Barrons had talked like killing a vampire was pretty much impossible.

For a moment, I just stood there, my weapon buried in his stomach, hoping it would do something. If it had any effect on him at all, I sure couldn't tell. I stared stupidly into those feral yellow eyes, glowing in that white, white face. Then my wits returned and I tried to pull the spear out for another stab at him, this time in the chest—maybe Barrons was wrong, I had to try *something*—but the razor-sharp tip had gotten lodged in a knot of gristle or bone or something and wouldn't yield.

He closed his hand on my arm. It felt cold and dead. "You little bitch! Where is my stone?" the vampire hissed.

I got it then—why he'd not brought it up before, when he'd first seen me. He was two-timing the Lord Master and couldn't risk the Rhino-boys knowing.

"Oh God, he doesn't even know you *had* it, does

he?" I exclaimed. The moment I said it, I realized my mistake. Mallucé had more to lose if the Lord Master discovered he was betraying him, than by owning up to inadvertently killing the *sidhe*-seer in the heat of battle. I'd just signed my own death warrant.

I yanked frantically on the spearhead. Mallucé bared his fangs as the weapon gave and I stumbled back. Off balance, I lashed out again—but a millisecond too late. The vampire backhanded me across the face and I flew backward through the air, arms and legs folded forward like a rag doll, just as I'd seen his bodyguard do that night at the House of Goth.

I slammed into the side of a stack of pallets that gave about as much as a brick wall. My head snapped back and pain ricocheted through my skull. I heard things in me crack.

"Mac!" I heard Barrons shout.

I slumped down the plastic-shrouded wall, thinking how weird it sounded, him calling me Mac. He'd only ever called me Ms. Lane. I couldn't breathe. My chest was locked tight, and I wondered if my ribs had broken and punctured my lungs. The spear was slipping from my fingers. That arctic wind was back, chilling me body and soul, and I understood dimly that the gate was open again.

My lids were as heavy as paperweights and I blinked slowly. My face was wet. I wasn't sure, but I thought I was crying. I couldn't be dying. I finally knew who'd killed my sister. I'd looked into his face. I hadn't avenged her yet.

Barrons swam before my eyes. "I'll get you out of here. Hold on," he told me in a slow-motion voice and was gone.

I blinked again, heavily. I still couldn't breathe and my vision was going in and out, especially in one eye. One moment it was all shadowy, then there was Barrons again. He and Mallucé were facing each other, pacing a tight circle. The vampire's eyes glowed and his fangs were fully extended.

As my grasp on consciousness failed, I tried to decide what on earth Barrons had just done to Mallucé that had sent the absurdly strong vampire slamming into a stack of pallets and crashing into a forklift; how I'd gotten into his arms, and just where he thought he was taking me at such breakneck speed.

To a hospital, I hoped.

I regained consciousness several times during our flight.

Long enough, the first time, to realize I hadn't died, which I found dimly astonishing. The last time I'd seen Mallucé slam someone into a wall, the man had been way bigger than I, and he'd died instantly, bleeding from multiple orifices.

I must have muttered something to that effect, because Barrons' chest rumbled beneath my ear. "The spear did something to him, Ms. Lane. I'm not sure what or why, but it slowed him down."

The next time I regained consciousness, he said, "Can you hook an arm around my neck and hold on?" The answer was yes—one. The other one wouldn't move. It dangled limply from my shoulder.

The man could run. We were in the sewers, I could tell by the splash of his boots and the smell. I hoped I wasn't deluding myself with optimism, but I didn't hear the sound of pursuit. Had we lost them? All of them?

"They don't know the underground like I do," he said. "Nobody does."

How weird. I was a chatterbox and didn't even know it, reeling off question after question despite the pain I was in. Or was he reading my mind?

"Not a mind reader, Ms. Lane," he said. "You think all over your face sometimes. You need to work on that."

"Shouldn't I go to the hospital?" I asked muzzily when I woke up for the third time. I was back in bed, in my borrowed bedroom at Barrons Books and Baubles. I must have been out for a while. "I think things are broken."

"Your left arm, two ribs, and a few fingers. You're bruised all over. You were lucky." He pressed a cold compress to my cheek and I inhaled sharply with pain. "At least your cheekbone didn't get shattered when he struck you. I was afraid it had. You look a little worse for the wear, Ms. Lane."

"Hospital?" I tried again.

"They can't do anything for you that I haven't already done and would only ask you questions you can't answer. They'll blame me if I bring you in looking like this and you won't talk. I already set your arm and fingers," he said. "Your ribs will heal.

Your face is going to look...well...yeah. You'll be fine in time, Ms. Lane."

That sounded ominous. "Mirror?" I managed weakly.

"Sorry," he said. "Don't have one handy."

I tried to move my left arm, wondering when and where Barrons had added casting to his seemingly endless resume. He hadn't. My arm was in a splint, as were several fingers on that hand. "Shouldn't I have casts?"

"Fingers do well with splints. The break in your arm isn't acute and if I cast you, it will only cause your muscles to atrophy. You must recover quickly. In case you haven't noticed, Ms. Lane, we've got a few problems on our hands."

I peered blearily up at him through my one good eye. My right one was swollen completely shut from the contusion on my cheek. He'd called me Mac back there in the warehouse, when Mallucé had hit me. Despite my doubts about Barrons, and my worries over whatever arrangement he had going on with the Shades, he'd been there for me when it mattered. He'd come after me. He'd saved my life. He'd patched me up and tucked me into bed and I knew he would watch over me until I was whole again. Under such circumstances, it seemed absurd to continue calling me Ms. Lane and I told him so. Perhaps it was time I did better than "Barrons" myself. "You can call me Mac, er...Jericho. And thanks for saving me."

One dark brow rose and he looked amused.

"Stick with Barrons, Ms. Lane," he said dryly. "You need rest. Sleep."

My eyes fluttered closed as if he'd spoken a spell over me and I drifted into a happy place, a hallway papered with smiling pictures of my sister. I knew who her killer was now, and I was going to avenge her. I was halfway home. I wouldn't call him Jericho if he didn't like it. But I wanted him to call me Mac, I insisted sleepily. I was tired of being four thousand miles away from home and feeling so alone. It would be nice to be on a first-name basis with somebody here. Anybody would do, even Barrons.

"Mac." He said my name and laughed. "What a name for something like you. Mac." He laughed again.

I wanted to know what he meant by that, but didn't have the strength to ask.

Then his fingers were light as butterflies on my battered cheek and he was speaking softly, but it wasn't in English. It sounded like one of those dead languages they use in the kind of movies I used to channel-surf through quickly—and now regret not having watched at least one or two of because I probably would have been a whole lot better prepared for all of this if I had.

I think he kissed me then. It wasn't like any kiss I'd ever felt before.

And then it was dark. And I dreamed.

TWENTY-FIVE

No, not like that. You're *gooping* it on. The first coat's supposed to be light," I told him. "This isn't a cake you're icing. It's a fingernail."

We were sitting on top of Barrons Books and Baubles in a lush rooftop conservatory I hadn't even known was there until Fiona, who'd shown more distress over my injuries than I'd expected, had told me about it. I spent the late-afternoon hours sprawled in a chaise, pretending to be reading but not really doing much of anything. When blazing floodlights, mounted on all sides of the roof, had come on shortly before dark, illuminating the garden, I'd taken a good hard look at my ragged nails, gone down for my manicure kit, come back up, and spread my tools on a pretty glass-topped wrought-iron table above the facade of the bookstore, right under one of the brightest floodlights, and given it my best shot. But no matter how hard I'd tried, I'd not been able to paint the nails on my right hand with my splinted left arm. Then Barrons had arrived and I'd wasted no time putting him to work.

A muscle leapt in his jaw. "Tell me again why I'm doing this, Ms. Lane?"

"Duh," I said. "Because my arm's broken." I waved my splint at him, in case he'd forgotten.

"I don't think you tried hard enough," he said. "I think you need to try again. I think if you angle your splint out like this"—he demonstrated, in the process tipping fingernail polish onto the tiled patio— "then twist your arm around like this." He nodded. "Give it a try. I think it'll work."

I gave him a cool look. "You drag me all over the place, making me hunt for OOPs, but do I complain the whole time? No. Suck it up, Barrons. The least you can do is paint my nails while my arm's broken. It's not like I'm asking you to do both hands. And I'm not asking you to do my toes at all." Although I really could have used some help with my pedicure. A proper foot grooming was a two-handed job.

He glowered at the prospect of having to gloss my toes a matching shimmery, gold-frosted Ice Princess Blush, which, by the way, had always seemed oxymoronish to me, like jumbo shrimp. None of the ice princesses I'd known in high school and college had been the blushing types.

"Some guys," I informed him loftily, "would *jump* at the chance to paint my toenails."

Barrons bent his head over my hand, applying pale pink polish to my ring finger with exacting care.

He looked big and muscular and male and silly painting my fingernails, like a Roman centurion decked out in a frilly chef's apron. I bit the inside of my cheek to keep from laughing.

"I'm sure they would, Ms. Lane," he said dryly.

He was still calling me Ms. Lane.

After all we'd been through. As if he'd not found my map with the pink dot I'd stabbed on it, followed me into the Dark Zone, rescued, splinted, iced, bandaged, and, I think, even kissed me.

I narrowed my eyes, studying his dark, bent head. I knew how he'd found me. Fiona had told me she'd called him right after she'd seen me go walking into the abandoned neighborhood. From her guilt-tinged distress over my injuries, however, I was pretty sure she hadn't called him *immediately* after, if you know what I mean.

But that was about all I knew. I'd spent most of the three days since I'd gone to 1247 LaRuhe in a deep, drugged sleep, surfacing only long enough for Barrons to feed me something before ordering me to sleep again.

My back and hips were bruised, various parts of me were bound and immobilized, my ribs were wrapped and it hurt to breathe, but on the brighter side of things, my eye was almost completely open again. I hadn't been brave enough to look in a mirror yet, nor had I showered in four days, but I had other things on my mind right now, like some of those questions that had been burning holes in my gut all day.

"Okay, Barrons, it's time."

"I am not helping you shave your legs," he said instantly.

"Oh please. As if I'd let you. I meant for questions."

"Oh."

"What are you?" I dumped the question on him like a bucket of ice water.

"I don't follow," he said with one those elegant Gallic shrugs.

"You dropped thirty feet in that warehouse. You should have broken something. You should have broken *two* somethings—like legs. What are you?"

There was another of those shrugs. "A man with a rope?"

"Ha-ha. I didn't see one."

"I can't help that." The look he gave me was dry, bored, and just enough to make me doubt what I'd seen that night. After all, I had been pretty wigged-out at the time. I couldn't absolutely guarantee there hadn't been one of those sophisticated thin cables thieves always used in movies. I tried another tactic. "You sent Mallucé flying through the air. Smashing into pallets, then a forklift."

"I'm strong, Ms. Lane. Would you like to feel my muscles?" He showed his teeth but it wasn't really a smile and we both knew it. Two weeks ago it would have intimidated me.

"I don't care how strong you are. Mallucé is super-strong. He's a vampire."

"Maybe. Maybe not. His followers seem to think he's dead."

"Oh, happy day," I said fervently. "One down."

Only a thousand or so to go, in my estimation, though I was afraid I might be way off, as in seriously underestimating.

"Don't celebrate yet, Ms. Lane. Don't believe anything dead until you've burned it, poked around in its ashes, and then waited a day or two to see if anything rises from them."

"You're kidding. Some things are *that* hard to kill?"

"Some things, Ms. Lane," he said, beginning the second coat of my manicure, "are impossible to kill. However, I'm not certain Mallucé was one of them. It remains to be seen."

I fired my next question at him. "Why do the Shades let you walk in the Dark Zone, Barrons?"

He painted my entire index finger pink. Then had the nerve to glare up at me, as if *I'd* done it.

"Darn it, Barrons, they were looking good until you did that!" I yanked my hand away. "Dampen one of those cotton balls with this." I thrust a bottle of polish remover at him.

He took it, with a hard look. "You spy on me, Ms. Lane?"

"Serendipity, Barrons. I just happened to be glancing out the window when you happened to be doing something nefarious, which only makes me wonder how many nefarious things you're doing when I'm *not* glancing out the window. Where's the Maybach?"

An instant smile curved his lips; the quick, possessive smile of a man with a new toy. "O'Bannion didn't need it anymore. The police don't even see the—what did you call it—Dark Zone? It would have sat there forever. What a waste."

"Oh, you are just cold," I breathed. "That man wasn't even dead a day."

"Spoils of war, Ms. Lane."

"Couldn't you have at least moved those piles while you were at it?"

He shrugged. "You quit seeing them after a while."

I hoped not. It would mean a part of me was as dead as him. "What kind of deal do you have with the Shades, Barrons?"

I expected evasion, even a counterquestion, but I wasn't prepared for the one he lashed back at me with. "Why didn't you tell me you'd encountered V'lane, Ms. Lane?" he said silkily.

I jerked. "How did you know?"

"V'lane told me."

"How do *you* know V'lane?" I demanded indignantly.

"I know everything, Ms. Lane," he said.

"Oh really?" I said, saccharine-sweet. "Then who and what is the Lord Master? Answer me that." Not Fae, for sure. But he hadn't seemed...altogether human, either.

"Your sister's boyfriend," he said flatly, "and knowing that, just what should I make of *you*?" When I stared at him blankly, he said, "I found the photos in your jacket."

I nearly smacked myself in the forehead. The pictures! I'd forgotten all about the things I'd looted from the Lord Master's residence. "Where did you put the other things that were in my jacket?" I asked. I couldn't recall having seen either the two albums or the Franklin Planner in my bedroom. I needed to go over her calendar with a fine-tooth comb. There could be all kinds of valuable information in there: names, addresses, dates.

"There wasn't anything else in your jacket."

"There was too," I protested.

He shook his head.

"Are you sure?"

"Positive."

I searched his face. Was he telling me the truth? Had they fallen out while I'd been fighting? Or had he taken them for some reason? With a sinking feeling, I realized I might just have to go back to 1247 LaRuhe again to be certain. "I didn't know he was my sister's boyfriend, Barrons," I defended. "She didn't, either. Remember her message? She said he'd been lying to her all along. That he was one of them and she never knew it until then. He tricked and betrayed her," I said bitterly. "There, I answered your question. Now you answer mine. Why do the Shades let you walk in the Dark Zone?"

He didn't say anything for a long time, just glossed my nails a topcoat and touched up my cuticles in silence. He was better than most nail technicians; the man was a perfectionist. I'd just about given up hope of him answering when he said, "We all have our ... gifts, Ms. Lane. You are a Null. I am ... other things. What I am *not*—is your enemy. Nor am I in league with the Shades. You're just going to have to trust me on that."

"It'd be a whole lot easier to trust you if you'd just answer my question."

"I don't know why you ask, anyway. I could lie to you a million ways to Sunday. Look at my actions. Who saved your life?"

"Yeah, well, OOP-detectors don't work so hot dead, do they?" I pointed out.

"I managed just fine before you came along, Ms. Lane, and would have continued swimmingly without you. Yes, you can find OOPs, but frankly, my life was a great deal less complicated before you barreled into my bookstore." He sighed. "Bloody hell, I miss those days."

"Sorry I've been such an inconvenience," I retorted, "but *my* life hasn't exactly been a bowl of cherries since then, either." We were both quiet for a time, looking into the night, thinking our own thoughts. "Well, at least now I know who killed Alina," I said finally.

He looked at me sharply. "Did you hear something in that warehouse I missed, Ms. Lane?"

"Well, *duh*, her boyfriend was the Lord Master and she didn't know it. She must have followed him one day and found out who and what he was, just like I did. And he killed her for it." It was so obvious I couldn't believe Barrons didn't see it himself.

But he didn't. Skepticism was written all over his face.

"What?" I said. "Am I missing something? Are you saying I shouldn't go after him?"

"Oh, we should definitely go after him," Barrons said. "Note the 'we' in that sentence, Ms. Lane.

Head off one more time by yourself after something big and bad, and I'll hurt you worse than the monsters do. I want the Lord Master dead if only for one reason: I don't want any more bloody damned Unseelie in my city. But if there's one thing I've learned in life it's this: assume makes an ass out of 'u' and 'me.' "

"Cute," I said, spelling ass-u-me out in my head.

"I'm not trying to be cute. I'm saying don't assume you know who your sister's killer is until you've got solid evidence in your hand or a confession. Assumptions," he said darkly, "can make even worse things than an ass out of the best of us."

I was about to ask him "like what?" when I was suddenly so nauseous that I couldn't speak. Bile splashed the back of my throat without warning and somebody suddenly poked a knife through my skull—a twelve-inch-long blade I just knew had to be sticking out both temples.

I lurched to my feet, crashed into the table, and ruined every last one of my nails trying to catch myself. I would have hit the ground and probably re-broken my arm if Barrons hadn't grabbed me. I think I vomited.

Right before I passed out.

When I regained consciousness, I was lying in the chaise and Barrons was bending over me, his expression stark. "What?" he demanded. "What just happened to you, Ms. Lane?"

"Oh G-God," I said faintly. I'd never felt anything like that before and never wanted to again. That was it. I was going home. Abandoning it all. Quest for vengeance—over. I quit. I was turning in my formal *sidhe*-seer notice.

"What?" he demanded again.

"I c-c-can't st-stop sh-sh-sh..." I trailed off. "Shivering" was what I was trying to say, but my teeth were chattering too hard for me to get it out. My blood was ice in my veins. I was cold, so cold. I didn't think I'd ever be warm again.

Barrons shrugged off his jacket and draped it over me. "Better?" He waited all of two seconds. "So? What?" he asked impatiently.

"It w-was here," I finally managed, gesturing with my good arm toward the edge of the roof. "Somewhere d-down there. I think it was in a c-car. It was moving fast. It's g-gone now."

"What was here? What's gone?"

With a last violent shiver, I got my chattering under control. "What do you think, Barrons?" I said. "The *Sinsar Dubh*." I took a deep breath and released it slowly. I knew something about that elusive book I'd not known before: It was so evil it corrupted anyone who touched it—no exceptions. "Oh God, we're in a world of trouble, aren't we?" I breathed.

Though neither of us had brought it up, I knew we'd both been thinking about all those Unseelie who'd come through the dolmen that day and were even now being introduced into our world, trained to cast glamours so they could interact with us, and prey on us.

When everything is in place, the Lord Master had said, *I will open the portal and unleash the entire Unseelie prison on this world.*

I had no idea how big the Unseelie prison was and never wanted to know. But I had an awful feeling we were going to find out.

"Are there more *sidhe*-seers out there, Barrons?" I asked. "Besides us?"

He nodded.

"Good. Because we're going to need them." A war was coming. I could feel it in my bones. A war to end all wars.

And Mankind didn't even know it.

Glossary
from Mac's Journal

DARK ZONE: an area that has been taken over by the Shades. During the day it looks like your everyday abandoned, rundown neighborhood. Once night falls, it's a death-trap. (Definition Mac)

DEATH-BY-SEX FAE (e.g. V'lane): a Fae that is so sexually "potent" a human dies from intercourse with it unless the Fae protects the human from the full impact of its deadly eroticism. (Definition ongoing)

DRUID: in pre-Christian Celtic society, a Druid presided over divine worship, legislative and judicial matters, philosophy, and the education of elite youth to their order. Druids were believed to be privy to the secrets of the gods, including issues pertaining to the manipulation of physical matter, space, and even time. The old Irish "Drui" means magician, wizard, diviner. *(Irish Myths and Legends)*

FAE (fay): see also Tuatha Dé Danaan. Divided into two courts, the Seelie or Light Court, and the Unseelie or Dark Court. Both courts have different castes of Fae, with the four Royal Houses occupying the highest caste of each. The Seelie Queen and her chosen consort rule the Light Court. The Unseelie King and his current concubine govern the Dark. (Definition J.B.)

FOUR STONES, THE: translucent blue-black stones covered with raised runelike lettering. The key to deciphering the ancient language and breaking the code of the *Sinsar Dubh* is hidden in these four mystical stones. An individual stone can be used to shed light on a small portion of the text, but only if the four are reassembled into one will the true text in its entirety be revealed. *(Irish Myths and Legends)*

GLAMOUR: illusion cast by the Fae to camouflage their true appearance. The more powerful the Fae, the more difficult it is to penetrate its disguise. The average human sees only what the Fae wants them to see, and is subtly repelled from bumping into or brushing against it by a small perimeter of spatial distortion that is part of the Fae glamour. (Definition J.B.)

GRAY MAN, THE: monstrously ugly, leprous Unseelie that feeds by stealing beauty from human women. Threat assessment: can kill, but prefers to leave its victim hideously disfigured and alive to suffer. (Personal experience)

HALLOWS: eight ancient relics of immense power: four light and four dark. The Light Hallows are the stone, the spear, the sword, and the cauldron. The Dark are the mirror, the box, the amulet, and the book

(*Sinsar Dubh* or *Dark Book*). (*A Definitive Guide to Artifacts; Authentic and Legendary*)

MANY-MOUTHED THING, THE: repulsive Unseelie with myriad leechlike mouths, dozens of eyes, and over-developed sex organs. Caste of Unseelie: unknown at this time. Threat assessment: unknown at this time but suspect kills in a manner I'd rather not think about. (Personal experience)

NULL: a sidhe-seer with the power to freeze a Fae with the touch of his or her hands (e.g. me). The higher and more powerful the caste of Fae, the shorter the length of time it stays frozen. (Def. J.B.)

OOP: acronym for Object of Power, a Fae relic imbued with mystical properties. (Definition Mac)

PRI-YA: a human addicted to Fae sex. (I think. Definition ongoing)

RHINO-BOYS: lower mid-level caste Unseelie thugs dispatched primarily as watchdogs for high-ranking Fae. (Personal experience)

ROYAL HUNTERS: a mid-level caste of Unseelie. Militantly sentient, they resemble the classic depiction of the devil, with cloven hooves, horns, long satyr-like faces, leathery wings, fiery orange eyes, and tails. Seven to ten feet tall, they are capable of extraordinary speed on both hoof and wing. Primary function: sidhe-seer exterminators. Threat assessment: kills. (Def. J.B.)

SEELIE: the "light" or "fairer" court of the Tuatha Dé Danaan governed by the Seelie Queen, Aoibheal. (Def. J.B.)

SHADES: one of the lowest castes of Unseelie. Sentient but barely. They hunger—they feed. They cannot bear direct light and hunt only at night. They steal life in the manner the Gray Man steals beauty, draining their victims with vampiric swiftness, leaving behind a pile of clothing and a husk of dehydrated human matter. Threat assessment: kills. (Personal experience)

SIDHE-SEER (SHE-seer): a person Fae magic doesn't work on, capable of seeing past the illusions or "glamour" cast by the Fae to the true nature that lies beneath. Some can also see *Tabh'rs*, hidden portals between realms. Others can sense Seelie and Unseelie objects of power. Each sidhe-seer is different, with varying degrees of resistance to the Fae. Some are limited, some are advanced with multiple "special powers." (Def. J.B.)

SIFTING: Fae method of locomotion, occurs at speed of thought. (Seen this!)

SIFTING SILVERS or **SILVERS**: an elaborate maze of mirrors once used as the primary method of Fae travel between realms, until Cruce cast the forbidden curse into the silvered corridors. Now no Fae dares enter the Silvers. (Def. J.B.)

SINSAR DUBH (she-suh-DOO): a Dark Hallow belonging to the Tuatha Dé Danaan. Written in a language known only to the most ancient of their kind, it is said to hold the deadliest of all magic within its encrypted pages. Brought to Ireland by the Tuatha Dé during the invasions written of in the pseudo-history Leabhar Gabhåla, it was stolen along with the other Dark Hallows, and rumored to have found its way into the world of Man. Allegedly authored over a million years ago by the Dark King of the Unseelie. *(A Definitive Guide to Artifacts; Authentic and Legendary)*

SPEAR OF LUISNE (a.k.a. Spear of Luin, Spear of Longinus, Spear of Destiny, the Flaming Spear): the spear used to pierce Jesus Christ's side at his crucifixion. Not of human origin; it is a Tuatha Dé Danaan Light Hallow, and one of the few items capable of killing a Fae— regardless of rank or power. (Def. J.B.)

TABH'RS (TAH-vr): Fae doorways or portals between realms, often hidden in everyday human objects. (Def. J.B.)

TUATHA DÉ DANAAN or **TUATHA DÉ** (TUA-day-dhanna or Tua-DAY): (See Fae above) a highly advanced race that came to Earth from another world. (Definition ongoing)

UNSEELIE: the "dark" court of the Tuatha Dé Danaan. According to Tuatha Dé Danaan legend, the Unseelie have been confined for hundreds of thousands of years in an inescapable prison. Inescapable, my ass.

Turn the page for a sneak peek at the next novel
in the Fever series, *Bloodfever*

ONE

You're a difficult woman to find, Ms. Lane," Inspector O'Duffy said as I opened the diamond-
paned front door of Barrons Books and Baubles.

The stately Old World bookstore was my home
away from home, whether I liked it or not and, despite
the sumptuous furnishings, priceless rugs, and endless
selection of top-rate reading material, I didn't. The
comfiest cage is still a cage.

He glanced sharply at me when I stepped around
the door, into full view, noting my splinted arm and
fingers, the stitches in my lip, and the fading purple
and yellow bruises that began around my right eye
and extended to the base of my jaw. Though he raised
a brow, he made no comment.

The weather outside was awful, and so long as the
door was open, I was too close to it. It had been raining
for days, a relentless, depressing torrent that needled
me with sharp wind-driven droplets even where I
stood, tucked beneath the shelter of the column-flanked

archway of the bookstore's grand entry. At eleven o'clock on Sunday morning, it was so overcast and dark that the streetlamps were still on. Despite their sullen yellow glares, I could barely see the outlines of the shops across the street through the thick, soupy fog.

I backed up to let the inspector enter. Gusts of chilly air stepped in with him.

I closed the door and returned to the conversation area near the fire where I'd been wrapped in an afghan on the sofa, reading.

"Dreadful weather," he observed, stepping to the hearth and warming his hands before the softly hissing gas flames.

I agreed with perhaps more enthusiasm than the fact warranted; the endless deluge outside was getting to me. A few more days of this and I was going to start building an ark. I'd heard it rained a lot in Ireland but "constantly" was a smidge more than a lot, in my book.

"How *did* you find me?" I asked the inspector. When I'd last spoken to the *Garda* a week ago, he'd pressed for a way to reach me. I'd given him my old address at The Clarin House, where I boarded for a short time when I first arrived. I don't know why. I guess I just don't trust anyone. Not even the police.

"I'm a detective, Ms. Lane," O'Duffy told me with a dry smile, and I realized he had no intention of telling me. The smile vanished and his eyes narrowed with a subtle warning. *Don't lie to me; I'll know.*

I wasn't worried. Barrons had once said the same thing to me, and he has seriously preternatural senses. If Barrons didn't see through me, O'Duffy wasn't going to. I waited, wondering what had brought him here. He'd made it clear he considered my sister's case unsolvable and closed. Permanently.

He moved away from the fire and dropped the satchel slung over his shoulder onto the table between us.

Maps spilled across the gleaming wood.

Though I betrayed nothing, the cold blade of a chill caressed my spine. I could no longer see maps as I once had: innocuous travel guides for the disoriented traveler or bemused tourist. Now when I unfold one I half expect to find charred holes in it where the Dark Zones are—those chunks of our cities that have fallen off our maps, lost to the deadly Shades. It's no longer what maps show but what they *fail* to show that worries me.

A week ago I'd demanded O'Duffy tell me everything he knew about the clue my sister had left at the scene of her murder, words she'd scratched into the cobbled stone of the alley as she lay dying: *1247 LaRuhe.*

He'd told me they'd never been able to find any such address.

I had.

It had taken a bit of thinking outside the box, but that's something I'm getting better at every day—although I really can't take much credit for the improvement. It's easy to think outside the box when life has dropped a two-ton elephant on yours. What is that box anyway but the beliefs we choose to hold about the world that make us feel safe? My box was as flat, and about as useful, as a tissue-paper umbrella in all this rain.

O'Duffy sat down on the sofa next to me, gently for such an overweight man. "I know what you think of me," he said.

When I would have protested politely—good southern manners die hard, if at all—he gave me what my mother calls the "shush wave."

"I've been doing this job for twenty-two years, Ms. Lane. I know what the families of closed murder cases feel when they look at me. Pain. Anger." He gave a dry laugh. "The conviction that I must be a chuffing idiot who spends too much time in the pubs and not enough time on the job, or their loved one would be resting in vindicated peace while the perp rotted in jail."

Rotting in jail was far too kind a fate for my sister's murderer. Besides, I wasn't sure any jail cell could hold him. He might draw symbols on the floor, stamp his staff, and disappear through a convenient portal. Though Barrons had cautioned against assumptions, I saw no reason to doubt the Lord Master was responsible for my sister's death.

O'Duffy paused, perhaps giving me a chance to deny his words. I didn't. He was right. I'd felt all that and more, but weighing the jelly stains on his tie and the girth overhanging his belt as circumstantial evidence, I'd convicted him of loitering overlong in bakeries and cafés, not pubs.

He selected two maps of Dublin from the table and handed them to me.

I gave him a quizzical look.

"The one on top is from last year. The one beneath it was published seven years ago."

I shrugged. "And?" A few weeks ago I would have been delighted for any help from the *Garda* I could get. Now that I knew what I knew about the Dark Zone neighboring Barrons Books and Baubles—that terrible wasteland where I'd found 1247 LaRuhe and nearly been killed—I wanted the police to stay as far out of my life as I could keep them. I didn't want any more deaths on my conscience. There was nothing the *Garda* could do to help me anyway. Only a *sidhe*-seer could see the monsters that had taken over the abandoned neighborhood and turned it into a death trap. The average human wouldn't know they were in danger until they were knee-deep in dead.

"I found your 1247 LaRuhe, Ms. Lane. It's on the map published seven years ago. Oddly enough, it's *not* on the one published last year. Grand Avenue, one block down from this bookstore, isn't on the new map, either. Neither is Connelly Street, a block beyond that. I know. I went down there before I came to see you."

Oh God, he'd walked into the Dark Zone this morning? The day was barely bright enough to keep the Shades hunkered down, wherever it was the nasty things hid! If the storm had blown in even one more dense, sky-obliterating cloud, the boldest of those life-suckers might just have dared the day for a human Happy Meal. O'Duffy had been waltzing cheek-to-cheek with Death, and didn't even know it.

The unsuspecting inspector waved a hand at the pile of maps. They looked well examined. One of them appeared to have been balled up in shock or perhaps angry disbelief, then resmoothed. I was no stranger to those emotions. "In fact, Ms. Lane," O'Duffy continued, "none of the streets I just mentioned are on *any* recently published map."

I gave him my best blank look. "What are you saying, Inspector? Has the city renamed the streets in this part of the city? Is that why they're not on the new maps?"

His face tightened and his gaze cut away. "Nobody renamed the streets," he growled. "Unless they did it without notifying a single person in authority." He looked back at me, hard. "I thought there might be something else you wanted to tell me, Ms. Lane. Something that might sound, er, a bit...unusual?"

A Note About the Fever Series

————————

Every now and then a writer gets a gift: a tale complete from beginning to end, wrapped up in a box, tied with a pretty bow, and deposited on the doorstep of his or her subconscious. All that is required is a willingness to open the door, unwrap the box, release the world within, and do your best to transcribe that world into word.

When the Fever series arrived on my doorstep, I was shocked to find so much Thanatos in my Eros. I'd been writing romance novels for years, and had enjoyed every minute I'd spent with my Highlanders and the women who stole their hearts.

The world that came in the Fever box wasn't pretty like my romance novels. There were monsters in every corner, people dying, everyone was keeping secrets, all the characters were too flawed to be heroic, and there was no traditional romance to be found. The protagonist was a virtual Barbie with little ambition or interest in the world around her, and about as far from my personality type as the sun from the moon.

I sorted through the box, hunting for the elements I recognized as the trademarks of my writing, wondering if the FedEx Story Idea Guy had gotten the addresses mixed up again. He does that from time to time. Every now and then he seems to think it's funny to drop one of Stephen King's boxes on my porch. Things move around under the cardboard, and the noises they make come from the dark night of the soul. The few times I've been suckered into opening one of those misplaced gifts, I've duct-taped the box securely, propped a chair under my doorknob, and refused to go out onto my stoop again until it was gone.

"There are only two themes worth writing or reading about" writer F. Gonzalez-Crussi says, "love and death, Eros and Thanatos."

When I was thirteen I had two reading experiences that changed my life and shaped the writer I would become. I picked up Harlan Ellison's *Deathbird Stories* from the library of the Catholic Academy I was attending—the irony is apparent if you've read the book—and one of my aunts gave my mother a box of romance novels.

Eros and Thanatos. Love and Death.

Both came in the Fever box left on my doorstep, in a more fascinating blend than anything I'd tried to write before.

As my imperfect protagonist walked me through the craic-filled, historic Temple Bar District of Dublin and introduced me to her world, I was riveted by the tale of an ordinary, flawed young woman thrust into an extraordinary, terrifying dark world where the heroes and villains looked startlingly alike.

I followed her into the Dark Zones—parts of our cities taken over by deadly Shades that no longer appear on any of our maps, although you might stumble into one around the next corner if you're not careful; deep into underground labyrinthine caverns where monsters of the worst sort dwell—the kind that lie within us all; and eventually into the most treacherous place known to Man—Faery, with its irresistible illusions, lethal seductions and killing lies.

I couldn't close the box, which was probably a good thing. There was no return address on the package, and I haven't seen the FedEx Story Idea Guy since. I don't think he'll be coming around again until I'm done.

Sometimes you don't get a choice. A story shows up on your doorstep and stalks you until you tell it. You do your best and hope the passion you feel for it brings it to life in your readers' minds as vividly and thrillingly as it exists in your own.

Welcome to Mac's World—and Stay to the Lights!

Karen

Karen Marie Moning is the *New York Times* bestselling author of the Fever series, featuring MacKayla Lane. She has a bachelor's degree in society and law from Purdue University and is currently working on a new series set in the Fever world.

www.karenmoning.com